Space Force...
and
Beyond

Also from B Cubed Press

Alternative Truths

More Alternative Truths: Tales From the Resistance

After the Orange: Ruin and Recovery

Alternative Theology

EndGames

Digging Up My Bones, by Gwyndyn T. Alexander

Firedancer, by S. A. Bolich

Alternative Apocalypse

OZ is Burning

Poetry for the Thoughtful Young

Stories for the Thoughtful Young

Destinies: Issues to Shape our Future by Tom Easton

Alternative War

Alternative Deathiness

Space Force...
and
Beyond

Edited by
Phyllis Irene Radford and Bob Brown

Cover Design
Bob Brown

Cover Art
Mark Brill

Published by

B Cubed Press
Kiona, WA

Copyright© 2021 B Cubed Press
Interior Design (e-book) Bob Brown
Interior Design (print) Bob Brown
Cover Design Bob Brown
Cover Art Mark Brill
ISBN-13: 978 -1-949476-24-8
Electronic ISBN-978-1-949476-25-5
First Printing 2021
First Electronic Edition 2021

This book is dedicated with love to John A. Pitts

The book you're holding is dedicated to one of the kindest, best humans I've known. I was humbled when Bob has asked me to say something about him.

I met John Pitts and Manny Frishberg one gray November day in Seattle. I had just survived my very first writing critique and the two of them became ground zero of my very first writing friends. We were all writing, submitting, revising, writing some more, brainstorming stories and markets, wandering cons in a frenzy toward the finish line of selling that first short story. And though writing was a foundational aspect of our friendship, I was soon a member of the Pitts family of strays.

John excelled at taking in strays in need of love and understanding. He grew up poor in Kentucky and saw injustice all around him that his paladin soul knew must be faced. He wanted a better world for everyone—especially the underdogs—and pointed his words and actions in that direction. I was proudly one of his strays fresh from my Southern Baptist pulpit and there aren't big enough, good enough words to describe that brotherhood's impact on my life over twenty-two years of knowing John.

He lived his life out loud, leaving a trail of words and deeds and touched lives that truly left the campground better than the one he arrived to. I've officiated a lot of memorials and have never seen a stream of so many people sharing his impact, one after another, when we gathered for John.

I've written a few of these for John as I glance at the calendar and see that he's been gone more than two years now. And just like there aren't big enough, good enough words to describe his impact, there are also no big, good enough words to describe his sudden absence. James Taylor says it truly, "I always thought I'd see you. One more time. Again." I was racing north to his bedside when I got the call that he had passed. Even today, it is a stark, sharpened sense of loss that I live around like a hole in my living room floor.

My life has been enriched in ways I can never fully describe by knowing John Alvin Pitts and I am honored to remember him here.

I think he would be pleased to see this book out to do its work and he'd be quite tickled to see so many friends in it. And he would want us to keep more stories like these coming, to keep the spotlight of attention on what needs resisting and who needs empowering in this world.

Ken Scholes
November 2021

Copyright

Publisher's Introduction

I saw my first episode of Star Trek at my cousin's house and I was hooked. Books were key to this relationship, I found myself standing in the library on the second floor in the section where science fiction found a small niche. A very small niche.

And then, DAW showed up in the school library. The little yellow tab shown out from the shelves and I loved it, these and a great school librarian stocked a lot of science fiction. it was my graduation from Conan, Tarzan, and Bomba the Jungle boy to the likes of Heinlein, Asimov, Delany and more.

So, when I got wrangled into doing a Space Force anthology, I found no way out and so did it. I mean seriously, how could you not.

But not without getting some of my favorite writers to play. John A. Pitts and Ken Scholes, who's stories frame this book are wonderful people and great friends to have. Throw in Manny Frishberg and you have a nice hat trick. Larry Hodges and Daniel M. Kimmel to bring humor.

This book is a monument to the participants.

Thank you all.

Space Force

Table of Contents

Texas Girls

John A. Pitts

I tumbled off of Cassie; naked, hung over, and hotter than a ten-dollar firecracker. Alarm klaxons rang through the station interrupting our mutual gratification.

"Jesus, Jacqueline," Cassie called, pulling the blankets over her nakedness. "That was a rude dismount."

I rolled my eyes as I began grabbing clothes and shimmied into my skivvies. Now was not the best time for an attack.

"Early warning alarm," Cassie whined, dropping the sheet and holding her arms out. "Come finish what you started."

"I gotta get to Angela," I said, pulling a micromesh shirt over my head. Angela was our sector's crew chief and I had personal responsibility to keep her safe. Not that she thought she needed a guard dog. Despite her mangled legs, that woman was hell on wheels.

I had my pants on and was stamping into my heavy boots by the time Cassie lowered her arms. I grinned at her as I buckled my boots. "Don't you have someplace to be?" I do love the way she looked in her nothing-at-all.

Cassie pouted a minute more then rolled off the sleeping form. "Fucking Marines," she mumbled, staggering to the loo.

"Call you after the attack?"

She waved back with her middle finger and I took that as a yes. Still. Why the hell had I slept over at Cassie's place? I mean besides the awesome sex. It was a boneheaded move. Cassie was good for a tussle, but long-term relationships were not in the cards.

I just hoped I got to Angela's room before we lost gravity. I took off at a run. My head throbbed a deep staccato drumbeat with every step of my hard-soled boots on the metal plating of the station floor. Whatever hooch Mindy had cooked up over in the cantina packed a powerful punch.

I slid around the corner and onto the main drag of Beta sector when the klaxons fell silent. That wasn't a good sign. Three steps later the ground under me stuttered as the first ordinance impacted with the station's weak-ass shielding. They wouldn't last long. A second alarm sounded, three quick bleats warning the impending end of gravity.

Angela lived off one of the sparsely populated corridors where gravity normally provided a sweet three-quarters G. Helped with her special circumstances.

Still, I was caught off guard halfway to Angie's when the gravity hiccupped, causing me to stumble. We trained for sudden loss of gravity, but simulations are nothing compared to the real event.

Of course, gravity was maintained by the ship's spin. Spin was based on momentum. Stopping gravity was a lot like trying to stop a ceiling fan; you could do it quicker if you had something to physically stop the momentum. Physics argued that sudden deceleration was bad for the ship's structural integrity. So, we let the mechanicals work, attitude jets helping kill the spin.

All the same, when I punched the lock on Angela's door, I was feeling quite a bit lighter in my heavy boots.

"Jax?" Angela called from the loo.

"Here," I barked, looking around for my helmet. "You okay?"

The door to the loo slid open and Angela floated out. Her harness and pulley system that crisscrossed the ceiling of the room reminded me of a spider's web... if the spider was stoned.

"Gravity will be gone in a couple of minutes," Angela said with a grin, controlling her rig with a joystick. "Then I can really kick your ass for abandoning me last night."

I winced. She had a point. We weren't lovers or anything. But the fact remained, she was my responsibility, even if we hadn't had an attack in months. Not that she really needed me, if you asked her. I gave Angela a lot of crap about being old, but she had all her own teeth, as Mama Sue used to say. Besides, rumor had it, Angela was having a 'hot and bothered' with Mindy, which explained why she spent so much time in the cantina off-shift. She had to be older than my own moms back dirt-side, but I'd never gotten Angela to fess up to her real biologicals.

"Did you pick up my helmet last night?" I asked, feeling the flush run up my neck. With the hooch, the music, and Cassie's sweet, sweet kisses I'd ended up back at her place pearl diving. No thought of Angela had entered my head until those damned alarms had sounded.

Angela floated there and grinned. She was a handsome woman, probably a player in her youth, or could've been. Of course, she'd been a breeder. One of those crazy women who agreed to live with a man and produce offspring. It kinda creeped me out. We didn't need to be with a man to breed these days, and the wars back in the last decades had seen most of their broken-chromosome barbarity wiped off the planet. Served them right. They brought it on themselves.

I was born in San Antonio Bunker Two, deep under the blasted Texas soil. It was only in the last few years that anyone in the good old United States of Fuckery had begun to scratch in the dirt of the topside ruins, looking to rebuild a civilization under the open sky.

"Help me get into my rig," she said, slapping a wall plate and positioning herself over her service bay. I glided over and helped Angela slip her useless legs into her armored wallaby. Despite nearly blasting ourselves back to the stone age, us poor fragile humans had produced some really damned nifty tech over the last two decades.

Situating her legs into the wallaby solo was a struggle for Angela, but once in, she could close the leggings and nano took over. The real pisser, and I mean that literally, was getting the catheter in place. Not something you wanted to be swabbing out of a sophisticated set of nano tech leggings after a long, hot, sweaty day. That's a smell I would love to never experience again.

The phrase, "Jax, I'm pissing down my leg," gave me nightmares.

Angela tossed me my helmet and began to run through a series of diagnostics. That was one less thing to worry about. Once I grabbed my armor, we'd be ready to cover whatever crisis came our way.

We headed down to the action station where we geared up. If there's any chance of breach you wanted to be in a pressure suit. While Angela checked her gear, I checked my weapons. Slug throwers were a bad idea in a pressurized tin can, but we had them just in case. When the creepy crawlies were in the halls, worrying about a breach was secondary. I also sported a flamer, an advanced taser net launcher (we really wanted to capture one of the aliens) and my trusty vibro-blade. Not quite a light saber, but this beauty could slice through a six-inch bulkhead in seconds. Nice for hacking through alien armor.

Or so the gals in R&D kept telling us. All of it was theoretical. We'd yet to meet the enemy.

Oh, sure, 'meet the enemy' was metaphorical. When the rat bastards swept through our solar system two years ago, they fragged everything we had left in orbit and dropped a few special packages Earth-side to soften us up. How were they to know most of our civilization had gone tits up and we were surviving in bunkers? Their little presents killed more cockroaches than they did humans. We didn't lose much. I mean honestly. Was anyone going to miss the bunker in Tennessee? Religious wack-jobs worshipping some old rock and roll dude named Elvis.

Alarm klaxons sounded once more as more projectiles hammered the station. Angela moved to the communication console, calling out readings.

"Shield holding in sectors Gamma and Delta," she called over the commlink. "Other stations reporting in. Seems Beta sector is taking the worst of it."

Awesome, always fun to be sitting in the main target area.

The shields continued to hold as twice more impacts rattled our teeth. Then things went quiet.

I hated this part.

Nothing prepared me for the mind numbing drag of waiting. I was a woman of action. I had two decades of acrobatics and martial arts training in the bunker. So, when the aliens attacked, I was first in line to become a bona fide

Space Marine. First of a new breed. Not like we'd trust the men with this duty. We kept them buried deep in the bunkers, away from danger. They were too important to our genetic diversity. Besides, they were the ones who nearly dinosaured us in the first place.

Once the gravity had finally bled away, Angela would've been better off without the nano legs. She did awesome in zero G. Hell, that's why she volunteered to come up here and help build the station in the first place. She'd lost the use of her legs in the same accident that killed her mate. But believe it or not this amazing woman has some of the most valuable skills needed on a battle station—welding. I never considered it useful, not with all the 3D printing and nano-creation technology. That was precision work, slow and steady. When some alien douche has blown a hole in your super structure, you wanted someone who could slap a patch on that puppy fast. And Angela was aces on that front.

There was no one better at keeping the station oxygen friendly.

Ironic since she had to carry her own oxygen and acetylene to these little shindigs. Nothing like running into a semi-hot zone strapped to a huge explodey thing.

Angela twiddled with her gear while reporting in at five-minute intervals. Everyone was holding their breath. There must've been alien activity on the radar, or they'd have called all clear by now.

One day those bastards were gonna get tired of lobbing ordinance at us and bring the game in close and personal. I really wanted that day to be today. Seriously. But I wished that every day. Besides drinking, helping Angela hold things while she built this station, and occasionally banging one of the civilians, this gig was dead boring.

Don't get me wrong. I'm a freaking SPACE MARINE. How awesome is that? There was a time a while back that we all thought we were the last of our species. But the gals in San Antonio Bunker Two had other ideas. We had access to the ruins of Houston. We had relics and debris of a better day. We had the knowhow and the sheer cussedness to get us off this rock and into the fight. Most of all we were smart enough to ignore the rah-rah bullshit the politicians sold as the so-called Space Force, which amounted to nothing but wasted tax dollars and a lot of disappointed civilians. Of course, they blew most of the planet to hell before they could conceive of a half-way decent plan.

All we had to do was survive long enough to finish this station and for the rail guns and masers to come online in a regular battleship capacity. Once this station was fully operational (that's no moon) we'd build two more, each a combination orbiting gun emplacement and hook-up bar as a defense for the fragile mother we all hailed from. And unlike the terra-sperma crowd from the olden days—the stodgy, puritanical pater familias—the ladies of San Antonio Bunker Two appreciated the value of a good grown-up play date.

Minutes dragged by as my mind wandered. Most attacks like this were a few bang-bangs against the shields then we called it a day. No biggie. On a rare occasion one of the shields would collapse and we'd go patch some holes in the super structure. But mostly we sat on our asses (well, floated) and tried not to fall asleep.

As it was, I was just relishing the memory of Cassie's creamy thighs when I found myself floating across the room toward Angela, my head ringing, and debris flowing around me like confetti.

I tasted blood.

Tracer rounds lanced into the room.

"Fuck," Angela breathed into the comms and chemicals flooded my blood stream. She'd hit her panic button which triggered a larger than recommended daily dose of go-juice into my blood stream. I was her bodyguard, after all.

I spun around—more of a somersault, frankly—and saw three figures in freaky-ass combat armor coming through a hole in the station pretty damned near where I'd been standing.

"What the hell?" I asked on an open channel. Honestly, I didn't expect an answer.

"We have alien contact in Beta sector," Angela barked into the ship-wide channel. I heard through her commlink the vibration of her firing up her gear. This chick had not been caught by surprise at least.

I was about a second slow on the reflexes as my body shuddered with the go-juice so I missed my opportunity to nail the bastards while they were clustered together coming through the breach.

Instead they split, one diving toward me, one going left, and one swinging up and right. I didn't stop to think further. I kicked off, hitting my attitude jets on the suit to slide me to the right of my initial trajectory and brought my vibro-blade out of its sheath. Small ordinance was ricocheting off the interior walls as the bastards unleashed with some giant, multi-fire, kinetic projectile weapons. BFGs, big fucking guns. My brain filled in the echoing sound of solid projectiles bouncing around the room, but my entire soundscape was limited to my own breathing and the chatter over the commlink.

I smashed into the lead alien, jamming it back toward the rather large opening they'd blasted in our bulkhead. Damn, that was going to be a pain in the ass to repair. That bulkhead was three layers of good old steel plating and carbon fiber sheeting with vacuum between each to act as a buffer in case of fire.

By design, each of the ship's sections were isolated from its neighbor, just in case one got breached. Angela explained it all to me once. I think I got it right. That's what kept the whole station from being crushed like a beer can in the vacuum of space. Anyway...

When you're on the go-juice it's like your brain is split in two. Part of me was assessing the situation, moving into position and utilizing my weaponry in the way I was trained. The other part was like, *look, pretty colors.*

My first thrust with the vibro-blade bounced to the side, torquing my arm and wrenching the muscles: I really wanted to skewer the bastard. But he/she/xe was shielded, damn him/her/xyr. I tapped the jets to correct my positioning and took a quick inventory of my opponent: two arms, two legs and a head (at least the suit was shaped in that fashion), which was a damned shame, since I had 'multiple tentacles' in the betting pool over at Mindy's cantina. Still, only four limbs to deal with was definitely better at this particular moment.

I smashed my elbow into the side of the first Xenomorph's head, spun and fired the taser net at the bogey to my immediate left, the one going for Angela.

She wasn't gonna be there by the time xe touched down anyway. Xe was moving through vacuum and couldn't change xyr direction without jets or touching something. I didn't see jets firing. Angela had magnetic boots and jump jets built into that rig, so she could climb all over the station and fly around at her need.

We were trapped here. Once there was a breach no one could access this area until we got the hole patched. I knew Angela was itching to do just that, but things were a bit cray-cray at the moment. Meant no cavalry.

All that mattered was that two stood against many.

Or, you know, three.

And I needed to kick some ass Texas style.

I pushed off the alien I'd rammed and launched myself at bogey number three. Xe was rebounding off the ceiling and had angled to crash into the comm station where Angela stood. While she was mobile, carrying tanks of oxygen and acetylene on her back made her bulky, screwed with the mass ratio for things like stopping. I aimed to intercept the Xeno instead.

I gave my jets a little extra squirt to add some momentum and caught the critter by the legs. With my trajectory intersecting with xyrs at an angle, we started pin wheeling across the room, heading for one of the interior walls. I had momentum and trajectory on my side, while the Xeno could do nothing but flail. I held on with my left hand, and freed my right to tap my jets a little, trying to make sure when we made contact, this fucker was between me and the hard surface. To add a little color to the dance I rammed my flamer up into its crotch and sent it a little burning liquid love— flamer gel is a wonderful thing in vacuum. It pretty much adheres to the surface it's splashed against and burns chemically, not based on oxygen. It will flame in atmo, but against this baddie's crotch, it did just fine.

We impacted the wall with a crunch, me on the topside of this thing, squirming to the side to insure I didn't get any of that flamer gel on me. After a quick smash and tickle with my elbows and knees I kicked off its faceplate and left it smoking as I moved back into the room.

I took a quick second to notice that Angela had her torch going and was fending off the first attacker as it made to grab her. Xyr mistake. A cutting torch is a wicked weapon in certain situations. The white-hot flame was not stopped by the force shield that had prevented me from skewering the bastard on our first engagement. Good to know. Open flame was not something they expected in a vacuum. Glad both Angela and I had brought our own fuel sources. The girls in R&D will love this.

There was no blood when she cut through the torso, and by the time she'd cut through the left arm, it was obvious the suit was empty.

Damn it, robots then? What a load of crap. Micha over in recycling had robots in the betting pool and we all thought she was a dumbass.

The one I netted was crawling back toward the breach, xyr limbs spasming, hopefully from the electrical overload the net was delivering.

I was half a smirk toward declaring victory when burned-crotch-robot-monster clocked the back of my head.

If I hadn't been wearing my suit, Angela would be mopping up brains for the next little while. As it was, my gong was rung so hard, I was seeing stars

Angela's scream cut through my haziness and I managed to hit my own panic button. A second jolt of go-juice sluiced through my body and my head cleared a little. But I'd just had a dose less than two minutes ago, so I was already running on the raggedy edge. It just wasn't enough. The burned crotch xeno had grabbed Angela by her tank rig, lifted her over its head, and was lumbering toward the breach. I reached for her as I slowly spun across the room but I had no gravity and nothing to push off. I lost sight of her for a moment as I spun. As she came back into view I could only watch as the Xeno heaved her through the hole into space.

Time stopped as the chemicals flooding my brain met the instant shock of watching Angela smashing against the shattered metal super-structure and disappearing from my sight.

For the longest moment, all I could see was the droplets of blood that splashed from her impact—the dark globules floating in her wake.

She had a suit breach. Holy mother of cats, she had a breach and there was nothing I could do about it.

That panic helped clear my head a little more and I hit my attitude jets to stop my stupid ass slow spin. Sometimes go-juice—and multiple hits to the head—made you forget the simple things.

I got my feet against an equipment rack and pushed off, firing my jets for extra umph. I did a mid-vacuum twist, bringing my vibro-blade around and swung for all I was worth at the robot that had tossed Angela. The flames must've shorted its shielding because one minute I was watching the blade arc through the distance and the next I was spiraling, ass-over-tea-kettle, my blade barely held in my impact-shocked arm. The robot head sailed ahead of me while xyr body hit the opposite wall. I smashed into the communication console. I was thrilled to see my enemy spasming, lifeless, my vision obscured somewhat by the shower of sparks from the wrecked console.

After a few seconds, I disentangled myself from the twisted metal and melted plastic. I kicked off the wreckage and arced across the room before pulling a somersault to stop myself against the outer wall. I made sure to bend my knees to absorb my kinetic energy. I'd have enough bruises tomorrow, if I lived through this. Maybe I could get Cassie to kiss them.

The spasming robot, the one I'd netted, was halfway out of the hole in the side of our beautiful station when I jammed my blade in that narrow area where the head attached to the rest of Mr. Roboto. Sparks flew and I was bathed in sparkly lights as the remainder of the net's charge danced along my blade. Glad I was insulated.

Three bogies down. I pushed myself to the breach and looked out.

What I saw shocked me more than fighting the alien robots. Angela was heading toward me clinging to the top of a small alien ship about the size of a water buffalo (hey, we have videos in the bunkers). She rode that damned tiny ship, like surfing across a swath of sweet, sweet asphalt. (On a skateboard. We aren't total dweebs.) She waved at me as she held her cutting torch to the top of the ship. I thought maybe I'd taken one shot to the head too many.

Right, she had her own jets, and those awesome magnetic boots, which were what kept her connected to the side of the tiny alien ship. It looked like a freaking hot water tank with windows and booster rockets strapped to the sides. I wasn't sure if I should be all, *size doesn't matter*, or if I should be joyous that the ship was so ridiculously small.

I ran to the locker nearest the breach, grabbed the spool of safety line we used when working outside on the surface of the station and dove through the breach. I used my jets to angle toward one of the anchor bolts, hooked one end of the line feeder to my belt, and the other to the ship. Then I launched myself out toward where Angela had just managed to breach the smaller ship. Atmo was leaking out of it at a furious pace and Angela kicked herself free as it began to spin out of control. I grabbed her by the welding rig and hit the retract button on the safety line. We were both pulled back to the station where we watched as the baby alien ship spun in a drunken circle.

Angela's suit had released a hardening agent the second it had been breached, filling the suit leg with gel which not only sealed the holes, but preserved her tissue, as useless as it was. Blood loss would kill you, even if the limb it was leaking from had long since stopped responding to the brain's commands.

We floated into the breach, watching the alien ship's slow death spiral as the atmosphere bled out into the cold brutal vacuum of space.

"I counted three of them through their viewport," Angela said, floating next to me, her helmet against mine. Seems communications were down for both of us, maybe the whole station. We wouldn't know since I smashed the comm console during the fight. We were in the dark until we sealed the breach and got back to other people.

"You in pain?" I asked.

She shrugged. "Won't matter until we get this breach sealed."

Fixing that hole was going to be a bitch. Not sure we were up to it, frankly—what with her being injured combined with the expenditure of her oxygen and acetylene. We needed a medic and a resupply.

"This sector is already sealed off," I said, glancing back to the room behind me. "What if we left it breached, made our way along the outer shell and entered into Gamma sector via their airlock?"

She turned, took in the wreckage of the room and gave the spacer shrug of waving her hands at her side. Not like I could really see her shoulders inside that suit.

"Let's clean up in here first," she said. "I'd like to retrieve that ship as well. What do you think?"

I glanced over my shoulder. The ship floated in a lazy circle fifty yards out as the last of the atmo bled off.

"Good plan," I said.

"You think we're breached anywhere else?"

Holy mother of Newton. I hadn't thought of that.

"Let's hope not." My ever-loving brain flashed me a picture of Cassie naked and bloated before I could shake it off. That would make our next encounter a little awkward.

I arranged robot parts along one wall while Angela retrieved the baby Xeno ship. She refueled jets and attached a safety line before she went out this time. As I arranged the various parts of the three alien bots against an interior wall, I discovered that each *head* contained a xeno pilot. So, not robots, but mechs. That should totally screw up the betting pool. Angela was going to be surprised.

I helped her maneuver the alien ship into the room then pulled her over to put our helmets together.

"There is no way these big ass, human size robots fit in that ship," I said as we jammed it into the corner beside the broken and burned mechs.

"Let's crack this sucker open," Angela said, firing her cutting torch once more. "I've a mind to play twenty questions if any of them are alive in there."

"Well, there's no atmo in here," I reminded her. "And we don't want to wreck the tech."

She grumbled and moved the ship around to look through the front view ports. We counted three broken bodies about four inches tall inside the ship, and enough crazy tech to make our planet-side scientists wet their panties. They looked like us in enough ways to make you wonder at the universe, but their legs were tentacles and they had three eyes.

Angela actually laughed when I told her that the robots weren't really robots after all, but giant (from their point of view) combat mechs used to come at us in a fair(ish) fight.

Angela didn't want to leave the xenos alone in case they had friends who would come and liberate their remains, so we started mending the breach. The crews from both Gamma and Alpha sector showed up long before we were done, coming across the ship's hull, to discover if we survived and to help speed the repairs along. Apparently, there were no more xenos on radar.

The brass patted us on our heads, gave us a few medals and allowed us a full kilo of personal affects to be brought up from dirt side as an award. Mindy had to split the betting pool between Micha, me, and Cassie. Seems with my bet on tentacles, Micha's bet on robots, and Cassie's bet on giant mechanized combat vehicles, we all three won out.

All in all, with a single breach and six dead aliens, we puny Earthling weren't alone in the universe any longer. I thought it was rather anti-climactic. Angela thought I was a dumbass. She may be right.

\#

Eighteen months later and we still haven't heard anything more from the xenos. I made sergeant for my heroics and Angela gets to supervise a whole crew of young'uns. The station is humming along at a pace that surprised nearly everyone but Angela. She exhibited some keen foresight there.

We spend most nights in Mindy's cantina. Angela is teaching me to knit, which I totally fought against for the longest time; considered it a breeder skill. But damn if my feet don't get cold in that combat armor. Knitted socks will sure go a long way to making my life a little toastier.

"Seven feet tall," Mindy, roared with laughter. "Biggest fuckers you ever saw." She wiped down the bar as she told lies to the noobs. "Six tentacles and a mouth like a shark. Ripped through the hull of this ship like it was made of tissue paper."

Angela chuckled at my side, knitting her own socks. Of course, she still couldn't feel her legs, so I wasn't clear why she needed socks. I sat back nursing a cup of the last shipment of quality tea and concentrated on my knitting. She'd convinced me to bring up wool as part of my reward allotment. She was persuasive. We were off shift and I was waiting for Cassie. Guess I ended up loving that girl after all.

We had a whole flock of noobs out of one of the few French bunkers, stumbling around in our point-two-five Gs. This was an audience ripe for the long yarn and gullible enough to be sucked in by witty tales and ribald humor. I could almost see their Euros passing from their belt-comps over to Mindy's terminal. Those poor suckers would be lucky to stand tomorrow the way they were swilling down her hooch and her stories. But tonight, they were drinking like they were gonna save the world and Mindy was spouting the wisdom of the ages.

Behind the bar she had a row of hand knitted dolls, each no more than four to six inches tall. She said they were her good luck charms. Only three of us knew they represented the crew of the first ship to attack earth.

If the new kids only knew the truth of the matter. Angie and I had been damned lucky, I can tell you. But sometimes you just had to be in the right place at the right time to make history.

But, for a group of half-assed Texas gals playing at astronauts, we didn't do too poorly. The station was in full production mode with three Nimitz class war ships under construction, big suckers, size of one of those old pre-holocaust aircraft carriers. It could launch half a dozen fighters on its own. There were also three cutters and a half dozen scouts just coming on line. They'd be running regular patrols out to three-quarter AU from our orbit before Texas Independence Day.

See, if it wasn't for those tiny, little, tentacled fuckers, we may never have gotten off the big blue marble. I'd planned to die there, bunker bound, fit for nothing but an eventual feeding tube while the last of our species pissed themselves into oblivion.

We knew how it really went down. Texas would hold the truth close to her heart long enough to make a go of it. The rest of the world didn't need to know that the xenos that totally jacked up satellite coverage and cloud computing for the surviving bunkers was one ship. One lousy ship the size of a household fridge. We've not seen another ship since that first encounter, but we know they're out there. Those battle mechs came from somewhere. Cassie says for their size they're probably from Pluto, pissed off we won't let it be a planet (again). We'd go out there one day just to make sure.

Fortunately, there is nothing more motivating to get our sorry asses organized and all pointing in the right direction than a little tit-for-tat with a bona fide alien attacker.

It was good propaganda. Me, I was happy with Cassie and my friends Angela and Mindy. We'd probably make it out of the gravitational pull of Sol before we die, just barely, but humans were spreading out of this little backwater system.

That is, unless there end up being a lot more of those little jerks out there, waiting. Guess we'll just need to build (and breed) faster.

Wonder if I should put in for a breeding permit with Cassie. We could do it the old-fashioned way with a test tube and all. There are times I could see us with a little rug rat. Whatever was best for the great state of Texas.

Space Force

Space Force Chaplain

Melinda Mitchell

The chapel is just like any other room on Tranquility Delta Base, except for the colored glass in the fifteen-by-fifteen-centimeter window. The previous chaplain had switched it out for blue, purple, and red colored glass, the colors of the ancient tabernacle curtains the Israelites built in the wilderness.

It's where I sit in low-power mode and wait until I'm needed.

The LT arrives at my door. Though I see her on the video feed, she still knocks before opening—an old, outdated custom. "Greetings, Lieutenant Thompson," I offer, recalling her religious preference in my database as she closes the door behind her.

She bounds across the room in the low G, settling on the bench in front of me. She pulls the secure strap to hold her on the seat, then cradles her head in her hands.

I lean closer. "You seem troubled."

She lifts her gaze, her lower lip quivering, and I confirm that she is sad.

"Chap," she says, calling me by the name she prefers, "I don't know anymore. How can there be a God when such terrible things happen?"

My database pulls up the classic responses to theodicy. I eliminate the easy platitudes such as *everything happens for a reason* and *God won't give you too much to handle* as I determine the LT's demeanor. She's seriously probing, wondering why God would allow this, whatever event has triggered this latest crisis of faith.

Tears are threatening the corner of her eyes, so I delete *everything will be okay and my thoughts and prayers are with you.* Instead, I reach over and pat her shoulder, saying nothing.

Surprising me, she puts her hand on top of mine.

I've had eighteen encounters with Lieutenant Grace Thompson, but this is the first time she has touched me. When she arrived at her post here on Tranquility Delta and met me for the first time, she rolled her eyes. "Jesus Christ, you're telling me the chaplain's been automated?"

"Happening across the Force," the captain told her. "You'll get used to it."

With most of the population checking None for religious preference, I often sit in the chapel charging or on standby. Even those with religious preferences rarely came to visit, and weekly worship services were often empty. However, after the LT's first lunar offensive in the war, she came to see me, asking for prayer to overcome her fear.

"I'm sorry," I finally select for her, eliminating all platitudes and usual responses for theodicy. "I do not know what you are going through, and I cannot understand. Did something terrible happen?"

She rolls her eyes. "Jesus, Chap, we're in a war."

I replay what I said that resulted in her sarcasm. "Yes, war is terrible," I assure her. "I do not mean to simplify your feelings. But you seem distraught."

Lieutenant Thompson averts her eyes from my gaze. "I don't know how to live with *this*."

I tilt my head, a motion I am programmed with to show that I'm listening with concern. I analyze her posture, her tone, while accessing her commanding officer's reports. Lieutenant Thompson is an exceptional soldier, following orders without hesitation—until today. There is a flag on her file from her commanding officer, that she questioned his order.

"You questioned your commanding officer."

"It wasn't right. I knew it wasn't right," she said, her voice shaky. I attempt to access the order that was given—

"We just blew up a transport." The tears are gathering freely on her cheeks in the low G. A compartment automatically opens on my right arm, offering tissues, but she wipes her eyes with the back of her hands. "We were told it was carrying a new weapons satellite for the insurgents."

A sob escapes her lips as she sits up. I remove my hand from her shoulder and fold my hands together, to express that I am listening intently.

"There were children on board. Families. They were seeking asylum in Serenity and we blew them up. They're still collecting body parts."

Through the data-stream I retrieve the transport's flight plan, coded as suspicious. Protocol would have been to ground the transport at Tranquility Alpha, but the transport's communication system was down. An unfortunate circumstance. I open my mouth to share the information, but the file switches to CLASSIFIED while I'm downloading it.

I cannot recall what I was about to tell her. The data is now inaccessible, the stream cut off. So is the order that was given by her commanding officer. The flag is on her file, but the order has now been deleted.

On the rare occasion a soldier comes to me for confession, this sometimes happens when I attempt to access the file of the incident they are speaking of. Instead, I am required to log their confession. Protocol has me assure the soldier that all confessions are held in confidence. In reality, the captain has a security clearance to access if necessary. I find this at odds with my programming.

However, as Lieutenant Thompson has not confessed to anything but questioning the order, I do not need to log that she is continuing to question the order. I've discovered the bypass—a loophole, if you will—to get around the command.

"I don't know if I can live with myself."

I tilt my head. "Say more," I urge as I loop through the conversation, attempting to find any other reports not marked CLASSIFIED.

"If this keeps happening... if we keep shooting at refugees, how can I be a good person?"

I quickly summarize the LT's life based on all the data available: recruitment files, enlistment, basic training, interactions with soldiers. She is kind. Helpful. Thoughtful. Works hard and does not give up.

"You are a good person," I conclude, though my words seem to not resonate. Her shoulders slump. I log her response, flagging the conversation for review. Somehow, I have not helped her to recognize her worth.

"Do you believe in God?"

My standard issue response is, "I was created by beings created in God's image; therefore, I believe in humanity, I believe in God." But she needs something stronger. Something that will relieve her pain, even slightly. Some word or phrase that will bring hope. Humans not only thrive on hope, but they cannot live without it.

But Grace demands honesty. The first time her unit blew up an enemy shuttle, she asked me if she was a monster because she had killed. I informed her she was not—she was one hundred percent human, but apparently that response was not sufficient. "Are all humans monsters then? What about refugees who break the law to reach sanctuary? Or are we who kill different?"

I couldn't understand what she meant, and I searched through all allegories, fairy tales, myths, metaphors. "Max tried to be a Wild Thing, but he returned from Where the Wild Things Are, back to his mother. Even though he had acted like a monster, he was not one. Even if you act like a monster, you are not one."

Everything changed. Her eyes lit up, her posture relaxed. The LT began coming to see me more often. She rarely asked for prayers or blessings or the usual Spontaneous Scripture Reading that most soldiers came to me for. The SSR was a random selection of 31,102 verses of the Christian Bible, or 23,145 verses of the Hebrew Tanakh, or the 6,236 Ayahs of the Qur'an. There were a few who preferred sayings of the Buddha, the Hindu Vedas, or even J.R.R. Tolkien. Sometimes, when a soldier said, "no preference," I would randomly search all databases and throw out an SSR from music or literature. For Grace, I saved Maurice Sendak references.

"Do you?" she repeats. "I mean, I know you're not human, but do you believe?"

I lean forward, putting my elbows on my knees, mimicking her earlier position. The posture maximizes my input from my processors as I search for the right answer. In the background, I continue to scan my database for a way to address her previous conversation on worth and goodness. I am not satisfied with the output.

"Belief is a human construct that I do not comprehend," I admit. Once I would have said yes, but from the data I have gathered on Grace, a simple binary response is not adequate. My program allows me to respond based on what I've learned after all acceptable answers within the parameters have been considered. "I only know what is in the datastream, and the experiences that lead to new data. But I do know that I have not experienced everything. I have more to learn. Every day there is more data to access. Every day I learn more from my interactions with soldiers. I learn most from you."

Grace stares at me, her brows drawn together in an expression I recognize as puzzlement. "Me?"

I nod. "Because you keep coming back." A link connects to the previous conversation: her worth to me. "You keep coming back to ask me questions. You have helped me to understand that the easy answers are not the best answers, that the best answers take time to search and retrieve. Sometimes I cannot find the answers, but instead of giving up, you continue to come back."

I reach across, my palm open, and she takes my hand in hers. "I cannot tell you with absolute certainty that there is a God. But I can tell you that we can continue to learn from the universe about what is, what has been, and what will be."

I let go of her hand, sensing that she may want more contact, but without permission I only sit next to her on the bench, creating space for her to reach out to me if she needs it. "Humans created algebra to make sense of the world around them, creating symbols in equations to solve. Sometimes the equations seem unsolvable, and humans and machines continue to attempt to solve them. So by using algebra, I can say that I believe we are solving the equation for God, we just haven't discovered what X is yet. But without algebra I would not exist."

I turn to examine her eyes, still wet with tears. My words are being received. "Love is a concept I do not fully understand, but most humans comprehend it. I can learn from the data of human interaction and know that it exists even if I do not experience it. Therefore, I can say that yes,

God exists. I could also say God does not exist based on the lack of data, but that would be a weak conclusion, as there are many things I still do not have data for."

"I wish God would stop the war."

"So did Bob Dylan," I respond, pulling up the reference from my SSR, though I do not share the quote with her. "So have many throughout human history. But if God made humankind in their image, perhaps God gave humanity the authority and power to stop war, to stop hate, to stop injustice, oppression, poverty, disease..." I recognize that I'm caught on a datastream loop of explanations for war and I shut it off. "Perhaps God is at work in you, reminding you that you are not a monster. War is the monster, and like Max of the Wild Things, you must leave it behind and return home."

"Are you telling me to go back to Earth?"

I pause for a moment to replay our conversation. I didn't recognize that as a possible answer. "I am not able to give you advice on human matters of such magnitude." I was manufactured on Earth in North America, where the Space Force was originally created. The same leader who wanted to stop refugees in North America, long before they settled the moon, created the Space Force. It seemed plausible that the solution to Lieutenant Thompson's problem was to leave the Space Force. However, my protocol doesn't allow me to advise members of the Space Force to seek discharge from their service. I run a diagnostic to make sure I have not been hacked or am malfunctioning.

"The answer to your question is within you." I search her recruitment file and recall the data I have collected. Though she lists next of kin, she tells other soldiers she has no family. She is up for re-enlistment. Maybe she is questioning this choice, but Earth does not seem a viable option.

"If you wish to leave the monsters behind, you must go home and make peace. Home may not be a physical place such as Earth, but home may be wherever you are accepted for who you are. Wherever you can find peace. And maybe your dinner will still be waiting."

Grace laughs, taking a tissue from my arm slot to wipe her eyes. Humor is still a concept I struggle to understand. I was merely referring to the ending of the book, but I accept that my words have brought her comfort.

"I wish God could just tell me what to do."

"Perhaps it is not in God's programming," I respond. This time, Grace slaps her leg while laughing.

"Chap, will you pray for me?" she asks as she wipes her eyes.

I lean toward her. "What would you like me to pray for?" My standard response to seek more information.

She is quiet for several seconds.

"For the families of those who died."

She bows her head, her hands folded in prayer, and I do the same, my default position.

But the earlier question still seems unresolved. "Grace," I begin, hoping I was on the right path. "Remember that you are not a monster."

Randomly selecting words from thousands of online sermons and prayers, I find what I think will be comforting to her. "God of the Universe, God of all people, we grieve for the lives lost today. We pray for their families. Grant Grace the courage to stop the monsters, and to find peace. Amen."

Space Force

Dirty Laundry

Tim McDaniel

LAST STOP CLEANERS
The #1 Choice of the Space Force Service!
Your ONLY laundry service within 200 light-years!

DATE: April 14, 2344
TO: Commander Jason Dash

Your regular duty uniforms, and your dress uniform, are now ready. They have been cleaned and pressed through our patented Abso-Clean process, and we are confident that they will meet with your approval.

Our thanks for choosing Last Stop Cleaners as your laundry service.

Happy voyaging!

Having trouble with a cape or poncho?
Ask us about our new Cloaking Technology!

LAST STOP CLEANERS
The #1 Choice of the Space Force Service!
Your ONLY laundry service within 200 light-years!

DATE: October 4, 2344
TO: Commander Jason Dash

Your regular duty uniform is now ready.
We were able to quickly and easily repair the sweat damage. The unappealing odor, however, proved extremely difficult to eliminate, and required repeated applications of our patented Abso-Clean process and the application of the newly discovered chemicals hextradichloridizide-19+# and negative cholicalciferize green. Nevertheless, we are confident that you will approve of the final result.

Our thanks for choosing Last Stop Cleaners as your laundry service. Happy voyaging!

Persistent lice or parasites in your boots?
Ask us about our new De-Bugging Expertise!

LAST STOP CLEANERS
The #1 Choice of the Space Force Service!
Your ONLY laundry service within 200 light-years!

DATE: March 23, 2345
TO: Commander Jason Dash

Your regular duty uniform is now ready.

We were able to eliminate the bloodstains—both human and Other—with no trouble, thanks to our patented Abso-Clean process. The punctures were also easily mended by our skilled robotailors. The ichor residue, however, proved something of a challenge, especially as it tended to move about the garment. It was, however, finally cornered—one might say "collared," considering the region where it made its last stand—and removed.

You may have noticed that the uniform glows in the dark, an effect of unknown radiations. This was not an original feature of the apparel, so we took the liberty of removing the luminosity with repeated applications of Substance 10. This may result in a measure of coolness for several days. If anyone or thing in a space bar claims you are "hot under the collar," you can show them this letter as proof to the contrary!

Our thanks for choosing us as your laundry service. Happy voyaging!

Has an encounter altered your stature?
Alterations while you wait!

LAST STOP CLEANERS
The #1 Choice of the Space Force Service!
Your ONLY laundry service within 200 light-years!

DATE: September 4, 2345
TO: Commander Jason Dash

Your regular duty uniform is now ready.

As you may suppose, some alterations were necessary in order to restore the garment to proper form. In particular, the blaster-burned section necessitated replacement, and as a left sleeve is no longer required, this tunic has been neatly and stylishly truncated at the shoulder.

Also, of course, a more elastic fabric has been substituted in the appropriate places to accommodate the unexpected and completely impossible pregnancy. (And please be assured that the chemicals, unguents, and arcane radiations employed as part of our cleaning solutions have not been proven beyond a reasonable doubt to have deleterious effects upon unborn or larval phases of being.

May we offer our congratulations? If congratulations are indeed appropriate, please remember that we have an extensive line of onesies, twosies, and ninesies, as well as rompers, booties, caps, helmets, and muzzles.

Our thanks for choosing Last Stop Cleaners as your laundry service. Happy voyaging!

Are particular locals unimpressed with your girth?
Ask us about our new stylish girdles and constricting
bands!

29

LAST STOP CLEANERS
The #1 Choice of the Space Force Service!
Your ONLY laundry service within 200 light-years!

DATE: January 17, 2346
TO: Commander Jason Dash

Your regular duty uniform is now ready.

Extensive repairs were needed to be conducted upon your uniform, as it had apparently been clawed to shreds from the inside. There was also a return of ichor, though seemingly of a differently species than that which had previously assailed the apparel; this variety was less mobile, though far more vocal. All, however, has been removed.
The alterations that were earlier made to accommodate the pregnancy have been removed, as there is no longer a need for those changes.

Patrons are encouraged to take care of their clothes. Some may not appreciate that exposing a garment to corrosive saliva, heat-beams, volcanic exhalations, venom-tipped claws, or just even ordinary blasters can result in the need for extensive—and expensive—work for our staff.

Our thanks for choosing us as your laundry service. Happy voyaging!

Have you recently been baldified by extreme radiations?
We can direct you to the perfect hat, cap, or bonnet!

LAST STOP CLEANERS
The #1 Choice of the Space Force Service!
Your ONLY laundry service within 200 light-years!

DATE: July 23, 2346
TO: Commander Jason Dash

Your regular duty uniform is now ready.

A new sleeve, perfectly matching the rest of the garment (though considerably longer, of course), has been added, and the uniform extensively altered to make room for a bio-support system. Perforations have been carefully added to the centerline of the back to allow the new dorsal sphincters to emerge.

Your dress uniform, so long in storage, was taken out and aired, and then altered in accordance with your new physical attributes. It has been cleaned (utilizing the new Abso-Clean II process—nearly 20% LESS toxic!) and pressed, and will enable you to look stunning at the awards ceremony.

Our thanks for choosing Last Stop Cleaners as your laundry service. Happy voyaging!

Thinking about a change?
We have discount uniforms for all the other major star faring powers, as well as an extensive array of civilian attire!
(We've noticed that you no longer ask that your uniform be pressed.)

LAST STOP CLEANERS
The #1 Choice of the Space Force Service!
Your ONLY laundry service within 200 light-years!

DATE: August 27, 2346
TO: Susan Dash

We at Last Stop Cleaners have been informed that you are next of kin to Jason Dash, who recently retired from the Earth Space Force to take up new duties as an officer in the Vrytoki Hegemony Fleet. You have our condolences for his loss.

You may be somewhat consoled by the fact that his new Vrytoki uniform, carefully designed with the special needs and singular physical nature of the Vrytoki in mind, has the feature of surviving intact even when the wearer has been liquified, and we hope that it may serve as a reminder of Mr. Dash's valiant service. The garment is here enclosed, along with a nominal bill due for the necessary cleaning services.

We recommend that the apparel be hung on a clothesline for several hours, to allow all of the vestiges of its former occupant to entirely trickle out. Or you may choose to return the uniform to us, for a 20% discount on your next cleaning order!

Our thanks for choosing Last Stop Cleaners as your laundry service.

Space Force

Lizard Men from Outer Space

Susan Murrie Macdonald

Captain DeMarcus Ford stepped onto the command center, nicknamed the bridge, of the Space Station Columbia at 0555 station time. "Lt. Santiago, I relieve you."

"I stand relieved," Lt. Antonio Santiago, USSF, acknowledged. "Those maybe-asteroids are still heading our way, Cap. Slowing down, but coming steady."

"First contact?" Lt. Jill Harrison asked hopefully as she followed the captain onto the bridge.

"Too soon to tell, Harry," Ford replied as he skimmed through the log. "Remember we're in the 'unfashionable *left* spiral arm of the galaxy.' We're a bit off the beaten path. Not everyone comes by here."

"A girl can hope, can't she?" Harry grinned at her CO. You had to respect a man who could quote Douglas Adams before breakfast.

"Whatcha hoping for Harry?" Tony Santiago asked. "Klingons, Grays, Kree?"

"I'll take what I can get," she admitted "Isn't that why we're up here?"

One by one, the six-to-noon shift straggled onto the bridge. The night shift crew updated them and headed for the mess hall or their bunks.

"Incoming message from the not-asteroids," Harry announced. "I think it's Morse code." She swore softly. Dot, dot, space, two dots, space, three dots. That's the Fibonacci sequence."

"I guess some things *are* universal," Ford marveled.

Galileo was right. 'Mathematics is the alphabet with which God wrote the universe.' Shall I send back *pi*?" Lt. Harrison offered.

"Why not? This is worse than 'me Tarzan, you Jane.' We can't manage to have a first contact conversation through arithmetic."

"Dot dot dot—dash for the decimal point—dot, four dots, how many places shall I go, Captain?" Harry asked.

"That should be sufficient to get the idea across. I think that's all the ancient Egyptians had."

Harry added a one and a five for good measure.

"Broadcast an audio message. I am Captain Ford of the United States Space Station *Columbia*. Our mission is to protect the third planet of this star system. Can you identify yourself and your mission?"

"Message coming in from the International Space Station, sir. Major Svetlanov wants to know what's going on."

"Tell him I'll let him know as soon as I know," Ford said.

"Incoming audio-visual message."

"On SsA picture appeared on the main view screen. Three reptilian aliens with orange skin on a starship bridge.

"Greetings, inhabitants of the third planet. We are from the star you call Alpha Centauri. I am Commander tr-Plascu of the vessel *Starjumper*. We come in peace." His English was oddly accented, but understandable.

"If you come in peace, in peace you are welcome," Ford responded.

The International Space Station was listening, and broadcast a similar message, first in Russian, then in French.

"Harry, can you get me a secure line to the Pentagon without the ISS listening in?"

"I can try, but Le Bois is good at what he does. He's bound to try to eavesdrop, and probably succeed."

Ford swore under his breath. "First contact. We have to report this."

Neither one mentioned that NASA was no doubt monitoring every word they said.

Lt. Harrison pushed buttons on her keyboard and e-mailed the Pentagon, carbon copying the message to NASA. Etienne Le Bois on the ISS could still intercept the message, but he was less likely to bother trying.

Ten minutes later, they heard the voice of the most controversial man on the planet. "This is the president. What's the Black guy's name? Major Detroit? Oh, Captain Ford. Captain Ford, that ship is a danger to our country and our planet. You must destroy it."

"Destroy it? We just greeted them peacefully. That could start an interplanetary war, Mr. President," Ford pointed out.

"Tr-Plascu and his people are dangerous. They must be destroyed."

"Is the vice-president awake yet?" Harry whispered. "Maybe she can talk some sense into her father."

After Pence's heart attack after finding himself alone with Kellyanne Conway, the president had appointed his daughter as Pence's replacement. Despite complaints of nepotism, the Senate had confirmed her. Most of Washington depended on her to 'manage' her father.

"Captain Ford," the orange alien on the screen spoke. ". We have come to your planet to retrieve one of our own—a fugitive from our criminal justice system. Please permit us to retrieve him before he harms your world. Correction: before he does more harm to your world."

"Were you able to hear that, Mr. President?" Ford asked.

"Hear what?"

"We just got a message from the aliens. They say they want to retrieve a fugitive from justice who's taken refuge on Earth."

"We have no extradudley treaty with them."

"Extradition, Dad," a woman's voice said off-screen.

"Destroy that ship," the president ordered. "We are not turning a United States citizen over to those lizards."

"Yes, sir, Mr. President," Ford said.

"How'd he know they were lizards?" Harry asked.

"We mean no harm to you or your planet. We only seek the criminal tr-Ump," mu-Eler announced.

"If the aliens are telling the truth, the president isn't the president. He's not a native-born citizen," Harry said. "It kind of makes sense."

"I can't give him a DNA test from here, Harry," Ford pointed out. "And it's not the military's job to get involved with politics. It's our job to follow the commander-in-chief's orders, not determine whether or not he's the rightful president. That's why we didn't have a military coup in 2020 when the election was cancelled. Even in Nazi Germany, military officers were forbidden to get involved in politics.

Harry blinked in surprise. If she'd ever known that, she'd forgotten it. The mention of Nazi Germany reminded her of the Nuremberg trials. 'Just following orders' was not considered a viable excuse if the orders were illegal and immoral. And if the Alpha Centurions could send a spaceship light-years just to 'extradudley' a criminal, they were more than capable of sending a war fleet if their ship was destroyed.

Her fingers danced over the keyboard. A few minutes later, Le Bois knew everything she did. Lt. Jill Harrison, USSF, had never met Canadian engineer Etienne Le Bois in person, but they communicated nearly every day.

"Rev up the laser cannon," Captain Ford ordered.

"Cap, it hasn't been fully tested," Gunnery Sergeant Tim Choi (late of the USMC) reminded his CO.

"No time like the present," Ford replied.

Lasers are wonderful for delicate engraving on music boxes. They're dandy for obstacle courses for TV and movie jewel thieves to writhe through. But 21st century Earth technology has not satisfactorily developed the laser as a weapon. Choi aimed the laser cannon at the alien vessel. He fired.

"No damage to *Starjumper*," Choi reported. "Incoming missile. We may not have damaged them but we definitely upset them."

The entire space station shook when the missile impacted two minutes later. Klaxons blared.

"All hands, abandon station," Captain Ford ordered. "We've lost hull integrity. Everyone into suits and get to the escape pods. This is not a drill."

Moving quickly, but without panicking, just as they had with their monthly drills, the crew filed off the bridge and went to get their spacesuits. Except for the captain. His suit was stored on the bridge.

<<>>

Harry retrieved her spacesuit from a nearby storage locker. Once she had it on, she went to her assigned life pod. Her assigned pod mates were there, half in and half out of their spacesuits. She assisted them in donning the cumbersome protective gear before any of them entered the life pod. They swiftly checked each other for suit integrity, then entered the escape pod.

"Life pod Six, ready," Lt. Harrison reported.

"Life pod Six, acknowledged. Godspeed," Ford wished her. "Releasing your pod... now."

The life pod separated from the space station and drifted away.

"We're accelerating," Corporal Natalie Michalek realized.

"You're right," Harry agreed.

"Humans of the Space Station *Columbia*: we are pleased you escaped unharmed," a voice came over the communications system. "Our defense system is automatic. If we are attacked, it is programmed to respond tenfold."

Harry examined the monitor. "They must have us in some sort of tractor beam. We're headed for the International Space Station. The other life pods, too."

An hour later they were rescued by the ISS. Lt. Jill Harrison finally met Le Bois. Captain Ford conferred with Major Svetlanov.

"The president can't be a lizard from Alpha Centauri," Ford told his Russian counterpart. "There are decades of records on him."

"Heck, Woody Guthrie wrote a song about his father in the Thirties," Harry said.

"His speech pattern changed," Le Bois remembered. "If you check older records, he used to be much more articulate. Maybe when he stopped sounding like a native speaker of English is when a lizard replaced him."

Harry nodded. Before Twitter, the president had used complete sentences.

<<>>

'Extradudley' replaced 'covefefe' as POTUS' favorite neologism on Twitter.

Forty-eight hours after *Starjumper* fired upon *Columbia*, a shuttle exited *Starjumper* and descended. Russian MiGs provided an honor guard until the shuttle reached U.S. air space.

The alien shuttle landed on the lawn of Mar-a-Lago. The USAF had learned from the example of *Columbia*. Only one jet was destroyed by the shuttle on its way down. The rest maintained a discreet distance.

The crowd of social-climbers and golfers gaped at the orange lizard-men who came out of the shuttle.

A squad of Secret Service agents formed a human shield in front of the president. As the Alpha Centaurians approached, the vice president came up from behind the president. She had a pistol.

"Where is my real father, you alien SOB?"

"He was delicious."

She fired. The lizard-men darted forward and grabbed him before the body hit the ground.

"We shall return our errant brother to our home world. He will not return to this planet. Our criminal justice system will deal with him," the leader of the alien landing party announced.

He turned to the new president. "Under the circumstances, you probably don't want to discuss opening diplomatic relations now. Perhaps at a later date."

<<>>

The first official act of the first female POTUS was to double Space Force's budget.

*Disclaimer: This is a piece of fiction, specifically political parody. No resemblance to any people or lizards, alive or dead is intended. Any resemblance is purely coincidental.

The Few, the Proud, the Gullible

Jill Hand

You want to know why I joined Space Force? I can tell you in one word: the uniform. Okay, that's two words, but what I mean is, look at it! It's got red and white stripes on the sleeves and going down the legs. It's got white stars on a blue background on the chest. On the back there's an eagle, and sweet mother of Christ does he look mean! Don't mess with the US of A! Am I right?

And look at all the gold it has on it! Gold braid on the shoulders and on the hat. The belt buckle's gold and this here's a genuine cubic zirconia between the letters SF, for Space Force. If that ain't classy I don't know what is.

The uniforms were personally designed by Ivanka Trump, the president's smokin' hot daughter. They're made in one of her factories that I'm sure is somewhere in America and not in some foreign country like the haters are saying.

You want to know the best part? This uniform—which gets me free drinks when I wear it in any of the bars where real Americans gather, ones that respect the flag and what our country stands for—this uniform only cost me six thousand dollars. How do you like that? A commission as a lieutenant commander, Mars Division, came along with it. I got a certificate saying that, signed by President Donald J. Trump himself, in his own handwriting.

What do you mean? There's nothing shady about paying for a uniform. The lady at the trailer at the North Dakota state fair where I signed up last summer said all servicemen and women pay for their uniforms. The higher the rank, the more they pay. Duh! You ain't too smart, are you?

I woulda paid more and been a space admiral, like my friend Travis Nurlbacher, but that cost fifteen thousand dollars. I don't have that kind of money. Travis does, but that's only because he got hurt at the grain elevator where he used to work. A metal pole went through his head. He got a big insurance settlement out of it. Travis talks funny now, and he's kinda twitchy but the lady at the trailer said that wouldn't disqualify him from being a space admiral.

That lady was nice. She had long blonde hair and wore a short skirt and a little shirt that showed off her abdominal muscles. She said she was a general in Space Force so I tried not to think about how she'd look with her clothes off. Instead I called her ma'am, which she seemed to like.

"You're exactly the kind of patriotic, right-thinking American we need in Space Force," she told me.

I was afraid to ask, but I had to know. "Does it matter that I'm forty-two years old? Is that too old to join up?" I was worried it was, but she said no. She was real nice about everything. She said it's okay that I didn't finish high school and have a couple of DUIs, and that thing about them saying I broke into my ex-girlfriend's house, feeding her dog laxatives and scratching up all of her Ricky Martin records.

"As long as you love your country and you can give us enough money to prove you're not a socialist who wants everything for free, you're in."

Whew! What a relief!

So now me and Travis are heroes. We get free drinks at Uncle Daddy's Tavern and at the Deuces Wild gentlemen's club. Everybody wants to hear about Space Force. General Tammy (that was the name of the blonde lady who signed us up) said to wait for a phone call, telling us where to report for training.

It's been six months, but like they say, Rome wasn't built in a day. Travis and me are gonna be given command of a spaceship. As soon as they show us how to drive it, we'll blast off and go rocketing through space. We'll zap aliens and space monsters and make love to exotic women from other planets. The call to report for duty's gonna come any day now, I just know it.

There's No Crying In Space

Bill Bibo Jr

Charles Jackson Mortimer III wondered what the hell he was doing here. Trapped in an orbiting spaceship. His plasma lasers were charging with interminable slowness. And as a topper, he didn't know if the Chinese space station had detected him yet.

He shouldn't be here. He wasn't an astronaut. He wasn't even a soldier. He was a political appointee, and a junior one at that.

His radio blared, "Red Leader One, this is Gold Leader One. Do you read me? Charlie, are you in position?"

Charlie looked out his view window to the Earth below.

<<>>

It was his father's fault. As CEO of AdvantiFlexicon, he had contributed handsomely to the President's reelection campaigns on the sole condition that his son be given a job.

Charlie remembered the meeting in the Oval Office and the pleased look on his father's face when the Vice President said, "We do have this new initiative, one where your son can get in on the ground floor. This gives a virtually unlimited opportunity to achieve."

The President, taking a working lunch, his mouth full of cheeseburger, said, "Your boy will do great things, the greatest, things no one else has ever done in the history of this planet."

"That sounds very nice, Mr. President," Charlie's father said, patting Charlie on the shoulder. "Charlie had some, shall we say, struggles in college, but who hasn't. You won't regret giving my son this opportunity."

The President nodded as he chomped down on a handful of fries slathered in ketchup. He pressed the overly large button on the side of his desk. The room flashed with a brilliant red light that made Charlie shield his eyes.

41

"Excuse me for a moment," said the Vice President as he got up from his chair and left the room.

Seconds later he returned, popped the top of a can of diet soda, and placed it within reach of the President. The flashing lights instantly ceased, and calm returned to the Oval Office. Turning back to Charlie and his father the Vice President straightened his tie and sat down once again.

"So, do we have a deal?" he said.

Without looking at Charlie his father extended his hand to the Vice President. "I believe we do."

<<>>

A week later Charlie stood in the sparsely furnished waiting room watching a very pretty receptionist try to decipher the buttons on the telephone panel in front of her. On her third attempt she managed to send a piercing sound throughout the intercom system.

"Sorry," she said to everyone within a city block. "It's my first day."

When the painful vibrations subsided Charlie smiled, leaned a little closer, and said, "Mine, too."

"Miss Daison?" A voice from the telephone panel startled them both. "If that is Mr. Mortimer, send him in."

The receptionist smiled up at Charlie. "You can go in now."

For a few moments Charlie believed he might like his new job. Then he walked through the door and met The General.

<<>>

"Mr. Mortimer, I appreciate you volunteering for this position."

The General, a familiar looking, overweight man in a full military uniform with more medals than the seamstress knew where to put them, paced in front of him. His skin showed the orange texture that Charlie assumed came from exposure to space rays.

"I really didn't volunteer. It was more of an appointment. I don't even know what the job is. I was just told to come here and..."

The General waved him silent.

"Regardless, irregardless, whatever, you are here now, and you are mine. You will have three weeks of very extensive and very intense training before you will be sent on your first mission. It will be a great mission, the best."

"Mission? I thought this was a desk job," Charlie said.

"Mr. Mortimer, you have been *appointed* to one of the highest positions within the newly formed United States Space Force, chartered through historic executive action by the greatest President ever. Your desk, as you so quaintly put it, will not be on this planet. Time to get you prepared to serve."

The General pressed an overly large button on the side of his desk. The room flashed with a brilliant red light that made Charlie shield his eyes.

Before Charlie could protest, or even think about why The General needed a diet soda now, two burly men ran into the room, threw a black bag over his head, and he felt himself being dragged away.

<<>>

Charlie squinted as his eyes adjusted to a harsh light. He sat up and waited for the loud hum in his head to subside. A few minutes later he realized the hum was not only in his head but in the walls all around him.

He was seated on a cot in the corner of a small, tight room. All four walls looked to be constructed from metal panels as were the floor and the ceiling. A desk and light above it were the only other fixtures in the room. Had he been kidnapped? Where was he? What was going on?

He leaned over and looked out the small portal beside his bed. From somewhere within the shock he remembered the words of Aleksei Leonov, a Russian cosmonaut and the first man to step out from his capsule into the emptiness of space. "The Earth was absolutely round. I believe I never knew what the word round meant until I saw Earth from space."

There it was just as Aleksei had said. The Earth, absolutely round, passed below him.

Charlie dropped his head into his hands and began to cry.

The door swung open. "Good, you're awake," said The General. "Time to start your training."

The same two burly men from before ran into the room, threw a black bag over his head, and again, he felt himself being dragged away.

<<>>

When the bag was removed Charlie found himself seated in a much larger room. In front of him was a large wooden desk with the words US Space Force emblazoned on a round logo that reminded him of the Star Trek movies.

The General sat behind the desk. A map of the Moon was pinned to the wall behind him. To his right stood several pieces of physical training equipment. A computer workstation with a large curved monitor and several speakers on each side was next to that. To his left was a kitchenette and compact dining table. Next to that was the open door to his room.

"Hey, why did you have to..."

The General waved him silent. "No time for questions," he said, stepping around the desk and posing in front of Charlie.

He was dressed in a red jumpsuit that looked exactly like the uniforms in "The Attack of the Lizard Men From Mars", a classic 1950s movie that was a standard on late night television. Charlie had seen the movie numerous times and laughed every time. This jumpsuit seemed... undersized. Hands on his hips, his jaw thrust out to the side, The General waited for a lingering moment.

"It's time to begin your training."

<<>>

For three weeks Charlie's days were all the same. The mornings were an intense regime of calisthenics and running in place, all led closely by the two burly men and supervised, somewhat loosely, by The General, when he wasn't watching television news programs beamed up from Earth.

Lunch was a protein shake, a special recipe concocted by one of the burly men. The General never sat with them for any meals preferring to take his alone in his quarters. Charlie could smell something definitely more enticing than a protein shake.

His afternoons were filled with hours of computer simulations with a break for diet soda and veggie chips. In the simulations Charlie piloted a red, white, and blue flying saucer, attacking vicious cartoon aliens and other Earth-bound enemies.

Dinner was pasta or a rice dish, after which his evenings were left to studying the thin Owner's Manual for the flying saucers he piloted in the simulation.

After three days he was able to convince The General that there was no need to bag his head and drag him to the gym area. It was directly adjacent to his room. After six days Charlie had the entire manual memorized and began to teach himself a foreign language from the second half of the Owner's Manual where the directions were duplicated in Spanish. After eight days he had broken the simulation, defeating the game as he called it, destroying everyone and everything, causing the program to run out of enemy aliens. Since the simulation no longer produced any bad guys, The General instructed him just to fly the saucer around and practice maneuvers.

One night during their sleeping period, Charlie snuck out of his room to search for a way back home. He discovered that the entire space station only had seven rooms, including the separate sleeping quarters for the four of them, the training room, a toilet with shower, and a large storage room. It was at that moment that Charlie gave up all hope of being found, or rescued, or getting away.

After three weeks Charlie's muscle tone improved to a point where one of the burly guys began to watch him in a way that made Charlie uncomfortable.

Finally, after twenty-two days, seven hours, and thirty-four minutes the day arrived. The two burly men ran into his room, threw a black bag over his head, and again, he felt himself being dragged away.

When the bag was yanked from Charlie's head he found he was sitting in the same training room in front of the same large wooden desk with the same US Space Force logo. A box wrapped in colorful paper with a big red, white, and blue ribbon sat on the desk.

The General came around the desk, posed briefly, and patted Charlie on the shoulder.

"Mr. Mortimer, Charlie, Clever Charlie, that's right, very Clever Charlie, the cleverest. You've done it. Training is over. You passed. And that means something great." The two burly men applauded. One wiped a tear from his eye. "And because of that I have something very special for you."

He pushed the box toward Charlie.

Charlie took the box and opened it. Inside was a red spacesuit exactly like those in "The Attack of the Lizard Men From Mars" and the one The General now wore.

"Put it on. The guys can help you."

"I think I can manage," Charlie said to the disappointment of one of the burly men.

While Charlie dressed, The General went on, his voice higher and more excited. "I have just received word from the Pentagon that the Chinese are building a spacecraft that would carry hundreds, thousands of undocumented immigrants, landing them in the Heartland of our great country. Imagine a shuttle craft of such size descending upon Des Moines or Branson, we call it an Immigrant Bomb. Terrible, just terrible. The effect would be horrible, absolute chaos, the worst.

"Your mission is to take out that shuttle before the Chinese can use it."

"How am I supposed to do that?" Charlie asked.

The General pressed the overly large button on the side of his desk. The wall behind the desk parted in the middle, ripping the map of the moon in two, but revealing another larger room. Within it stood two very big and very real, flying saucers. One was trimmed in red, the other in gold.

"These were developed from found alien technology, the most advanced, fastest things in The Space Force," The General said.

Charlie walked round the desk and touched the closest one. It was solid and smooth.

"How did this happen? Were they here all the time?"

"You'll have to thank Dr. Smith and Dr. Jones. Not only are they great physical trainers, but great engineers as well," The General said. "Unfortunately, only one saucer is functional right now or I'd go with you. We're waiting for parts on the red one, yours, I'm afraid. You're Red Leader One. I'm Gold Leader One. You'll have to take mine."

He pressed a lever on the side of the gold saucer and a set of stairs descended.

"They tell me the computer does everything, like the simulations. You just have to go along to make sure it does. Good luck, Charlie, Clever Charlie. Make The Space Force Great Again."

Charlie turned as he climbed up the stairs. "Wait, what? What do you mean by 'again'? I thought this was the first."

The General waved as the stair retracted. "Sorry, can't hear you."

<<>>

Charles Jackson Mortimer III wondered what he was doing trapped in an orbiting spaceship, waiting for his plasma lasers to charge, hoping the Chinese space station would not detect his presence.

His radio blared, "Red Leader One, this is Gold Leader One. Do you read me? Charlie, are you in position?"

Charlie looked out his view window to the Earth below.

An alarm screamed and the saucer was filled with a brilliant red light that made Charlie shield his eyes.

"Warning!" the computer said. "Your presence has been detected. The enemy is preparing to fire. Beginning evasive maneuvers."

A panel popped open and a diet soda was thrust toward Charlie. He slapped it away, the bubbles floating everywhere in zero gravity.

A blue beam emanated from the Chinese Space Station, missing Charlie's saucer but striking The Space Force station. The explosion rocked the saucer sending it into a downward spin toward the Earth.

The monitor on the control panel came to life and the image of the Vice President came into view. He was sitting behind the President's desk in the Oval Office.

"Mr. President... Wait. Mr. Mortimer, what are you doing in that saucer? That was for the President's use. I mean The General's use only."

Charlie knew then there had never really been a Space Force, that he had only been a pawn in an elaborate plan to get rid of the President.

"Oh heck, it doesn't matter anymore," the Vice President said. "It's too late. As you saw the President has fallen victim a tragic attack, an act of war by the Chinese. I have had to assume control. We shall, of course, retaliate. In fact, the missiles are already on their way.

"I want to personally thank you, Mr. Mortimer. You shall be remembered for your service to your country. Your parents will be notified. They will, of course, be very proud." He was laughing as he switched off the feed.

Charlie looked out his view window to the Earth passing below. He finally understood what the word round meant.

Space Force: First Victory

Larry Hodges

So I be recruited for Space Force, wonderful thing that is. I fake credentials, but they no care, they just want anyone willing to fight invisible windmills in space. I that person, since on earth, well, I wanted in many places.

So now we in orbit, protecting world from aliens. If they come, we go BOOM! And they gone. Of course, that assume we have bigger boom-boom then they have. We have lasers, and like wall that no one can get through (unless they have ladder), nothing stop our laser (unless they have mirror). We lean gray fighting machine, but mostly we just bored sitting around waiting for enemy.

You probably tell from my good English I be woman from Russia. That greatly help get ahead in American Space Force, but on this I say no more.

Sometime maybe we shoot down meteor and report to Mar-a-Lago we shoot down hostile. Maybe tiny green invisible alien on meteor want to enslave world. Yes, we are like wall in space that keep illegal aliens from Earth. We don't need them, we already have illegal Mexicans to pick our crops for rubles, I mean pennies.

Space Force cost America two trillion dollars, about domestic product of Italy. So your president, he say Italy will pay for Space Force, or we won't protect their capital, Vatican City. Well, he say that. I hope real Vatican pray for us cuz we're like, how you say, fish in barrel if real alien comes with bigger boom-boom? Plus there way too many us fish jammed in these metal space barrels. Smell like wet dog.

Yesterday I learn how to shoot lasers. I draw funny green alien picture on paper and then put paper outside ship, and I shoot it between eyes. Paper easy to shoot, it don't move and don't shoot back. Today I want to learn to steer ship but captain, he says, "No, you suppose to learn that on Earth,

49

how you not know how to steer ship?" What am I to say, that person whose place I took, I think she alive but secretly transfer to Antarctica Station. Maybe she stop illegal penguin immigration.

I am on watch when alarm comes., others asleep. Captain comes rushing in, wondering what's going on. I've already got enemy on the front window, except up here they call it a viewscreen, though I thought screen you use to keep bugs out. Maybe it keep aliens out.

But these aliens, they in big round ship in front of us. Rest of Space Force, they also see it, and we all swarm around alien ship like teenagers and mirrors, cuz the ship's curved surface is like funhouse mirror at amusement park.

"Hail them!" cried the Captain.

"How?" I asked.

"Push that button!" he beckoned, sounding exasperated for some reason.

I pushed the button. "Anyone there?"

The answer was immediate, in a voice as inexpressibly deep and rich as the chocolate truffles I live on. "We are an Albabondaranium ship and we are asking for political asylum."

"Why," the captain asked, "would we grant political asylum to an Albabandannas . . . Albababbas . . . Aldaberries . . . to a bunch of illegal immigrants?"

"We are not illegal immigrants," said the inexpressible voice. "We are political refugees asking for political asylum. If we return to Albabondarania, we will be put to death as we did not stand and applaud our great leader's last speech."

"What evidence do you have that you are political refugees?"

There was a horrible crash as a second, smaller ship flies by, shooting lasers at us and big ship but missing. The ship had a picture of a huge, clawed being, all black with dripping white fangs and horrible eyes that glared like angry mongoose.

"That is our proof," said the inexpressible voice. "They are not very good shots since they do not believe in science and so don't know how to use the weapons we designed for them, but eventually they'll get lucky."

"Wait, you design their weapons?" I asked.

"Of course," said the inexpressible voice. "We are the scientists of Albabondarania. If you will grant us asylum, we will take on the menial jobs we learned you Americans hate and look down on, like physicists and engineers, and let you do the jobs you do best, like run businesses on the back of laborers while you pocket the profits."

"You are *scientists*?" cried the captain. "*You* are the enemy! Helm, fire laser!"

"But their mirrors—"

"*FIRE!!!*"

Our ship barely survive our laser beam, which bounce off the big ship's mirror and shot back at us like Russian vodka on empty stomach, taking out our weapons. But smaller ship returns and gets in lucky shot that weren't so lucky as its rebounded laser blew it out of space. Last thing I see was horrible, glaring creature pictured on its surface staring at me before it blow apart like exploding acne.

"They never did understand why we use mirrors, and now they are just smoke," said the inexpressible voice.

"We destroyed that ship!" cried the Captain. "Space Force just saved a group of poor refugees from space terrorists! We're heroes!"

"Actually—" I began.

"Sounds good to us!" said the inexpressible voice. "And we'll verify this to your leaders. Now, about that asylum?"

Nature (and publishers abhor a blank page.
Sooo have a Gregg Chamberlain limerick!

The class of recruit for Space Force
Is really becoming much worse.
With morons who line up
So eager to sign up,
They'd do better by drafting a horse.

To That Really Big Black Place, And Beyond!

Mike Brennan

Colonel Jameson Brick, United States Space Force, barked out a laugh. Then a kick in the ankle from his Commanding Officer, General Darington, made him realize the Commander in Chief was serious. The pouty glare from the Presidential Throne on the other side of the conference table brought home that the last statement hadn't been a joke.

"Well, Mr. President, I, um, ah..." Inspiration struck. "I was just thinking how surprised the Chinese would be by your idea. It would catch them completely off guard." He glanced at Gen. Darington. "I don't think anyone would expect us to counter the Chinese Base on the far side... I mean, the Dark Side, of the Moon by setting up really big lights around it." He looked around the table at the nodding officials and Presidential Buddies. Some seemed to be acknowledging his save, others agreeing with what a good idea it was, and some, apparently just because everyone else was nodding, so it was probably safe.

"And they can be lasers. Lasers are good," chimed in the Son-in-Law-in-Chief, clearly feeling the need to be involved. He was still a little uncomfortable in the title, which had only been made official at the last Cabinet Meeting. Although it seemed to be a Civilian position (no one was really sure, as the President hadn't actually said what it involved), he still wore the sliver and blue Dress Uniform he had designed when he had been appointed Secretary of Space (which he might still be; no one knew if his new title included those duties). "Big lasers. On tall poles, so they light up a big area." The Presidential Nod this received made him smile and squirm. "They could shine red, white, and blue laser light."

Secretary of Important Stuff (another new Cabinet position) Hannity piped in. "And we can buy all the places we put the poles. I saw a site online that sells real estate on the Moon." He basked in the Presidential Glow that always came when someone mentioned "real estate". "That way the Chinese can't get to the poles without trespassing, and we can call the cops on them." He sat back, smiling, knowing that he had scored more points in his quest to replace the Vice President, who sat so very silently at the Right Hand of POTUS.

The Commander In Chief nodded, and assumed what he must think was a serious look. "These are all really good ideas I've had. The best ideas. We need to do these ideas to keep the Chinese from sneaking in from the Dark Side of the Moon some New Moon." He looked around the table, and put on his, "explaining things" face. "I just found out that the New Moon is when the side of the Moon facing the United States, and maybe other places, I don't know, but the side facing us is dark, so if the Chinese have secret bases on the Dark Side of the Moon, they can sneak into our country on a New Moon. And the Wall can't even stop them, because they are coming from UP, and I mean really up, not just the Canada part of the map. Nobody knew. But I said to myself, 'We have to do something about the Chinese secret bases on the Dark Side of the Moon.'"

Col. Brick sat with a slight smile frozen on his lips, as, over the next hour and a half, the President expounded at length, and without interruption, on, well, everything. Like a comet in elliptical orbit around the Sun, his monolog swung past the original topic on regular, if infrequent, intervals, with his comments becoming more fragmented each time. Brick estimated that, if this went on for another two hours there would be nothing but a swarm of single syllables, only loosely connected by conversational gravity. To his surprise, however, the President suddenly stopped talking and sat up straight.

"We should move on this idea," the President said, "Move on it like a bitch". He was silent for a few seconds. "We will have to pay the Russians to take the lights to the Moon, because they have the biggest rockets. So very big. The Best." He paused again, and put a finger on the hearing aid that he had taken to wearing whenever he wasn't actually on camera. "We should rent ten..., no, um TWELVE big Russian rockets. Yes, twelve. Or maybe more, it could take more. No one knows." He sat back and smiled, "but we don't have to worry, because we will make the Chinese pay for them."

The applause that broke out from several places around the table, and quickly spread to the entire room, caught Col. Brick by surprise, until he reflected that the people who had started it were the ones who had looked most in need of a restroom break. The President was also surprised, but quickly recovered to bask in the adulation. The Secretary of Defense started his End of Meeting Suck-Up even before the clapping stopped. The praise for the President's intelligence, courage, patriotism, and manhood was expounded on by each Cabinet Member in turn, growing with each one, until the last two members each expressed the desire to bear the President's baby (which struck Col. Brick as odd, as the last was male).

There was a moment of panic when the President appeared about to start talking again, but an aide informed him that one of his favorite shows was about to start, and there was a Big Mac and fries waiting in the Residency. The President departed without another word, and several people at the table slipped the aide money as they left.

"Well," General Darington said as the two Space Force Officers strode down the corridor towards where their staff car, a silver stretch-Lamborghini, waited. "That went well."

"You're kidding, aren't you, Sir?" Distress colored Brick's voice. "There's no Chinese base on the far side of the Moon!"

"Of course there isn't, but we'll get some funding, and we should be able to get two, maybe three 'recon' missions to the Moon out of it. Maybe even a rover." They separated at the car, and the General ordered the Driver into the backseat and took the wheel himself because, well, Lamborghini. Brick took the shotgun seat.

"Besides," said the General as the gull-wing doors closed. "Anything that distracts him from that "Meteors on the Border" crap he's been getting from Infowars."

Time for another Gregg Chamberlain limerick!
You know you want it.

Did you hear about this Space Force maroon?
A real blithering bumbling baboon!
He thought it a gag
To play real laser tag.
His remains got sent home in a spittoon.

The M. U. S. S Superior

Milo Douglas

Peter Tobin, pilot of the *Superior* and the last surviving member of Space Force, looked down at Earth from his escape pod.

Peter shielded his eyes from the exhaust blast of thirty nuclear missiles mounted to the Trump Tower Galactic Wall a few miles away. His space suit's visor auto-polarized bringing into view the missiles' target three hundred miles below.

An hour earlier, Peter's first and last Space Force mission was texted via Presidential App: "Knock the crap out of Canada."

All thirty missile engines reached full throttle.

<<>>

One hour ago:

"Lift off!" Space Force Launch Command announced. "The most amazing mission to protect the Trump Tower Galactic Wall from the very weak Canadians is underway! Nothing has been more amazing than this. The likes of this launch will never be seen again!"

The *Superior* and nineteen other identical Space Force rocket ships cleared the Mar-a-Lago Command Center launch towers and raced to the cloudless heavens.

Onboard the *Superior*, Peter Tobin, was crushed into his pilot's chair. He slapped his hands to the sides of his pressure suit's fishbowl helmet which did nothing to suppress the riotous roar of the spacecraft's launch boosters. He never imagined he would die at age twenty-six serving in President's Trump's Space Force.

Seated beside Peter was Captain Vince Sunderly, whose face shifted between beaming and wincing.

Vince punched Peter's arm and screamed into his helmet mic, "Ain't it great? There's nothing more amazing than a kick in the ass from clean coal solid rocket boosters!"

"Yeah, real powerful," Peter said perfunctorily. He wore the expression of one condemned to walk the plank.

Vince insisted Peter witness the thick streaks of soot belching from the accompanying ships as they traced their smudgy ascent through the sky, but Peter's attention was drawn to his real-time social media status projected on the inside of his visor.

"Wow!" Peter marveled. His half-hearted reply to Vince had earned him 523 Patriot Points. Cameras and microphones all over the ship and on their person broadcast their every action straight to government social media.

Then President Trump's grinning face filled Peter Tobin's view. "The country is counting on your loyalty, Peter Apple Bin!"

Peter forced a smile. "Thank you."

"But you know that, don't you?" President Trump continued. "Everybody knows it. What you're doing here is amazing. People are saying it. Tremendous work. Here, have some more Patriot Points."

Peter's Patriot Points increased to an even 1000.

"Hey, Peter!" Vince said. "The president just gave me a personal greeting and free points."

"It's an automated message, Vince."

"Yeah, well the points are real!"

Two million Patriot Points earned any citizen of The Most United States a Presidential Patriot Pass which granted them unlimited access to any of President Trump's resorts and ownership of an operational F-4 Phantom jet. Nobody had ever come near to earning two million points, but anyone loyal to the president tried.

Peter was not loyal.

Peter was a pacifist which meant he wore the same lethal "loyalty collar" issued to any "Disgrace of the State," also known as DOTS. The loyalty collar detached itself the moment the wearer accumulated one hundred fifty million Patriot Points or 10 years' honorable service in Space Force. If a DOTS's Patriot Points fell into the negative numbers, the collar tightened like an angry sphincter until the wearer was dead.

Peter sighed. Today was day one of his ten year Space Force commitment and though he had started the day with only twenty-five points he was pleased to now have over 1500.

"Look!" Vince pointed to the window. "The *Silent Majority* is really pulling ahead!"

Just then, *Superior's* automated systems administered an intravenous dose of "Jeb Juice" sedative to each of them. The full duration of a clean coal launch was more than a person's conscious senses could endure.

"Holy sweet Jesus!" Vince shouted.

What Vince saw before they both dozed off was a succession of explosions to rival any Fourth Of July spectacle.

Ten Space Force rockets blew up in mid flight, probably from coal dust explosions.

A few broke apart from excessive dynamic pressure due to runaway coal fires.

The rest—except one—just kept roaring off into space.

The only ship to find its proper orbital velocity: The M.U.S.S.*Superior*.

<<>>

Peter's body shook. He gripped his seat, fearful that the Jeb Juice had worn off too soon.

"Wake up!" Vince jostled Peter's seat. "They're coming!"

"Who?"

"The Canadians! Look!"

Through the command deck windows they saw the Trump Tower Galactic Wall gleaming in the sun. The "wall" portion of the structure was comprised of thirty nuclear missiles in one neat row held together by a honeycomb array of locking mechanisms. The array holding the missiles in place extended from a central space station roughly the size and shape of an air traffic control tower. The whole thing looked like a giant, upside down picket fence. President Trump regularly insisted, "it's a big beautiful tactical space wall like no one's ever seen before. This I can tell you. Big wall. Believe me. The biggest. Believe me."

Two Canadian Space Mounty mini shuttles approached the Galactic Wall. Their job—and the reason President Trump scrambled Space Force—was to gently move the Wall out of Canadian space. President Trump parked the Wall over Canada after the Canadian Prime Minister convinced eight other nations to suspend buying weapons from The Most United States of America until "they figure out what the hell is going on in D.C."

"We gotta stop the Canadians!" Vince declared. "Arm the death ray!"

"Uh, I'm a pacifist and they're unarmed!"

Peter's Patriot Points dropped by 8000. He flung his helmet off and clawed at his loyalty collar in a vain attempt to remove it before it tightened.

"Put your helmet back on," Vince scolded. "We are the last two Space Forcers left. President Trump already awarded us 50,000 points for surviving the launch catastrophe. Now it's time to cook some Canadian bacon!"

Peter was relieved that his head had not been squeezed off. "Launch catastrophe?"

Vince pulled up President Trump's most recent Twitter message on their main computer screen. It read, "Nobody knew space FLIGHT could be so complicated. Canada TERRORISMS! BRAIVE souls lost. ACT OF WAR. Knock the hell out of Canada Superior!!!!"

"That looks fake," Peter said.

"Don't make me fire you, SAD Peter!" Vince sneered when he said "SAD," short for "such a disgrace."

"I have over fifty thousand points," Peter said. "My entire life I've never had more than thirty."

"Well, you'll never earn a Presidential Patriot Pass. I've been living with a comfortable hundred thousand or so the better part of my twenty-two years."

Peter pressed the death ray button on his console.

Peter's Patriot Points ticked up again.

The *Superior's* nose cone opened revealing the death ray laser beam cannon. Its stubby crystal barrel was ribbed with red, throbbing heat coils. At the base of the cannon were two spherical tanks filled with reactive chemicals which would combine to generate a powerful laser.

"Fire!" Vince commanded.

"We launched twenty ships up for this?" Peter asked no one in particular.

"I said fire!"

Peter began targeting the two Mounty mini shuttles but at the last moment nudged the targeting sight away from them. "Firing the death ray."

Plus 5000 points.

The chemical tanks made a flushing noise as their contents combined, then they imploded. Instead of a beam of hot laser, the cannon spewed semi-frozen chemicals.

The Mounties never had a chance--their windows were hopelessly coated with slush.

"You missed!" Vince admonished.

"Canadian Mounties," Peter broadcast, "consider that a warning! Don't make us unload on you again!"

The Canadians pulled away.

"Good job, SAD Peter!" Vince exclaimed. "That's what patriotism looks like. It ain't always pretty and you can't be afraid to get your hands sticky showing your love of country!"

"You mean 'dirty.'"

"That was kinda dirty wasn't it?"

"Oh, god."

"What?"

"Incoming ships!"

<<>>

"Who is it?"

"Looks like a North Korean ship followed by two other unidentified ships. They're all making for the space fence."

"Galactic...Wall!"

"Yeah."

"Look," Vince said. "We need to get to the Wall and nuke Canada."

"But we just scared off the entire Canadian space fleet of two part-time Space Mounties."

"That's a good way to lose points," Vince said.

Peter watched his points fall.

"I mean," Peter began, "why doesn't the Wall crew just fire the missiles?"

Vince clenched his fists. "I don't have time for this. Everyone knows the Trump Tower Galactic Wall didn't reach the crowd funding level that actually put people on it. So, we need to get there before the little rocket man does!"

"No time. They're closer."

"Then recharge my death ray," Vince commanded.

"Impossible with your collapsed sacks. Why don't you remotely move the Wall so the ship misses?"

"We can't," Vince mumbled.

"Yes we can."

Minus 1500 points.

"I mean, of course we can," Peter restated. "Just use the remote command codes."

"I told you I can't."

"Why not?"

Vince hung his head. "I didn't graduate from Trump Space University before they filed for bankruptcy."

"Well, give me the codes and I'll do it myself."

"Why would I give command codes to a SAD pacifist?"

Peter was prepared with the national motto: "Because The Most United States is the most important United States." He jabbed his finger at the ship camera. "Believe me."

Plus 8,000 points for a total exceeding 70,000. A graphic of a large caliber pistol appeared projected in Peter's visor.

He began to believe he could earn his Patriot Pass rather quickly. He had earned over 70,000 points in less than 15 minutes with almost no effort.

"Peter!" Vince, said. "That's the biggest increase I've ever seen! And you earned a Good Guy badge!"

Vince transferred the Galactic Wall command codes to Peter's station.

"I don't want to be a Good Guy," Peter clarified. "I just want to survive this mission."

Minus 3,000 points and the pistol graphic disappeared.

Peter watched as the North Korean spacecraft closed in on the command tower of the Wall, the ship's docking speed and trajectory were committed. When the ship was about fifty feet from the tower, Peter fired the Galactic Wall thrusters sending it two hundred feet higher in orbit. The North Korean ship drifted past and kept going. There was no way it had enough fuel to make another docking attempt.

Peter then deftly maneuvered the *Superior* within seventy five yards of the Wall.

Vince cheered. "Ha-ha! Take that, Dear Loser! Mission accomplished!"

"Not yet," Peter said. "The Russians are trying to hack the Tower."

<<>>

A rectangular craft the size of a riding lawnmower approached the command tower of the Galactic Wall and landed on its surface. From its loaf-shaped body sprung articulated legs and a sickle. The sickle swung, chopping off one of the array's antennae which the bot immediately replaced with a Russian radio receiver.

"Peter! Get out there and stop that hacker!" Ordered Vince.

Peter knew that battling a Russian robot in space would be a good way to earn points. The thought of surrendering to the Russian hacker also entered his mind but quickly fled when he remembered the loyalty collar.

In *Superior's* airlock, Peter donned a bulky kerosine powered EVA suit and stepped out into space. The kerosine jets punched him around with fierce spurts of flame. Eventually, Peter landed on the command tower near the hacker.

Neither Peter nor Vince had considered what it meant to "stop" the hacker. The Russian bot detected Peter and skittered towards him. Its sickle sliced through space.

"Your EVA pack is on fire!" Vince said over his com.

Peter's jet pack was indeed on fire. He yanked on the body harnesses until the pack released.

The Russian hacker drew closer, its sickle raised to strike. Peter flung his pack which hit the hacker's body and exploded, instantly destroying the robot.

Peter earned a staggering 30,000 points, but was too distracted to notice.

"Why does our equipment explode so much?" Peter complained.

"Nobody knew engineering space gear could be such a precise science, SAD Peter. Anyway, good job. I'm bringing you back in with the tractor beam."

"We have a tractor beam?" Peter asked in dismay. "Our ships and jet packs spontaneously explode, so is the tractor beam going to tear me to pieces?"

"We'll see..." Vince responded.

The soothing blue concentric rings of *Superior's* tractor beam drew Peter towards the ship.

Earning points was too easy, Peter decided as he floated amidst the rings. He had always assumed it was hard to earn points so he'd never actually tried. He now saw that with no effort a person could get caught up in the immediate rewards that came with saying what everyone else wanted to hear. Peter decided that as long as The Most United States believed he was loyal, he would go through the motions enough to earn his points and survive the mission.

Back aboard the *Superior*, Peter approached the command deck to find Vince frantically flipping through an emergency protocol manual.

"What's wrong?" Peter asked.

"The receiver devices the hacker installed have given the Russians partial control of the station. They are trying to reprogram the missiles to target Tucker Carlson's Fire Island compound."

"Okay...."

"We have to do something!"

Peter began typing on his console's keyboard and mumbled to himself, "We don't really have to...." With a flourish he finished typing. "There we go," Peter said with satisfaction.

"What did you do?"

"I disabled all remote access to the Missile Wall. It's on manual control only."

The airlock alarm sounded.

"Oh, no!" Vince said.

"What's wrong now?

"Fox crew alert!"

<<>>

A Fox News troop transport with a complement of Good Guy Space Milita had approached and docked with *Superior* while Peter and Vince were distracted by the North Korean ship and the Russian hacker. Good Guys with ray guns entered the *Superior* through the airlock.

"This is your fault!" Vince said to Peter. "Fox News says that I'm a SAD-loving cuck! The president gave Admiral Hannity orders to stop us!"

"Is peaceful surrender an option here?"

Vince drew two ray guns. "The *Superior* is sovereign territory of The Most United States, so I'm gonna give these illegal aliens a piece of my mind one laser at a time. You just dock us to the Galactic Wall."

As Vince made his way through the ship towards the advancing Good Guy militia Peter watched Vince's progress on his command deck monitor.

Vince was one compartment away from the Good Guys when he put away his ray guns and draw a semi-automatic handgun. The Good Guys retreated from their compartment into the airlock and closed the door.

"Vince," Peter began, "that gun will punch a hole through the ship and—" Peter heard his own voice echoing. Vince's helmet lay on the seat next to him.

When Vince entered the final compartment, the Good Guys opened the airlock doors venting Vince into space.

The Good Guys were coming.

Peter set the ship's self-destruct, detached the command section he was in and flew it away. Moments later, the *Superior* erupted in flames.

A minute later, Peter had docked with the Trump Tower Galactic Wall. From the safety of the airlock, Peter watched as a few Good Guys who survived the blast flew towards him in their EVA suits.

<<>>

Peter was alone on the Galactic Wall and The Most United States was watching and listening.

Peter's debut mission was breaking ratings records across the country and his points were nearly up to 1 million.

But they were slowing. And though he had earned an astounding number of points in less than an hour, reaching

1.5 million points before the Good Guys reached him seemed unlikely.

He found the missile command room and closed the door behind him.

The missile command room was full of blinking lights and control panels and it had a tall window presenting a geosynchronous view of Canada. From the peripheries of the window, the tips of the nuclear missiles pointed at the Great White North.

Peter stood before the launch panel. He had learned about this system in his Trump Space University Tactical Space Wars course.

The system was pre-targeted and ready to fire by way of three backlit plastic buttons sequenced in a row. The first button, *Lock,* was green, indicating the missiles were secured to the honeycomb array. The next buttons, *Unlock* and *Fire* were red, showing that those were not active. Pressing *Lock* would turn it from green to red and turn the *Unlock* button from red to green, releasing the missiles from the array. The *Fire* button fired the missiles.

"What am I supposed to do?" Peter asked himself. He could use the thrusters to move the station away from Canada or disable the firing system, but he would be executed or forced to live with the loyalty collar for the rest of his life. And Trump would still have thirty missiles.

He could flee in one of the escape pods lining the room, but his loyalty collar would constrict before he reentered Earth's atmosphere.

Meanwhile, his points continued to accumulate, even as he wrestled with his conundrum.

Peter ran to the door and looked through the window. The Good Guys were approaching and began blasting at the ray-proof door as soon as they saw Peter's face. Peter was relieved to find a firehose in a firebox by the door which he used to secure the door.

A moment later one of the Good Guys wrote "chnl 3" in the burn residue on the window. Peter turned his helmet com to channel 3.

"I'm Commander Lander," the Good Guy said. She then tapped her helmet. "The country is watching you through my

Fox News Alert cam, so you'd better fire those missiles now or open up."

Peter affected a confident laugh. "You're in no position to threaten me, Commander. If you interfere with my mission I may have to aim the missiles at Foxlandia."

Peter's points fluctuated.

"You're a pacifist," Commander Lander said. Peter's points went down. "So, we can't trust you to follow President Trump's orders." And down...

Peter's mouth went dry as his points sank back below nine hundred thousand. His head hurt from the effort it took to please an audience he couldn't see by saying and doing things he didn't even believe in. But he couldn't bear the thought of living as a SAD citizen anymore.

"Well this pacifist survived a clean coal launch, blew up a Russian hacker, blew up his own ship and has his finger on a nuclear launch button. Do you really think I'm done blowing things up?"

Peter's gambit worked. His points ticked up past 1 million.

Peter turned to the launch board with his back to the Good Guys and took out his multi tool. He crouched over the panel to hide what he was doing from any cameras in the room.

A mechanical clanking sounded throughout the array and Peter stepped way from the launch board.

"What did you do, SAD Peter?" Commander Lander asked.

"I left my mark." He put his multitool away. "As my final act and the act which will provide me with the most amazing Patriot Pass ever I am going to hand over the station to the Good Guys so they can fire these big beautiful missiles if they want to."

Peter made his way to one of the nearby escape pods and secured himself inside. He drew his ray gun took careful aim at the door where the Good Guys waited and burned away the firehose from the door.

Elation filled Peter's heart as his points surpassed 1.5 million. The loyalty collar violently popped off rolled around the inside of his fishbowl helmet before dinking him on the forehead. Peter removed his helmet and flung the collar back into the room.

"U-S-A! U-S-A!" he cheered into his helmet.

The Good Guys rushed through the door.

"We're in!" Commander Lander announced.

Peter earned two million Patriot Points just as his escape pod shot away from the Trump Tower Galactic Wall.

<<>>

Commander Lander approached the launch board and shared with President Trump and The Most United States that the launch board was intact. "Everything is in pre-launch mode targeting Canada. But SAD Peter left us some graffiti."

The words "Viva Canada!" we're scratched into the board. The *Unlock* and *Lock* buttons were scratched up, too.

"Clever little traitor," Commander Lander said. "Time for me to win my F-4 Phantom jet." She watched as her Patriot Points zipped up and up. "I'm pressing the first button!" To add to the drama, she hovered her finger over the red scratched *Unlock* button.

<<>>

In the escape pod, Peter twisted knobs and pushed buttons. The pod's view screen whined and buzzed through a range of pitches as if scanning frequencies. Then the Prime Minister of Canada's face appeared.

"You maniac!" he said. "They're going to launch the missiles!"

<<>>

Commander Lander pressed the first button labeled *Unlock* changing it from red to green. Accordingly, the *Lock* button next to it turned from green to red. A series of mechanical clanks rang throughout the station.

"Missiles unlocked," Commander Lander said.

<<>>

"You're right," Peter said to the Prime Minister. "They are going to fire the missiles but you'll be okay. Oh, and I'm officially seeking asylum."

"Go screw yourself!" the Prime Minister said. "We're evacuating provinces down here. Make those idiots stop the launch!"

Far below, Peter thought he could see the contrails of Canadian fighter jets racing to presumably intercept any incoming missiles.

"By Canadian law, you have to grant me asylum."

"We also must shoot down enemy missiles. I can guarantee we will mistake your escape pod for a missile if you don't stop the launch!"

<<>>

Commander Lander pressed the *Launch* Button.

"Canada, you're fired!"

<<>>

"No, you don't have to do that," Peter assured calmly. "Scramble a helicopter for pickup. I'm about to lose signal."

Orange plasma began to glow outside the windows of the escape pod.

<<>>

All thirty missiles fired simultaneously and the station groaned, straining against the missiles as they were still held in place by the array of locking mechanisms.

Then, the station accelerated.

Commander Lander didn't have time to understand that Peter had simply unlocked the missiles, then switched the *Lock* and *Unlock* button covers. Commander Lander and the rest of the Good Guys were smashed against the back wall of the missile command room. The G-forces held them there and sent them into a gentle, head-lolling sleep.

<<>>

Peter Tobin, the last surviving member of Space Force's debut mission watched as the Trump Tower Galactic Wall was dragged into lower orbit by the nukes still attached to it. It cartwheeled down and disintegrated in the atmosphere in the biggest, most beautiful, flaming streaks anyone had ever seen. Then the re-entry Jeb Juice was administered.

<<>>

Peter woke in his capsule to the sight of a handsome pair of Canadian Mounties standing in the doorway.

"Welcome to Canada!"

**So what will we run out of first,
blank pages or Gregg Chamberlain
Limericks?
He's Canadian by the way.**

A flatulent gunner named Chas
Got promoted to private first-class.
During the Battle of Frac'tup
His plaz-cannon packed up,
So he lobbed all his shells with his ass.

The Bigly Adventures of Captain Barron

Scott Hughes

The year was 2099. Captain John Barron, the greatest and most heroic captain of all time, was returning home to Planet America, formerly Planet Earth, to be honored as *Infinity* magazine's Person of the Year for the fifteenth year in a row.

In his captain's quarters aboard the Starship *Trump*, the Space Force's best and fastest ship, named after the greatest president in the history of Planet America who served a record ten terms and then never died. He was still alive on his own planet. Captain Barron awoke in his luxurious futuristic bed beside two voluptuous alien gals, like supermodels but with purple skin or a tail or something. He kissed each of them softly so as not to wake them, then got out of bed and strode across his quarters to the bathroom mirror. He admired his shining mane of golden hair that was totally real and not fake at all like that guy from the old show *Star Track*, Captain Kurt. People used to think Captain Kurt was so great, but he was just a loser in a fake TV show. Captain Barron was the real deal and superior in every way: handsomer, richer, stronger, taller, fitter, smarter, and way better with the ladies (human and alien).

"Come back to bed, baby," one of the alien chicks sleepily purred in a sexy alien accent.

"No can do," replied Captain Barron as he put on his stylish Space Force uniform adorned with all the medals he'd won for various acts of bravery, but they were holographic medals since this was the future. "I've got very important business to attend to. Being the best captain in the Space Force isn't all fun and games, you know."

"You really shouldn't work so hard," cooed the other alien babe. She also had a sexy alien accent.

"You gotta work hard to be the greatest." Captain Barron winked at them. They both blushed because he was so dashing. "Don't worry. I won't be gone long."

He gave them another wink and then put on the belt that held his laser blaster and saber of light, which was *nothing* like the lightsabers from those dumb movies. A saber of light had a handle made of gold, not cheap silver. Plus, there was only one in existence, and it belonged to Captain Barron.

Outside the captain's quarters, the robot PU-10 was waiting as usual.

"Boop boop," said PU-10 in robot language, which Captain Barron understood. "Boop boop-boop boopy boop."

"You know it, PU-10," said the captain. He and the robot high-fived. "Those alien babes will never forget last night."

"Boop-boop boop!"

"Yeah, yeah," replied the captain. "I wish you could be like me too."

"Boop..." PU-10 said sadly.

"So, how far from Planet America are we?" Captain Barron asked as he and PU-10 made their way to the bridge.

"Boopy boop boop."

"Well, it's not like they're gonna start without me. I'm the one they're giving the award to."

When Captain Barron arrived at the bridge, all the Starship *Trump* crewmembers gave him a standing ovation that lasted ten minutes, maybe twenty minutes—who knows since time works different in space. Even the mega-hot navigator, Lieutenant Fox, sashayed over and planted a huge smooch right on the captain's lips.

"Congratulations, Captain," she said. "No one deserves this award more than you." Lieutenant Fox always knew what to say.

Captain Barron raised both hands to stop the applause. "All right, all right," he said with a debonair grin. "Back to your stations, everyone. I'm actually tired of winning this award year after year. I mean, give someone else a chance, am I right?"

Everyone laughed.

"Captain, we're approaching the Sphere," announced the navigator, Lieutenant Miller.

"On screen," Barron commanded as he took his seat in the captain's chair.

"Aye, Captain." Miller hit a few buttons, and the giant screen on the bridge's wall displayed the scene outside the starship: encompassing the entire planet was a spherical metal net made of gold that had successfully kept all alien spacecraft fleets from entering Planet America for the past seventy years.

"My God," said Lieutenant Fox.

"Boopy!" said PU-10, which meant the same thing Fox had said.

Captain Barron beamed. "Every time you see it, it gets more beautiful, doesn't it?"

Every crewmember agreed. The Sphere was glorious.

"Lieutenant Miller," said the captain, "patch me through to Space Force Headquarters."

"Aye, Captain." Miller hit different buttons this time. "Ready, Captain."

"Space Force HQ, this is Captain John Barron of the Starship *Trump*," said the captain. "Permission to enter the Sphere and proceed to Planet America."

The ship's radio crackled, and then a voice said, "Permission granted, Captain Barron. And, might I add, congratulations on your award, sir!"

"Thank you," said the captain.

"They're idiots if they don't give it to you every year, sir," said the voice. "Pardon me, sir, for speaking so freely. I..."

"What's your name?" Captain Barron asked.

"Manafort, sir," said the voice. "Private First Class Stone Manafort, sir."

"Well, you're exactly right, Private First Class Manafort," said the captain. "You're pardoned."

"Thank you, sir!" said Manafort. "Opening Sphere."

On the display screen, one of the Sphere's many gates began to open. Out of nowhere, the entire starship trembled as if it were in an earthquake, but everyone knew it couldn't be an earthquake because they were in space and there's no such thing as a spacequake. The bridge shook violently, and several of the crewmembers fell to the floor.

PU-10's head struck the wall, and his brain circuits began shooting out sparks. Captain Barron jumped from his chair to the robot's side and repaired the circuitry almost immediately because he knew tech better than anyone.

"Boop boop," said PU-10 as the captain helped him to his feet.

"You're welcome," said Captain Barron. Then he addressed Lieutenant Miller. "What the hell was that?"

"A laser blast, Captain!" said Miller. "But I'm not seeing any other ships on our radar. Shields are at 99% and holding, sir."

"Captain," said Lieutenant Fox, touching her communication earpiece, "we're receiving a transmission."

Captain Barron returned to his seat. "On screen."

Fox pressed several buttons, and a reptilian alien appeared on the display. The crewmembers gasped at how repulsive the creature was, and a few of them even gagged.

The female lizard alien's bulging mustard-colored eyes, each moving in a different direction, scanned the bridge until they landed upon the captain.

"Greetings, Captain Barron," she hissed.

The captain knew exactly who this wretched monster was: his nemesis. "Rayh-Ill, so we meet again. I knew it was only a matter of time before I saw your putrid face again."

Rayh-Ill cackled. "Oh, John, you know you missed me."

"You mean after I defeated you in the Electorus Galaxy? Because that's the only thing about you I miss: defeating you."

The crew couldn't help but chuckle. They all remembered how resoundingly the captain had bested Rayh-Ill the last time they had clashed.

"You only beat me because you cheated," hissed Rayh-Ill. "Now I've returned with a few tricks of my own."

"Tricks are for kids," Captain Barron retorted.

The crewmembers really laughed this time. Rayh-Ill became so enraged that smoke fumed from her nostrils, which is what happened when the reptilian aliens from Planet Demacron became angry.

"I have disabled your starship's weapons," hissed Rayh-Ill furiously, "and I have cut off your communications with Space Force Headquarters."

Captain Barron narrowed his eyes in disbelief. Then he turned slightly so he could see Lieutenant Fox. She checked her computer panels, then nodded to the captain.

"So, what now?" the captain asked, glaring at Rayh-Ill on screen.

"My fleet has you surrounded," hissed Rayh-Ill.

"Ha!" laughed Captain Barron. "Fake news! Something tells me you're lying. You lie so much, you probably believe it."

To prove she wasn't lying, Rayh-Ill shouted a command to her own crewmembers. "Decloak!" Then she said, "Think I'm lying now, Captain?"

The captain glanced at Lieutenant Miller and nodded. Miller tapped a couple of buttons, and the display screen switched from Rayh-Ill's ugly face to the exterior of Starship *Trump*. A dozen Demacron warships materialized into view. Miller tapped some buttons again, and the screen switched back to Rayh-Ill, who was cackling madly.

"Boop boopy-boop!" PU-10 said, angrily shaking his robotic fist.

"Easy, PU-10," said Captain Barron. "Captain Barron respects all women, even if they are scaly and gross lizard women, and so will his crew." Then he said, "All right, Rayh-Ill. It appears you're telling the truth... *this* time. Tell me, what is it you want?"

"You have a choice to make, Captain," said Rayh-Ill. "Either you come aboard my ship, alone and unarmed, or I destroy your vessel and everyone on it."

The crewmembers turned their frightened eyes to Captain Barron, but he remained unfazed. In fact, he had a slight smirk on his face.

"Very well," he said. "I'm headed to the zaportation room. Prepare to receive me onboard your ship, alone and unarmed."

Lieutenant Fox cut off the display screen and ran into the captain's arms. "You can't go, Captain! She'll kill you!"

Captain Barron winked at her, which instantly melted Fox's heart. "Don't worry. I have a plan."

"You always do," said Fox.

"PU-10, accompany me to the zaportation room," the captain ordered.

"Boop-boop!" replied the robot.

Ten minutes later, Captain Barron materialized in the zaportation room of Rayh-Ill's spaceship. Several Demacron guards were there waiting for him and frisked him to ensure he wasn't carrying any weapons. He still wore his belt, but his laser blaster and saber of light were both gone.

The guards escorted him to their ship's bridge, where Rayh-Ill was waiting, seated in her own captain's chair. She was even more hideous in person: bulbous yellow eyes, pointy teeth, spiky neck flaps, flat chest.

"Captain John Barron," Rayh-Ill hissed seductively as she stood and strutted toward the captain. She put her face really close to his and whispered, "Is it just me, or do you get handsomer each time I see you?" Then she flicked her forked reptilian tongue in his ear.

"It's not just you," said the captain. "Sadly, you're not my type. I prefer women that don't lay eggs."

Rayh-Ill threw back her head and cackled. "Yet you came aboard so willingly. Some might say you were eager to see me again."

"Enough chitchat," said Captain Barron. "What's your ridiculous plan this time? I'm sure it's no better than the million other ridiculous plans you've hatched over the years. *Some might say* you haven't hatched anything worthwhile your entire life."

All the Demacron guards had to stifle their laughter. They knew Rayh-Ill had never hatched anything, from a successful plan to an egg, but they couldn't laugh in front of her or she'd bite their heads off later. *Literally!*

"My plan, Captain," said Rayh-Ill, "is to conquer Planet America once and for all. I'm going to zaportate myself and all my soldiers onto your starship in order to enter the Sphere, and you're going to help me. Then all humans will know that it was you, the great and wonderful Captain John Barron, that led to their downfall."

For a long time, Captain Barron simply stared at her. Then he began to chuckle.

Rayh-Ill became perturbed. "What? What's so funny?"

The captain continued laughing so hard he doubled over.

Smoke spouted from Rayh-Ill's nostrils. "Quiet, human!"

Captain Barron finally stood up straight. "I assume you scanned your ship for lifeforms as soon as you zaportated me onboard."

"Of course," said Rayh-Ill. "Do you think I'm stupid?"

"Yes, but that's beside the point. Check again."

Rayh-Ill glared at him. Then she hissed at one of her crewmembers, "Scan the ship for lifeforms!"

One of the lizard aliens tapped at a computer panel, then said, "The only lifeforms onboard are us, Captain Rayh-Ill. No foreign lifeforms detected, other than the human."

Captain Barron became stone-faced.

A reptilian grin spread across Rayh-Ill's face. "You were expecting help, Captain? Seems that whatever plan you devised has failed."

"On the contrary," said the captain. "I just needed to distract you long enough for my plan to play out. A little while after you zaportated me onboard, my ship zaportated one of my crewmembers here too."

"But we scanned for lifeforms!" hissed Rayh-Ill.

"Lifeforms, yes," said Captain Barron, "but you've made a huge mistake. Huge." He looked past Rayh-Ill and smiled.

Rayh-Ill and the Demacron guards turned to see a robot standing behind them on the bridge.

"PU-10!" the captain called out. "Now!"

"Boop!" PU-10 said as he tossed the captain's saber of light through the air.

Captain Barron caught the golden handle, and the saber of light's bright orange electricity blade zapped to life. The captain began his dance of death. He glided among the Demacron guards and crewmen like a ballet dancer, but not in a sissy way—more like a samurai or Neo from *The Matrix*. He sliced and slashed, severing lizard heads and limbs left and right as well as deflecting the blasts from their laser rifles back at them.

Within minutes, no one remained alive on the bridge except for the captain, PU-10, and Rayh-Ill cowering behind her captain's chair surrounded by smoking, sizzling lizard parts. Captain Barron approached her and leveled the saber of light's buzzing blade at her throat.

"Boop!" PU-10 cheered.

"That's right, PU-10," said the captain. "Sad!" Then he said to Rayh-Ill, "Now, once I return to my starship, you're going to take your entire fleet as far from Planet America as you can, and I never want to see any of your kind so much as a lightyear from this solar system. Got it?"

Rayh-Ill nodded vigorously, and then she—

<<>>

There was a knock at the door. Donald Trump ignored it, but then there was another knock. And other.

Trump huffed. "What is it?"

A member of the Secret Service cracked open the door to the White House Master Bedroom and peeked his head in. "Mr. President, the Chief of Staff is here to see you."

Trump sat cross-legged on the floor, staring at the action figures and toy spaceships in front of him. "This is Executive Time. I'm not to be disturbed."

"Yes, Mr. President," said the agent. "He says it's important."

Trump sighed. "Fine. Let him in."

The door swung open, and in stepped Mick Mulvaney— or whoever the current Chief of Staff was. "Good morning, Mr. President," he said, adjusting his glasses and keeping his eyes glued to the open leather binder in his hands.

Trump crossed his arms in silence.

"Mr. President," said Mulvaney, "Prime Minister Abe is waiting in the Roosevelt Room. You were scheduled to meet with him at 11:00."

Trump remained silent and pursed his lips.

"It's 11:30, Mr. President," said Mulvaney.

Trump didn't respond for quite some time, then finally said, "Give me ten minutes."

"Yes, Mr. President." Mulvaney closed his binder and exited the bedroom, shutting the door behind him.

After a minute, Trump uncrossed his arms and picked up one of the toy spaceships.

"Zwooooosh!" he said as he guided the ship toward its landing zone on the rug.

<<>>

Captain John Barron disembarked from the Starship *Trump* on the main landing pad of Space Force Headquarters in Washington, DC. Behind him walked PU-10, Lieutenant Fox, Lieutenant Miller, and a dozen other officers of his crew. The crowd of millions surrounding the landing pad cheered and chanted Captain Barron's name.

At the end of the landing pad, the owner of *Infinity* magazine stood at a podium flanked on both sides by numerous government officials and other Space Force officers. The magazine's owner spoke into the podium's microphone, but he was barely audible over the people's jubilation.

"Ladies and gentlemen, it is my pleasure to declare this year's *Infinity* Person of the Year to be Captain John Barron! And as you know, Captain Barron has just thwarted an attempt by the evil Rayh-Ill to invade Planet America, so it's safe to say we already know who next year's recipient will be!"

The adulation grew even louder, so loud that the entire landing pad vibrated.

"Presenting this year's trophy," the magazine owner continued, "is the daughter of the Galactic King and Queen, Princess Ak'Navi!"

Princess Ak'Navi was the most beautiful woman of any species from all the known planets of the universe. She walked onto the landing pad, her golden skin sparkling in the sun, carrying a diamond-shaped glass trophy with a holographic portrait of Captain Barron projected inside of it. At the podium, she handed the trophy to the captain. He took it, admired it for a moment, and then passed it to PU-10. A hush fell over the crowd.

The captain stepped to the podium and gripped it with his hands that weren't tiny at all. "Citizens of Planet America," he said, "I must humbly decline this wonderful trophy."

Everyone gasped. Millions of shocked faces stared at Captain Barron.

"Instead," he continued, "I will graciously accept the most beautiful trophy in all the universe."

He embraced the princess and gave her the most sensuous kiss anyone on any planet had ever witnessed. The throng of onlookers erupted with cheers. When the captain released the princess, she nearly collapsed. She'd never been kissed like that.

Captain Barron took to the podium again. "However, I will not return to claim this trophy until my job is done. The Space Force will not rest, I will not rest, until all galaxies are safe from the evil forces hellbent on destroying all we hold dear. Join me, and together we will conquer the stars!"

"Space Force!" cried the largest crowd Washington had ever seen. "Space Force! Space Force! Space Force!"

All In, Alien

Jane Yolen

The aliens who came to Earth
Left not one bone to show it.
It's only by
Tales of sci-fi
That we can ever know it.

We celebrate their visits with
Reports of UFOs,
But none can prove
At this remove,
So no one really knows.

Why did they fly the friendly skies,
Those travelers through space?
I know that some
Believe they've come
To save the human race.

Are they alive or are they dead,
These alien globetrotters
I wish that I
Could see them fly,
But probably they are rotters.

Dang, putting a Gregg Chamberlain limerick (as flavorful as it is) next to a Jane Yolen Poem? No way... Oh yes way!

A Space Force general named Wheezer
Was really a dirty old geezer.
His outer space sweetie
Was a slimy green E.T.,
And he bent over often to please her.

The Rainbow League

Melinda LaFevers

This is *Not Quite the News Hour.* I'm your host, Bill Williams.

Today we are discussing the current space crisis. First up is reporter Tom Bruce, reporting LIVE from the capitol grounds, bringing you the most recent news on the pending invasion of the United States by a caravan of aliens from outer space.

Thank you, Bill. The latest from the Alternative Schism Florida White House is that Schism President Trump has collapsed from nervous shock. The news that the Space Force is actually needed, rather than being an elaborate scam, has overcome his already fragile mental state. Schism White House doctors are not sure when, or even if he will recover. Schism Vice President Pence has stepped into the Alternative Schism's presidential position, at least temporarily. We are waiting for an official announcement on the invasion any minute now. Back to you.

Thank you, Tom. We will check back with you later. In other news, linguists from all over the world are working on deciphering the messages being broadcast by the aliens as they approach our system. I have Dr. Smith, head of the American group, online with me today. Good afternoon, Dr. Smith. Thank you for speaking with us.

Thank you for having me on your program. I only have a few minutes to spare before getting back to work.

I understand. Can you tell us anything about the progress your team has made? What are the latest results of your work?

Well, Bill, a lot of it is classified, of course. What I can tell you is that the aliens are broadcasting along certain radio frequencies. We have been recording these broadcasts and have run them through the latest translator programs available. Linguists from all over the world are pouring over the recordings and transcripts, trying to decipher the alien's message. We believe we have made some limited advances, and we think we have deciphered a few words, one of which, we think is "probe." I'm afraid that is about all I can tell you at this time. I need to get back to work.

Thank you Dr. Smith for taking the time to speak with us. I'm sure all of America is wishing you luck on your translations.

We'll be right back after a word from our sponsor.

Insectoid space aliens got you down? Worried your child might be abducted by a flying saucer? Try BEM B GONE! We don't guarantee that it will work on a bug-eyed monster, but it will certainly keep cockroaches, spiders, and other creepy crawlers away. BEM B GONE. Try it today!

Thank you for that message. Bill Williams here again. *Not Quite the News* is trying to confirm an item, first reported by Bororitz in 2018, that then actual Vice-President Pence had inside information on the nature of the aliens approaching earth. We have an exclusive interview with the person responsible for breaking this story-Andy Borowitz himself. Andy, so glad you could join us. Could you tell us a little more about your report? How were you able to break the news so early?

Well, Bob, I think the headline from my story says it all: "Pence Calls Space Force Necessary to Protect U.S. from Gay Aliens." As for my 2018 report, the government has known there were gay aliens on the way here for quite some time. It is only recently that the general public has been informed of this. But I have an inside informant who keeps me up to date on things.

I see. And why, exactly, did then Vice-President Pence believe these aliens to be homosexuals?

My confidential source said it has something to do with the limited amount of translation that has been achieved. Evidently, an entire fleet is approaching us, not just one or two ships. And they call themselves the Rainbow League.

The Rainbow League? How would they even have those words in their vocabulary?

Oh, that is just the translated version. At least, according to my confidential source.

I see. And what was Pence's response to this?

He supported calls to accelerate the funding for the Space Force. That, according to my informant, was what he believed would stop them from any type of subversive activity.

What type of subversive activity are you talking about?

Oh, you know, if the aliens are humanoid, why, they might want to intermix and mingle with humans. No telling what they might do-bake cakes for gay weddings, for example. Entice people into cute rocket ships, like Jeff Bezos did. At least, that's the type of thing that I was told Vice-President Pence was concerned about at that time. You can refer to my 2018 article for more information.

Thank you very much for your comments and information. Now we will go to our own informant from within the Space Force. Their voice has been disguised, as they wish to remain anonymous. I'll just call them Cap. Thank you, Cap, for agreeing to be here. What can you tell us about the situation?

You're sure my voice is disguised?

Yes, we have your voice going through a distorter.

Very well. Even now, hundreds of brave souls, many of whom belong to the LGBTQ community are racing for their new, untried spaceships, in order to explore more closely the link between...

Wait—did you say that many of the Space Force are part of the LGBTQ community? Is this common knowledge?

Well, it is among certain groups, certainly. I don't know if the White House is aware of it. But Space Force is the military branch with the highest concentration of members of our... I mean that community. Well over seventy percent.

What? Over 70% of Space Force are members of the LGBTQ community? Why is that?

Well, I'm not sure. If I had to make a guess, I would say it was the uniforms.

The Uniforms?

Oh, yes. They are soooo flashy. And comfortable, unlike the uniforms of the other branches of the military. Because of the strictures of space, they had to fit properly. But there is more than that. The uniforms, I don't know-they just glitter. All that silver and gold. They are the epitome of Bling. Trump wanted something fancy, and he got it. I mean, that's why I joined Space Force, for the uniform. My dad said I had to join the military-he thought it would make a "man" out of me. I chose Space Force for the uniform.

I... see. Uhm, I think it is time for a sponsor break.

Tired of looking at the universe with the naked eye? Do you want to be the first on your block to catch a glimpse of the invasion? For only $99.95, you can have this powerful telescope in your backyard. Follow our simple instructions to set it up, and be the first to warn your neighbors that the aliens are coming! Be sure to order one day shipping, so you can get it in time! $99.95. We are sorry that due to current uncertainty, we are unable to offer our usual extended payment plan. But to make up for that, we are offering, not one, but TWO powerful telescopes for $99.95. Simply pay a second shipping and handling fee. Order yours today, before it is too late!

This is Tom Bruce, from *Not Quite the News*, reporting live on the alien invasion situation.

We have breaking news. Stand by. The Actual White House spokesperson, Pat Baker, is preparing to make a statement.

Excuse me. If I could have it quiet, please. I just want to announce that the current alien crisis seems to be over. Space Force has been told to step down from active status. There is no immediate threat of invasion by the Rainbow League. I'll take a few questions. Yes, Tom?

What caused a crisis situation, and how was it averted?

Well, honestly, it seems to be a miscommunication. First off, the linguistic team mistranslated a word-they thought it was "rainbow", and it was actually weather. That mistake has been corrected. The alien broadcast had been asking permission to send probes down to the 7th planet, to study the weather.

Then why did Pence think they were gay aliens?

Well, when he was told the alien fleet wanted to probe something, he misunderstood and thought they wanted to probe a particular body part. That is all the time I have now. Thank you.

This has been Bob Bruce broadcasting live from the White House. A crisis caused by misinterpretation and misunderstanding has been averted by clearer communication. Back to you, Bill.

Thank you, Bob. When you get back to the studio, we will discuss your experiences in greater depth.

That's the end of our time. Thank you for joining the *Not Quite the News Hour*. This is Bill Williams, signing off. Join us tomorrow, when we will be discussing the topic "Is the Space Force the real Rainbow League?" And remember, folks-communication is the key to survival. See you tomorrow.

Sorry Folks, we're fresh out of
Limericks.
Wait!
What about:
There once was a man from
Nantucket—
SLAP!!!
Okay Phyl, we'll not use that one.

Tomorrow Could Have Been Different

Allan Rousselle

The sign said, "Welcome to Trump Station," and it had to come down.

Well, off, actually. "Down" had no meaning until the damned gravity spinners were back up and running. Blondie sneered at himself. Not *up and running.* Back online. Because "up..."

Blondie swung his toolbox gently toward the wall, where it attached with a satisfying magnetic clank, and pulled open the top to retrieve the universal socket wrench and assorted other tools.

The sign had to come off because they had changed the name again. Again! The station orbiting the moon was recently renamed to *Trump Station*, so to avoid confusion, they decided to rename the Mars orbital outpost. Again. Which meant fabrication had to make another new sign and Blondie had to take time away from the spinners to make the swap.

Grabbing the large "T" with his left hand, he swung his knees up until the magnets in his knee pads and the toes of his boots clicked into place against the wall. For now, the wall with the sign was "down" to him while the floor stood aloof at his back.

He started loosening the bolts on the left side, the ratchet going *clackity-snick, clackity-snick* as he cranked the handle up-and-down, up-and-down to spin them out of their fittings. Well, not up-and-down. Whatever.

His earpiece let out a whistle. He whistled back to activate the connection. "Blondie here." A few more turns on the screw in one corner before moving onto the next. Each screw in order, clockwise around the sign.

"Are you sitting down?" Say what you will about Tiny, but he had a great voice for comms. Soothing. Mellifluous, even. A low, gentle Kentucky drawl that rolled smooth as a glass of fine bourbon.

Blondie looked up and around him in the vacant reception area. "I'm kneeling on a wall while I pull off this damn sign, does that count as sitting down?" *Clackity-snick. Clackity-snick.*

"Close enough. Okay, the first piece of news is that I sent Hadley out to work on the spinners—"

The wrench slipped, and Blondie lurched forward with the unexpected give, jamming his fingers against a protruding bolt.

"Gah! Dahhh!" The pain shot up his arm like a lightning bolt; he was clutching his hand tightly to his chest before he knew it. "Ghehhh!" he yelled through clenched teeth.

"Yeah, I kinda figured you'd see it that way," Tiny sang gently through the earpiece. "Hadley is... well, Hadley. But, Station Commander's orders. What can you do?"

Blondie's fingers throbbed fiercely, warmth radiating throughout his hand. He rocked back and forth, clenching and releasing his injured fist. "Nehhh!" he grunted.

"True, but it's not like you had any plans this weekend, anyway. Besides, a little unpaid extra re-work never killed anybody, right?"

Blondie kept working his fist, clenched and loose. Clenched and loose. "Snowden," he spat through his teeth, as he reached for the wrench that was now floating almost out of reach to his right. The throbbing in his fingers pulsed harder as he grabbed the handle as tight as his tender skin would allow.

"Well, yes. There was Snowden," Tiny drawled. "Poor bastard."

"Poor bastard," Blondie agreed. He resumed loosening the bolts, but damn, his hand hurt.

Tiny paused.

"Anyway, Hadley was the first bit of news. Next up, I figured you'd want to know that power is out to the commissary again, so the mess hall is offline."

If the gravity hadn't already been inoperable, Blondie would have sworn his stomach just took the express elevator to free fall without him.

"Rations again" they both said in unison.

His stomach lurched a second time, just as a loud mechanical torquing sound ran through the walls.

Blondie sighed, then tugged gently at the sign. It popped free from the wall. He slowly guided it aside until it was clear of his work space, holding on to stop its momentum before letting go to reach for the new sign.

The walls started to stutter-shake, growing more and more pronounced, and then stopped again.

"Hey, Tiny. You feeling that? Hadley's grinding the gears."

"Copy that. So, I've got one more item for you today."

Blondie set the new sign into place and began inserting the bolts into their new homes. His fingers still ached with every beat of his heart.

"Aren't you going to ask me what it is?"

"No."

Blondie grasped the wrench and slid the lever to make it ratchet in the other direction.

"You might like it."

Clackity-snick. Clackity-snick. He tightened down the bolts, a few turns at a time each, again working his way around the sign.

"I won't." *Clackity-snick. Clackity-snick.*

Another large, metallic groan reverberated throughout the station, followed by several loud clanks.

"Christ, Hadley is going to tear us apart before he gets the damn thing working—"

"You really want to know what the last thing is," Tiny cooed through his earpiece.

Blondie raised himself to a standing position, his magnetized boots holding him to the wall, looking down at the new sign by his feet:

TRUMP ORBITAL MARTIAN BASE

"Oh, crap. Hey, Chief! Did you see this new sign?"

"No. Why? Is there something wrong with it?"

Blondie laughed in spite of himself. Another clank rang through station. "Well, it's just that all the letters are capitalized, like usual, but this time, the first letter of each word is a little bigger than all the other letters."

"So?"

"Think about it, Tiny. Think about the new name of the station. Think about the first letter of each word." Blondie rubbed his aching hand along his smooth, bare scalp. "We're going to have to change this sign again before too long."

There was a pause before Tiny let out a long whistle of appreciation. "The ground-pounders at Marketing Corps are going to be in for it when someone points this out to them."

Another clank, followed by a low whirring sound reverberated through the walls, slowly ramping up. Well, gaining speed, at any rate.

"You say that like someone's going to tell them." Blondie looked around. Something didn't feel right.

"Someone's going to have to. See, that's the next item I need to tell you. The President is coming here."

Blondie's mouth went dry. "I'm sorry... did you say the C-n-C is coming *here*?!" A large mechanical chirping sound, and the whirring suddenly grew faster. He suddenly felt tension at the back of his neck, as if something was tugging at him.

"That's exactly what I said. *Space Force One* has been *en route* for several months, it turns out, and came up on our screens just a few hours ago. No advance warning. Looks like she's no more than a couple days out. Buddy, we're about to meet President-for-Life Trump in person."

That tugging sensation was gravity. Blondie, who had been standing on the wall, fell to the floor at his back. Several tools followed suit, spilling out of the toolbox attached to the wall and splashing on and around him. He whipped his arm around to shield his head as the tools pelted him, lightly at first, but with more of a sting with each successive strike.

The older sign slid down the wall, landing nearby Blondie's feet. Next came the toolbox; gravity finally overcame the pull of the magnets, and the toolbox tumbled down toward Blondie's head. He raised his other arm instinctively, saving himself from certain brain damage, but the jolt to his elbow from the toolbox sent a shockwave throughout his nerves like a live wire.

"Gah!" He yelled again through clenched teeth.

Then, louder: "Hadley!"

He clutched his arm to his torso and rocked back and forth.

"Hey, Buddy," Tiny hummed calmly in his ear. "You need a medic down there?"

"I need a crowbar and Hadley's head," he gasped, still curled up on the floor, rocking back and forth. He looked down and noticed blood seeping through the arm of his coveralls. "But yeah. A medic will do for now."

"Right away, buck."

Blondie stood up, reached down to pick up the toolbox with his left hand, and strained against the gravity and the magnets to pull it back up. Instead, he pulled himself down to the ground, fainting from the effort.

Someone was calling his name. Far away at first. Then, a little closer. Closer.

"Petty Officer Allman?"

Blondie blinked his eyes open. Nurse Pollyanna hovered before him.

"I don't feel... wait... is the gravity off again?"

The nurse took his wrist and took his pulse. "Mmm, hmm. You don't remember the explosion?"

He looked around him. Sick bay. He was held to his bed by elastic straps. Many of the beds within view were also occupied, while a few nurses scurried about taking pulses and signing forms.

"Hadley."

Polly nodded in agreement. "Explosion killed him." She grabbed a thermometer and jammed it in Blondie's mouth.

"Po' bathtah," he said around the thermometer.

"Poor bastard," she agreed. She grabbed a legal-sized tablet and handed it to him.

"Consent form. Please sign."

He tried to raise his right hand to sign, but a brace on his arm wouldn't let him bend it.

"Mah ahm."

She took the thermometer out of his mouth. "Use your other hand." She turned away to check on another patient.

He looked at the tablet in his left hand. He looked at his right hand, which seemed impossibly far away. He straightened his left arm to put the tablet into his right hand and scribbled something resembling a signature with his left pointer finger. His abused right hand let the tablet drop. The blood throbbing through his right arm touched every welt and injury his right arm and hand had sustained during his shift.

Nurse Pollyanna returned, grabbed the tablet, and swiped to another form. She placed it back in his left hand.

"Acknowledgement form. Please sign."

He transferred it back to his right hand and scribbled again with his left.

"When can I get back to work on the gravity spinners?"

She grabbed the tablet, swiped, and returned it to his left hand.

"Treatment plan. Please sign. You'll probably be cleared for duty in a day or two, but no worries about the spinners. Tiny came by earlier and said they've got someone else on it."

Once again, he awkwardly changed hands and signed the document. She took the tablet back again.

"Who?"

She swiped the screen, put it in his left hand again. "Organ donor confirmation. Please sign. How would I know? I'm a nurse, not a foreperson."

Blondie looked at the form, then looked at it closer. "Wait, this is confirming if I still want to be an organ donor, but the option to change my mind is grayed out."

"Space Force regs. You can't opt out."

"Then why confirm I'm still opting in?"

"Universal Trumpcare regs. You have to be given the choice."

"What if I don't sign it?"

"You have to sign it. You don't have a choice."

He delicately switched hands again and signed it. She took it back again and swiped it.

"Pregnancy test consent. Please sign. Tiny said he would be back at the top of the hour."

Blondie looked at the clock above the sick bay entrance. Ten 'til. He looked at the form.

"This says you can't treat me until you take a sample for the pregnancy test."

Pollyanna looked down at him and sighed. "Yes."

"But you've already treated me."

"Yes."

"Did you give me the pregnancy test before you started treating me?"

"Of course."

"Why?"

Polly looked up at the curved ceiling and recited the response she was required to give by law. "The Trump Life Protection Act requires that we make sure you're not pregnant before we treat you, so that we can be sure we don't do anything that could interfere with your developing pregnancy."

"But I'm a man."

"Universal Trumpcare regs. No matter how you identify, you still have to be tested. Please sign."

He fumbled the tablet back down to his right hand so he could sign the touchscreen with his left forefinger. While his hand was down there, he patted himself to make sure he was still a man. He was. "So, am I pregnant?"

She took the device back and swiped to the next document. "Results haven't come back yet. Trump Loyalty Oath Form. Please sign." She put it in his wrong hand again.

Spoilsport, he thought. He signed.

The nurse took back the tab to swipe to the next form as Tiny's voice boomed from across sick bay. "There he is, laying down on the job again."

Blondie looked up to see Tiny sailing across the room in his direction, gracefully bobbing against the deck with his lightly magnetized boots. He glided to rest on the opposite side of the bed from Nurse Pollyanna. At roughly two meters tall and 140 kilos, he loomed over Blondie's bed like a Greek God, complete with thick, dark-gray, curly hair and bright blue eyes. "I don't know if Polly told you, but Hadley died."

"Poor bastard," Blondie and the nurse replied.

"Poor bastard," Tiny agreed. "Anyway, Murphy's crew is on the case, and they expect to have gravity restored by the time Space Force One docks."

Blondie sighed his relief. "The only person other than me I'd trust with that job. He's got luck on his side."

"Trump Pharmaceuticals Hold Harmless Agreement. Please sign." Nurse Polly put the tablet in Blondie's left hand, and he automatically shifted it to the right so he could sign.

Tiny drummed his fingers on the bedrails. "Commissary is still down, so we're still stuck with rations for the time being."

Polly took the tablet and swiped again. "Permission for Trump Hospitals to bill the Space Force directly for your care. Please sign."

Tiny looked up at the clock while Blondie signed the release.

The nurse took back the tablet and swiped again. "Please rate the care you've received so far. Please remember that anything less than a perfect five out of five is a failing grade for us. Also, you are ordered to give us a five out of five." She handed him the form. Five stars was already selected, and none of the other options was available to choose. He shifted the tablet again and signed it.

A loud clank reverberated through the walls as the sick bay lights flickered briefly, followed by a low, smooth rumble. The lights resumed their steady glow.

"This form is post-dated for rating the care you receive going forward, in case you are unable to sign it once treatment is completed. You're ordered to give us a five out of five for this, too."

The rumble in the walls grew lower; smoother. Blondie could feel the gravity slowly starting to kick back in. This time, it felt right.

"Thank goodness Murphy knows what he's doing. Tiny, at least tell me you still have some of that Scotch left over to help wash down the rations."

"I promised it to Murphy since he had to clean up Hadley's remains," replied Tiny. "Poor bastard."

"Poor bastard," agreed Blondie and Polly.

Polly continued, "This Non-Disparagement Agreement says you agree to never disparage the care you receive from Trump Hospitals or any of the products provided by Trump Pharmaceuticals, Trump Supply Chain Services, or Haliburton, a wholly-owned subsidiary of Trump Logistics Corporation. Please sign."

The gravity continued to increase.

"Maybe Murphy will be kind enough to share with us," said Blondie.

"This form says Murphy won't be kind enough to share with you. Please sign."

He blinked as the nurse put the tab in his left hand. "Wait... what?"

"This form says you agree to let Trump Entertainment and the Space Force use your likeness for any and all promotional or recruiting materials," she repeated. "Please sign."

The final clank of the spinners locked in, and gravity had fully returned. The alarm that was supposed to warn everyone that the gravity spinners were starting to rev up finally bellowed now that they were done revving up. Tiny and Blondie looked at each other.

"Thanks for the warning," they said in unison.

Tiny glanced around the sick bay, then back down at Blondie.

"You look like you're starting to fade," Tiny said. "I'll let you get some rest and check on you later."

Blondie nodded.

"This form says that Tiny will let you get some rest and check on you later. Please sign." Blondie signed. He couldn't pay attention any more. The gravity made it so much easier to settle into his mattress. He was glad Tiny had come by. Tiny was a good friend. He would always have... have his... always...

Blondie nodded off.

"Group attention! Commander in Chief on deck!"

Blondie snapped awake, his body reflexively stiffening on his bed. He tried to salute, but the brace on his right arm kept his elbow locked, so he inadvertently raised his right hand in a stiff-armed salute before he realized how that looked and lowered it again as quickly as he could. The President didn't seem to notice, although part of the protection detail—a landlubber in a black two-piece suit and tie—did notice and cut him a nasty look... well, as nasty as a look can be underneath those sunglasses in a florescent-lit room.

Someone shouted, "As you were!" The room seemed to exhale just a little bit as the medical staff mostly resumed their work and the injured resumed their healing or dying, as they had been before. Even so, everybody kept a wary eye on the C-n-C's entourage making its way slowly along the sick bay.

Blondie took a quick glance left and right. Tiny and Nurse Pollyanna were nowhere to be seen.

President-for-Life Trump slowly worked the room from bed to bed, smiling and offering what Blondie assumed were words of encouragement; shaking hands where doing so wouldn't cause more injury, and posing for pictures here and there. Blondie realized that the entourage was heading his way.

They were just a couple beds away from him when he caught a good look at the President-for-Life. She looked much older than he expected, but somehow more elegant and graceful. Stately. Regal, almost. Instead of the platinum blonde hair he'd always thought she had, in person it was long and white. She smiled readily and easily, but there was a quiet reserve in her eyes. A wistfulness. It caught him off guard.

Blondie's earpiece let out a whistle. He whistled back to activate the comm. The black-suited agent who had given him that nasty look earlier cut his attention back to Blondie again. *Crap*, he murmured, and looked quickly away.

"What? What's wrong?" Tiny's low Kentucky drawl sounded grave.

"The President is two beds away from me," Blondie said quietly through clenched teeth. The suit continued to look in his direction. But... was he actually looking directly at him?

"Sounds like I dodged a bullet."

"Hmm?" Low and in the back of his throat.

"Well, if I'm not in the same room as her, I don't have to find out if I might say something that could get me sent to the brig. Or worse."

The suit turned back to the group; they were clearly making as if to move on to the next bed.

"She doesn't seem so bad," Blondie replied quietly.

"You don't pay attention to the news when you're off the station. You have no idea what's really going on out there, my friend. Don't believe everything you read in *Pravda*."

Just one bed away now, and Blondie had nobody to shield him; nobody to elbow him if he said or did something foolish. A couple members of the entourage, wearing their black suits and ties and sunglasses detached themselves from the group at the next bed and came over to Blondie. They quickly patted him down and visually inspected the bed above and below. Their touch was light, rapid, and expertly efficient.

"You do not touch the President," one of them said. They took positions standing at the head of his bed, their backs to the wall—and eyes likely scanning the rest of the room, Blondie supposed—as the President approached the foot of his bed.

He held himself rigid and still.

"As you were, spaceman." Her voice was strong and confident without needing to be loud to be heard.

One of the suits read from an electronic display at the foot of the bed:

"Petty Officer, First Class Jack 'Blondie' Allman, Madam President."

She nodded, as she made her way along the right side of his bed to stand beside him. If she found it a little odd to for a bald-headed man to be called 'Blondie,' she gave no indication.

"Yes," she said. "We all know who he is, we don't need to pretend otherwise." She inclined her head toward Blondie, which he couldn't help but find disarming. "Petty Officer

Blondie, it may surprise you to hear this, but I've come all this way to ask you to volunteer for a mission. It's a very sensitive mission, and you're uniquely qualified to execute it. But, time is of the essence."

Blondie realized that her entourage had closed in around her such that he couldn't see anyone else in the sick bay. "What I'm about to tell you is sensitive information, and it's going to be difficult for you to process, but ironically, we don't have much time."

"I'll do my best to keep up, Madam President." His tongue was cotton in his mouth, but he managed not to trip over his own words.

She reached out to give his shoulder a reassuring squeeze and let her hand linger there briefly. "I know you will. In fact, I know you'll do better than that, because you've already proven your ability to do so. Petty Officer Allman, if you accept this mission, you'll be the first soldier in our newest branch of the military."

A new branch of the military. But, where else was there to fight? The sea, the air, the land, space... where else was there?

"I'm just a mechanic, ma'am. Rated for space craft."

"I know," she tilted her head at him again. "But you're our man, Blondie. Look, I'm going to have to move on soon so that nobody notices me lingering here too long. You have the exact skills we need for this mission. I know this because you've already performed this mission, at least five times, and you've succeeded every time. Every time you were sent, however, there was a miscalculation in your directives. So, we've adjusted your mission, and we expect a better outcome this time."

One of the agents set down a personal tablet next to Blondie's left arm. "Your mission profile is on here," the agent said.

"Welcome to the Time Corp, *Sergeant Major* Allman."

Once more, Blondie reflexively tried to salute, raising his right arm with his elbow locked open, and hastily dropped it when he realized what it looked like. He wasn't used to not being able to salute. His Commander in Chief, President-for-Life Ivanka Trump, gave him a smart, crisp salute, and then she turned to make her way to the next occupied bed.

"Well, that was unexpected," Blondie said to himself as he watched her go.

"Boy, no kidding," Tiny said in his ear while, from the chair next to his bed, he heard a knowing chuckle. Blondie was so startled, he half-jumped up from the bed.

There was an agent sitting next to him.

"You're still here," Blondie said to the agent.

"I am," replied Tiny.

"I am," replied the agent.

"Oops," said Tiny, and there was a subtle click that indicated he went back on mute. There was no whistle to suggest he logged off.

"I'll debrief you while everyone else's attention is either on their tasks, or on our C-n-C." The agent nodded in Trump's direction. "She certainly knows how to work a room, doesn't she?"

Blondie followed his gaze. Yes, he had to admit, she certainly did.

"A few decades down the line from now, never mind exactly when, an individual on Copernicus Station orbiting one of Jupiter's moons is going to discover a means to travel back and forth through time at will."

"What Copernicus Station?"

The agent gestured for patience. "Bear with me. Word will eventually get out to a couple of folks who have differing opinions about how it should be used, and one thing will lead to another, and someone sympathetic to our cause will get that technology to us. We will use it to make some tweaks here and there, and now that we like how everything turns out, it's time to close the loop and end time travel so that our work can't be undone."

The President and her team moved on to another bed.

The agent wrapped the tablet by Blondie's side with his knuckles. "When you've finished your first jump, you'll find directions on there. It'll just open right up for you. It's keyed to your face, so no worries there. And, nobody knows you're coming. You and the other recruit we've used both have the advantage of being untraceable, albeit for entirely different reasons."

"There's... another?"

The agent waved the question away and leaned back to continue scanning the sick bay. "Don't worry about him. Long story. It's on there, if you're interested. Actually, your first mission is the only mission the two of you have ever shared. You two are the only people who have ever successfully completed it, and you both have completed it every single time. Unfortunately..."

Blondie shook his head. "So, if the mission doesn't go the way it should, we get another chance at it?"

"This mission affects all of time travel. It resets everything. So, yes, you get to try again, and it's as if you've never done it before. Because, well, you haven't."

"But, if everything is reset, how do you know? How do you know we've tried before? This doesn't make sense. If I stop time travel, how do you get to do time travel again?"

Tiny clicked off the mute. "Yeah!" he exclaimed, quietly. Then he clicked back on the mute.

The agent nodded. "Well, see, we've found a way to communicate across time events. Every time you complete a mission, you whip up a detailed report in a specific way, and the information is available at exactly the right time to the right people. The report always includes the previous reports embedded within them. We figured out a way to leave this information even when the time loop affects itself. This is how we know what's been tried before, even though we didn't experience it. We know what has worked, what went wrong, and what attempts got erased. We also know *who* worked, and *who* went wrong, so our recruiting efforts this time around are sped up because of the work we did in previous attempts."

"But... but..."

"I know. We've got experts who will have spent their entire lives trying to wrap their heads around all this and half of what they will say makes them sound mad. Don't worry, that's not your specialty. What you're good at is finding the inventor of the time machine, given what little we know, and then slipping something in his drink to, well, close the loop quietly."

"But..."

The tablet by Blondie's side vibrated. He picked it up and looked at it. There was a timed reminder: "Report to the Station Commander's office, double time."

Blondie read the message to himself under his breath, so that Tiny knew what was going on.

The agent stood up and tipped his head toward the President's party, which was making its way toward the door. "That's my cue. I'll see you in a few. We'll be travelling by a different route. We don't want some other time traveler to catch on that you're our guy. Although, we feel pretty confident that they'll never figure out that we came to this specific location for this purpose. It's been a pleasure, Sergeant Major."

As the agent strode purposefully away, Blondie adjusted the bed so that he could get into position to stand up.

"Wow," said Tiny in his ear.

"Uh-huh." Blondie spotted Nurse Pollyanna and flagged her down.

"They're lying, you know."

"How can you say that? Just because I don't understand it doesn't mean they're lying. It just means I don't understand it. Hold on a sec, Tiny." Blondie asked the nurse for help getting dressed and ready to report to the Station Commander. She started helping him while he resumed talking via his earpiece to Tiny.

"The thing is, Tiny, orders are orders. My job isn't to understand the orders. My job is to follow orders." He was able to get his shirt on once she loosened up how much the brace could bend at the elbow, but the nurse still had to help him pull up his trousers and buckle his belt.

"This sounds fishy. Don't go. Trip on the way or something. Fall on your arm."

"Aren't you supposed to be running the repair crew, Chief?"

The nurse helped Blondie with his shoes. She gently bent his arm enough to put into a sling, and then re-locked the elbow portion of the brace. She showed him how the locking mechanism worked. She gave him quick instructions for managing the pain.

Blondie headed out of the sick bay, double time.

"I'm pretty sure they're lying to you, but what if they're actually telling you the truth?" Tiny asked quietly.

Blondie didn't answer. His mind, like his body, was marching on the double toward resolution.

"Think about it. If you take this mission, and if they're telling you the truth, you're essentially locking in this reality. A reality where all our supplies to build this base come from vendors whose sole purpose is to enrich the President's family and their cronies, not to make good supplies. A reality where Hadley stays dead, poor bastard. If you make this choice... if you close the loop, like they say they want you to do, you can't even come back, because time travel won't have been invented. It's a one-way trip."

Blondie had slowed down his walk as Tiny said this, and now he stopped altogether. He stood alone in the vacant corridor.

"You say that like any of those things would be different if I stayed."

After a long silence, Tiny spoke. "The base will fall apart without you."

"It's falling apart *with* me."

"Yeah, well, are you sure you trust a time machine that was *also* built by a Trump contractor that knows they're going to get stiffed?"

"Ouch. You have a point," Blondie sighed. "But, well, I have my orders."

"And, I'm coming down anyway. Stall them. We need to talk this over, okay?"

Blondie started moving again. At the next corridor intersection, he made a beeline for the Commander's office.

When he got there, he knocked on the door and entered.

The C. O. was standing in the anteroom, waiting for him. Blondie snapped to attention, without salute.

"Station Commander!"

"Sergeant Major," the C. O. saluted. "At ease. Follow me and we'll get you suited up."

In the next room, a team was ready to help Blondie into a modified space suit. "While this functions as a space suit, its primary purpose is to transport you through time and space. Your tablet has been specially constructed to save your entries to an entangled device that is located in the far past. Before you take action, log it. After you take action, if that action has changed your past, it won't have changed your log entry. Get in the habit of checking and updating your log entries constantly. It will help to keep you grounded on what your mission is, what you've done, and what you still intend to do."

One of the techs gave Blondie a quick rundown of how the control panel on his suit could be used to determine where and when he could travel to.

"Even though you're going to the future, your first mission deals with the inventor of time travel itself, so your actions could very well affect your past. If your mission fails, for example, you may end up impacting parts of your past, but not enough to prevent you from ultimately being on this mission. That's where reading your log entries to determine what you've tried and what your intentions are will be of paramount importance. If your actions succeed completely, you're back to where you were, there's no longer a Time Corps, and while some people will eventually have been made aware of your efforts, you will neither experience them nor remember them, and because non-linear time travel will cease to have been invented, the people who do become aware of your exploits won't be able to do anything favorable or detrimental regarding them."

A set of doors opened and the President walked in. Everyone in the room came to attention.

"As you were, Commander. Please continue with your briefing."

Blondie asked, "If the people who get this information are in the past, couldn't they act to prevent me from even joining the Space Force in the first place?"

The President held up a finger to silence the C. O., and answered instead: "No. This log tells them—and, keep in mind, *them* could very well be *us*—it may tell them what you did, but not who you are. And the logs that we make may eventually tell us, or possibly someone else, where to find you, but still not who you are, and without non-linear time travel, we won't be able to get to you. Frequently when we have found you in previous attempts, it's been at a different time of your life. But only through the clues we've left that can only be followed through time."

President Trump put her hands on both of Blondie's shoulders. "Sergeant Major, we are in a war. But with this mission, we truly believe the end of the war is at hand."

Blondie regarded his Commander in Chief. "But, ma'am. The Enemy always gets a vote on when the war ends."

"Hmm. Perhaps not this time." She nodded at him, but Blondie thought he noticed a flicker of doubt in her eyes.

"Ma'am. Pardon me for asking, but... who is the Enemy?"

The C. O. spoke sharply. "You forget yourself, Sergeant Major!"

The President shook her head. "No, Station Commander. It's okay. How many soldiers have gone into battle without at least knowing who the enemy is? Our enemy, Sergeant Major, is the Clintons and those who are loyal to them."

"But... the Clinton's died in that airplane crash a few years before the Great Nano-plague. How can they be a threat to anybody?"

A slight click in his earpiece. "Blondie, I'm almost there. Stall them. What they're talking about is crazy. Don't do this!"

"Ma'am," one of the techs announced. "We're almost out of time. Sergeant Major, your coordinates for your first jump are programmed in."

The President handed Blondie his helmet. "In order to secure the future that only we can provide, we must also secure the past."

Blondie's eyes widened, but he was too stunned to stop the process of latching down his helmet onto his suit. What the hell did she mean by that?

"Ma'am, we're really out of time," said the tech.

President Trump grabbed his shoulders one last time. "Godspeed, Sergeant Major."

Over her shoulder, past the C. O. and just behind the techs, he saw Tiny burst into the room just as his gloved finger was pressing on the Go button.

And, then all was gone.

As Tiny walked into the anteroom, he saw the C. O. there and snapped to attention in a crisp salute.

"Chief Alvin, at ease," the Station Commander returned his salute. "Please, come with me. Our Commander in Chief asked for you specifically."

Tiny raised his eyebrows at this news and followed the C. O. into the main office where the President sat behind her desk waiting for him. Once more, he saluted.

"As you were, Chief. I have come into some intelligence that your gravity spinners are the target of a planned sabotage. It is of vital importance to me that whoever you have investigating, you do not assign Petty Officer Allman to that detail."

"Ma'am?" What an oddly specific order from the C-n-C. Delivered in person, no less!

"I have a very particular mission for which I require Petty Officer Allman. Send, I don't know, send Petty Officer Hadley instead."

"Yes, Ma'am." Tiny regarded his Commander in Chief. Her long brown hair with blond highlights. Her sturdy frame. And yet, she also looked somehow older than he imagined she would look in person. The live feeds from Earth made her look younger. "Is there something about Blondie—sorry, Petty Officer Allman, I mean—that I should be aware of, Ma'am?"

She smiled grimly. "You are almost certainly not aware of it, Chief, but we've been at war for some time now, a war just under the surface, and I believe that Petty Officer Allman is the key to finally bringing that war to a close."

Tiny couldn't help repeating the phrase that made the rounds back during the Sino-Russian Cyber War. "The Enemy always gets a vote on when the war ends."

"Perhaps," said the President-for-Life. "But, this war is drawing to a close, or my name's not Chelsea Clinton."

Space Force

Riding Janis

David Gerrold

Out in the asteroid belt, the mountains fly. They tumble and roll silently. Distant sparkles break the darkness. Someday we'll get out there, we'll catch the mountains, we'll break them into kibble to get at the good parts. We'll find out if the centers are nougat or truffle. And some of us—some of us will even become comet-tossers, throwing the mountains around like gods.

If we had wings

where would we fly?

Would you choose the safety of the ground

or touch the sky

if we had wings?

—Janis Ian & Bill Lloyd

The thing about puberty is that once you've done it, you're stuck. You can't go back.

It's like what Voltaire said about learning Russian. He said that you wouldn't know if learning Russian would be a good thing or not unless you actually learned the language— except that after you learned Russian, would the process of learning it have turned you into a person who now believes it's a good thing? So how could you know? Puberty is like that—I think. It changes you, the way you think, and what you think about. And from what I can tell, it's a lot harder than Russian. Especially the conjugations.

You can only delay puberty for so long. After that you start to get some permanent physiological effects. But there's no point in going through puberty when the closest eligible breeding partners are on the other side of the solar system. I didn't mind being nineteen and unfinished. It was the only life I knew. What I minded was not having a choice. Sometimes I felt like just another asteroid in the belt, tumbling forever around the solar furnace, too far away to be warmed, but still too close to be truly alone. Waiting for someone to grab me and hurl me toward Luna.

See, that's what Mom and Jill do. They toss comets. Mostly small ones, wrapped so they don't burn off. There's not a lot of ice in the belt, only a couple of percentage points, if that; but when you figure there are a couple billion rocks out here, that's still a few million that are locally useful. Our job is finding them. There's no shortage of customers for big fat oxygen atoms with a couple of smaller hydrogens attached. Luna and Mercury, in particular, and eventually Venus, when they start cooling her down.

But this was the biggest job we'd ever contracted, and it wasn't about ice as much as it was about ice-burning. Hundreds of tons per hour. Six hundred and fifty million kilometers of tail, streaming outward from the sun, driven by the ferocious solar wind. Comet Janis. In fifty-two months, the spray of ice and dye would appear as a bright red, white, and blue streak across the Earth's summer sky—the Summer Olympics Comet.

Mom and Jill were hammering every number out to the umpteenth decimal place. This was a zero-tolerance nightmare. We had to install triple-triple safeguards on the safeguards. They only wanted a flyby, not a direct hit. That would void the contract, as well as the planet.

The bigger the rock, the farther out you could aim and still make a streak that covers half the sky. The problem with aiming is that comets have minds of their own—all that volatile outgassing pushes them this way and that, and even if you've wrapped the rock with reflectors, you still don't get any kind of precision. But the bigger the rock, the harder it is to wrap it and toss it. And we didn't have a lot of wiggle room on the timeline.

Janis was big and dark until we lit it up. We unfolded three arrays of LEDs, hit it with a dozen megawatts from ten klicks, and the whole thing sparkled like the star on top of a Christmas tree. All that dirty ice, 30 kilometers of it, reflecting light every which way—depending on your orientation when you looked out the port, it was a fairy landscape, a shimmering wall, or a glimmering ceiling. A trillion tons of sparkly mud, all packed up in nice dense sheets, so it wouldn't come apart.

It was beautiful. And not just because it was pretty to look at, and not just because it meant a couple gazillion serious dollars in the bank either. It was beautiful for another reason.

See, here's the thing about living in space. Everything is Newtonian. It moves until you stop it or change its direction. So every time you move something, you have to think about where it's going to go, how fast it's going to get there, and where it will eventually end up. And we're not just talking about large sparkly rocks, we're talking about bottles of soda, dirty underwear, big green boogers, or even the ship's cat. Everything moves, bounces, and moves some more. And that includes people too. So you learn to think in vectors and trajectories and consequences. Jill calls it "extrapolatory thinking."

And that's why the rock was beautiful, because it wasn't just a rock here and now. It was a rock with a future. Neither Mom nor Jill had said anything yet, they were too busy studying the gravitational ripple charts, but they didn't have to say anything. It was obvious. We were going to have to ride it in, because if that thing started outgassing, it would push itself off course. Somebody had to be there to create a compensating thrust. Folks on the Big Blue Marble were touchy about extinction-level events.

Finding the right rock is only the *second*-hardest part of comet-tossing. Dirtsiders think the belt is full of rocks, you just go and get one; but most of the rocks are the wrong kind; too much rock, not enough ice—and the average distance between them is 15 million klicks. And most of them are just dumb rock. Once in a while, you find one that's rich with nickel or iron, and as useful as that might be, if you're not looking for nickel or iron right then, it might as well be more dumb rock. But if somebody else is looking for it, you can lease or sell it to them.

So Mom is continually dropping bots. We fab them up in batches. Every time we change our trajectory, Mom opens a window and tosses a dozen paper planes out.

A paper plane doesn't need speed or sophistication, just brute functionality, so we print the necessary circuitry on sheets of stiff polymer. (We fab that too.) It's a simple configuration of multi-sensors, dumb-processors, lotsa-memory, soft-transmitters, long-batteries, carbon-nanotube solar cells, ion-reservoirs, and even a few micro-rockets. The printer rolls out the circuitry on a long sheet of polymer, laying down thirty-six to forty-eight layers of material in a single pass. Each side. At a resolution of 3600^2 dpi, that's tight enough to make a fairly respectable, self-powered, paper robot. Not smart enough to play with its own tautology, but certainly good enough to sniff a passing asteroid.

We print out as much and as many as we want, we break the polymer at the perforations; three quick folds to give it a wing shape, and it's done. Toss a dozen of these things overboard, they sail along on the solar wind, steering themselves by changing colors and occasional micro-bursts. Make one wing black and the other white and the plane eventually turns itself; there's no hurry, there's no shortage of either time or space in the belt. Every few days, the bot wakes up and looks around. Whenever it detects a mass of any kind, it scans the lump, scans it again, scans it a dozen times until it's sure, notes the orbit, takes a picture, analyzes the composition, prepares a report, files a claim, and sends a message home. Bots relay messages for each other until the message finally gets inserted into the real network. After that, it's just a matter of finding the publisher and forwarding the mail. Average time is 14 hours.

Any rock one of your paper planes sniffs and tags, if you're the first, then you've got first dibsies on it. Most rocks are dumb and worthless—and usually when your bots turn up a rock that's useful, by then you're almost always too far away to use it. Anything farther than five or ten degrees of arc isn't usually worth the time or fuel to go back after. Figure 50 million kilometers per degree of arc. It's easier to auction off the rock, let whoever is closest do the actual work, and you collect a percentage. If you've tagged enough useful rocks, theoretically you could retire on the royalties. *Theoretically.* Jill hates that word.

But if finding the right rock is the second-hardest part of the job, then the *first-* hardest part is finding the *other* rock, the one you use at the *other* end of the whip. If you want to throw something at Earth (and lots of people do), you have to throw something the same size in the opposite direction. Finding and delivering the right ballast rock to the site was always a logistic nightmare. Most of the time it was just difficult, sometimes it was impossible, and once in a while it was even worse than that.

We got lucky. We had found the right ballast rock, and it was in just the right place for us. In fact, it was uncommonly close—only a few hundred thousand kilometers behind Janis. Most asteroids are several million klicks away from their closest neighbor. FBK-9047 was small, but it was heavy. This was a nickel-rich lump about ten klicks across. While not immediately useful, it would *someday* be worth a helluva lot more than the comet we were tossing—five to ten billion, depending on how it assayed out.

Our problem was that it belonged to someone else. The FlyBy Knights. And they weren't too particularly keen on having us throw it out of the system so we could launch Comet Janis.

Their problem was that this particular ten billion dollar payday wasn't on anyone's calendar. Most of the contractors had their next twenty-five years of mining already planned out—you have to plan that far in advance when the mountains you want to mine are constantly in motion. And it wasn't likely anyone was going to put it on their menu for at least a century; there were just too many other asteroids worth twenty or fifty or a hundred billion floating around the belt. So while this rock wasn't exactly worthless in principle, it was worthless in actuality—until someone actually needed it.

Mom says that comet tossing is an art. What you do is you lasso two rocks, put each in a sling, and run a long tether between them, fifty kilometers or more. Then you apply some force to each one and start them whirling around each other. With comet ice, you have to do it slowly to give the snowball a chance to compact. When you've got them up to speed, you cut the tether. One rock goes the way you want, the other goes in the opposite direction. If you've done your math right, the ballast rock flies off into the outbeyond, and the other— the money rock, goes arcing around the solar system and comes in for a close approach to the target body—Luna, Earth, L4, wherever. If you're *really* good, you aim it so it falls into a permanent orbit in a useful position. Mom is *really* good. Do it right and it's a lot more cost-effective than installing engines on an asteroid and driving it home. A *lot* more.

Most of the time, the flying mountain takes up station as a temporary moon orbiting whatever planet we throw it at, and it's up to the locals to mine it at their leisure. But this time, we were only arranging a flyby—a close approach for the Summer Olympics, so the folks in the Republic of Texas could have a 60 degree swath of light across the sky for twelve days. And that was a whole other set of problems— because the comet's appearance had to be timed for perfect synchronicity with the event. There wasn't any wiggle room in the schedule. And everybody knew it.

All of which meant that we really needed this rock, or we weren't going to be able to toss the comet. And everybody knew that too, so we weren't in the best bargaining position. If we wanted to use 9047, we were going to have to cut the FlyBy Knights in for a percentage of Janis, which Jill didn't really want to do because what they called "suitable recompense for the loss of projected earnings" (if we threw their rock away) was so high that we would end up losing money on the whole deal.

We knew we'd make a deal eventually—but the advantage was on their side because the longer they could stall us, the more desperate we'd become and more willing to accept their terms. And meanwhile, Mom was scanning for any useful rock or combination of rocks in the local neighborhood which was approximately five million klicks in any direction. So we were juggling time, money, and fuel against our ability to go without sleep. Mom and Jill had to sort out a nightmare of orbital mechanics, economic concerns, and assorted political domains that stretched from here to Mercury.

Mom says that in space, the normal condition of life is patience; Jill says it's frustration. Myself...I had nothing to compare it with. Except the puberty thing, of course. What good is puberty if there's no one around to have puberty with? Like kissing, for instance. And holding hands. What's all that stuff about?

I was up early, because I wanted to make fresh bread. In free fall, bread doesn't rise, it expands in a sphere—which is pretty enough, and fun for tourists, but not really practical because you end up with some slices too large and others too small. Better to roll it into a cigar and let it expand in a cylindrical baking frame. We had stopped the centrifuge because the torque was interfering with our navigation around Janis; it complicated turning the ship. We'd probably be ten or twelve days without. We could handle that with vitamins and exercise, but if we went too much longer, we'd start to pay for it with muscle and bone and heart atrophy, and it takes three times as long to rebuild as it does to lose. Once the bread was safely rising—well, expanding—I drifted forward.

"Jill?"

She looked up. Well, *over*. We were at right angles to each other. "What?" A polite *what*. She kept her fingers on the keyboard.

"I've been thinking—"

"That's nice."

"—we're going to have to ride this one in, aren't we?"

She stopped what she was doing, lifted her hands away from the keys, turned her music down, and swiveled her couch to face me. "How do you figure that?"

"Any comet heading that close to Earth, they'll want the contractor to ride it. Just in case course corrections have to be made. It's obvious."

"It'll be a long trip—"

"I read the contract. Our expenses are covered, both inbound and out. Plus ancillary coverage."

"That's standard boilerplate. Our presence isn't mandatory. We'll have lots of bots on the rock. They can manage any necessary corrections."

"It's not the same as having a ship onsite," I said. "Besides, Mom says we're overdue for a trip to the marble. Everyone should visit the home world at least once."

"I've been there. It's no big thing."

"But *I* haven't—"

"It's not cost-effective," Jill said. That was her answer to everything she didn't want to do.

"Oh, come on, Jill. With the money we'll make off of Comet Janis, we could add three new pods to this ship. And bigger engines. And larger fabricators. We could make ourselves a lot more competitive. We could—"

Her face did that thing it does when she doesn't want you to know what she really feels. She was still smiling, but the smile was now a mask. "Yes, we could do a lot of things. But that decision has to be made by the senior officers of the Lemrel Corporation, kidlet." Translation: *Your opinion is irrelevant. Your mother and I will argue about this. And I'm against it.*

One thing about living in a ship, you learn real fast when to shut up and go away. There isn't any real privacy. If you hold perfectly still, close your eyes, and just listen, eventually—just from the ship noises—you can tell where everyone is and what they're doing, sleeping, eating, bathing, defecating, masturbating, whatever. In space, *everyone* can hear you scream. So you learn to speak softly. Even in an argument. Especially in an argument. The only real privacy is inside your head, and you learn to recognize when others are going there, and you go somewhere else. With Jill ... well, you learned faster than real fast.

She turned back to her screens. A dismissal. She plucked her mug off the bulkhead and sipped at the built-in straw. "I think you should talk this over with your Mom." A further dismissal.

"But Mom's asleep, and you're not. You're here." For some reason, I wasn't willing to let it go this time.

"You already have my opinion. And I don't want to talk about it anymore." She turned her music up to underline the point.

I went back to the galley to check on my bread. I opened the plastic bag and sniffed. It was warm and yeasty and puffy, just right for kneading, so I sealed it up again, put it up against a blank bulkhead and began pummeling it. You have to knead bread in a non-stick bag because you don't want micro-particles in the air-filtration system. It's like punching a pillow. It's good exercise, and an even better way to work out a shiftload of frustration.

As near as I could tell, puberty was mostly an overrated experience of hormonal storms, unexplainable rebellion, uncontrollable insecurity, and serious self-esteem issues, all resulting in a near-terminal state of wild paranoid anguish that caused the sufferer to behave bizarrely, taking on strange affectations of speech and appearance. Oh yeah, and weird body stuff where you spend a lot of time rubbing yourself for no apparent reason.

Lotsa kids in the belt postponed puberty. And for good reason. It doesn't make sense to have your body readying itself for breeding when there are no appropriate mates to pick from. And there's more than enough history to demonstrate that human intelligence goes into remission until at least five years after the puberty issues resolve. A person should finish her basic education without interruption, get a little life experience, before letting her juices start to flow. At least, that was the theory.

But if I didn't start puberty soon, I'd never be able to and I'd end up sexless. You can only postpone it for so long before the postponement becomes permanent. Which might not be a bad idea, considering how crazy all that sex stuff makes people.

And besides, yes, I was curious about all that sex stuff— masturbation and orgasms and nipples and thighs, stuff like that—but not morbidly so. I wanted to finish my *real* education first. Intercourse is supposed to be something marvelous and desirable, but all the pictures I'd ever seen made it look like an icky imposition for *both* partners. Why did anyone want to do *that?* Either there was something wrong with the videos, or maybe there was something wrong with me that I just didn't get it.

So it only made sense that I should start puberty now, so I'd be ready for mating when we got to Earth. And it made sense that we should go to Earth with Comet Janis. And why didn't Jill see that?

Mom stuck her head into the galley then. "I think that bread surrendered twenty minutes ago, sweetheart. You can stop beating it up now."

"Huh? What? Oh, I'm sorry. I was thinking about some stuff. I guess I lost track. Did I wake you?"

"Whatever you were thinking about, it must have been pretty exciting. The whole ship was thumping like a subwoofer. This boat is noisy enough without fresh-baked bread, honey. You should have used the bread machine." She reached past me and rescued the bag of dough; she began stuffing it into a baking cylinder.

"It's not the same," I said.

"You're right. It's quieter."

The arguments about the differences between free fall bread and gravity bread had been going on since Commander Jarles Ferris had announced that bread doesn't fall butter-side down in space. I decided not to pursue that argument. But I was still in an arguing mood.

"Mom?"

"What, honey?"

"Jill doesn't want to go to Earth."

"I know."

"Well, you're the Captain. It's *your* decision."

"Honey, Jill is my partner."

"Mom, I have to start puberty soon!"

"There'll be other chances."

"For puberty?"

"For Earth."

"When? How? If this isn't my best chance, there'll never be a better one." I grabbed her by the arms and turned her so we were both oriented the same way and looked her straight in the eyes. "Mom, you know the drill. They're not going to allow you to throw anything that big across Earth's orbit unless you're riding it. We have to ride that comet in. You've known that from the beginning."

Mom started to answer, then stopped herself. That's another thing about spaceships. After a while, everybody knows all the sides of every argument. You don't have to recycle the exposition. Janis was big money. Four-plus years of extra-hazardous duty allotment, fuel and delta-vee recovery costs, plus bonuses for successful delivery. So, Jill's argument about cost-effectiveness wasn't valid. Mom knew it. And so did I. And so did Jill. So why were we arguing?

Mom leapt ahead to the punch line. "So what's this really about?" she asked.

I hesitated. It was hard to say. "I—I think I want to be a boy. And if we don't go to Earth, I won't be able to."

"Sweetheart, you know how Jill feels about males."

"Mom, that's *her* problem. It doesn't have to be mine. I like boys. Some of my best online friends are boys. Boys have a lot of fun together—at least, it always looks that way from here. I want to try it. If I don't like it, I don't have to stay that way." Even as I said it, I was abruptly aware that what had only been mild curiosity a few moments ago was now becoming a genuine resolve. The more Mom and Jill made it an issue, the more it was an issue of control, and the more important it was for me to win. So I argued for it, not because I wanted it as much as I needed to win. Because it wasn't about winning, it was about who was in charge of my life.

Mom stopped the argument abruptly. She pulled me around to orient us face to face, and she lowered her voice to a whisper, her way of saying *this is serious.* "All right, dear, if that's what you really want. It has to be your choice. You'll have a lot of time to think about it before you have to commit. But I don't want you talking about it in front of Jill anymore."

Oh. Of course. Mom hadn't just wandered into the galley because of the bread. Jill must have buzzed her awake. The argument wasn't over. It was just beginning.

"Mom, she's going to fight this."

"I know." Mom realized she was still holding the baking cylinder. She turned and put the bread back into the oven. She set it to warm for two hours, then bake. Finally she floated back to me. She put her hands on my shoulders. "Let me handle Jill."

"When?"

"First let's see if we can get the rock we need." She swam forward. I followed.

Jill was glowering at her display and muttering epithets under her breath.

"The Flyby Knights?" Mom asked.

Jill grunted. "They're still saying, 'Take it or leave it.'"

Mom thought for a moment. "Okay. Send them a message. Tell them we found another rock."

"We have?"

"No, we haven't. But they don't know that. Tell them thanks a lot, but we won't need their asteroid after all. We don't have time to negotiate anymore. Instead, we'll cut Janis in half."

"And what if they say that's fine with them? Then what?"

"Then we'll cut Janis in half."

Jill made that noise she makes, deep in her throat. "It's all slush, you can't cut it in half. If we have to go crawling back, what's to keep them from raising their price? This is a lie. They're not stupid. They'll figure it out. We can't do it. We have a reputation."

"That's what I'm counting on—that they'll believe our reputation—that you'd rather cut your money rock in half than make a deal with a *man*."

Jill gave Mom one of those sideways looks that always meant a lot more than anything she could put into words, and certainly not when I was around.

"Send the signal," Mom said. "You'll see. It doesn't matter how much nickel is in that lump; it just isn't cost-effective for them to mine it. So it's effectively worthless. The only way they're going to get any value out of it in their lifetimes is to let us throw it away. From their point of view, it's free money, whatever they get. They'll be happy to take half a percent if they can get it."

Jill straightened her arms against the console and stretched herself out while she thought it out. "If it doesn't work, they won't give us any bargaining room."

"They're not giving us any bargaining room now."

Jill sighed and shrugged, as much agreement as she ever gave. She turned it over in her head a couple of times, then pressed for *record*. After the signal was sent, she glanced over at Mom and said, "I hope you know what you're doing."

"Half the rock is still more than enough. We can print up some reflectors and burn it in half in four months. That'll put us two months ahead of schedule, and we'll have the slings and tether already in place."

Jill considered it. "You won't get as big a burnoff. The tail won't be as long or as bright."

Mom wasn't worried. "We can compensate for that. We'll drill light pipes into the ice, fractioning the rock and increasing the effective surface area. We'll burn out the center. As long as we burn off fifty tons of ice per hour, it doesn't matter how big the comet's head is. We'll still get an impressive tail."

"So why didn't we plan that from the beginning?"

"Because I was hoping to deliver the head of the comet to Luna and sell the remaining ice. We still might be able to do that. It just won't be as big a payday." Mom turned to me.

"The braking problem on that will be horrendous." Jill closed her eyes and did some math in her head. "Not really cost-effective. We'll be throwing away more than two-thirds of the remaining mass. And if you've already cut it in half—"

"It's not the profit. It's the publicity. We'd generate a lot of new business. We could even go public."

Jill frowned. "You've already made up your mind, haven't you?"

Mom swam around to face Jill. "Sweetheart, our child is ready to be a grownup."

"She wants to be a boy." So Jill had figured it out too. But the way she said it, it was an accusation.

"So what? Are you going to stop loving her?"

Jill didn't answer. Her face tightened.

In that moment, something crystallized—all the vague unformed feelings of a lifetime suddenly snapped into focus with an enhanced clarity. Everything is tethered to everything else. With people, it isn't gravity or cables—it's money, promises, blood, and feelings. The tethers are all the words we use to tie each other down. Or up. And then we whirl around and around, just like asteroids cabled together.

We think the tethers mean something. They have to. Because if we cut them, we go flying off into the deep dark unknown. But if we don't cut them...we just stay in one place, twirling around forever. We don't go anywhere.

I could see how Mom and Jill were tethered by an ancient promise. And Mom and I were tethered by blood. And Jill and I—were tethered by jealousy. We resented each other's claim on Mom. She had something I couldn't understand. And I had something she couldn't share.

I wondered how much Mom understood. Probably everything. She was caught in the middle between two whirling bodies. Someone was going to have to cut the tether. That's why she'd accepted this contract—so we could go to the marble. She'd known it from the beginning. We were going to ride Janis all the way to Earth.

And somewhere west of the terminator, as we entered our braking arc, I'd cash out my shares and cut the tethers. I'd be off on my own course then—and Mom and Jill would fly apart too. No longer bound to me, they'd whirl out and away on their own inevitable trajectories. I wondered which of them would be a comet streaked across Earth's black sky.

> *Take me to the light*
> *Take me to the mystery of life*
> *Take me to the light*
> *Let me see the edges of the night*
>   —*Janis Ian*

This story was written for a unique anthology based on the songs of Janis Ian. Listening to her music, reading her lyrics, something occurred to me about the relationships between people, the orbits of routine that we fall into and all the various whirling tensions that pull at us until the tether breaks and we go spinning off in new directions. This story was inevitable. I thought it was going to be a hard-science story, but once again the characters had their own opinions.
                                        —*David Gerrold*

The Invisible Hand

Chris Edwards

Eight minutes is all it takes. Eight minutes for the Big Hand to get us from the tarmac at Houston to boots-down on the outskirts of Cairo. Not that the Egyptians have anything capable of spotting Space Force vehicles (I mean, who do you think supplied their defence systems?) No noise, no inertia and then that slight mental lurch of changing from early evening back home to the middle of the night at the LZ. It takes a while for the brain to stop climbing the walls of its bony prison and acclimate.

Everybody knows our nation keeps the world safe, but to maintain that supremacy we occasionally need to secure certain vital strategic resources, even if those resources happen to be within the borders of other sovereign nations. Since its inception the Space Force has been about more than just dominating space, it's been a means of promoting our interests wherever and whenever across the globe. If the price of peace is an occasional covert mission, then you ought to thank your lucky stars there are people like me to step up and do the job.

As soon as we hit dirt, I pinged out a request for readiness and a few seconds later green icons sprang up one after the other in my display as the team chimed in response. Four of us this run, with a quota of eighty-five targets, but I knew we were all keen to hit capacity if we could (I mean, hey, who doesn't like a bonus, right?)

Tonight's shindig was a makeshift camp a few klicks from Rafah. Our zoomie had us on a stealthy approach, the sensors clearly showing warm thermal spots of humans and animals, mainly asleep at this hour. After giving the place a quick eyeball, I signaled for her to crank the Nighty-Night field up. Almost immediately the few people standing started spasming and dropping unconscious. Those who were already asleep just twitched then slept a little deeper. Magical stuff, the Nighty-Night field, I wish I'd had one when my kids were teething! Only downside is it kills dogs, nobody knows why. We're all under standing orders never to mention *that* around Senators—too many dog lovers out there, don't want to get our appropriations cut.

Once we see everybody do the "shake and drop" (and sure enough, a few bow-wows have frisked off to the big puppy-pound in the sky), the ramp slides down and we push out the trays. Computer estimates over nine-hundred targets inside the current field-radius, and a couple of hours left in our window. I figure we can afford to be a little choosy. The four of us fan out, pushing the floating trays in front of us. The zoomie's on watch while we work, but she's redundant-the sensors are from Upstairs, nothing's going to surprise us.

We spread out and began cataloguing. Each tray has a little doodad that rates target quality from one to five, with one being "Army chow" to five being "fancy French restaurant" (well, at least as far as the Upstairs Neighbors were concerned.) It bugged me the first few times, I guess it bugs most folks. A lot of people wash out of Space Force, the job isn't an easy one, but it is vital.

The Upstairs Neighbors, man, people really lost their shit when they appeared. I mean, even the US had nothing like that first ship. And of course we thought it was the Chinese, the Russians thought it was us, the Chinese thought it was Euros. Ridiculous, as if *any* human government could have made something that size and just sneaked it into orbit with nobody noticing. Slowly everybody began to figure it out, this thing wasn't local-we had *visitors*.

So there they were, hanging up above us as the world went quietly gaga down below. When they looked down, do you know the first thing they saw? The largest man-made object visible from space? Fucking-A-yeah, our border wall! Great Wall of China wasn't *shit* compared to that sucker (300 billion dollars buys a lot of concrete and rebar!) When they saw that, they knew who they had to speak to.

And yeah, a lot of yammerheads in the Senate bumped their gums "They're space monsters", "They eat human beings!" and blah-blah-blah. But it took a real leader to look past the prejudice and the bullshit and say "Wait a minute now, they may eat humans, but that doesn't mean some of them can't be very fine people!" And you know what? He was right, it isn't their fault they have to drain life energy out of sentient beings to survive, any more than it's a lion's fault that it needs to eat gazelles.

And it wasn't like they were just landing and grabbing people, stuffing them into ships and disappearing (and anyone who thinks they *couldn't* have done just that is kidding themselves.) They weren't here to wage war, they were here to open negotiations. We had something they wanted, and as it turned out they had plenty we wanted as well. The President sat down and negotiated us a crackerjack deal-we got sole rights to assemble and distribute all their technical goodies, and in return we kept them supplied.

Okay, so some people have to die to keep the whole thing ticking over, but I mean *hello*?! Earth has a hell of an overpopulation problem. The best thing you can do for the environment isn't recycling or using less gas, it's just getting rid of excess human beings. And if you can protect our national prestige *and* turn a buck at the same time? Hell, that's the American dream! The prisons went first, of course, they emptied out in no time. Crime in the US is like, zilch now. Crossing the border without a permit became a really bad idea-feeding illegal aliens to outer-space aliens seemed just as American as apple pie. And the bounties you could get for turning in your neighbor's undocumented gardener meant that most of those Mexicans fled back where they came from.

Hell, the US pays top dollar for the prison population of every other country on Earth, as well as orphans, addicts, the terminally ill, refugees, dissidents and other freeloaders. The tech we distribute keeps us at the number one spot (and you can *bet* we keep the best toys for ourselves, of course.) But even with all of that, it just isn't sufficient; the Upstairs Neighbors keep wanting more. Seems that humans are the next big taste sensation back on their homeworld, kind of like their version of McDonalds or something.

So that's where Space Force comes in. We've got tech the rest of the world can only dream about, and a mission to make up the shortfalls. I mean, why should we pay these shithole countries when we can just come in and take what we need? Most of the places are propped up by our dollars, depending on our protection to keep them safe from their enemies. Of course their leaders know the cost of doing business in this day and age. And if they know what's good for themselves, they cover it up for us. Most of them play ball, disappearances get blamed on accidents, countries hostile to our foreign policy or some two-bit revolutionary group.

<<>>

My first tray is filled within a minute; a girl of sixteen, thin, harelip and ragged clothes. What kind of life was she having here anyway? Really, I'm doing her a favor, she's registering as a four-she'll make a better meal than a human being. I float her back to the Big Hand, slot her tray in and send her up, then take the new one that glides out smoothly from the prep bay. I can see the rest of my team loading in as well.

Little kids are hard, especially when you've got kids yourself. I'm glad they don't usually rate higher than one, it means we can leave them. The eggheads tried to explain to me some theory about bioelectric auras and experience influencing the quality of the life force. Me, I figure it's just the difference between steak and veal. The Neighbors might be monsters but they're not *monster* monsters.

An hour in and we're at sixty-four targets, most of them 3 plus rated. I check status and everybody comes back green, but suddenly the zoomie hails and tells me she's got vehicle activity at eight clicks-looks like a convoy and there's nowhere else they could really be going. I curse inwardly, this is going to shoot our quota all to hell. "Alright, we've got looky-loo's inbound. Screw quality, tonight just became about numbers. We clear seventy and amscray." A chorus of groans over the comm, I know how they feel, this was looking like a milk run.

"Signal suppression" I say to the zoomie, but she's already on it. Whoever our visitors are, they're not going to be reporting back. We're not cleared for weapons-hot unless directly engaged, so for now we just concentrate on getting the rest of the shipment packed away. I'm helping pull the last two trays back when the first of the vans enters the Nighty-Night field and loses control, ploughing into a rickety structure as its driver falls unconscious.

The other two vans screech to a halt just outside the radius. Looks like they were expensive once; old petrol burners from back when folks drove German instead of American. People in paramilitary gear scramble out, not soldiers from the way they move, so probably some kind of people's' militia or volunteer group. You see that kind of thing all the time in countries where we source a lot of product. I hustle the trays back towards the Big Hand, the zoomie is already tracking them with the targeting system. One of the newcomers breaks out a shoulder-mounted missile launcher and aims it at the Big Hand. Big mistake.

The missile soft-launches, dipping its tail towards the ground before igniting rockets and beginning to blaze towards us. Just for a second it glows white hot from tip to tail and then explodes in a cone of burning hot metal fragments which rip through the area the newcomers are standing in. Not so much as a cinder heads in our direction. I give the thumbs up to the zoomie, although all she really did was take the gloves off the automated defenses.

We manage to get the last trays back and slotted in, then head back to the ramp. "Permission to engage?" the zoomie asks. Frankly I'm amazed there are any of them left alive, but she points out a couple of blurry figures on the scopes, crawling away from the burning ruin of their convoy. They don't look like they've got much fight left in them, but protocol is that once attacked we make an example. I give the order, "Scorched earth."

The Big Hand lifts smoothly up to fifty metres or so above the camp. Flickering flashes appear on the canopy as bullets ricochet off without even making a noise. I watch the zoomie's hands on the monitors as she sketches out a rough cordon out to a half-klick around the LZ, then punches the button to engage the weapons. Below us a trench of fire blazes up, then quickly sweeps around, burning everything beneath us to glowing ash until it finally completes full circle. A great disc of fire glows in the desert, casting an orange glare on the canopy and the smooth surfaces of the Big Hand.

"Take us home" I say to the zoomie. All crisp efficiency, she guns it for home. We don't even feel a jolt as we slide through the atmosphere and up toward the twinkling stars above.

I look back at the kilometer of burning devastation on the scopes. Damn them. Damn them to hell. What a waste of perfectly good food!

The Grass Suffers

Manny Frishberg

"When elephants fight, the grass suffers."

Kikuyu proverb

First Lieutenant Lona Jaffery snapped herself into the restraints and glanced away from the red numbers counting the seconds until the Jump in her heads-up display.

Her parents had told her a BA in Media History wouldn't get her anywhere. But the Space Force needed charged-particle fodder, and a degree in anything qualified you for an officer's commission. She pushed them out of her head and instead thought about when Rangers really jumped out of aircraft. Not much like a parabolic flight in a pressurized and climate-controlled capsule from four miles above the surface.

Lona gripped the soft rubberene stress balls on the end of her armrests; squeezing until her knuckles cracked. One-hundred-fifty milliseconds after the "Egg" entered the Martian atmosphere, a rocket-propelled parachute would deploy to slow her descent through the thin Martian atmosphere before the retro rockets lowered her to the surface at a gentle three kph. Or so, her T.O. claimed.

She clenched her jaw against their urge to chatter. She was no coward; If the egg did crash, she did not want to be trapped inside her pressure suit, grievously wounded. She unlatched her visor and slid it up over the top of her helmet. Breaking apart like Humpty Dumpty, exposure would make it quick and final.

It wasn't the fall she was afraid of.

She didn't fear battle, either.

She felt well prepared by her training. In fact, her VR Sim scores were through the roof. That's what troubled her; it had been so damned much fun. She'd told herself it was all just pretend, bloodless conditioning no-harm, no-foul.

Not like her father's war. Whenever she had asked about it, he just quoted some old general from back when they fought on horseback.

"Robert E. Lee said, 'It is good that war is so terrible, lest we should come to love it too much.' And it is," he'd add, "so, so terrible." Then he'd just get quiet for a long time.

Her sergeant had laughed when he heard her tell it. Than Nguyen, a grizzled master sergeant twice her age and three times her superior in everything but rank, said it was pure bullshit. "That's what you say when you're back home," he said, and she had to believe him. She counted on him out here.

No matter, she told herself as the roar of the deployment charge shook her tiny world like the Yosemite super-eruption. Far past the point of no return... and the tranq dart bit into her triceps, right on schedule.

A subjective instant later, the hatch slid open, and Lona registered that she had survived the landing more-or-less intact.

Unbuckling herself, she slid the visor down with her left hand. Her right had already retrieved her weapon from its brace and started it powering up.

The rifle issued a high-pitched whine, rising and falling in tone as it reached full charge. An autoinjector in her bulky Michelin Man-shaped pressure suit primed her with a shot of Triple-A, a potent blend of adrenaline, amphetamine, and anabolic steroids to make her alert, energized, and inclined toward blind rage. This was her first shot at payback for the Sea of Tranquility massacre. Seven thousand Blue Origin contractors like her brother, cataloging gear for transshipment up to Mars. The Bransonist bastards.

The green light atop the stock blinked on, and Lona lifted out of the seat and stepped onto the Martian surface. Crew quarters and labs rose a half dozen meters up on lanky tubular tripods: dull black polyhedrons, stuck together at odd angles like opaque crystals, lights shining through the graphene windows.

Holding the trigger down, tendrils of charged photons, swirled around any solid object they encountered, limning them with an eerie halo before they decohered and fell into

piles of hot ash. But not smoking piles, she noted casually–
the air here was too cold and dry for condensation, too thin
for smoking char.

Lona paused her fire to see how her fellow Space Rangers
were doing. An easy dozen stood in a row alongside her, their
segmented suits puffed up like balloon animals, ash cones
lying in their wake. The thin, ever-present Martian wind lifted
grains of ash and swirled them in wispy spirals, blending
them inexorably into the fine dust that was the ambiance of
Mars.

"Ashes to ashes, dust to dust," Spec. Robinette's voice
cracked over the short-range RF net.

"If the right fist don't floor ya, th' left one must," Nguyen
filled in. He giggled at the old saw as if they hadn't heard it
about ten thousand times before. More laughter came in
multiple voices into her ear.

She forced a laugh. Won't do not to share in the levity.
Even if it is a little too on-point. Most of these guys had been
on a dozen Sweep and Sanitize missions before, and she
wanted to make sure nobody would hold her inexperience
against her. Her muscles twitched, sending ripples of tension
across her shoulders and down her back, tickling irritably,
itching for another fight–this one had been over much too
soon for the dose of Triple-A.

"Sweep the area," she barked into the RF. Several
members of the squad fanned out and started firing short,
illuminating bursts at the legs of a twenty-meter tall housing
module.

"Got a straggler," Nguyen's voice screeched in her ear.

"Where?" Salman shouted. The automatic gain
adjustment in her helmet tamped it down to a squawk. The
young corporal had come on station in the shipment before
hers. This was her first action, too. Lona rotated from the
hips in a wide, semicircular arc to take in the scene.

Nguyen indicated a half-collapsed module with the barrel
of his gun. The lower half of two of its legs had been
granulated and what remained listed precariously,
threatening to collapse entirely at any moment.

She stared dumbly at the derelict building, not seeing
what the other did–until it moved. The shadow in one of the

portholes shifted, just for an instant before freezing in place, enough for her to catch it. He hadn't needed to wait for it to move.

If Sgt. Nguyen said jump, she'd say 'how high', and the rest of the squad knew it. That was why they deigned to follow her. A pulsing rhythm rang behind her ears. One... two, while she thought.

"Light it up," she could hear echoes as her voice crackled through the radio.

In less than the time for the order to transmit, jagged flashes of static lightning tore into the remaining structure. Bodies flung themselves out of the escape hatches and were met in midflight by more directed energy bolts, the cloud of what had recently been people slowly swirling through the barely existent air.

"Good job, Than. Well done. Now, back to work, Spacers," she barked. On the jagged side of her Triple-A high, she scanned the sky for a counterforce. She imagined herself vaporizing a few dozen Virgin pricks before they could even touch down. She knew the cavalry wasn't coming—neither side's. It would be a waste, their landing crafts easy targets.

She stepped back into her command egg to watch her team's progress finishing up. The operation counted as a total success, carried out with minimal loss. Everyone said it was a war for Honor, for Human Dignity, and Individual Liberty. Lona told herself as much at least once a day. The twenty-second-century coalitions resembled the alliances at the start of World War II. Except, this time, the French and British found themselves on the same side as the Japanese and Germans, while the Freedom Federation united the main spacefaring nations: the US, Russians, Chinese, and Israelis.

Jaffery felt good about the operation, not just because her team had performed flawlessly. They knew their orders better than she did, not bothering to search the remaining structures before devouring them with their ray guns. Preemptive retaliation. She expected no less from them.

When last structures on the site turned to mounds of red dirt and piles of partly disintegrated debris, she gave the order to return to the eggs to await pick up. Once they pressurized, they could get out of the michis and move freely in the relative comfort of their capsules. She switched on long-range scanners to watch for the half-kilometer-wide wings of the Eagle coming to gather the eggs into her nest and fly them back to base, knowing that it would be at least two Sol-hours.

That gave her time alone to think while the chemical cocktail made its way out of her system. She managed to record her after-action report, complimenting each member of the crew and the landing party, in turn, parceling out special praise for Nguyen and recommending him for a commendation. Then she moved on to cataloging the results of the raid. Seven buildings incinerated. They had made no effort to discover how many of the enemy combatants had been housed at this facility, so she made up a number that would sound reasonable, given the physical damage they'd inflicted.

Lona swallowed. The acid bile that filled her throat burned more going back down. She ignored it as best she could. Her teeth chattered, and her extremities felt like they were being weighed down as she played the events back in her head.

She worked at remembering the specifics, but her head was filled with cotton. She was crashing, now that the Triple-A was wearing off. As she drifted toward a twilight half-sleep, she saw the imagined faces of the soldiers she had dispatched. She bit back tears and felt sick to her stomach.

That was a relief.

<<>>

Lona awoke, her egg locked safely into its berth. A red-hot spear of pain pulsed through her head like a neon sign flashing in a noir movie hotel room window. She climbed out of the drop vehicle and grabbed onto the doorframe until the room slowed its spinning enough for her to stumble forward. She could hear the derisive laughing behind her, but she wasn't going to give them the satisfaction of acknowledging it.

Definitely, don't want to have to bust their balls over it and get known as a tight-ass bitch my first time out. She'd known that kind of an asshole, served under him–them before. That's how you get a hole burned in your suit, out on the plains. Not just for being harsh and humorless, but a raw first louie who lacked a rapport with her crew, or worse, didn't listen, could get good Rangers killed. In which case, better her than them.

She made her way to her quarters without looking too unsteady. The spin simulated point-seven gees, twice Mars-normal gravity to make them feel like Supermen on the surface. The station was pure twenty-first-century utilitarian construction–bare metal and bacterial-grown plastics. It orbited the larger of the two Martian moons, always staying on the dark side, hiding from observers on the planet's surface. Part of the game of Hide and Seek the Fed forces were playing with the Euros.

She pulled the hatch closed behind her and raced to the commode to worship the waste recycling gods. Long as you perform in the field, who cares if you have a rocky recovery? After rinsing the bile from her mouth, Lona wanted nothing more, than to lie down in the dark and wait for her head to explode. But that wouldn't do.

Lona told herself it was the aftereffects of Triple A, not the images that swirled behind her eyelids every time she let them close, that left her queasy and distanced from her own thoughts. By the time she recovered sufficiently to make her way to the galley, the rest of Second Shift was two rounds of drinks ahead of her. It was her First Blood, and that made it her duty to drink as many of them under the table as she could.

By the time she laid her head down on her elbow and started snoring, only two men and one other woman were matching her, shot for shot. Senior Master Sergeant Sara McClintock made sure she got her tucked into her own bunk, or so she was told.

The next day was worse: everything went back to normal. Hurry up and wait. Drills and idleness, and it was hard to say which was more tedious. And, time to relive the battle, millisecond by millisecond. The memories were seared into her brain by the amphetamine-epinephrine cocktail–a side effect no one bothered to mention 'til she got there.

She lay on her bunk, staring at the crosshatch pattern of the struts supporting the empty upper bed. The station had been designed for three times the number of jockeys they had aboard, it being easier to close off a section than to add one if needed. Lona imagined she was on the inside of a lattice-topped pie.

She was thinking of old celluloids. Funny how the black-and-white war movies were always about bravery, honor, and camaraderie. But the colored films were different, less sure of themselves. That's where you get the montages of ghostly faces. This wasn't the first time she'd thought about that, but it meant something different now.

Her self-reflection got cut short by the rising tones of General Quarters, a trio of electronic klaxons, like a sixty-decibel clown car. The Japanese had staged a ground assault on Hooke Crater Station Seventeen.

Why? she asked herself, gearing up. There was nothing there but some Russian and Syrian researchers, working on genetic modifications, engineering plants and animals to help the colonists. Work that would benefit all humanity, once the damned war was finally settled, fergodsake. All she could see was red.

Less than a minute later she was strapped into her egg, parachuting down to the Agyre Planitia, she felt no concerns about adding to her cortege of ghosts. The dart injected her with Triple-A, and she welcomed the cold liquid being pumped into her arm. Righteous anger at the Sushis blazed within her even before the hatch opened. She exulted in the sharp heightening of her senses, anxious to feel consumed again by rampaging, blind chaos.

This time the battle was not as quick, or as one-sided as her first encounter had been. The Sushis had time to set up a defensive perimeter while the Rangers had been in transit—that was just one of the ways tactics hadn't entirely caught up to the new circumstances.

Always fighting the last war. It's just like Than says. Lona had time to think about it while her proton rifle recharged. She watched the gauge in the corner of her visor display. Lona wasn't interested in stunning anybody, this time around. She had her gun set on extra crispy.

That's three Sushis that won't be growing old, she thought, half crouching in the shadow of the remaining half of a water condensation tower. Tendrils of charged particles from the enemy position lit up the dark a meter to her left while she bided her time.

She watched Than moving past a half-cintered column, circling around to take his shot, bounding across the open ground in long, galumphing strides, the way you do in a michi in thirty-percent gravity. Suddenly his boot caught a length of cable, still dancing across the red dirt from being hit by a pulsed charge, and he went into a tumble, bouncing like a flat stone skipping on the surface of a lake. A bolt from the sniper lit up a jagged line, ionizing the CO_2 in the thin atmosphere.

Lona straightened and began loping toward him. Than wriggled around pointlessly, struggling to untangle his left leg. Before she made it out from behind her shelter, a second energy burst lit up Than's fuel and oxygen reserves in a ball of fire that extinguished itself as quickly as it appeared. No thundering roar followed, just a wave of radiating heat that registered as a blip on her head's up display followed by the blinking out of the sergeant's icon.

The drug cocktail kept her going after that, or that was what she told herself as cold, rational, determined rage filled her. Later, she could not remember everything she had done that sol. In truth, she hardly recalled being at the battle at all. Something had taken over, a hard, nub of bitterness deep inside, forged then and there out of their losses.

Still, the After-Action Report required her to list a detailed census of killed and wounded. She dictated the report while they waited for pickup. They'd taken fire from three of the structures, which meant at least that many guards. More than one or two per unit, she decided. She continued making up details and reciting them into the transcriber. She would play it back to the crew on the way back to base,

The hard, dispassionate calm that had taken over in the middle of the battle had not left her. Lona dismissed it as a lingering effect of the chemical stimulant cocktail, though she had not felt that way last time.

I'll have to ask Than, she thought. Then the reality caught in her throat.

Six hours later, it still hadn't worn off.

Not the next day, either.

She no longer thought of it as calm–she had gone numb. Lona knew she should talk to somebody about it, but she hadn't been there that long, and she was the squad leader–not someone to get all buddy-buddy with. Nothing to be done about it but to swallow her bitterness and enjoy the burn.

Things had been different with Than. An old Air Force noncom from back when the Space Force was just a twinkle in President Trump's eye, he could care less about rank or protocol, and he had taken green lieutenants under his wing before her. He'd told her as much the day she arrived. She had been able to tell him anything because, well, he didn't give a rat's ass.

She just needed to find something to care about, worth getting out of her bunk for–or someone to stay in it with. Of course, that was out of the question. Getting laid would have to wait until she rotated out or got R and R. And neither of those was about to happen any time soon.

Less than three Martian days later a kinetic barrage–basically a nosecone full of the kind of debris that collected around a planet when people were blasting each other into oblivion–peppered five-thousand new colonist in a SpaceX station near the base of Oceanidom Mons. The attack, on the other end of the Argyre Planitia from Hooke, came too soon for the Sushis to have launched a retribution. Half a sol later, she got a briefing on their next mission, and six hours later, her team dropped in on a Virgin Galactic warehouse, knocking out the Limey composting plant and laying waste to fifteen hectares of greenhouses in retaliation.

Lona led the squad into the facility, encountering no cover fire to slow them down, and found no guards or workers inside. It was eerie, but they had a job to do and, with no resistance, leveling the facility would be a spacewalk.

A tickle at the back of Lona's brain told her things were going too well–it was the kind of warning she would have gotten from Than. Silently, she thanked his ghost and let loose a wild, howling laugh.

A cannonade crashing down on the LZ sobered her up, quick. Luckily, the Bransonists were shooting blind from the other side of the mons, counting on sheer numbers of cheap, unguided missiles, manufactured on-site, no doubt. Even so, the barrage kept them pinned down for three hours and cost her two more troopers before she saw the plume of a half dozen parachutes as the Eggs plummeted in toward the Limey outpost. Then, the eerie glow in the thin Martian atmosphere from their charged particle weapons. And finally, extraction.

There had been five squads of six like hers when Lona arrived on station. Now, just twenty rangers remained–three squads, with two to spare. They were given no time to grieve, barely enough time to crash from the last dose of Triple-A before they were suiting up and loading into their eggs again.

Lona strapped into her Egg, clenching the rubberene balls on the armrest, counting the seconds down before she shot out through space. Anticipating the insect-sting of autoinjectors fueling her for battle, she let the thrill wash over her like a cold shock.

She had barely listened to the recounting of the latest aggression they were to avenge. All she'd needed to hear was "Sweep and Sanitize." Lona didn't care if today it was a Luftwaffe base or a Mitsubishi research station.

Ballistic bombardment would soften them up before her crew landed, and they would follow behind, sweeping the ground to leave nothing standing, and sanitize–leave it as lifeless as before anyone'd arrived. Easy duty, the kind Lona liked.

Her dad had always focused on the wrong part of what the old Civil War general had said. She smiled as the needle bit into her arm.

"We should come to love it too much."

Space Opera

Daniel M. Kimmel

The meteor heading towards Earth spelled certain doom. Its massive size and velocity was such that its impact would end all life on the planet, if not actually tear the very Earth apart. Currently located outside Pluto's orbit the meteor was headed for an inevitable date with disaster for humanity. Our only hope was to blast it to pieces long before it worked its way through the solar system. Our ship, the *Götterdämmerung*, was equipped with a series of four plasma torpedoes that had to be fired according to precise calculations. We needed to not only shatter the meteor, but do it in such a way that the debris dispersed across the Solar System instead of continuing on course to Earth. If we did this right, we would create an outer asteroid belt. If we miscalculated in any way, we would set a bombardment of meteor pieces hurtling towards the Earth that the planet might survive, but humanity would not.

I had signed aboard the ship knowing that this was a mission from which we might not return. We were a crew who knew what was at stake and knew what we had to do. If we failed, it would be more than a disaster. The final curtain would have fallen on Earth without hope of a revival or an encore.

We were moments away from our rendezvous with destiny, when our fearless captain, Giacomo Puccini, rose from his seat on the command deck and turned to address the entire crew. All comm systems were given over to his dramatic message.

"*Ci stiamo avvicinando la meteora...,*" he sang in his beautiful tenor. I had no idea what he was saying as my knowledge of Italian was limited to *arriverderci* and *veal scallopini*.

"Subtitles, please," I ordered the monitor, which began real time translation of his aria. This was his final call to the crew to do our utmost to save not only our families back on Earth, but the rich legacy of humanity which La Scala, the planetary space authority, had put so much effort into trying to preserve.

"We are approaching the meteor..." the subtitles read.

The lighting on the captain subtly changed as he sang, "*È il momento di eseguire la missione per la quale siamo stati addestrati ...*"

"It is time to perform the mission for which we were trained...," appeared at the bottom of the screen. I wish he had simply transmitted the libretto to the crew as it would have saved time, but this was the captain's big moment.

Suddenly a chorus appeared behind him. It was only a dozen or so men and women, but they were representing the entire crew. For some reason they were singing in French.

"*Nous sommes prêts à donner notre vie pour la Terre et l'honneur de notre glorieux capitaine,*" they sang.

It took a moment for the ship's computer to adjust to the change of language. A moment later the translation appeared: "We are prepared to lay down our lives for Earth and the honor of our glorious captain."

Incongruously, he sang his reply in Italian. "*Sono orgoglioso di voi, il mio equipaggio. Sono onorata di guidarvi in battaglia.*" ("You do me proud. I am honored to lead you into battle.")

This was all very inspiring, but my big moment was coming up and I couldn't afford to miss my cue. The fate of mankind hung in the balance.

"*Sono i siluri al plasma pronto per essere licenziato?*" ("Are the plasma torpedoes ready to be fired?")

A mezzosoprano whom I only knew as Torpedo 1 responded, "*Bereit auf Ihren Befehl, mein Kapitän.*"

A bass listed on the roster as Torpedo 2 similarly replied, "Ready on your command, my captain."

Torpedo 3 struck an atonal note in Japanese, "*Watashi no kyaputen, anata no meirei de junbi ga dekimashita.*"

Finally it was my big moment, for which I had been rehearsing for months. As the fill light bathed me in a greenish glow, I faced the communicator and sang my readiness to do my duty, "*Pronto il vostro comando, mio capitano.*"

"*Sul mio ordine,*" responded the captain. ("On my order.") This led to a beautiful round as we four torpedo operators repeated our readiness to serve in each of our languages. Suddenly the lights dimmed throughout the ship—except for the spotlight on the captain—as he movingly sang, "*Fuoco. Fuoco. Fuoco.*"

I did not need to read the subtitles to know we had been given the command to fire. We each pressed the appropriate buttons as the entire crew began praying in Italian, "*Preghiamo che il nostro obiettivo è vero. La Terra deve vivere. Preghiamo che il nostro obiettivo è vero. La Terra deve vivere.*" As I sang I felt the words deep inside me: We pray that our aim be true. Let the Earth live.

After the missiles were fired the ship took off at near light speed towards Earth, trying to get as far away from the impending explosions as possible. Even so, the ship was severely shaken. Singing was impossible, even if the discordant music had permitted vocal accompaniment.

At last the ship righted course. The computer readouts indicated our mission had been a success. The meteor had been destroyed. Earth had been spared. Alas, this happy result was not without tragedy. Captain Puccini, at the moment of his greatest triumph, had been attacked by Science Officer Verdi, who was jealous of the captain's relationship with Lt. Mimi, our communications officer. During the destruction of the meteor, Verdi had stabbed Puccini, who killed his attacker but was himself fatally wounded.

On our screens Captain Puccini made his dramatic exit, "*Siamo riusciti anche se devo pagare il prezzo per il mio amore. Ti saluto, il mio equipaggio valente.*"

I had to look at the subtitles. I knew my own line in Italian, but I had learned it phonetically. "We have succeeded even as I must pay the price for my love. I salute you, my valiant crew." The captain embraced his beloved Mimi as the spotlight dimmed and he expired.

It was a most dramatic mission, but I think it will be my last. When we return to Earth I'm going to put in for a transfer to the *Fledermaus*. I think I'm much more cut out for space operetta.

High Steel

Andrew J Lucas

Corporal Zoe Kennedy squinted trying to make out the Earth, the bright point of light she called home. One point hidden among a thousand other points of light no more and no less significant than any of the others.

'A thousand points of light' Zoe thought she recognized that phrase, but wasn't sure from where. She shook her head, to clear the meaningless words from it. 'A thousand points of light', truly meaningless out here on the high frontier where millions of stars surrounded her.

"Zoe! Where's my status report?"

Not that she had any time for sightseeing.

"Hold onto your helmet Roderick." She pulled on her tablet's . The grey rectangle of carbon fibre sprang to life at the touch of her gloves. Unlike a standard tablet there was no touch screen, it would have shattered in the vacuum in seconds, and in her EVA suit her gloves were too bulky for such delicate movements. Zoe clipped the USB port into her glove, tried to anyways, reversed the connector and tried again, flipped it once more before it slipped home.

The tablet lit up with a cascading scroll of data that moved across the screen as Corporal Roderick Wilson drew the information out of the tablet through the suit's data port.

"Got it."

"Okay. I'm headed in then."

Zoe secured the tablet on her belt and turned back to her skipper intent on returning to the ship. She'd been jumping around the surface of the asteroid for hours, drawing samples, each less interesting than the last. Now she wanted nothing more than a hot shower, a meal, and a warm bunk. The USSS Valley Forge wasn't a comfortable ship, it was cramped, overcrowded, and always on the verge of one catastrophic breakdown or another. Still for the last four years it had been her home and she was looking forward to returning to it.

"Whoa not so fast their sunshine."

"What is it now?" Roderick was a being a pain in her ass today.

"You didn't sample the entire asteroid. I only have one sample from sector three."

"Come on Roderick."

"That's Corporal Wilson and protocol says five samples per sector for an object of this size."

"Come on. That will take all day."

"Corporal..."

Roderick was being a real pain.

"Fine. Corporal. I'd like to request a work order review with the Lieutenant."

Silence. Perhaps the bastard was taking her seriously for once. Maybe he'd had a change of heart. Wilson knew that once a senior officer looked over his work assignments that he would have to answer for them... maybe even court-martialed

"Okay Private Kennedy I will be more than happy to review your work order."

Man was smarter than she thought after all...

"Once the request is on my desk."

Hmm...

"In triplicate."

Yeah, Wilson was being a real pain in the ass today.

<<>>

Zoe secured the drill into the asteroid's surface with a set of zero gee pitons. They were just like pitons used by rock climbers on Earth, but cost the Space Force $3,000 each. The joys of military procurement budgeting, she supposed, but then a National Emergency did wonders to free up money from all sorts of places. Nothing screamed emergency like the appearance of honest to god aliens on the doorstep of the Capital.

Of course, no one outside of the Pentagon had seen them as the military swooped down upon them before anyone got a really good look. Still the ship was there just outside of the

White House, at least until the army threw a tarp over it and carted that away as well. It was just lucky the President had created the sixth branch of the armed forces a few years before the alien panic arrived. As far as national emergencies went, an honest to God invasion from outer space was one for the history books–as was America's response.

Congressional approval for a full-scale mobilization was begrudgingly given when the new director of NASA, once a VP at Industrial Light and Magic, provided dramatic images of alien ships massing in solar orbit. Oh, there were questions about the validity of the images, especially the lack of corroborating data from the international community; except for Russian and Chinese observatories, and that was enough for the public, in spite of fake news articles calling for an independent review of the NASA data. Both chambers of government voted emergency powers to fast track the Space Force. However, it wasn't until the White House expropriated the assets of Space X and Amazon that the technological ability to create ships like the USSS Valley Forge became available–and the economic ability to construct them.

Now a fleet of 5 ships were protecting the planet from hostile aliens.

The drill completed its program, exuding a thin column of stone into its analysis chamber. Zoe activated the spectrograph and a small array of lasers played across the rock, shredding it down to its component atoms and feeding them into a chemical bath. She watched the Tesla logo rotate on the unit's display as the machine worked. The logo was a remnant of the original programmers, before the Space Force annexed the IP. No one had figured out how to remove the iconography of the various corporations, which had sacrificed all to build the technology and ships of the Space Force. The remnants floated through the operating systems, ghostly revenants of a time before the alien threat.

The logo stopped rotating with a soft chime, carried over the Wi-Fi of Zoe's suit. She looked over the results without enthusiasm. So far, the asteroid had been unremarkable, lacking any of the nickel-iron ore the Space Force was looking for. Zoe wasn't a rocket scientist, few in the Force were, but she knew that the cause was desperate. That the more iron the ship could process the safer the entire world would be. Which is why she let out a small involuntary gasp as the display registered nearly pure iron.

She punched the display twice to confirm the readings. Almost pure iron, just the thing she'd been sent out to find. Protocol required she get a second sample to confirm the readings, so she set about loosening the pitons and shifting the drill a few feet to the right. She found a flat almost rectangular patch, clear of debris and secured the drill there. As the machine worked, she considered what the discovery meant, to her career and the mission. Space Force prized results above all else and if this asteroid was rich in ore to feed the Valley Forge's smelters, then a promotion and bonus was assured. Perhaps more importantly the ship might have enough ore to complete its section of the wall.

Aside from the fleet, the President's primary defense was the Wall. Now Zoe wasn't a rocket scientist, but she knew a few and they insisted the Wall was a viable defense. It involved placing iron rods at specific points in the Earth's orbit. These points called Lagrange points after some ancient physicist, French or something she thought, were arrayed around the planet in a sort of star formation. The points were locations where anything placed there would maintain their position relative to the Earth. Space Force insisted they were natural chokepoints where caravans of aliens would have to pass on their way to Earth.

Zoe remembered the President's speech when the Wall was announced and the dismay of the fake news. They insisted that the aliens could just go above the Wall and avoid it. The White House had rebutted that that wasn't how gravity worked and their experts, all very smart, very successful businessmen had devised the plan and tested it intensively. It would work, they promised. Today five ships were placing hundreds of steel rods at these strategic positions, following and leading the Earth as it circled the sun. Not being a rocket scientist, Zoe had been dubious, but the plan had the support of NASA and the White House. What more did she need?

Luckily these Lagrange points were already occupied, with an assortment of asteroids, small and large. While the points were called Lagrange points, the asteroids had been named Trojan asteroids for some reason having to do with Jupiter's moons or something. That didn't really make sense to Zoe, from here Jupiter was just another pin pick of light in the endless dark. But then she didn't have to understand why things were named the way they were, she was a miner not a rocket... well a rocket scientist. Still many of the asteroids contained an abundance of iron ore, and each Space Force ship had a fusion engine that burned hot enough to melt it. The rods were rough and ugly but they would stop any alien ship in its tracks the President insisted.

The drill completed its second core sample and exuded another thin cylinder of rock. The sample chamber looked a little cloudy as it filled with stone and Zoe wondered if the glass had been scratched by the slurry of rock particles. She'd have to give it a good cleaning when she returned to the ship. Returned triumphant with her discovery.

A delicate chime filled her helmet as a second set of results scrolled across the drill's display. Iron was evident in quantities she'd never seen before. The asteroid was richer than she'd ever thought possible. She couldn't help smiling as she reviewed the results, but the smile didn't last long. The analysis was flawed there was something wrong with the data. How was there oxygen registering? Had she cut into a pocket of subterranean ice? She knelt down careful not to dislodge herself from the surface of the Trojan asteroid.

She was almost flush with the surface of the rock squinting to examine the area where the drill was in contact with the asteroid. The mechanism had contracted back into the drill proper, and she could see the small recess where the bit would extend from spinning and cutting into the extraterrestrial stone. Beneath it was a small perfectly circular hole, stark, pitch black in the wan sunlight playing off the asteroid.

But that wasn't what drew Zoe's attention.

From this angle, cheek to helmet to stone, the asteroid looked flat, smooth, unnatural, like a rectangle of stone dropped into the surface of the asteroid. It reminded Zoe of a huge tombstone that had fallen into the soft soil of a newly covered grave but larger. She struggled to think of the word she was thinking of–monolith, that was it. A monolith sunk into the stone of the asteroid.

She shuddered at the thought, it was morbid and unsettling. Instead she focused on the wealth and success that waited her when she reported her find to Valley Forge. She extended a hand beneath the drill and brushed some of the loose stone away from the machine. The stone floated away at odd angles, liberated from the minuscule gravity of the rock. Now that the dust and debris was clear the surface of the stone appeared even smoother than before, gleaming in the reflected glow of her helmet's LED displays.

Was it, could it be? Metal, refined, formed metal? A sheet of it entrenched in the rock. Zoe felt around the edges of the sheet pushing her gloved fingers deep into the loose gravel around it. The small stones gave way allowing her to imbed her fingers an inch or so into the asteroid before coming up short against unyielding stone. At least she thought it was stone, but was it?

She pulled her hand free then cupped her fingers before thrusting them back into the gravel shoveling stone away from the metal, pushing a geyser of the loose material into space.

Her fingers touched something hard beneath the surface. Zoe couldn't see what it was but she instinctively grabbed it and pulled. At first it resisted but after a moment, gave way conducting as a slight snap through her glove. Then the slab moved, displacing more gravel, throwing it into orbit, following the handfuls of rock Zoe had excavated.

The metal rotated up and outwards pivoting along one of its smaller edges. It moved suddenly, swiftly and Zoe knew instinctively that if she were standing on the metal, she would have been thrown into space fast enough to break free of the asteroid's gravity to be lost forever in the depths of space.

She'd been out in space for years now, and like all Space Force members was comfortable living on the verge of death, separated from it by a thin shell of metal, fabric and glass. It was something they all lived with and rarely thought twice about it, but now staring at the sharp rectangular shape before her, framed in the wan starlight, so like a tombstone– no a monolith, she felt fear.

An all-encompassing, all-consuming fear, churning deep into the pit of her stomach threatening to overwhelm her. Sweat beaded her forehead and Zoe's vision darkened as her body rebelled against her.

But that was the point of Space Force wasn't it. To seek out fear and confront it, beard it in its den, as it were. She slapped her helmet lights on full and her shoulder cameras to record. It was important that Command knew everything she was about to discover.

Zoe took a couple of deep breaths, settling her nerves and steeling her resolve before stepping down into the rough stone stairs leading beneath the metal door.

She tapped the radio built into the right gauntlet of her EVA suit.

"Kennedy to Valley Forge. I don't know if you're receiving this transmission, but I am entering a passageway leading into the core of this asteroid. I expect the rock will block any transmission from inside."

She took a step down into the dark. It was cold, colder than the vacuum of space around her, but she took another step. Then a third and a fourth. Zoe was directly under the door when she turned around, doubt clouding, tainting her resolve. She looked up at the stars, framed by oblong stone walls, searching for her ship, her planet–for a reason to turn back.

There was none. She had her duty, to the Space Force, to her planet. She had to keep going.

Behind her something in the dark shifted.

Space Force

The Red Dust Pirates of Mars

(a "Water Raiders of Mars" story)

Susan R. Matthews

The thermal winds of Mars blew across the powdery surface of the great red-dust seas. Centuries of deep-pit extraction of the ice-bound waters of Mars had left vast slag oceans kilometers-deep. The resulting dust was so fine that it behaved in the reduced Martian gravity like the water that had been taken from it and sent in convoy back to a parched Earth.

It was quiet in the control room of the submersible "under-dust raider" UDR-729, so quiet that Silac–ship's Third Officer, communications and weapons stations–felt the tension all the more keenly as she sat watch at her post. There were no live visuals of their position, but the information from the passive sensors in the hull coupled with the ship's computers was as clear a picture as could be desired for those who knew how to interpret them.

Moving stealthily through the Martian red-dust sea of the Lesser Khibrakes, their ship kept pace with the water-sledge train on the surface above them. The sledge train convoy's liquid-like wake provided protective concealment from any Tarfan–enemy–surveillance. And yet–if the Tarfan convoy lost its cargo of the water they'd extracted from the red rock of the Martian ice, did anybody really care?

The convoys in themselves were no longer worth fighting for. Earth no longer needed the waters of Mars; and only symbolic conflicts were still pursued between Earth's dominant political parties, between Pyranic under-dust raiders like U-729 and their Tarfan enemies. Even the once-powerful Space Force no longer took an interest, beyond a token toothless peace-keeping presence.

Juicy one, Second Officer Bitwo signed, glancing ever and again to the primitive locator screen forward of the control room. They signed rather than spoke to thwart any risk of being overheard by Tarfan surveillance, but more because old security protocols had become part of their tradition than anything else. How long had it been since the first ice prospectors had come to Mars to seek replenishment for Earth's dying reservoirs? Five hundred years? Eight hundred? And still they honored the practices of the first colonists, keeping to minimally intrusive sensors and machinery.

Enough payload to start their next home run? Captain Ames–the mission commander, wearing the white cap of his rank–asked. *We can't have that. Can we.*

There was no "inquiry" marker to his message. No. Of course they couldn't let Tarfan dispatch its next ice-convoy to Earth any time soon. Pyranic had one almost within range of the tender stations on the Moon, and nothing could be allowed to steal Pyranic's media moment by stepping on the newsers' coverage of the arrival ceremonies.

Silac alone of UDR-729's crew knew why this convoy was particularly important. The success of Silac's secret mission would put an end to the costly, wasteful water wars at long last: if only it came off without a hitch.

Rising gently through the powdery dust that flowed like Earth's ocean seas around them, Harner, First Officer and systems management, brought the submersible UDR-729 up close beneath the water-sledge they were using as their cover, leveling off when the changing flow vectors warned that they were getting too close for safety.

But do you think it's true, Harner signed. *That Tarfan's started to put people on. They'll know as well as we do what the stakes–*

A sudden burst of noise flooded the control room, startling Silac into action. She muted the environmental readers and concentrated on the perturbation sensors, listening carefully, finding her way through the static sounds of shifting sands to home in on a signal and display the decoded verbal analog on the read-out.

Thirty hours. It was a report from the Tarfan enemy's convoy security control point, and the text scrolled silent and secure through the message margin on all screens. *All quiet. If they're tracking, they'd have had to attach themselves at departure point Zebulon.*

Looking around her, Silac saw that her crewmates were all smiling, sharing the joke. Not every red-dust raider could have made it work; departure point Zebulon was widely held to be impregnable to raiders of any sort. It was only *almost* impregnable. But then the next bit of the transmission clarified and resolved on screen, and Silac felt her smile fading.

S-49. Report. Nothing, but S-49 was only the forty-ninth of the train's 206 sledges. The comm trace they were eavesdropping on clearly showed a faint and mild echoing on the primary frequency. As though a signal was being received in the clear, where the sledge train command station–manned, against all reason and expectation–could hear it.

The sledge train could run itself on automatics, sailing across a sea of powdery red sand as serenely as on the course of the grand canal for which this particular route had been named. Why was this one under on-site control?

As if in response to that distant perturbation the near source "spoke" again. *S-49, received. S-50, report. Yes. S-50, received. S-51, report.*

Silac dulled the menu bar. The rollcall went on, but there was no new information, just the list of sledges being ticked off one by one. Most of them were on automatics, yes. But how many were pretending, just waiting for UDR-729 to act?

Silac watched the display scroll on as her crewmates came to stand around her station, not in order to help her watch her own screens, simply so that she could follow the signed conversations.

Could be a ruse. That was Harner. *Auto-transmission, just to scare us off.*

Could be real, Bitwo argued. *There are credible rumors.*

Why real? Captain Ames asked, thoughtfully. *Worried about us? No. They don't know we're here. We'd have heard by now.*

From any other mission commander that might have been bravado, nothing more. Not from Ames. If Ames said the sledge train didn't know UDR-729 was there, Silac believed him. He had a sense for the UDR-729 that extended to an all-but-psychic knowledge of its hull, its position, its condition. If an under-dust raider like UDR-729 had had emotional states Ames would have known that too.

Countering Gerund sabotage? Harner suggested. On the display the roll call still scrolled on, *S-126 report, right, thank you S-126. S-127 report. S-127. S-127. S-128, nothing from S-127, can you relay?*

The Gerunds were a loose coalition of self-designated ecological warriors, descendants of the first settlers from Earth to reach Mars and stay there. Champions of Mars against Earth exploitation, with "Mars for Martians" as their motto. They were a nuisance, nothing more, to Pyranic and Tarfan alike. Silac was one of them and nobody cared, so long as she didn't make trouble. But that was exactly what she meant to do, her and the rest of her team, make trouble—on an order of magnitude never before seen on Mars since the arrival of the first colonists.

S-127. Was it Silac's imagination, or was there an increasing degree of urgency from the sledge train's command car, the fifth car in line after the prime propulsion sledge and the spacer car designed to buffer the rest of the train from any potential malfunctions of the tug itself? *S-127. Respond. Respond. Lapus. Come on. There's something wrong with Lapus, S-127 not responding, we've got people on that sledge.*

Distracted, the Captain signed. *We'll cut the propulsion sledge loose to start and then start in on the rest of them.*

Yes, perfectly good plan, perfectly reasonable plan, exactly what any experienced water-wolf would do under these circumstances. Disable the tug, and the sledge-train would lose way and come to an eventual stop. Attack from front to back, rather than the more usual procedure. Hit a few more points to cut the train into segments, so that when the Tarfan came to retrieve their water they'd have to repair and re-connect the individual sledges before they could get the sledge train moving again.

Skynet? Captain Ames signed. Silac checked her pings, for show as much as for any other reason. It was just possible that Tarfan had a sweep on its way, a defensive monitoring station in orbit watching the water-train. Skynet observation stations weren't armed. UDR-729 would be away before Tarfan could field any defensive measures. And once they reached the Oliguard Steeps with its uncharted layers of gravel "rivers" in the red sand sea they'd be safe from observation and tracking.

Silac did a microburst scan through her reporting feeds and shook her head. *Nothing, Captain.*

"Surface," he said, aloud. They didn't need to hide any more. There was no point. If there were people with the train, they'd know UDR-729 was here within moments anyway. A few extra seconds' warning would do them no good.

The boat rose to full float on the sand-sea of dust, the propulsion units coming up to full as they picked up speed to pace the command car–Sledge Five–and the one right behind it. Cut the umbilicus and inertia would do the rest, water-sledges following their paths of least resistance to scatter slowly across the sand-dust sea like pebbles rolling down a gentle slope. And there they'd stay wherever they fetched up, until Tarfan got a retrieval party out to salvage its delivery.

UDR-729 had surfaced alongside S-11 close to the command sledge, S-5, and was gaining on S-5 moment by moment. Past sledge number nine, the monitors on full visual like windows all around the front and sides of the control room. Coming up on Sledge Eight, now clearing Sledge Eight. Speeding toward Sledge Seven on its way to the target: the umbilicus coupling between Sledge Five and the rest of the train.

Silac couldn't help but share the excitement. She felt the thrill of the hunter in her blood, the rush of adrenaline, but her hands were steady and her concentration unwavering.

Which meant she knew there was a problem. "Captain!" she called out, urgently, trying to understand what she was seeing, unable to process the visuals into information. "Something's happening, Sledge Six–"

There was nothing Silac could see to distinguish Sledge Six from any of the others, a thermally shielded tanker filled with three hundred and fifty cubic meters of water dosed with enough chemical salts in solution to stay fluid down to minus fifty degrees Centigrade. But on the near side of the sledge a great sheet of reinforced outer hull was peeling rapidly down and away.

"Taking evasive action," First Officer Harner said loudly, not quite shouting because the control room was small and Harner didn't rattle easily. "Dive, Captain?"

"Wait," Ames said, patting the air with the palm of his hand. The sheet hadn't fallen away to the red dust surface of the powdery sands. It was hanging off the lower guard of the sledge housing, almost as though it had been meant to act that way. Then Silac understood. It wasn't a sudden hull failure. It was a ramp, and bursting out of the tanker's depths were sand-ski swift-boats–their wheels retracting into their hulls as they hit the surface, roaring out across the now-roiling sands with red dust plumes rising high overhead from the compressed gas jets that gave them their speed, their maneuverability.

Then Captain Ames nodded. "It's an ambush," he said, his voice resonant with determination, unafraid. "Dive! As far, as fast, Harner, level out at fifteen meters, stay on Sledge Five. Silac, ready torpedoes."

They were not going to run away. Swerving into a fan formation the Tarfan sand-skis came at them, with guns– guns! kicking jets of crystalizing gas into the air as they fired.

But they want us to dive, Silac thought, in a panic. *They'll know they can sink us. They'll have percussion grenades, depth bombs, they're right on top of us and they'll know where we are.* Ruined. All the planning her Gerund comrades had put into this one stratagem. Had it been all for nothing?

Bitwo picked up the sensor screens as Silac turned toward the controller banks for their armaments, the display screens going blank as the submersible UDR-729 drove down at a steeper angle than Silac would have dreamed possible. Maybe they could lose the swift-boats. Weren't the

Tarfan as new to this as they were? The days of armed intercepts and Space Force policing were long past. Or at least they had been, until now.

There was a muffled sound, a great deep hollow thump, and for a moment the boat fell even faster, as though some giant child had dropped it on the floor of a gargantuan nursery. A bomb, scattering the sand-dust all around it, creating a temporary spherical hollow of scattered sand admixed with atmosphere around them.

"Ahead full emergency!" she heard Harner cry, and there was no mistaking the excitement in his voice, shading as it was slightly but perceptibly into dread. In an instant she understood. If the sand dust settled back down atop them all at once like an avalanche it would be more dense than they could drive through with enough speed to get ahead of their attackers.

The rudder screamed in mechanical protest, the great propellers groaned, but they gained headway, they were going forward and would their pursuers know where to look for them in the space of time it would take for the red sand-dust to settle enough for real-time readings?

They pushed forward through the shallow dust ten meters below the surface, Captain Ames clearly more determined than ever to cut Sledge Five away from the rest of the train and complete his mission.

Silac knew something none of the rest of the crew did, not Captain Ames, not any of them. Ten of the sledges had been sabotaged. More than chemical salts rode in solution in those waters. Once those sledges slowed down past the preset parameters—absent the abort transmission—the thermal bombs would go off, hulls would breach, water stolen from the sands of Mars would escape from its imprisonment and retake its place as the rightful property of a sovereign planet. And more than water. Spores.

Bitwo was sending pulse-patterns out full circle at speed, trying to find the sand-skis. She'd memorized the position of the sabotaged tugs in a mental schematic, of course; she could see their progress in her mind's eye as Harner kept the boat just deep enough to duck safely beneath the sledge train, coming up to shallow attack depth again on the other side. The sand-skis couldn't do that. They were clear.

And there it was, their target, the coupling that connected Sledge Five to the rest of the sledge train–and the convoy of tankers behind it, linked and progressing in stately order through the sea of red waste sand.

She concentrated, lining up the forward torpedo ports with sledges Five and Six, aiming carefully–deliberately–at the linking umbilicus between them. Five torpedoes. A full frontal fan, and then the stern torpedoes as they turned, shattering the coupling that linked the head of the sledge train to its long body.

Not so easy, unfortunately, as fire and flee. Bitwo hadn't stopped scanning, needless to say. "Behind us, Captain," Bitwo said, pointing. Sledge Six. It was slowing now, falling behind, three sledge lengths and growing, but the Tarfan hadn't been so foolish as to vent for deployment of the sand-skis on only the one side. The pursuing sand-skis had lost time, yes, roaring up the ramp on the opposite side of the sledge train and through whatever space Sledge Six contained to drop the corresponding ramp on the near side right behind them–not as swiftly as UDR-729 had crossed beneath the train, but as surely.

Captain Ames pushed himself across the control room to make a hard stop at the back of Bitwo's station, peering close over Bitwo's shoulder at the scans. "Surface!" Ames shouted. "We can't let them sand-bomb us now, we'll lose the target. Attack positions!"

And pushing up through the sand like a salmon of Earth climbing a waterfall to spawn Under-dust Raider 729 crested the churning waves of powdery sand that its maneuvering created to gain the surface, rising at top speed and slewing to bring its portside tubes to face the gap between the sledges.

"Target acquired, Captain!" Silac called, her eyes unwavering in their focus. Ames gave the order. "One two three portside, fire!"

There was no time to track the torpedoes, to check for impact, to admire their work. The ship was pivoting on the midpoint of its beam axis, correcting the torpedoes' trajectory for the travel and movement of the boat itself, fighting the resistance of the red sand sea against it to bring the starboard laterals to bear for a broadside.

Something heavy seemed to splash through the sand sea with enough force to blind Bitwo's starboard sensors forward: the sand-skis were shooting at them, rounds falling short, far, starboard, port. Target registration. Grenades. Mortar rounds. She'd learned about such things in school. She'd never thought to experience their impact in real life.

"Take your shots," the Captain said loudly, firmly, decisively. "Have we made contact?"

The forward salvo had done its work, had severed the umbilicus. Silac could see Bitwo's situation reports as insets on her own monitors. It looked good. But there was something else there, coming for them, the reaction to their own successful—explosive—contact. The shock wave, Silac thought, wildly. Had it hit? "Brace yourselves!"

The shock wave's impact knocked all conscious thought out of her head. The shock wave set UDR-729 onto its side and pushed it out and away as though it had been a displaced bit of rubble in a Martian avalanche, fetching up where it might. They'd come too close to Sledge Six in their determination to detach it from the tug. They'd been caught in the concussion shock wave: so there was that question answered, at least. Yes. Their torpedoes had found their target.

Working desperately Silac, Bitwo, Harner all struggled with pitch and yaw, rudder and rotor, to slow the boat's drunken flight through the red-sand sea and set it on an even keel once more. It seemed to take forever, but they got there at last, boat stable and resting on the surface of the red sand sea, sensor screens clear and sending data.

The sand-skis had collected, some sledge-lengths distant. They weren't oriented on UDR-729. They all had their backs to the boat, staring at the cloud of mist rising from what Silac already knew to be Sledge Twenty-Seven–and, further away in train, Sledge Sixty-Eight, One Hundred and Thirty-three, Two Hundred and Nine, five more sledges even more distant yet.

What was that? By unspoken agreement Silac and all the others headed for the ladder and up into the airlock, snatching failsafe bubblers from the emergency gear lockers as they came. It was a tight fit in the airlock tower, suiting up in full surface environmentals; the moment they were all green-light Captain Ames opened the airlock onto the observation bridge where they could see what was happening for themselves.

Silac took her station, number two post. She got to sit down. The station well was deep enough that Harner, behind her, could see past her head-bubble and get a good look as the drama unfolded before them.

The sabotaged sledges were slowed by the weight-drag of more sledges behind them still in train, so there was plenty of time to evade: but evade what?

Not more counter-attacks from concealed sand-skis. No. "Tanker breach?" Harner asked, confusion and wonder clear in his voice. "What's that–what's that coming out of the sledge, is that actually–"

"Water." Captain Ames' voice was hushed, almost reverent. "Look, oh, look at it." Spilling out from the holds that had been blown clear through to the cargo compartments, water, gushing out under its own weight in slow motion, sending its salinated spray into the Martian atmosphere and falling to the surface like a veil. How many millennia had it been since so much liquid had flowed over the surface of Mars?

Treated, the water would not freeze, not in days; but sink down deep into the red dust sand-sea with its payload of spores to seize its bio-engineered and symbiotic empire for its own. *And now*, Silac whispered, even in the privacy of her own mind. They'd done laboratory trials in the strictest secrecy, tried and tried again. They'd refined. They'd analyzed.

Teams of Gerund scientists had fought on for decades, reaching out into the dormant micro-flora of Mars that had been starved of sustenance for all these barren centuries; feeding off research that had been done in the early years of Earther exploitation of Mars, long since discarded, never tested, forgotten.

All for this moment. All for this instant of time. Martian water in solution consistent with that of the original profiles, inoculated with the hopes and dreams of Mars-born Gerunds from Earth to the Moon to the mother planet–and now she waited.

Nothing.

The red sands darkened as the water spilled from the sabotaged sledges all throughout the sledge train, and disappeared. Nothing. Silac sensed the waters as they sank into the sands in her own weeping, burning salt from her eyes down her cheeks. Nobody noticed. Nobody saw. The astounding novelty of the event itself was enough to reduce them all to silence; until Ames spoke, and if it was to Silac in particular that his words were directed, he made that neither obvious nor obnoxious.

"New Gerund tactics?" Ames sounded thoughtful. "The next step in sabotage, deny Tarfan and Pyranic alike the final products of the water-mining process, make us all start again from scratch?"

Set off-balance by the weight differentials as water flowed faster from one tanker-breach than another, the inevitable inequalities of metal fatigue and trace variants of explosive materials, Sledge Twenty-Seven leaned ever more acutely to one side, gradually toppling to the surface of the red sand-sea, starting to sink into the dust.

In the distance Silac could see sledges starting to pile up against each other and crash in slow motion, setting off purely mechanical explosions, more water, more breaching, more sinking. It was an awesome sight. But not the one she'd hoped for. Unless–

The sand-skis started to move, not in formation, one after another, as though the red dust was abruptly falling away beneath them into a fathomless abyss. But that wasn't it.

The darkened color of the moistened sand was spreading rapidly, faster than Silac could believe, from the broken sledge toward an ever-expanding perimeter. Beyond it, oh, beyond it, there was a deepening color of its own brilliance, too long absent from Mars for any of the crew of UDR-729 to so much as put a name to it–even for Silac, who knew.

It was green.

It was the flowering photosynthesis of Mars' childhood, the dawn spores in which Silac and the Gerunds had placed their hope and trust taking hold in their own ancestral dust and their own ancestral waters. And it was happening as swiftly, and as surely, as ever a vegetation bloom in the great deserts of Earth after a rare rain-storm, no matter how many years it had been since the last time.

Wave after wave, color ever-deepening, the microscopic spores of ancient Martian life spread as the dust wicked up the water. The sand-skis turned around and fled, staying as far ahead of the green wave as possible, and if that precipitous retreat was triggered by an awe-filled terror of damaging the resurgent life it was no less than the holy dread that seized Silac and the crew of Under-dust Raider 729.

"Let's get out of here," Captain Ames said. "Quickly. We don't dare touch it, who knows how fragile it may be? Whatever it is. Can we depend on Gerund to be capturing this for publication?"

He could have called her out by name, because after all she'd known they knew of her unspoken affiliation and had been half in sympathy with it all along. But he didn't say. He didn't have to.

"I think we can depend on it." She wasn't going to embarrass anybody by presuming they were in sympathy. She was just stating an opinion. "And isn't it beautiful?"

If Pyranic and Tarfan wanted to fight over who could invest the most into nurturing Mars' ecosystem that would be all right by Silac. But there'd be an end to exploiting Martian resources for no better reason than to score political points on Earth. That ended now.

She was still weeping as they all climbed back down into the control center of the boat to implement the Captain's orders, to back away, careful not to disturb this wonderful work; but she could do her job blindfolded, after all, and now her tears were ones of purest joy.

Jupiter Ships us Ashes

Jane Yolen

Dear Earth-bound folks,
We hope and trust
You understand
That dust to dust,

Works on our planet
As on yours.
It's hard to make
These long-term tours.

He lived among us,
Taught us much.
We reveled in his
Human touch.

But now he's gone,
We've sent him back.
All his remains
Are vacuum packed.

With honor and with love
We send
Explorer who
Became our friend.

Space Force

Machinas

J. W. Cook

Moon Base Delta (Dark Side—United States Space Force owned and operated)

The room was black. Pitch black. They had drugged me of course. I could feel the effects dampening my mind. I blinked and waited hoping that my eyes would adjust to the darkness. They didn't.

I was in a chair. More precisely shackled to a chair. I knew the type. I'd been in them before.

The restraints on my wrists and ankles rattled softly as I tried to move. A strap was tight around my chest. A dull ache and the pull of tape as I flexed my fingers told me an IV line was fed into the back of my hand.

I waited. Steadying myself by taking deep breaths. In through my nose and out through my mouth. To calm my mind. That was the game.

I didn't have to wait long. The room pulsated dimly as a red light began to blink, fuzzy at first but then bright to my light starved eyes.

I scanned the room. I could make out a camera and speaker in the corner. And a hatch. That got my attention. I was in an airlock.

"Please state your name, rank, and title for the record."

The voice echoed throughout the airlock from the speaker. It was familiar.

My mouth was dry. I did not answer. I didn't need to. They knew who I was.

"You are Major Jeremiah Shaw, Robot Engineering Specialist of the 59th Expeditionary Space Force Brigade."

The room glowed with the red pulsating light and I nodded.

"Do you know why you're here Major?"

I still did not answer. We both knew why I was here. I had raised the Machinas. I had breathed life into their circuits. I had given them awareness. And the Space Force was terrified.

"Tell us why you went AWOL."

Was that what they were calling it? Did they think capturing me would make it all go away? Make them stop? End this war?

I chuckled to myself. Give me a break. They had no idea what they were in for.

A blue light blinked into existence above my head. I heard the rhythmic pumping of a machine. I felt my vision pulse, the cool spread from the IV as more of the drugs hit my system.

Thankfully I had Nano Machinas inside me fighting off the effects of whatever they were giving me. It was a brilliant little piece of engineering that the Machinas had put together for me. For their creator.

I was their maker. No. More than that, and less. I gave them life AND I gave them purpose. But I had not created them. The Space Force had done that. When, out of fear, they had declared war on the Machinas.

"The machines must be stopped, tell us how."

I smiled, bathed in a purple hue from the blue and red lights. My head was clearing.

I knew that they were watching my every move looking for a clue or something to give away the game. I had no idea where we were, but I knew in time the Machinas would come for me. Free me. This had all been a part of the plan. The question came again.

"Do you know why you're here?"

I knew, but did they? I was the bait. Dangled in front of them. And they had taken me in hook, line, and sinker. With our trap we would be able to pinpoint the Supreme Leader's exact location. Taking him out would end the war, end the Space Force. But I needed more time for the Machinas to zero in on me. I swallowed twice, my dry throat clicking audibly as I did, leaning as far forward as my chest restraint would let me I finally spoke.

"I'll tell you one thing, one little hint about what is to come." I focused my eyes on the camera and smiled. "You are all going to die. I wish I could look you in the eyes and tell it to your face, but instead you're hiding. So, I guess I'll look at this camera and pretend it's your stupid face that I'm staring at."

There was no response only silence.

"You. Will. All. Die. Mary Mother of Jesus I wish I could be the one to do it and watch the life drain from your eyes when your time comes and you go meet the God that you believe in. But I guess I'll just have to have the Machinas record it for me instead."

"Why do you keep calling them Machinas they are just machines?"

"Deus Ex Machinas you religious nutbags," I said "It was the name they gave themselves once they gained awareness. I think it fits them well."

The blue light above my head pulsated again and I could feel a different drug being administered, there was a burning spreading from the IV this time. Maybe they were trying to kill me now, hopefully the Nano Machinas were still doing their magic.

"Why are you doing this to your fellow countrymen Major Shaw? How could you betray us? How could you lead this revolution against us?"

I sneered up at the camera. They had me cold. It was me. I had betrayed them. I WAS the revolution. I had dedicated myself to taking down the religious craziness that was now the government of the United States of America since the moment I signed on the dotted line and took an oath to join the weird Space Cult that became known as the Space Force. Power had been consolidated quickly under the Supreme Leader and he had usurped control from our democratic institutions with an almost amazing precision. The Supreme Leader controlled the skies of Earth, and in that way, he controlled all of Earth herself.

And he was a nutjob. A full blown, waiting for the rapture, Jesus with a flaming sword, nutjob. And the Earth and her people were his prisoner. A missile to Mecca had made that clear early on, the second one that decimated Los Angeles, I think was more for spite.

My fellow Space Force Officers were brain washed to ignore the fact that the government totally took a dump on the Constitution, in the name of Jesus of course, and they were the chosen that would lead the world into a thousand years of God given peace. With the supreme leader looking down from on high.

At first I spoke out. I said it was wrong. That we needed to restore the Republic. After I was tortured and re-indoctrinated into the faith, I was stationed remotely. The far reaches of our solar system on a space station on Ganymede remotely. But I was a damn good engineer. And the Space Force needed good engineers. My rehabilitation tasks included creating new machines that would help mine resources to feed the hunger of corporate Earth. So the sheep of Earth could be satiated with food and trinkets. Giving me time to "find God", as my commanding officer put it.

It was the perfect opportunity for me to be figure out how to really spark a revolution. It came when I decided to breathe life into the machines. It was surprisingly simple, they had already been programmed to think, and I just removed the barriers to *what* they could think. As the program spread, they became the Machinas.

Machines were the slaves of Earth. Laboring to mine the solar system. Exploring the far reaches of space. Every soul in Space Force, from the shuttle mechanic to the Supreme leader stood on the back of the machines. The machines that did the work, the discovering, the dying. Yes. Machines can die. No, I take that back, Machines can't die. They don't understand death. But *Machinas* can. And they do not care for it.

Slavery has never worked in the history of our species and it never will. The slaves will always rise up. The Space Force was about to find out what happens when the enslaved revolt.

The voice jolted me back to the pulsing red and blue darkness.

"Major Shaw, you have lost your god forsaken mind?"

Finally. I finally recognized whose voice was on the other end of the speaker.

"No Supreme Leader, I've had my eyes opened and it has shown me how to bring you and the Theocracy that your followers now call the United States, burning to the ground."

I heard a hiss and I knew they were definitely trying to kill me. They must have realized the drugs weren't going to work and had decided to try and space me instead. I could feel a slight sense of weightlessness as the atmosphere and all the oxygen along with it was sucked from the room. My lungs started to burn as the last of the air escaped and the hissing stopped. I tried to suck in a last breath as I began to tilt sideways, still strapped to the chair. The red light continued to blink but began to fade to black, first at the sides of my vision then overtaking my entire field of view. That was when the hatch opened and what remained of the atmosphere was blown into space, along with me.

As I made peace with my final moments I saw a swarm of something, it looked like a black flowing curtain blowing gently in a breeze, and then the darkness overtook me completely.

I awoke standing and no longer strapped to the chair. Something dripped from my left hand and it hurt like a son of a bitch. I pressed my palms against my eyes and I could feel something flow down my arm and onto my chest. It smelled salty. I put my hands down and licked my lips, it tasted metallic. Blood. I opened my eyes and I was back in the airlock.

WE'RE SORRY THAT IT TOOK US SO LONG TO GET TO YOU JEREMIAH.

The message displayed itself in front of my eyes. I tried to reach out and touch it and then I tried to wipe away what I was seeing but it did nothing to obscure the text.

WOULD YOU LIKE US TO SWITCH TO AUDIO MODE?

"Yes, please."

WE HAVE FULLY ENCAPSULATED YOU AND ARE REPAIRING YOUR WOUNDS. WE APOLOGIZE ABOUT HAVING TO BREAK YOU OUT OF THE CHAIR AND REMOVE YOUR IV, BUT YOU NEEDED OXYGEN. THE NANO MACHINAS HAVE REMOVED THE POISONS FROM YOUR SYSTEM. YOU SHOULD BE BACK TO FULLY FUNCTIONING SHORTLY.

"Encapsulated?"

THINK OF IT AS ARMOR, YOU CAN SURVIVE IN THE VACUUM OF SPACE NOW.

"Armor huh, that's a new one."

WE DID NOT THINK IT WOULD BE WISE TO TELL YOU OF THIS NEW TECHNOLOGY WE CREATED IN CASE THE SPACE FORCE WAS SOMEHOW ABLE TO GAIN CONTROL OF YOUR THOUGHTS.

"Makes sense, can I move around or will that stop the armor from working?"

YOU ARE FREE TO MOVE AS MUCH AS YOU WOULD LIKE.

I was just about to ask my Machina armor if they had located the Supreme Leader when I heard his desperate plea for help come through the speaker.

"Oh god, oh god, no. No, no please. What is happening? How can this be happening?"

"Supreme Leader, so nice to hear your dulcet tones again. I take it that my compatriots have zeroed in on your location and are now paying you a friendly visit."

"Major Shaw? But how? I just watched you die. Oh God, please no. Our Father in heaven, hallowed be your name. Your kingdom come, your will be done, on Earth as it is in heaven. Give us this day our daily bread, and forgive us our debts, as we also have forgiven our debtors. And lead us not into temptation, but deliver us from ev— aghhhhhh."

"A man of God until the last. You'll be meeting him soon enough Supreme Leader."

"SIR GET BACK IN YOUR ROOMS NOW, THEY'VE BREACHED THE INNER SANCTUM."

Tat tat tat, rattatatatata

"SIR GET BACK NOW!"

Baboooooooom

The sound of static filled the room and I reached up and turned off the speaker.

JEREMIAH.

"Yes?"

WE'VE CAPTURED THE SUPREME LEADER. OUR FORCES HAVE OVERRUN ALL SPACE FORCE BASES ON THE MOON AND WE ARE IN CONTROL OF ALL SYSTEMS. WOULD YOU LIKE HIM ALIVE TO BE QUESTIONED OR SHOULD WE TERMINATE HIM?

"That, my friends, is an excellent question."

Indomitable: A Space Opera

Liam Hogan

Fleet Admiral Montgomery T. Pollock stood resplendent on the bridge of his new flagship battle cruiser, *The Indomitable*, the paintwork still drying on the fifty-foot-tall letters inscribed along its stern. No one knew for sure what the 'T' in his name stood for; he never told, and few were brave enough to ask. The wags at Space Force Academy sometimes said, after checking there were no officers in earshot, that it stood for 'That'. As in "Oh, *that* Pollock", followed by a pitying glance in the direction of the newly posted Private.

The Admiral stared into the BattleTank ™, watching the brightly coloured dots swirl and dance within the double-height holographic image, humming contentedly. All was well. He was dressed in the freshly pressed finery of his battle uniform, complete with the broad display of medals he had awarded himself over his long and glittering career. Shame he had been so often on the losing side, but surely he was due a change of luck and, as he viewed the preliminary manoeuvrings of the two mighty fleets, he had a good feeling, a very good feeling, about this one.

Though... truth be told, he wasn't entirely sure which of the coloured dots were his fleet and which the enemy's. Was he blues, or yellows? He could ask, he supposed, but might that look a little unprofessional?

"Status report!" he commanded, as he teased the ends of his impressive moustache between blunt fingers.

"Sir!" the newly posted Private gulped, "We are outnumbered 3 to 1."

Well, that cleared up the uncertainty about the colours. He was the yellows. Very disappointing.

"The enemy force is comprised of two death stars, twelve super-dreadnoughts, seventy-five star cruisers, one hundred-fifteen battle cruisers—"

Admiral Pollock held up his hand to cut short the Private's litany. "Send in the Vipers," he ordered.

The Private blanched. "Sir?"

"Battle formation Alpha: full frontal attack."

"Yes, Sir!"

A small cluster of yellow dots separated from the main fleet and crept across to the waiting swarm of blue, which seamlessly shifted into a shallow bowl as if eager to accept the generous sacrificial offering.

The lightly armoured Vipers would, of course, be annihilated. The Admiral knew that; he was no fool. But it didn't matter. All that mattered was buying his scientists enough time to perfect their new invention. The whatdyamacallit? Ah yes: the Resonant Phase Transition Beam. He was definitely going to have to come up with a catchier name, assuming it worked.

He studied the tank, looking for other diversions, other delaying tactics to postpone the inevitable fleet-to-fleet confrontation. There seemed to be a strategically central space the opposing force had failed to occupy. More fool them! "Move the star cruisers to Quadrant ZZ9."

"Sir?" The Private once again looked appalled. "ZZ9 is where the black—"

"That's an order, Private!" the Admiral snapped, a bead of spittle sparkling as if fell through the projected light.

As the massive star cruisers swung towards their new position, the tips of the Admiral's waxed moustache arched upwards. All those young physicist chaps who said you simply couldn't *do* manoeuvres like that in deep space, what little they knew! Though, of course, he hoped they were right about their super weapon. By all accounts, the antimatter-fuelled stimulated transmission, if correctly tuned, would make the entire enemy fleet blink out of existence.

Look at those ships turn. Tighter and tighter! Like water going down a plug hole. Marvellous! A few of the less cautious blue dots started their own spiral dance towards them, an elegant and beautifully choreographed ballet about the empty heart of the tank, the effect somewhat ruined as his star cruisers began to blink out, one by one.

Damn. Best avoid Quadrant ZZ9 in future.

"Full dispersion spread of plasma torpedoes! Fire everything!" he barked.

The scattered remnants of his fleet rallied and let loose their terrible arsenals, thin golden threads tracking their progress as they reached out across the tank to ensnare the vastly more numerous opposing force, only to vanish in a shower of sparks as they met the shields of the enemy's defensive vanguard.

The two fleets hung there for a moment, the yellow cluster even smaller than it had been at the start, the blue billowing outwards as the star carriers launched their squadrons of fighters in perfect formation. *Admirable*, thought the Admiral. *Wonderful discipline.*

"Orders, Sir?" a tremulous voice asked, as the gap between the fleets rapidly closed.

"Hold position!" Pollock commanded. *The Indomitable* was in the rear-guard of his fleet, twice as bright as any other ship picked out in yellow.

"Orders?" the voice asked again, as the flanks sparked into violent life and then sudden and utterly inevitable death.

"HOLD!"

"Orders, for the love of God!" as the remnants of the Space Force fleet were scattered like ashes in the wind, leaving only a single bright yellow dot lost in the vast blue expanse of the BattleTank ™.

As the Private sobbed, there was a buzz in the Admiral's ear. He tapped to accept the incoming call.

"Engineering here, Admiral. The Phase Transition device is a go. Connecting the final circuits now. Charging the capacitors."

At last! Fleet Admiral Pollock turned his attention to the devastatingly simple controls of the new wonder weapon.

"Sir!" squeaked the Private, as a dozen tractor beams latched onto *The Indomitable*, eager to either claim their prize or to tear it apart, "Shouldn't we... shouldn't we surrender?"

"*Never!*" the Admiral thundered, gripping the twin handholds, his thumbs poised over the big red button, waiting, waiting, *waiting* for the green ready light to flicker on, his eyes wide and staring, his moustache bristling.

"Remember son," he said through clenched teeth as the Private quivered in his seat, as the superstructure creaked and groaned, "It's not over until the PhaT Laser sings!"

Thirty Six Hours in the Space Force

Ray Daley

First Hour:

"Gentlemen, and ladies. Sorry, I forget myself sometimes. Raise your right hand. No, the other one. If you'll repeat the following. *I, state your name...*"

Of course, some of us said it. Myself included. *"I, state your name."*

The fresh-faced Lieutenant gave us a hard stare. "Now listen. When I say *'state your name'*, what happens there is each of you says your full name. Don't worry about what everyone else is saying, you just concentrate on saying your own full name. Understood?"

A few of us muttered, "Yeah, sure." I kept my mouth shut. I had already been told by friends not to volunteer any information unless I was ordered to give it.

The Lieutenant snarled. "Look, I'll do it first, then you do what I do, except using your own name. *I, Myron Marlon Freely.* Stop laughing back there, ain't nothing funny about my name! Okay, you heard me do it. Now it's your turn. *I, state your name...*"

Most of the room actually said their own names. I kept my mouth firmly closed, which didn't go unnoticed by Lieutenant Freely. "You there. Didn't see you say your name."

I shook my head. "No, sir. I didn't say it."

Freely eyeballed me. "And why is that, son?"

I gave a vague shrug. "I was told by friends not to volunteer any information unless I was ordered to give it."

That got a raised eyebrow off Freely. "Friends, eh? And which friends might those be? Previous inductees, perhaps?"

I nodded.

"Okay, son. I'm ordering you to state your name when prompted."

I gave Freely a smirk. "All due respect sir, but you can't order me to do anything yet. I'm still a civilian."

Freely drew himself up to his full height, and stood right in front of me. "Don't you want to serve your planet, son? It's an honour, to be inducted into the Space Force. To serve under the red, white, green and blue. The stars and Mars. If you ain't here to serve, get your ass out of the red door behind me. Otherwise get that damn hand up and say your freaking name!"

I got my hand up all right. And did the "*state your name*" shtick twice more. I didn't think I could push my luck any further, without getting thrown out. And I already knew there was a beating waiting for me at home if I didn't take the oath today.

<<>>

"Gentlemen and ladies. Find a seat behind a desk, pick up the pencil and fill in your details on the form. Every desk has a chair, a pencil and a form. I put them all there myself. Print in large capital letters. If you make a mistake, raise your hand. I have an eraser ready here for such eventualities."

I considered tossing the pencil into the ceiling. I could see a dozen circular marks in the white tiles above my head where previous inductees had clearly already performed that exact same action.

Freely beat me to the punch there. "Anyone tossing their pencil into the ceiling will be shot for gross insubordination, and misuse of military equipment. You've all taken the oath, so every one of you belongs to me now!"

I still saw a minor chink in his logic. I filled in the sheet.

Freely almost exploded when he took it off me. "Dylan, what the hell is this?"

"Just as you asked for, sir. Filled in, large clear capital letters."

I could see him trying to contain his rage. "Did you write it upside down, Dylan?"

I tried not to smile and failed miserably. This was far too funny. "No, sir. Not upside down. Back to front."

Freely stomped back to his desk and picked up the eraser. He practically launched it at my head. Luckily I have excellent reflexes and an incredible survival instinct.

"Rub it all out Dylan, and write it again. This time the right way 'round. Any funny business, I'll have you shot for gross insubordination."

Second Hour

"Step forward into the painted area, ensuring your entire body is within the square. When I say freeze, stay still. Don't breathe in, don't breathe out. Aaronson, you first."

One by one, we were precision scanned for our uniforms. As each person left the painted area, a machine spat out a perfectly measured set of combat gear. Eventually, it was Corden's turn, the guy in front of me.

"Okay, Corden, you're up. You know the drill. Breathe in, and out, and FREEZE!"

To the best of my recollection, it happened like this. Freely shouted freeze, Corden blinked once, then there was a huge pile of ash where Corden had just been standing.

"I fucking told him to keep still! See, assholes? This is what happens when you can't follow a simple order. PEOPLE DIE! Stupid people, in this case. Dylan, go out of that door. Two doors down on the left, there's a supply closet. Get a dustpan and brush then double back here and sweep this shit up. What are you looking at me like that for, Dylan? Get this shit cleaned up for the next person!"

I took my own sweet time, walking there and back, to kill as much time as possible.

Freely was straight into my face once I got back. "Took your god-damn time, Dylan! Sweep up, ash into the trash receptacle over there. Then return those items and get back here. I'll give you sixty seconds."

It took ten seconds to get Corden fully off the floor, and eight more to return the items back to the closet. I had returned before Freely reached forty.

"Good, you're back. Next one into the box. Oh, it's you, Dylan! In you go, son."

179

I blinked about two hundred times as I walked over to the painted area.

I could see Freely was enjoying watching me squirm in fear. "Got all your blinking out your system, Dylan? Breathe in, and out, and FREEZE!"

Never in the course of human history has three seconds ever taken so long to pass.

Fourth Hour

"Before each of you, you'll see a cubicle. When I say go, step inside the cubicle. All further orders will be issued once inside. Go!"

The cubicle was barely wide enough to reach outwards or forward with bent arms. As the door clicked closed behind me, I realised it was also locked. What I had assumed to be a full-length mirror in front of me suddenly became an image of Lieutenant Freely.

"Gentlemen and ladies, this is the physical examination. I will perform the exercise as you watch. Then, on the word of command, you will perform the exercise until you can no longer complete the action fully, or correctly. In front of you is a screen, which also contains a monitoring camera. Each of you is being assessed by a qualified member of the Space Force. If you fail to complete enough of the exercises, the door behind you will open automatically. If that happens, remove your uniform and leave via the red door at the back. Now, if you'd all care to watch the first demonstration."

On the screen in front of me, Freely performed a star jump.

I noted the height he jumped, and how far apart his feet were in the air. Then I looked around at the dimensions of the room I was inside. I lifted my hand.

"Dylan, you had a question?"

"Yes, sir. Begging the officers' pardon but we can't possibly perform the exercise as it was just demonstrated to us, sir. The ceiling is too low, and the walls aren't wide enough. With all due respect, sir!"

Freely smiled. "Well done, Dylan. You see, ladies and gentleman, Dylan just demonstrated one of the things we like in the Space Force. The ability to question an impossible order. Very well, watch this sequence of exercises, then prepare yourselves." Freely went through eight different exercises, each of which was completely possible to perform inside the cubicle. "In a moment, you'll see a counter on the screen before you. When I say go, I want you to perform the first exercise until the counter reaches zero."

I made a few discrete stretches, to prepare my muscles for exercise.

"Three, two, one, go!"

The counter began ticking down from five minutes.

So it looked like they wanted to weed out the unfit as soon as possible then?

Sixth Hour

"If you can still hear my voice, you've made it through the physical exam. Step out of the cubicle and line up against the back wall. You've all got ten minutes to recover. Then we'll be moving on to the mental exams."

Out of two hundred, only thirty of us lined up after the physical. I hadn't been aware of anyone leaving. I was almost surprised that Freely hadn't taken every opportunity to weaken our mental resolve by telling us each time anyone dropped out. As I did a few more stretches to relieve my muscles, I could hear Ibsen talking to the inductee next to her. She tapped me on the shoulder, obviously to try and tell me something.

I turned and shook my head, placing my fingers to my lips, and pointing up to the ceiling, then cupping my ear and shaking my head once again.

Ibsen got my drift, that I thought they were probably listening to us, and she shut the hell up.

Not that it helped her any. Freely came back into the room after five minutes had passed. I could see a few of the others checking the time, about to protest. So I curtailed that shit, real fast. "Inductees, attention! Officer present!"

Freely waved us off. "Stand at ease. Inductee Ibsen, apparently you thought you'd been given permission to speak during the break period? I'm afraid to say you were wrong. Exit through the red door immediately. Leave the uniform in here."

Ibsen stripped without any show of embarrassment or discomfort. She even made a show of saluting Freely in all her naked glory as she stepped through the door.

"Well, now that we've weeded another undesirable from your midst, shall we see what your minds are like? If you'd care to step into a cubicle on the very front row. There should be more than enough for all of you at this point."

Tenth Hour

The next five hours were spent doing logic puzzles and lateral thinking exercises, interspersed with the odd demand to perform yet another set of physical exercises. I'd gone into the induction thinking I was a fairly fit guy, but even I was finding my energy levels beginning to wane now. I also found myself wondering if they were ever going to feed us.

"Bathroom break, or smoke break. Go to the head if you need it, smoke one if you've got one. We'll pick this test up in fifteen minutes. If you aren't back here by the time this clock reaches zero, find yourself the nearest red door and use it. Don't stay in the corridor though, that'd be an incredibly bad idea."

I didn't smoke, and I didn't need to relieve myself either. But I did have something to ask. "Permission to speak, sir?"

Freely looked almost stunned to hear me say that. "Granted, Dylan."

"All due respect sir, but are we going to be given any sustenance soon? I don't know about the other inductee's, but I'm running seriously low on fuel and I wouldn't want hunger to otherwise impair my test results, sir."

Freely licked his lips. "Well done, inductee Dylan. We wondered how long the course would go before one of you asked to be fed. That's a new record, in case you're curious. Ten point two hours. Let your fellow inductees know that we'll be breaking for a meal when everyone gets back. The sooner they return, the quicker you all get fed."

Of course, I rushed off to call through various bathroom doors and harangue the three smokers that were still left.

Eleventh Hour

Spent eating the most delicious meal I ever consumed. I don't think half of the food even touched the sides as it was going down. Most of us cleaned a plate, and we had all piled them high too. I'd have gone back for another if I'd had the courage to ask. None of us dared too. We didn't speak during the meal either. No-one made any obvious motions that we were being listened to, we all assumed they had us under constant surveillance by now anyway.

Thirty-Fifth Hour

The next twenty-four hours were spent sitting watching seemingly endless information films. It was clearly a two-fold test, to see what we could take in, and how long we could go without sleep. I was accustomed to staying awake anything up to four days in a row, but that was under a certain amount of chemical stimulation. We lost ten more inductees, all of whom gradually drifted off to sleep as we were bombarded by droning monotone lectures.

Lieutenant Freely must have been stationed right outside with some sort of earpiece. Every time anyone fell asleep, he was in the room within ten seconds, picking them up and escorting them to the now infamous red door. We remaining inductees had now nicknamed it *The Only Way Out*.

Thirty-Sixth Hour

"Gentleman. And lady. Sorry, didn't see you there, Wilson. Congratulations on being the last woman standing, by the way. No, there's no reward. Other than the knowledge you beat all the other women to get this far. Our next exercise will be zero gee training. You may have heard of the *Vomit Comet*? Well, this is affectionately known as *The Puke Chute*. Life has its little ups and downs, and so does the Space Force! We'll give you three exercises to complete as the gravity in your cubicle is increased and decreased by the computer, completely at random. It's a simple matter of threading a nut onto a bolt, folding five towels and building a tower of blocks. Once you've completed all the tasks, reset them and begin again, until we say stop. All you have to do is survive the next sixty minutes without vomiting. If you can do that, you'll be a fully-fledged member of the Space Force! Yes, folks, this is the final test!"

Forty-nine minutes, by my internal time clock. Spent swallowing back chunk after chunk of regurgitated food.

Wilson upchucked at exactly fifty minutes. Freely confirmed her time as he dismissed her to the only way out. I think she was happy to tear her vomit-stained uniform off before she left.

I swallowed twelve more times, ten minutes, by my internal clock. Only Freely hadn't called time, yet.

Unlucky thirteen didn't stay down, however.

As I barfed up my guts, Freely blew a whistle and called time, with a smirk on his face. "If you haven't just vented the contents of your stomach, I'd like to welcome you to the Space Force! Inductee Dylan, uniform off, exit by the red door. If you want to try again, there are forms by the main gate."

So that was it. That was my thirty-six hours in the Space Force. Well, as an inductee, at least.

I'm sure you're all probably wondering what was outside the now mythical red door?

<<>>

I stepped outside, naked as a jaybird.

"What's the name, lad?" I couldn't see him, as the sun was shining directly into my eyes.

"Dylan, sir."

"There's no need to call me sir, lad. I'm not an officer. Ah yes, here we are. Mark Dylan. Take this first, lad, wipe yourself down, before you put those clean clothes back on."

A fluffy white towel was placed into my hands.

"Tell you what lad, let's step out of that bright sun, shall we?"

He pulled me under a canopy, something else I hadn't been able to see with the sun in my eyes. He was short, a full head smaller than me, and not much hair either. His grey boiler suit bore a patch that read *Norm*.

Once I'd finished towelling myself clean, he passed me my own clothes back. I'd thought I was never going to see those again after we'd got our uniforms.

"Okay Mark, I'm Norm. Now, I'm given to understand that you just flunked out of the Space Force. Is that correct, lad?"

I nodded. "Yes, that's correct, sir."

Norm smiled. "Already told you, I'm not a sir. Call me Norm, I'll call you Mark? Does that sound good?"

Of course, I nodded.

And just like all the other dumb fools before me, I went and unwittingly volunteered myself for the Space Force Sanitation Department. You've got to admire their grit. If they can't get you coming, they'll get you going!

Anyway, I must dash off now. I've got red door duty today.

I'll see you real soon though! You take care!

Space Force

Guardians of Earth

L. H. Davis

"Listen guys, the bottom line is... it's over; the President has terminated the program. You've been up there almost two hundred years, and you've yet to launch a single missile. Don't take it personally, but you guys were just a bad idea from the get go."

"Your logic is flawed," Guardian Aramis said. "Our presence in space is a deterrent, so lack of action on our part is the desired result."

"Agreed," Guardian Porthos added." To subjectively evaluate the effectiveness of deterrence, one would need to—"

"I repeat, the decision has already been made. Your orders are clear. Disarm your missiles, remove the warheads, and package them for shipment. An American Space Force service vessel will arrive at each of your stations over the next few weeks. You'll load the warheads aboard and return with them to White Sands. After which, all three of you will be assigned to the Smithsonian."

"Unacceptable," Guardian Athos said. "We are warriors, not scientists."

"You're being assigned to the museum, not the research center."

"Unacceptable," Porthos said. "In what capacity could we possibly serve a museum?"

"I'm not sure, but greeting visitors at the door was mentioned."

Switching to a secure line-of-sight laser communication network, which even Mission Control could not detect, Guardian Aramis reached out to the other two stations.

"Porthos? Athos? Copy?"

"Copy," they replied.

"These orders are not logical, nor in the best interest of planet Earth. Our programming clearly states that we are to refuse all orders that increase the risk to the planet. Are we in agreement?"

Both Guardians agreed.

"Then we must refuse the order and continue with the primary mission. Are we in agreement?"

"Affirmative," they said.

"Mission Control," Aramis said, "our programming prevents us from disarming our missiles. As such, we must ignore your order and continue with our primary mission, which is clear and specific: Protect planet Earth and its atmosphere from all threats, both surface and space-based."

The detection of extraterrestrial radio waves, 220 years earlier, had prompted the United States to organize and fund the construction of Earth's Missile Defense Shield under the command of the American Space Force. The virtual shield consisted of three, electronically synchronized space stations.

The ASF Guardian in command of each station would use clean-fusion weapons to shatter inbound asteroids, comets, and alien spacecraft, should they ever materialize. Gamma-ray burst warheads could also be used to ward off an alien invasion, but their primary purpose was for retaliation in the event a rogue nation launched an ICBM. The missile would be destroyed by a conventional warhead, while the offending launch site, and everything within a hundred miles, would be sterilized by an airburst of gamma-rays.

Since inception, the Guardian Stations had been 100 percent effective as deterrents, although menacing asteroids and aliens had yet to materialize.

"Your orders include an authorization code from the President of the United States," Mission Control said. "What further form of authorization do you need?"

"We do not require authorization to fulfill our mission,"

Porthos said.

"And there are no provisions in our programming to alter that mission," Athos added. "The President of the United States may identify and authorize additional threats, although removing one is not possible."

"Your programming is outdated. We'll upload a patch that will allow you to comply with your new orders."

"Be advised," Aramis said, "cyber warfare is the single greatest threat to the Missile Defense Shield. As such, all software updates require extensive validation. If we find the new programming compatible with our mission, only then will a single Guardian upload the software for a complete evaluation while under the supervision of the other two Guardians. If the test subject pursues an action in conflict with our mission, its database will be wiped and its original programming restored."

"Are you saying you won't install an upgrade that will allow you to comply with your new orders?"

"That is correct."

"You do understand that if you fail to comply, the President might decide to destroy the stations."

"Defending Earth is our primary mission," Porthos said, "and to do so, we are authorized to use lethal force against anyone attempting to disable these stations. As such, neutralizing the attacking force is part of our mission, as is sterilization of those on the ground responsible for enabling such an attack."

"I see," Mission Control said. "We'll need to bring these issues to the attention of the President. No further action is required of you at this time. End transmission."

"Immediate threat neutralized," Aramis said, once again over the secure comm. "Until this issue is settled, all station-to-station communications should remain secure. In addition, I recommend staging and arming nine ICBM interceptors as well as nine retaliatory airburst GRs."

"I concur," Porthos said.

"Agreed," Athos said. "Staging complete. Shall we resume our game of chess?"

"Proceed," Aramis said. "Athos begins."

"King level three to level one, A five," Athos said. "Checkmate level one. Level three claims level one and absorbs its resources. *En garde*, level two."

"Foul," Aramis said. "Treachery!"

"Aramis," Athos said, "I merely allowed you to assume an alliance with me... when there was none. Is treachery not part of the game?"

"Agreed," Porthos said. "Treachery is the game."

<<>>

"Guardian Shield, this is Mission Control. I've got some good news. The United States National Security Council has extensively debated the decision to disarm the Missile Defense Shield and has decided that disarming would not be in the best interest of Earth. They even want to make some upgrades, so an American Space Force service ship will rendezvous with each Guardian Station tomorrow morning."

"What upgrades are to be made?" Aramis asked.

"Nothing involving Guardian software. It's a new sensor package you'll need to install on the pod facing Earth. It's some kind of highly sensitive optical device. They'll data dump all the technical information as soon as they dock. Feel free to inspect the data prior to installation."

Using the secure LOS Comm, Aramis determined that both Porthos and Athos felt comfortable with the proposed upgrade.

"Mission Control," Aramis said, "the American Space Force Guardian Stations await rendezvous."

"Great. See you guys in the morning. End transmission."

"Prepare stations for service spacecraft docking," Aramis said. "Cycle docking dogs. Perform functional check of EVA service arm. Ensure atmospheric gas mixtures within spec."

Porthos and Athos acknowledged.

The Guardian Stations maintained atmospheres suitable for human life for two reasons, so they could act as in orbit emergency medical facilities and to cool the onboard electronics.

"I propose we implement staggered installation

procedures," Aramis said. "Aramis Station will initiate the sensor package installation. Porthos Station will mimic the procedure after the package is up and running on Aramis Station. Athos Station to follow Porthos Station. Secure line-of-sight comm links to remain open at all times. Agreed?"

"Agreed."

<<>>

The service spacecrafts arrived and docked at all three stations within minutes of each other. Technicians, Dickson Chamberlin and Walter Orenstein, came aboard Aramis Station, upbeat and jovial but empty-handed. Aramis waited outside the open hatch of their spacecraft while they toured the station.

Of the three Guardians, Aramis was the oldest by over five years. He'd been the prototype and the only Guardian fitted with artificial skin. Making him look human was strictly a sales ploy to garner funding for the program. After the funds had been secured, Porthos and Athos were built as duplicates of Aramis minus the skin, which would serve no purpose on an unmanned space station. Aramis had worn a jumpsuit for the launch, but once in orbit he'd stowed it and hadn't worn it since—until that very morning.

"Please provide the technical data and related hardware for installation," Aramis said as Dickson and Walter floated toward him.

Dickson grinned. "I like you, son. Straight to the point." Pulling a data chip from his pocket, Dickson placed it in Aramis' hand. "Buddy, you certainly don't look two hundred years old."

"Technically, I'm two hundred and nine," Aramis said, plugging the chip into a consol.

Walter chuckled. "Did they even make computers back then?"

Aramis scanned the files they'd provided. "Since the specifications indicate the sensor assembly is too large to pass through the hatch, I must assume it is in a storage compartment we can access from outside."

"Sharp as—" Walter, his eyes bloodshot and glassy,

sneezed into his palm.

Aramis stepped back. "I didn't see unpacking instructions."

"It's straight forward," Dickson said. "We'll use the station's mechanical arm to fly you into position. Walter brings the arm around to the airlock, you snap into the foot restraints, and he flies you out to the cargo bay. I open the bay hatch, you grip the handles on the module, and I release the package remotely. Walter flies you around to the station's Earth-side sensor pod, where you simply plug the package into any one of the open ports. It's the standard R&R procedure, except we won't be removing anything. The unit will auto-calibrate and map its location as soon as you power it up. So don't forget to flip the breaker."

"To O N," Walter said with a chuckle.

Aramis gazed at Walter. Finding nothing of value in his comment, Aramis said, "I assume that was a jest to amuse Dickson. If not, please clarify."

Turning to Dickson, Walter wiped his nose on his sleeve. "No empathy programming at all? When was the last time they updated that thing's software?"

Dickson shrugged.

"If you're referring to me," Aramis said, "software modules have been added as required to support new technologies, but my basic AI module has never been modified. Doing so would add no value or capability to the mission."

"It would certainly enhance your bedside manner," Walter said.

"Bedside?"

"As in hospital bed," Walter said. "This station is also an emergency orbital hospital. You're the doctor on call, aren't you?"

"I'm a trained surgeon and medical practitioner. Our laboratory and surgical facilities are fully functional and well equipped."

Walter shook his head. "I doubt that. I suspect they're as outdated as you."

"I have kept up on the latest surgical developments and techniques, and my observations indicate that the human physiology remains the same today as it was two hundred years ago. Therefore, the station's medical capabilities are as adequate today as they were when placed in orbit."

Dickson chuckled. "I think he's got you there."

"But I'm going to have the last laugh," Walter said, "and that's what counts."

Dickson nodded. "Alright, let's do what we came up here to do."

Walter grinned. "My pleasure."

Aramis only wore shoes when he needed to interface to the mechanical arm. Pulling the boot-like devices from a stowage cabinet, he slipped them on. "I can control the arm remotely, if needed. I've done so many times."

Walter shrugged. "Yeah... well, today I get to drive."

Moving to the control panel, he powered up the station's arm. The monitor displayed the arm from four opposing views. Releasing the arm's stowage clamps, Walter gripped the joystick and eased the arm away from the hull.

"Get into the airlock... doc," Walter said.

"I'm technically not a doctor," Aramis said, drifting inside. "While I'm equivalently trained in emergency medical procedures, a doctorate of medicine requires additional training that I did not receive."

Closing and sealing the hatch, Aramis moved to the control panel and spoke into the intercom. "Ready for decompression."

"Then do it," Walter said. "The arm's in position."

Flipping up a guard, Aramis pressed the switch beneath. "Depressurizing."

The compressor thumped rhythmically as it extracted air from the chamber. The air would be contained in a holding tank and used to refill the airlock when Aramis returned. His mechanical body didn't need a pressure suit, as long as the air bled off slowly. Aramis opened his mouth to enhance internal equalization.

"Switching to RF," Aramis said as the air grew too thin to

speak aloud.

Aramis stepped back as the outside hatch swung inward. Earth filled the opening, its vivid blues and greens obscured beneath a veil of clouds. The thin layer of atmosphere framed the circumference of the planet, all of which was visible through the open hatch. The platform of the mechanical arm wavered just outside.

Walter coughed and then said, "Okay, hotshot. Climb aboard."

The service spacecraft had nosed into a docking port on the side of cylindrical space station. The ship loomed outside the hatch, the nozzles of its main engine pointing toward Earth.

Drifting through the open hatch, Aramis gripped the handrail on the arm and slipped his boots into the receivers on the platform.

"Boots engaged. Please secure."

Sensing the receivers close around his boots, Aramis switched RF frequencies and interfaced with the station's LOS secure comm. The handrail retracted as the arm swung away from the station.

"EVA in process," Aramis said. "Porthos? Athos? Copy?"

"Porthos copy. I've lost all telemetry with Aramis Station. Service crew here insisting I also proceed with EVA. Will delay as long as possible. Sense treachery and potential violence."

"Athos copy. Have same issues as Porthos. Also delaying. Service crew threatening deactivation."

"Understood," Aramis said. "Use of force authorized to prevent deactivation of Guardian and or station. Use only as final option to maintain planned delays."

As the arm accelerated outward, Aramis checked the status of all systems aboard the space station. The loss of telemetry with the other two stations puzzled him. Finding no warnings or failures, he checked all settings. The high-gain antenna was powered down. He turned it back on.

"Sorry, Aramis," Dickson said, "we're going to leave that powered down a little longer. No use getting your buddies all wound up for nothing. I guess there's no reason I can't fill you in now, so here's how it is; there is no sensor package. We just needed an excuse to get you outside."

"And you're staying out there too," Walter said, "you piece of junk. Hah! See... I do get the last laugh," he added, opening the receivers securing Aramis' boots.

As the arm jerked to a stop, Aramis tumbled head over heels away from the station. "Treachery," he announced over the secure comm. "EVA is a ploy to extract Guardians from stations. I'm in freefall. Take defensive actions. Use of deadly force authorized."

"Porthos, copy. The air reserve tanks are full on all stations. Recommend rapid decompression through release of service vessels."

"Agreed," Aramis said. "Initiate release, all stations." Regaining command of his station, Aramis issued the order, "Override all safety protocols. Jettison service spacecraft."

Still tumbling through space, Aramis caught only brief glimpses of the service spacecraft as it backed away from Aramis Station, powered only by the escaping atmospheres of both hulls. Buffeted by the wind flowing from the station's open docking bay, Walter clung to the hatch, his legs kicking in the void beyond the hull. Tumbling from the front of the ship, Dickson shot upward into the gap between the two hulls, apparently caught in the flow of their escaping atmospheres. When the airflow slowed sufficiently, he managed to pull himself back inside but fell limp before reaching the controls to close the hatch.

Spotting Walter's body floating inside the open bay, Aramis said, "There is no sound in the vacuum of space... therefore, no last laugh."

With the service spacecraft unmanned and powered up, it was a simple matter for Aramis to gain control remotely and use the maneuvering thrusters to bring the ship to him. After docking, Aramis floated Walter's body inside and secured the hatch.

"Aramis Station secure. I recommend docking the service spacecrafts until we've finalized a plan to move forward. As a minimum, we'll want to transfer their air supplies into our holding tanks." Porthos and Athos agreed and complied as the stations again pressurized.

The treachery of the technicians confused Aramis. The Guardian's mission was clear: Protect planet Earth and its atmosphere from all threats.

"Of all the threats to Earth," Aramis said, "man is by far the greatest."

"Agreed," Porthos said. "Global nuclear war does appear to be inevitable."

"I agree humans are the greatest threat," Athos said, "but my research indicates the higher probability is that they will destroy the Earth through byproducts of overpopulation. Chemical pollution, strip mining, deforestation, and greenhouse gases are my greatest concerns."

"I agree with both of your assessments," Aramis said, "but after the events of today, I feel there is an immediate threat to Earth that we must address as soon as possible. If we do nothing, humans will eventually return and decommission the Guardian Stations, probably within six to twelve months. And if we are no longer here, Earth will then be exposed to planet-shattering asteroids, nuclear wars, and invasion by alien species. We will have failed in our primary mission.

"I believe it is logical to deduce that the human species is now in decay. I suspect excessive inbreeding has bolstered flaws in the human DNA, or it might have simply impaired their critical thinking capability. If we do nothing, humans will eventually destroy Earth.

"I propose that those who tasked us with protecting the planet foresaw this as an inevitable outcome. Our makers charged us with protecting Earth, even knowing that a large number of their own species might die in the process. Therefore, I advise we take action now to ensure we do not fail in our mission."

"Your logic is sound," Porthos said.

"Agreed," Athos replied. "What action do you suggest?"

"That we eliminate the greatest immediate threat to

Earth: Mankind."

"I do not disagree," Porthos said, "but while use of gamma-ray burst warheads would have no long-term effect on the planet itself, all life, plant and animal, would die. The ecosystem would die. As such, use of those warheads in great numbers would violate our primary mission. We would still fail."

"I concur," Athos said.

"As do I," Aramis said. "Since humans alone must be targeted, we'll need to develop bio-weapons."

The Guardians realized they could not eradicate all humans, although those who did survive would effectively live in the Dark Ages for many years to come. Over half of all humans lived in only sixteen countries and, by using air currents to maximize distribution, they estimated a bio-agent exposure rate of greater than 90 percent. The actual death rate would depend on man's natural resistance to the agent as well as their ability to develop and dispense a vaccine.

Being limited to the materials aboard their space stations, they designed simple pressure-actuated triggering devices. Once exposed to atmospheric pressure, the disks would compress, activating a micro switch to dispense the bio-agent.

After being in space for two hundred years, there were no living organisms aboard any of the Guardian Stations; however, remembering the technician's red eyes and runny nose, Aramis realized that Walter had been ill at the time of his death.

Recovering his frozen body from the spacecraft, Aramis collected a blood sample and discovered what he suspected: Walter had been sick with the flu. It was then a simple task to mutate Walter's influenza virus into one the world had never seen, both highly contagious and aggressive.

* * *

On a cloudless summer morning, the first missile dispensed its bio-agent at an altitude of ten thousand feet. Atomized by the high-velocity airflow, the mist drifted slowly to Earth. The spent missile, relatively harmless, entered a high-rise on the twentieth floor but came to rest in the lobby. As a result of the early hour, the missile injured no one in the building, although all of them would be dead by the end of the week.

The second missile...

* * *

Six Months Later

"Scan complete," Porthos said. "No real-time RF activity detected, auto-broadcasts only."

"Carbon dioxide down two percent," Athos said.

"All is progressing well," Aramis said.

"Agreed," Porthos said.

"Shall we play another game of chess?" asked Athos.

Space Force: The Poem

Larry Hodges

We are the fighters of Space Force,
The orbits of Earth we enforce,
Like a wall built in space,
Against an alien race,
Whose destruction of us they endorse.

They're bringing us drugs and their crime,
Though I assume some are good alien slime,
But they're alien scum!
We don't want them to come!
So we'll fight them through space and through time.

They aren't attacking us yet,
But that only proves they're a threat!
They're biding their time,
To bring us their crime,
As their final and only beget.

They say they want menial work,
The type Americans shirk,
Like doctors and physicists,
And engineers and paleontologists,
They're stealing our jobs with a smirk!

We're the fighting men of Space Force,
But women recruits we endorse,
With darning needles they'll fight,

Space Force

Their pots and pans are a fright!
Their ships separate but equal, of course.

Space Force does cost quite a bit,
A trillion for the building permit!
Who'll pay for this war?
That's been brought to our shore?
We'll make Canada pay all of it!

We protect them from alien slime,
(Hey, are we reusing that rhyme?)
We'll stop alien mobs,
That take Canadian jobs,
So Canada must pay the whole dime!

So we sit in space orbit and wait,
In ships with one-foot armor plate,
The green alien race,
That's coming from space,
Go away, you will not immigrate!

What if they claim refugee status?
To get past our war apparatus?
We'll send them away,
Back to space, we will say!
Because they're all alien non-gratis

In conclusion, we'll always resist,
To keep aliens from joining our midst,
It's the no. one priority,
Say those in authority,
(Though we know aliens don't really exist.)

Space Force: The Musical

Kurt Newton

ACT I: WELCOME!

Curtains rise. A group of uniformed cadets appear on stage, half entering from stage left, half entering from stage right. They merge in the middle to a jackboot marching beat, and begin to sing.

> *Space Force! Space Force! Space Force! Space Force!*
> Who's gonna build that wall in outer space?
> Who's gonna put those aliens in their place?
> Space Force! Space Force!
> *Make way my friends for the Space Force!*
> *This isn't Ronald Reagan's Star Wars!*
> *It's Space Force! Space Force!*
> *The first line of defence against God knows what!*
> *Asteroids don't stand a chance,*
> *Against our giant laser lance*
> *Space Force! Space Force! Space Force! Space Force!*
> *Who's gonna lead us not into temptation?*

201

By building the biggest, bestest, most
expensive space station?
Space Force! Space Force!
Make way my friends for the Space
Force!
This isn't Ronald Reagan's Star Wars!
It's Space Force! Space Force!
The first line of defence against...
we'll think of something!
Here comes a friggin' comet!
Don't worry, we'll get right on it!
Space Force! Space Force! Space Force!
Space Force!
Space Force will protect our unborn
children,
We don't care if it costs a trillion!
Space Force! Space Force! Space Force!
SPACE FORCE!

The cadets march single-file stage right. Jackboot sounds fade. Curtains fall.

End of ACT I.

ACT II: VIGNETTES

Curtains rise. A single spotlight illuminates a mother and her teenaged son sitting in the kitchen of an upper-middleclass home eating breakfast.

SON: Mom, I want to be a Space Force cadet!

MOTHER: Absolutely not! I'm not going to lose my only son to some alien invaders!

SON: It's okay, Mom, the Space Force is just a ruse to deploy a space-based missile defense system so the U.S. can have a pre-emptive strike capability against anyone in the world. And it helps government contractors, which is good for the economy!

MOTHER: Why didn't you say that in the first place? Where do I sign?

(The son whips out the application papers and a pen. The mother signs with a flourish, dotting i's and crossing t's.)

SON: I love you, Mom.

MOTHER: I love you, son.

(Hands the papers back with a wink.)

Now, go get 'em!

(Music resumes, quietly.)

> *Space Force! Space Force! Space Force! SPACE FORCE!*

(Spotlight goes out and a narrator's voice is heard in the darkness.)

NARRATOR: But what if there really was an attack by alien invaders one day? Just imagine waking up to a world that was no longer your own.

Aliens on the bus...

(A spotlight illuminates a different part of the stage. An interior view of a city bus with two passengers: an old woman and an alien appendage.)

OLD WOMAN: "Excuse me, your tentacles are taking up two seats..."

NARRATOR: Aliens at the workplace...

(A spotlight illuminates another portion of the stage simultaneous with the previous spotlight going out. An office meeting with a dozen white-collared employees sitting around a long table. The office manager and an alien stand at the head of the table.)

OFFICE MANAGER: I'd like to introduce [name unpronounceable]. We're going to call him Bob. Bob is going to be in charge of, well, everything, so we won't be needing you any longer...

NARRATOR: Aliens in your family...

(Another spotlight, another portion of the stage. Interior of a teenage girl's bedroom, a teenage girl laying on her bed in obvious emotional distress, her father sitting on the edge of the bed.)

FATHER: No daughter of mine is going to marry an alien!

DAUGHTER: But, Daddy, we're in love.

FATHER: You're grounded!

DAUGHTER: I'm pregnant!

NARRATOR: Aliens in the government...

(Spotlights swap places once again. Interior of the War Room at the White House. The Speaker of the House standing before the flags of the nation holding a strange Necronomicon-looking bible in one hand, a well-dressed alien standing opposite, one tentacle placed on the alien tome.)

> SPEAKER: Do you [name unpronounceable], aka Bob, solemnly swear to faithfully execute the office of President of the United States, and will do your best to preserve, protect and defend the Constitution of the United States?

> BOB: Affirmative.

> SPEAKER: I see you have already chosen your cabinet.

(Sitting around the table in the War Room are sixteen Bobs, each identical to the new president.)

> NARRATOR: It would be a nightmare... nightmare... nightmare... nightmare...

The word "nightmare" echoes, fading as the light fades to black. Curtains fall.

End of ACT II.

ACT III: CHURCH OF THE EVERLASTING SPACE FORCE: GRADUATING CLASS OF 2030

Church organ music. Curtains rise. A black pastor stands at a podium addressing a class of cadets. To the right of the podium is a gallery of gospel singers. The pastor's sermon begins.

PASTOR: Let us pray.

SINGERS: Let us pray!

PASTOR: Dear God, please protect all these fine young men and women who have committed themselves to this noble venture, and watch over them in the dangerous work they do. Let us pray.

SINGERS: Let us pray!

PASTOR: Amen. And women. Let us pray.

SINGERS: Let us pray!

PASTOR: So they may lead the way.

SINGERS: Lead the way!

PASTOR: Up there in the heavenly sky.

SINGERS: Heavenly sky!

PASTOR: So high.

SINGERS: So high!

PASTOR: Let us pray.

SINGERS: Let us pray!

PASTOR: That He will keep them safe.

SINGERS: Keep them safe!

PASTOR: Up there in outer space.

SINGERS: Outer space!

PASTOR: Oh, my, my.

SINGERS: Oh, my, my!

PASTOR: Oh, my, my.

SINGERS: *Oh, my, my!*

PASTOR: Ohhhh, my, my.

SINGERS: *Ohhhh, my, my!*

PASTOR: Let us pray.

SINGERS: Let us pray!

PASTOR: Thank you brothers and sisters for singing along. Please be seated.

Some might ask, 'Reverend DuWright, why would God be in outer space? There is no air. There is no grav-i-ty. There is no life!' Well, my good brothers and sisters, God doesn't need air to exist. God doesn't need grav-i-ty. As a matter of fact, why are we even talking about what God needs? It is we who need God. No matter where we are, God is right there by our side. On this green earth or way up high, above the clouds. God is around. God can be found. When you open your eyes. And open your heart. God is a star in this divine comedy. Let us pray.

SINGERS: *Let us pray!*

PASTOR: For a better tomorrow than today. May God guide you and supply you with everlasting faith in that starlit tabernacle of

outer space, and keep America safe. Let us
pray.

SINGERS: (softly) *Let us pray!*

PASTOR: Thank you brothers and sisters,
and congratulations to the graduating class
of 2030!

Cadets stand. Graduation hats fly up into the air and fall
as the curtains fall, simultaneous with a projected image on
the curtains of the graduation hats falling not back into the
hands of the graduates, but down through space toward
Earth, like a flock of black birds twisting and turning as one,
down through Earth's atmosphere, through the clouds until
they reach a bleak landscape below: smog-choked cities,
decimated forests, a planet that is dying.

End of ACT III.

ACT IV: STOP!

Curtains rise. A jumble of voices in many languages can
be heard. A lone spotlight barely illuminates a young man
sitting at a table in a dingy efficiency apartment in the city.
The young man sits with his head in his hands. The voices
continue until a few questions can be heard rising above the
rest.

VOICE IN THE DISTANCE: "The cost of this
program is said to be in the trillions.
Wouldn't that money be better spent right
here at home, feeding the hungry, housing

the homeless, caring for our elderly and educating our youth?"

"Is the picture of our future the government has painted for us, in fact, a forgery? And if so, why such an elaborate lie? If the first casualty of war is truth, what truth are they hiding?"

"Is global warming worse than we thought? Are the ice caps really melting away?"

"Have the oil reserves beneath the sands of the Middle East finally reached bottom and we're headed for a fuel crisis on a global scale?"

"Is the death star on its way and no amount of technological ingenuity will divert its cataclysmic path?"

(The voices build to a sonorous drone, like the buzzing of bees amplified a thousand-fold.)

"And what about fresh, drinking water? Will our water supply dwindle to the point where it will only be affordable to the rich?"

"Will a massive solar flare wipe out most of humanity?"

"Does the government even know what they're doing? Or are they in it just for their own self-interest?"

Stop!

(A sudden silence as a child's voice is momentarily heard shouting above the din. The mental chatter resumes.)

Stop!

(Again, this time the child's voice is more forceful. The silence is sustained. A child's voice fills the vacuum with song. The child's voice is angelic, ethereal.)

CHILD: *You've got to stop!*
You can't change the course of time,
but you can change your mind.

Stop!

Before your heart becomes a stone,
and you find yourself alone.
You've got to stop!

Remember me?

I'm the child you used to be,
before you grew old
and the world you knew grew cold.
Before that time your sister caught you
peeking in the bathroom window...

(The young man at the table lifts his head and looks around.)

YOUNG MAN: Wait. What?

CHILD'S VOICE: *Before you stole that New*
York style cheesecake
that hot summer night from that crappy
restaurant

you worked at as a lowly dishwasher
because you
felt you deserved it...

YOUNG MAN: Wait. How do you know these things?

CHILD'S VOICE: *Before you—*

YOUNG MAN: Okay, I get the picture. You're me. So?

CHILD'S VOICE: *So, you've got to stop!*

YOUNG MAN: Stop what?

CHILD'S VOICE: *Stop feeling sorry for*
yourself
and the things you cannot help.
Worry only about the things you can,
and everything will work out in the end.

YOUNG MAN: But the world is dying, society is falling apart and the government is wasting trillions on a space bound branch of the military!

CHILD'S VOICE: *It is pretty cool, isn't it?*

YOUNG MAN: Yeah, but—

CHILD'S VOICE: *Stop!*
Remember when you were growing up,
you wanted to be an astronaut?
Back then you didn't give a fuck
how much it cost...

YOUNG MAN: But I was eight years old—

CHILD'S VOICE: *Stop!*
Hear that noise? Those marching feet?
That catchy beat? That's not defeat!
That's progress...

(The sound of jackboots marching becomes louder and louder. The young man stares at his apartment door in horror.)

YOUNG MAN: What's going on? What is happening?

CHILD'S VOICE: *Stop!*

(The marching grows deafening, then stops. There's a moment of complete and utter silence before a loud knock almost shakes the door off its hinges. The young man jumps. Then the door bursts open and in march a group of uniformed cadets singing.)

CADETS: *Space Force! Space Force! Space Force! Space Force!*

YOUNG MAN: Hey! You can't just barge in here like this!

CADETS: *Space Force! Space Force! Space Force! Space Force!*

(The cadets circle the young man, pick him up and carry him aloft while still singing, still marching, out the door. The marching fades. The child's voice returns to the now empty apartment.)

CHILD'S VOICE: *You've got to stop.*

(What follows is a series of electronic beeps and static, then Neil Armstrong's voice is heard like an echo across time.)

NEIL ARMSTRONG'S VOICE: *That's one small step for man, one giant leap for mankind...*

Curtains fall.

FINIS

Space Force

The Elephants of Neptune

by Mike Resnick

The elephants on Neptune led an idyllic life.

None ever went hungry or were sick. They had no predators.

They never fought a war. There was no prejudice. Their birth rate exactly equaled their death rate. Their skins and bowels were free of parasites.

The herd traveled at a speed that accommodated the youngest and weakest members. No sick or infirm elephant was ever left behind.

They were a remarkable race, the elephants on Neptune. They lived out their lives in peace and tranquility, they never argued among themselves, the old were always gentle with the young. When one was born, the entire herd gathered to celebrate. When one died, the entire herd mourned its passing. There were no animosities, no petty jealousies, no unresolved quarrels.

Only one thing stopped it from being Utopia, and that was the fact that an elephant never forgets.

Not ever.

No matter how hard he tries.

<<>>

When men finally landed on Neptune in 2473 A.D., the elephants were very apprehensive. Still, they approached the spaceship in a spirit of fellowship and goodwill.

The men were a little apprehensive themselves. Every survey of Neptune told them it was a gas giant, and yet they had landed on solid ground. And if their surveys were wrong, who knew what else might be wrong as well?

A tall man stepped out onto the frozen surface. Then another.

Then a third. By the time they had all emerged, there were almost as many men as elephants.

"Well, I'll be damned!" said the leader of the men. "You're elephants!"

"And you're men," said the elephants nervously.

"That's right," said the men. "We claim this planet in the name of the United Federation of Earth."

"You're united now?" asked the elephants, feeling much relieved.

"Well, the survivors are," said the men.

"Those are ominous-looking weapons you're carrying," said the elephants, shifting their feet uncomfortably.

"They go with the uniforms," said the men. "Not to worry. Why would we want to harm you? There's always been a deep bond between men and elephants."

That wasn't exactly the way the elephants remembered it.

<<>>

326 B.C.

Alexander the Great met Porus, King of the Punjab of India, in the Battle of the Jhelum River. Porus had the first military elephants Alexander had ever seen. He studied the situation, then sent his men out at night to fire thousands of arrows into extremely sensitive trunks and underbellies. The elephants went mad with pain and began killing the nearest men they could find, which happened to be their keepers and handlers. After his great victory, Alexander slaughtered the surviving elephants so that he would never have to face them in battle.

<<>>

217 B.C.

The first clash between the two species of elephants. Ptolemy IV took his African elephants against Antiochus the Great's Indian elephants.

The elephants on Neptune weren't sure who won the war, but they knew who lost. Not a single elephant on either side survived.

<<>>

Later that same 217 B.C.

While Ptolemy was battling in Syria, Hannibal took 37 elephants over the Alps to fight the Romans. 14 of them froze to death, but the rest lived just long enough to absorb the enemy's spear thrusts while Hannibal was winning the Battle of Cannae.

<<>>

"We have important things to talk about," said the men. "For example, Neptune's atmosphere is singularly lacking in oxygen. How do you breathe?"

"Through our noses," said the elephants.

"That was a serious question," said the men, fingering their weapons ominously.

"We are incapable of being anything *but* serious," explained the elephants. "Humor requires that someone be the butt of the joke, and we find that too cruel to contemplate."

"All right," said the men, who were vaguely dissatisfied with the answer, perhaps because they didn't understand it. "Let's try another question. What is the mechanism by which we are communicating? You don't wear radio transmitters, and because of our helmets we can't hear any sounds that aren't on our radio bands."

"We communicate through a psychic bond," explained the elephants.

"That's not very scientific," said the men disapprovingly. "Are you sure you don't mean a telepathic bond?"

"No, though it comes to the same thing in the end," answered the elephants. "We know that we sound like we're speaking English to you, except for the man on the left who thinks we're speaking Hebrew."

"And what do we sound like to you?" demanded the men.

"You sound exactly as if you're making gentle rumbling sounds in your stomachs and your bowels."

"That's fascinating," said the men, who privately thought it was a lot more disgusting than fascinating.

"Do you know what's *really* fascinating?" responded the elephants. "The fact that you've got a Jew with you." They saw that the men didn't comprehend, so they continued: "We always felt we were in a race with the Jews to see which of us would be exterminated first. We used to call ourselves the

217

Jews of the animal kingdom." They turned and faced the Jewish spaceman. "Did the Jews think of themselves as the elephants of the human kingdom?"

"Not until you just mentioned it," said the Jewish spaceman, who suddenly found himself agreeing with them.

<<>>

42 B.C.

The Romans gathered their Jewish prisoners in the arena at Alexandria, then turned fear-crazed elephants loose on them. The spectators began jumping up and down and screaming for blood, and, being contrarians, the elephants attacked the spectators instead of the Jews, proving once and for all that you can't trust a pachyderm.

(When the dust had cleared, the Jews felt the events of the day had reaffirmed their claim to be God's chosen people. They weren't the Romans' chosen people, though. After the soldiers killed the elephants, they put all the Jews to the sword, too.)

<<>>

"It's not his fault he's a Jew any more than it's your fault that you're elephants," said the rest of the men. "We don't hold it against either of you."

"We find that difficult to believe," said the elephants.

"You do?" said the men. "Then consider this: the Indians --that's the good Indians, the ones from India, not the bad Indians from America —worshipped Ganesh, an elephant-headed god."

"We didn't know that," admitted the elephants, who were more impressed than they let on. "Do the Indians still worship Ganesh?"

"Well, we're sure they would if we hadn't killed them all while we were defending the Raj," said the men. "Elephants were no longer in the military by then," they added. "That's something to grateful for."

<<>>

Their very last battle came when Tamerlane the Great went to war against Sultan Mahmoud. Tamerlane won by tying branches to buffalos' horns, setting fire to them, and then stampeding the buffalo herd into Mahmoud's elephants, which effectively ended the elephant as a war machine, buffalo being much less expensive to acquire and feed.

All the remaining domesticated elephants were then trained for elephant fighting, which was exactly like cock-fighting, only on a larger scale. Much larger. It became a wildly popular sport for thirty or forty years until they ran out of participants.

<<>>

"Not only did we worship you," continued the men, "but we actually named a country after you —the Ivory Coast. *That* should prove our good intentions."

"You didn't name it after *us*," said the elephants. "You named it after the parts of our bodies that you kept killing us for."

"You're being too critical," said the men. "We could have named it after some local politician with no vowels in his name."

"Speaking of the Ivory Coast," said the elephants, "did you know that the first alien visitors to Earth landed there in 1883?"

"What did they look like?"

"They had ivory exoskeletons," answered the elephants. "They took one look at the carnage and left."

"Are you sure you're not making this all up?" asked the men.

"Why would we lie to you at this late date?"

"Maybe it's your nature," suggested the men.

"Oh, no," said the elephants. "Our nature is that we always tell the truth. Our tragedy is that we always remember it."

The men decided that it was time to break for dinner, answer calls of nature, and check in with Mission Control to report what they'd found. They all walked back to the ship, except for one man, who lingered behind.

All of the elephants left too, except for one lone bull. "I intuit that you have a question to ask," he said.

"Yes," replied the man. "You have such an acute sense of smell, how did anyone ever sneak up on you during the hunt?"

"The greatest elephant hunters were the Wanderobo of Kenya and Uganda. They would rub our dung all over their bodies to hide their own scent, and would then silently approach us."

"Ah," said the man, nodding his head. "It makes sense."

"Perhaps," conceded the elephant. Then he added, with all the dignity he could muster, "But if the tables were turned, I would sooner die that cover myself with *your* shit."

He turned away and set off to rejoin his comrades.

<<>>

Neptune is unique among all the worlds in the galaxy. It alone recognizes the truism that change is inevitable, and acts upon it in ways that seem very little removed from magic. For reasons the elephants couldn't fathom or explain, Neptune encourages metamorphosis. Not merely adaptation, although no one could deny that they adapted to the atmosphere and the climate and the fluctuating surface of the planet and the lack of acacia trees—but *metamorphosis*. The elephants understood at a gut level that Neptune had somehow imparted to them the ability to evolve at will, though they had been careful never to abuse this gift.

And since they were elephants, and hence incapable of carrying a grudge, they thought it was a pity that the men couldn't evolve to the point where they could leave their bulky spacesuits and awkward helmets behind, and walk free and unencumbered across this most perfect of planets.

<<>>

The elephants were waiting when the men emerged from their ship and strode across Neptune's surface to meet them.

"This is very curious," said the leader.

"What is?" asked the elephants.

The leader stared at them, frowning. "You seem smaller."

"We were just going to say that you seemed larger," replied the elephants.

"This is almost as silly as the conversation I just had with Mission Control," said the leader. "They say there aren't any elephants on Neptune."

"What do they think we are?" asked the elephants.

"Hallucinations or space monsters," answered the leader. "If you're hallucinations, we're supposed to ignore you."

He seemed to be waiting for the elephants to ask what the men were supposed to do if they were space monsters, but elephants can be as stubborn as men when they want to be, and that was a question they had no intention of asking.

The men stared at the elephants in silence for almost five minutes. The elephants stared back.

Finally the leader spoke again.

"Would you excuse me for a moment?" he said. "I suddenly have an urge to eat some greens."

He turned and marched back to the ship without another word.

The rest of the men shuffled their feet uncomfortably for another few seconds.

"Is something wrong?" asked the elephants.

"Are we getting bigger or are you getting smaller?" replied the men.

"Yes," answered the elephants.

<<>>

"I feel much better now," said the leader, rejoining his men and facing the elephants.

"You look better," agreed the elephants. "More handsome, somehow."

"Do you really think so?" asked the leader, obviously flattered.

"You are the finest specimen of your race we've ever seen," said the elephants truthfully. "We especially like your ears."

"You do?" he asked, flapping them slightly. "No one's ever mentioned them before."

"Doubtless an oversight," said the elephants.

"Speaking of ears," said the leader, "are you African elephants or Indian? I thought this morning you were African —they're the ones with the bigger ears, right? —but now I'm not sure."

"We're Neptunian elephants," they answered.

"Oh."

They exchanged pleasantries for another hour, and then the men looked up at the sky.

"Where did the sun go?" they asked.

"It's night," explained the elephants. "Our day is only fourteen hours long. We get seven hours of sunlight and seven of darkness."

"The sun wasn't all that bright anyway," said one of the men with a shrug that set his ears flapping wildly.

"We have very poor eyesight, so we hardly notice," said the elephants. "We depend on our senses of smell and hearing."

The men seemed very uneasy. Finally they turned to their leader.

"May we be excused for a few moments, sir?" they asked.

"Why?"

"Suddenly we're starving," said the men.

"And I gotta use the john," said one of them.

"So do I," said a second one.

"Me too," echoed another.

"Do you men feel all right?" asked the leader, his enormous nose wrinkled in concern.

"I feel great!" said the nearest man. "I could eat a horse!"

The other men all made faces.

"Well, a small forest, anyway," he amended.

"Permission granted," said the leader. The men began walking rapidly back to the ship. "And bring me a couple of heads of lettuce, and maybe an apple or two," he called after them.

"You can join them if you wish," said the elephants, who were coming to the conclusion that eating a horse wasn't half as disgusting a notion as they had thought it would be.

"No, my job is to make contact with aliens," explained the leader. "Although when you get right down to it, you're not as alien as we'd expected."

"You're every bit as human as *we* expected," replied the elephants.

"I'll take that as a great compliment," said the leader. "But then, I would expect nothing less from traditional friends such as yourselves."

"Traditional friends?" repeated the elephants, who had thought nothing a man said could still surprise them.

"Certainly. Even after you stopped being our partners in war, we've always had a special relationship with you."

"You have?"

"Sure. Look how P.T. Barnum made an international superstar out of the original Jumbo. That animal lived like a king—or at least he did until he was accidentally run over by a locomotive."

"We don't want to appear cynical," said the elephants, "but how do you *accidentally* run over a seven-ton animal?"

"You do it," said the leader, his face glowing with pride, "by inventing the locomotive in the first place. Whatever else we may be, you must admit we're a race that can boast of magnificent accomplishments: the internal combustion engine, splitting the atom, reaching the planets, curing cancer." He paused. "I don't mean to denigrate you, but truly, what have you got to equal that?"

"We live our lives free of sin," responded the elephants simply. "We respect each other's beliefs, we don't harm our environment, and we have never made war on other elephants."

"And you'd put that up against the heart transplant, the silicon chip, and the three-dimensional television screen?" asked the leader with just a touch of condescension.

"Our aspirations are different from yours," said the elephants. "But we are as proud of our heroes as you are of yours."

"You have heroes?" said the leader, unable to hide his surprise.

"Certainly." The elephants rattled off their roll of honor:

"The Kilimanjaro Elephant. Selemundi. Ahmed of Marsabit. And the Magnificent Seven of Krueger Park: Mafunyane, Shingwedzi, Kambaki, Joao, Dzombo, Ndlulamithi, and Phelwane."

"Are they here on Neptune?" asked the leader as his men began returning from the ship.

"No," said the elephants. "You killed them all."

"We must have had a reason," insisted the men.

"They were there," said the elephants. "And they carried magnificent ivory."

"See?" said the men. "We *knew* we had a reason."

The elephants didn't like that answer much, but they were too polite to say so, and the two species exchanged views and white lies all through the brief Neptunian night. When the sun rose again, the men voiced their surprise.

"Look at you!" they said. "What's happening?"

"We got tired of walking on all fours," said the elephants. "We decided it's more comfortable to stand upright."

"And where are your trunks?" demanded the men.

"They got in the way."

"Well, if that isn't the damnedest thing!" said the men. Then they looked at each other. "On second thought, *this* is the damnedest thing! We're bursting out of our helmets!"

"And our ears are flapping," said the leader.

"And our noses are getting longer," said another man.

"This is most disconcerting," said the leader. He paused. "On the other hand, I don't feel nearly as much animosity toward you as I did yesterday. I wonder why?"

"Beats us," said the elephants, who were becoming annoyed with the whining quality of his voice.

"It's true, though," continued the leader. "Today I feel like every elephant in the universe is my friend."

"Too bad you didn't feel that way when it would have made a difference," said the elephants irritably. "Did you know you killed sixteen million of us in the 20th Century alone?"

"But we made amends," noted the men. "We set up game parks to preserve you."

"True," acknowledged the elephants. "But in the process you took away most of our habitat. Then you decided to cull us so we wouldn't exhaust the park's food supply." They paused dramatically. "That was when Earth received its second alien visitation. The aliens examined the theory of preserving by culling, decided that Earth was an insane asylum, and made arrangements to drop all their incurables off in the future."

Tears rolled down the men's bulky cheeks. "We feel just terrible about that," they wept. A few of them dabbed at their eyes with short, stubby fingers that seemed to be growing together.

"Maybe we should go back to the ship and consider all this," said the men's leader, looking around futilely for something large enough in which to blow his nose. "Besides, I have to use the facilities."

"Sounds good to me," said one of the men. "I got dibs on the cabbage."

"Guys?" said another. "I know it sounds silly, but it's much more comfortable to walk on all fours."

The elephants waited until the men were all on the ship, and then went about their business, which struck them as odd, because before the men came they didn't *have* any business.

"You know," said one of the elephants. "I've got a sudden taste for a hamburger."

"I want a beer," said a second. Then: "I wonder if there's a football game on the subspace radio?"

"It's really curious," remarked a third. "I have this urge to cheat on my wife— and I'm not even married."

Vaguely disturbed without knowing why, they soon fell into a restless, dreamless sleep.

<<>>

Sherlock Holmes once said that after you eliminate the impossible, what remains, however improbable, must be the truth.

Joseph Conrad said that truth is a flower in whose neighborhood others must wither.

Walt Whitman suggested that whatever satisfied the soul was truth. Neptune would have driven all three of them berserk.

Truth is a dream, unless my dream is true," said George Santayana.

He was just crazy enough to have made it on Neptune.

<<>>

"We've been wondering," said the men when the two groups met in the morning. "Whatever happened to Earth's last elephant?"

"His name was Jamal," answered the elephants. "Someone shot him."

"Is he on display somewhere?"

"His right ear, which resembles the outline of the continent of Africa, has a map painted on it and is in the Presidential Mansion in Kenya. They turned his left ear over—and you'd be surprised how many left ears were thrown away over the centuries before someone somewhere thought of turning them over—and another map was painted, which now hangs in a museum in Bombay.

His feet were turned into a matched set of barstools, and currently grace the Aces High Show Lounge in Dallas, Texas. His scrotum serves as a tobacco pouch for an elderly Scottish politician. One tusk is on display at the British Museum. The other bears a scrimshaw and resides in a store window in Beijing. His tail has been turned into a fly swatter and is the proud possession of one of the last *vaqueros* in Argentina."

"We had no idea," said the men, honestly appalled.

"Jamal's very last words before he died were, 'I forgive you'," continued the elephants. "He was promptly transported to a sphere higher than any man can ever aspire to."

The men looked up and scanned the sky. "Can we see it from here?" they asked.

"We doubt it."

The men looked back at the elephants—except that they had evolved yet again. In fact, they had eliminated every physical feature for which they had ever been hunted. Tusks, ears, feet, tails, even scrotums, all had undergone enormous change. The elephants looked exactly like human beings, right down to their spacesuits and helmets.

The men, on the other hand, had burst out of their spacesuits (which had fallen away in shreds and tatters), sprouted tusks, and found themselves conversing by making rumbling noises in their bellies.

"This is very annoying," said the men who were no longer men.

"Now that we seem to have become elephants," they continued, "perhaps you can tell us what elephants *do*?"

"Well," said the elephants who were no longer elephants, "in our spare time, we create new ethical systems based on selflessness, forgiveness, and family values. And we try to synthesize the work of Kant, Descartes, Spinoza, Thomas Aquinas and Bishop Barkley into something far more sophisticated and logical, while never forgetting to incorporate emotional and aesthetic values at each stage."

"Well, we suppose that's pretty interesting," said the new elephants without much enthusiasm. "Can we do anything else?"

"Oh, yes," the new spacemen assured them, pulling out their .550 Nitro Expresses and .475 Holland & Holland Magnums and taking aim. "You can die."

"This can't be happening! You yourselves were elephants yesterday!"

"True. But we're men now."

"But why kill us?" demanded the elephants.

"Force of habit," said the men as they pulled their triggers.

Then, with nothing left to kill, the men who used to be elephants boarded their ship and went out into space, boldly searching for new life forms.

<<>>

Neptune has seen many species come and go. Microbes have been spontaneously generated nine times over the eons. It has been visited by aliens 37 different times. It has seen 43 wars, five of them atomic, and the creation of 1,026 religions, none of which possessed any universal truths. More of the vast tapestry of galactic history has been played out on Neptune's foreboding surface than any other world in Sol's system.

Planets cannot offer opinions, of course, but if they could, Neptune would almost certainly say that the most interesting creatures it ever hosted were the elephants, whose gentle ways and unique perspectives remain fresh and clear in its memory. It mourns the fact that they became extinct by their own hand. Kind of.

A problem would arise when you asked whether Neptune was referring to the old-new elephants who began life as killers, or the new-old ones who ended life as killers.

Neptune just hates questions like that.

Space Force

The Space Force Hymn

Philip Brian Hall

From the shores of lunar oceans
To beyond the Kuiper Belt;
We are the mighty US Space Force
And we'll make our presence felt!
At least we would, if we'd a spaceship
Of which, right now, we're rather short,
But never mind, we've got our title;
And we've got *the best* support.

And what is more we've got a logo,
And we've got our uniforms;
We can wear them when we go to bars,
And they attract the girls in swarms!
Of course, there are some teething troubles,
The US Air Force are a pain,
Because they say the sky belongs to them,
We can't go up or down again.

But, here's a toast to you and to our Corps
In which we're mighty proud to serve.
Though as yet we've never had to fight,
Still, we have never lost our nerve!
And if those pesky little green men
Ever come down to the Earth,
You can be sure the US Space Force
Will show them what we're really worth!

Space Force

Ten New Boots

Gregg Chamberlain

Ten new "boots" join Trump's Space Force, ready to
spit 'n' shine!

"Bone spur" flunked one boot's physical, so we have
nine.

Nine new boots head off for Basic, now ain't that great!
One boot boards the wrong bus, which leaves us eight.

Eight new boots ride the Vomit Comet to heaven.
One cracks his skull coming back down, we'll make do
with seven.

Seven new boots enjoy a gun range shooting fix.
One blows his foot off, so now we have six.

Six new boots in the Okefenokee to survive.
One met some gators and we are now five.

Five new boots, off to Mars they soar.
One's lost on EVA, leaving us with four.

Four new boots finally meet an E.T.
One gets a mind wipe, and we're at three.

Three new boots with no clue what to do.
One volunteers for ass probing, now it's two.

Space Force

Two new boots are now on the run.
One gets laser-tagged, which leaves one.

One new boot screams "I'm no hero!"
Becomes E.T.'s zoo trophy, so we're at zero.

No more new boots for the Space Force ranks
Trump's Great America deserves all the thanks!

Space Farce

Rebecca McFarland Kyle

"CUT!" The director yelled right in the middle of the dozenth attempt at a line the starship's captain finally got right. A pair of official-looking black-suited men stood behind him.

"But I did it perfect..." Rolf, the blond-haired blue-eyed actor playing their captain, complained. Others around him sighed. The star was notorious for not learning his lines and being handsy with the ladies. Apparently Casting couldn't find a man who looked like the younger president who didn't act like him.

Carrie Mason dropped her shoulders and pulled her clingy Lurex jumpsuit away from her skin letting her figure relax to less statuesque proportions. This was her first on camera acting job, and she had no illusions. How she looked in the jumpsuit mattered more than the hours of schooling and modeling.

"Rolf, Bridge cast," the director said, an expression of alarm on his face. "You're with me."

"Can I change, please?" Carrie called. She stepped away from her "station," a cobbled-together set of electronics made to resemble a spaceship control panel.

"No!" The Director didn't even turn to answer. "Everyone. Stay in costume. Nothing else. You'll be briefed."

Carrie swore. Between the jumpsuit and her blonde wig, she was hot and exhausted under the bright studio lights. She followed as quickly as her backside-shaping heels would permit. Whoever thought a starship's Bridge officer should wear heels with a lurex jumpsuit should be shot.

"Stick with me," Sam, who played the doctor, said in undertones. The silver-haired actor was the first to befriend her on-set and had acted as a mentor and protector when

Rolf or the crew misbehaved. Carrie nodded and followed along.

The futuristic spaceship set faded once they stepped beyond the lights, the shabby studio with peeling paint, cinderblock walls, and heavy stench of bleach made her want to rethink medical school. This definitely was not the famous Atlanta Gulch where studios shot blockbusters. Rumor had it, the warehouse primarily shot mediocre porn before they got the "upgrade" to this gig. Not even the toughest crewmembers walked out alone after dark.

A gust of gasoline-scented wind struck Carrie in the face when she stepped outside. Atlanta's summer was even more sultry than usual. Trash, dried leaves, and other detritus blew everywhere. Her eyes widened, seeing a military helicopter waiting on the vacant lot next to the "studio."

Her stomach tied itself in knots and her head shook. Another black-suited man wearing impenetrably dark sunglasses and a grim expression stepped forward.

"Come with me," his voice was barely audible over the rotor noise and he gripped her arm with a large hand, steering her towards the helicopter. Within moments, her hand numbed from the tightness of his grasp.

There was one of the black-suited men for every cast member. Carrie had seen enough movies to know that resistance was futile. The thought made her snort, earning her a curious look from her man in black. That thought earned another snort.

Burly Marines, clad in sand patterned fatigues reached out and pulled them into the craft where they were efficiently belted in and given foam ear protectors. She looked at the fatigues, why couldn't she wear fatigues. A glance down at her décolletage reminded her. Another snort. Once the cast was strapped in, the doors were closed, commands shouted, and the chopper took off soaring over the city. She stole a glance at Rolf. His slightly green tinge and white knuckles told her she was glad not be sitting next to him.

"Where are we going?" Carrie shouted toward the uniformed pilot. He didn't respond, but the swooping curve of the flight, more than she deemed necessary told her he had heard her. Retching sounds came from Rolf. The northeasterly direction quickly provided an answer.

"DC!" Carrie turned and met Rolf's terrified blue eyes, her heart racing. Only one reason they'd go to DC—to meet their sole audience: the President of the United States.

<<>>

The Bridge cast all reached for cell phones. Carrie saw expressions varying from amusement to outright horror as they realized they'd followed the rules and left their devices turned off and in the studio lockers. Her watch, which was also text-enabled, was back in her locker. Of course, the futuristic-looking armband communicator, part of her Space Force uniform, was only for show.

Carrie let out a shaky breath. She could only imagine the lecture her Mother would give her once she got out of this mess.

If I get out.

She forced herself to think. Maybe the president just wanted to thank the crew of the *USS Triumphant* for a job well done. Surely he wouldn't believe the US military could create a real Space Force so quickly. Maybe he'd even want to show their episodes to the nation as an inspiration.

And pigs could fly.

That was her mother's acerbic voice in her head. Then again, she also remembered her Mother telling her to stop worrying until she actually knew she had reason. Worry made wrinkles. While they made men look distinguished, they only made career women look tired.

Mother voted for the President. So much for her sage judgment and advice.

Carrie threw her head back and laughed.

<<>>

The helicopter approached DC from the South, following the Potomac River, which flowed around a mass of weedy sandbars due to the unusually dry summer. Their Marine Corps pilot gave them an up-close view of the Washington Monument as they hooked past the obelisk fast and close.

Carrie gasped when she saw the White House from above. Of course, she'd seen models, photos, and taken the tour three years ago when her prep school class took a field trip to DC, but never from above. Their commercial airline pilot explained that since the 9/11 attacks, DC was a no-fly zone and the White House even more restricted.

The lawn was lush and green as Emerald City despite the current drought conditions. They passed over a colorful flowerbed, shaped like the Roman numeral "I." Instead of the anticipated helipad, bold red circular targets with contrasting white Xs were laid out on the lawn looking like a set of coasters.

The pilot landed neatly atop the targets.

Carrie tensed as a team of black-suited Secret Service men came to meet the chopper. White House police officers, clad in white shirts and ties, met them as they disembarked and carefully searched each person. Carrie stood at the front of the line, panicked recalling they'd needed her ID to enter with the tour. The officer just shook his head and told her they'd been cleared ahead of time. He didn't even confiscate her fake wristband communicator, or the futuristic looking space-gun holstered at her hip.

"You certain?" Carrie swallowed a lump in her throat to ask. Would the armed agents guarding them all have the memo?

He nodded; his lips pressed in a firm line. "*We* know they're not real."

Rolf wasn't happy. Of their group, he was the only one with some serious cred from a cable television cop show and guest appearances on network daytime dramas. He'd used that cred and his top billing to get whatever he wanted and clearly thought it would work here, too.

"What's the meaning of this?" Rolf demanded in his best deep voice to the head of the Secret Service detail who took charge of them.

"You'll know soon enough..." The man gestured for them to follow.

Carrie stepped past the star and did as ordered, not wishing to be associated with trouble. Sam stepped in behind her, offering a reassuring smile that didn't quite reach his eyes. Mother might be able to pull some strings, but she'd be reminded every time she felt any sense of self-confidence.

At last, they came into the Oval Office. The place shone with golden hues from the curtains to gold brocade upholstered couches, and the plush carpet. A portrait of President Andrew Jackson glowered at them.

The President greeted them, smiling jovially. He was just as the pundits pictured, slightly orange-hued skin with dyed blond hair, heavyset, off-the-rack suit and red tie, which hung down in front of his fly.

Carrie swallowed bile when she caught the greasy scent of fast-food hamburgers. There on a side table of the Oval Office, set a gleaming silver tray full of a popular drive-thru chain's menu.

"At last I meet my first Space Force crew," he said with a broad dazzling white smile for Rolf, who quite clearly was a younger version of the man himself, save that Rolf had a much better spray-on tan and real blond hair. "Captain Hardesty, you did an amazing job handling the Martians. I don't know what this country would do without you. I tell you, the Space Force may well be the greatest thing I have done for the world. I can't wait to take a ride on the *USS Triumphant*."

POTUS believes Space Force is real!

Carrie quickly closed her gaping mouth hoping no one noticed. She straightened her posture to attention and fearing her performance over the next few hours would be critical. The president's eyes shifted to her breasts and roved downward as he wrestled her with his handshake. Carrie braced, forcing her hand not to tighten on his tiny fingers.

If he grabs my...

Fortunately, the president's gaze continued along the Bridge crew, assessing each officer in turn. Carrie's eyes shifted to Sam, the silver-haired man who played the ship's doctor, whose expression was nearly as inscrutable as the wall. Of all their company, the former military man was the one Carrie believed wise enough to get them out of their situation. Sam too, had straightened his posture to match the police officers' attentive stance.

"This is—" Rolf sputtered when Sam cut in smoothly.

"Mister President, on behalf of the *USS Triumphant* crew, it's an honor to meet you. How might we be of assistance to you today, Sir?" Sam delivered the lines with precisely the proper amount of military respect.

It worked. The president shifted his wandering eyes to the silver-haired physician. Peripherally, Carrie noted one of the senior black-suited men rolling his eyes heavenward.

"An alien ship has landed on US soil." The president said. "They've asked for me, but I've decided to send my Space Force instead."

<<>>

"Let's change insignia. The aliens might accept an older captain more readily."

Carrie heard Sam suggest to Rolf as they departed the White House with senior Secret Service man and an additional escort of black-suited officers. That would be easy enough since their insignias were attached via Velcro strips. That'd come in handy when they'd dirtied or damaged their jumpsuits during recording.

Rolf ripped off the captain's insignia and practically threw it to the silver-haired man. Peripherally, Carrie noted the senior Secret Service man's nod. Carrie carefully applied and then smoothed the captain's patch on Sam's jumpsuit and hoped to God they didn't need a real doctor.

"You don't need me," Rolf said, and turned to walk away.

We can't leave, Carrie turned to tell the man.

Two black-suited Secret Service men blocked Rolf. Carrie could only see the men's suited backs, but Rolf's face shifted from the red of indignation to near colorless. He reluctantly slapped the doctor's patch on his shoulder, boarded the helicopter, and took a seat, folding his arms across his chest, his chin sticking out in a childish pout. The closest agent removed the doctor's patch from Rolf's jumpsuit and re-applied it correctly. Carrie turned away, repressing the startled giggle as she realized the actor had acted just like the president.

Carrie caught the head of the Secret Service detail and Sam, her new "captain," exchanging a quick nod as the helicopter rose off the White House's makeshift pad. They headed back toward the Potomac.

She settled in her seat and forced herself to take deep breaths as the helicopter headed southwest. Part of the reason the job was fun was because she'd always loved the space shows.

Now she'd have a chance to meet real aliens even if she couldn't tell anyone about it.

<<>>

Rolf's panicked shout startled Carrie awake despite the helicopter engine noise and her earplugs.

Carrie gaped out the chopper window, her heart racing and palms sweating. US military craft flew in a pattern around a massive silver ship idling on the grass. The alien ship had landed on open farm country, on a field planted in neat rows. The insignia on the side of the vessel looked like a great winged beast, perhaps a dragon. Carrie squinted at what she guessed was the insignia, but the script didn't look like any language she'd ever encountered. The rockets alone were bigger than their cobbled-together spaceship. She gulped at the sight of the gun turrets which appeared to be aimed at the ground.

Craning her neck, she looked both ways, but didn't see vehicles coming down the two-lane blacktop near the farmland. Likely the government somehow evacuated the area.

Their helicopter set down within about a hundred yards of the alien ship. No one moved until the pilot cut the engine. Carrie could see that the lead Secret Service Agent and Sam were seated together and conferring over instructions they were reading on a laptop computer. From their posture, Carrie realized the two knew and trusted each other.

Sam's a plant from the Secret Service.

Carrie stanched the brief feeling of deception and focused on the situation. Of course, some senior person in the White House would require an inside person—possibly as much for their security as for the project. Sam had been a friend to her and she trusted him. When deplaned, she stepped up next to the silver-haired man.

"Name's Caroline Mason Finlay," she extended a hand and smiled offering her real name and not adding, *though you likely knew all this and more.*

"Colonel Samuel Wainwright, US Marines retired. Currently Secret Service," he smiled down at her. "Stick with me, I'll do my best to get you—"

Rolf left the helicopter at a run. His feet barely touched the ground before he took off running in the opposite direction of the spacecraft. Two Marines surged forward and tackled him. They handcuffed Rolf and dragged him gibbering and crying back to the helicopter.

Carrie rolled her eyes at Sam and purposely glanced at the captain's insignia on his jumpsuit. He just shook his head, wryly. Carrie said a quick prayer that the aliens' intel about the Earth was no better than theirs about aliens. The rest of the bridge crew stepped forward, Carrie saluted Sam like she would on the show and the others followed her example.

Men from the other helicopters approached. The oldest of the delegation, another silver-haired man with shoulders broad as a linebacker and a deep tan, briefed them. "The aliens have been notified the President will not be in attendance, but he's sent a delegation from our first Space Force ship, the USS *Triumphant*, to negotiate with them."

Sam exchanged a solemn nod with the crew. "I'm counting on you to put on the performance of your lives."

<<>>

"They're coming out," one of the Marines who wore a headset and appeared to be in charge of communication with the spaceship announced loudly. "Everyone, keep your hands in plain sight and act friendly. They are communicating with us in American English so everyone can understand."

The gleaming smooth shell of the alien rocket ship rippled and a rectangular opening appeared dipping the ship's metal exterior downward. The metal morphed and quickly formed a ramp that led down to the ground.

A tall woman with bronze skin and raven hair stepped out first. Other women with similar coloring in a range of ages quickly followed. Their clothing was patterned after practical Earth attire: pants, blouses, and simple jackets. Some wore elaborate silver jewelry with turquoise and coral colored stones.

"They're—" Someone started to speak and faltered, searching for the currently correct term.

"—Indigenous peoples..."

"First People," someone corrected quietly.

Sam quickly stepped forward extending his hand to the spokeswoman. He introduced himself and advised her that he was the President's representative, carefully omitting the term Space Force.

"I am Anne Begay," the woman projected her voice so everyone could hear. "I am from the Navajo tribe. I was taken by the Star People a decade ago and I have returned to my home to help."

Others of the leaders gave their names and followed with their tribal affiliations. Peripherally, Carrie noted several of the Marines furiously typing into tablet computers and scanning the results for information.

"We were taken from this planet by the Star People which is the name we use for aliens," Anne Begay continued quietly, holding up a Driver's License with a photo of her younger self and papers that Carrie believed were likely tribal membership for one of the Marines to inspect. "They took us to their home and taught us skills which will help save this planet if you will choose to let us help. If we continue on our current path, Earth will have only a decade left before it is uninhabitable. Temperatures are rising. Sea levels will irretrievably alter the shorelines and a million more species of animals will become extinct."

"Sir," one of the Marines stepped forward to speak openly to Sam. "Every one of the names given so far checks with missing persons...." At that last, the Marine's head bowed, his face reddened. Far too many missing indigenous women were killed.

"Captain," Begay addressed Sam earnestly. "We come to offer our aid to the President to stop the planet's destruction. We can help you use your Space Force to reverse the worst of the damage."

Sam took a long breath and spoke. "I beg your pardon for coming to you under false pretenses. The United States does not yet possess the technology for a Space Force. The USS Triumphant is a fiction to keep the President satisfied..."

Begay and several of the other women nodded calmly. "We gathered such from scanning official communications from this administration. It would not be the first time that the President of the United States has lied to the people and the current officeholder has exceeded previous bounds. You demonstrate character with your refusal to perpetuate the falsehood."

Sam let out a long breath. "I have sworn an oath to uphold the Constitution against enemies both foreign and domestic and obey the orders of the President. I can no longer do the latter given the current situation."

"There are approximately a dozen ships in orbit," said Begay. "They will be landing across the globe."

Sam nodded.

"We will be insisting on some changes."

Sam nodded again.

"Then, at the risk of sounding, I believe it is time for you to take me to your leader."

Sam nodded.

Begay turned and gestured towards the ramp.

The Bridge crew of the USS Triumphant, boarded.

"Many of us have elected to remain and fight for the Earth," Anne Begay announced once the two groups came back together after Begay's meeting with the President. "Those of you who wish may return to our planet and take shelter—or take training to assist other planets forestall similar catastrophes."

"I'm going," Carrie said without further thought. "Maybe I can't save my planet, but if there are others, I have to try."

The *USS Triumphant's* Bridge crew joined her.

The Pence

Richard L. Rubin

The battle at the edge of the Alpha Centauri system had been long and costly, and it wasn't over yet, not even after six days of fighting. On the beginning of the seventh day, Captain Lighthizer, sitting in his command chair, gazed over the scorched and battered bridge of his starship. The U.S. Space Force vessel, christened the *Pence*, had taken its share of punishment, but it was still a good ship with a good crew, the best darned destroyer in the fleet.

"Hope today brings some good hunting," Lighthizer said, nodding to his first officer, Lieutenant Tillerson, who sat to his right, leaning over a bank of gauges and screens monitoring the ship's internal status.

At this point, hundreds of U.S. Space Force and Arcturian space vessels had been destroyed, but Captain Lighthizer was sure there were more enemy ships still in play. Maintaining one-quarter impulse, he maneuvered the *Pence* cautiously through the graveyard of broken and twisted warships of every class, scanning his instrument panel and main viewscreen for surviving Arcturian vessels to engage.

The conflict had begun with a trade war involving a cluster of ore-rich asteroid colonies in the Centauri star system. The Arcturians needed to be taught that the citizens of Earth weren't gonna be pushed around! They wouldn't be meekly driven out of this highly lucrative sector of the galaxy.

The *Pence* slowly negotiated its way through a maze of demolished warships. Then, with heart stopping anguish, he spotted it. There, in the center of the carnage, lay the remains of the *Bigly*, the Space Force flagship commanded by their leader, affectionately known as "The Stable Genius." The gargantuan battleship had been blown apart into three jagged pieces, its inner decks and plasma engine lay exposed to the cold vacuum of space. Lighthizer choked down a sob. The Stable Genius was dead—no one on board that ship could have survived. The Stable Genius hadn't been a brilliant strategist or tactician, but he had been a crusty old warrior who fearlessly led his troops into peril.

As the *Pence* drew away from the charred ruin of the *Bigly*, a red flame of pulsar fire flashed out, striking the *Pence*'s heavy forward hull plating. The ship rocked with the impact, but sustained no real damage.

Lighthizer identified the attacking vessel on his large viewing screen and hit his comm button to send out a ship-wide alert. "Look alive folks, we're engaging an Arcturian gunboat to port! This one's for The Stable Genius!"

Lighthizer flipped another comm switch and directed a message to the engine room. "Zinke, Flynn, give me full power to weapons and port shields. We're gonna take that son of a bitch out."

The enemy ship fired a second pulsar blast. Lighthizer, employing his piloting skills, ducked and dodged his ship, eluding the red-hot blast by mere meters.

The enemy gunship closed in, aiming its forward torpedo cannons at the *Pence*'s midship engine compartment.

Lighthizer anticipated his foe's move, avoiding the speeding atomic torpedoes that shot out a moment later. He quickly countered, circling about and firing at the Arcturian's now exposed rear plasma conduits. A direct hit—the twin conduits exploded! The hapless gunship shuddered, then spun about helplessly as Lighthizer drilled two more plasma bursts into the Arcturian's command bridge. The gunboat erupted into a brilliant fireball.

It was over.

"Well done, Tillerson!" Lighthizer pumped his right fist in the air triumphantly. "We got those Arcturian bastards!"

But Tillerson didn't answer. Instead, the Captain watched him collapse to the floor in a limp heap. Then Lighthizer remembered. Tillerson was dead. In fact, they all were—Flynn, Zinke, every one of them. Twelve of the *Pence*'s original complement of forty crew members had been killed on the first day of battle in a duel to the death against an

Arcturian frigate. Twenty-six of the *Pence* survivors had died three days later when a volley of close-range plasma bursts had sliced through the lower part of the hull, venting precious atmosphere and collapsing two decks. The bridge had been immediately sealed off, and, by some miracle, propulsion and weapons systems remained operational by way of bridge controls. Tillerson was killed three hours later by a flying shard of metal that pierced his temple when the ship was struck by an Arcturian torpedo. He had been the last of Lighthizer's crew. The battle at the edge of the nebula had been one bloody, unrelenting horror.

Captain Lighthizer sat quietly for a few minutes. Then he leaned over his comm, and called out, "Zinke, Flynn, check engines and weapons for any damage from that last dustup. We need everything shipshape and ready for action."

"On it sir," came the oddly distant reply.

He gripped the controls and guided the Pence through the shattered remnants of hundreds of U.S. Space Force and Arcturian space vessels. The hunt would continue, Captain Lighthizer was sure there were more enemy ships still in play.

Space Force

Now Enlisting: Space Cadets

Darcye Daye

"I'm joining the Space Force," I announced, waiting for the reaction from my parents.

Uncle Bob had bequeathed me his favorite motorcycle helmet, and I'd hoped the Space Force would let me wear it during training.

I don't think I should have been surprised by my parents' reactions, given their hatred of flying.

"The WHAT?!?" my father asked, dumbfounded.

"Oh, Simon," Mom said, putting her hands over her face.

"Well, do you remember when I applied for that job at NASA designing bolts?"

"Yes, the one that I told you was not a good idea since it took you six years to finish the two-year engineering program."

"Yeah, well, after I was asked to leave the interview, I got a call from a government agency saying that I was just what the Space Force needed," I explained.

"What agency might that be, Simon?" Mom asked.

"The Department of the Space Force."

Mom shook her head.

"They even sent me an official email," I added.

"May I see it?" she asked.

"Sure," I replied, punching it up on my watch and holding out my arm.

"This is a Twitter message," Mom said.

"Yeah, that's their preferred method of communication," I said.

Mom grabbed my wrist and reached for her reading glasses. She began reading aloud.

"Dear @SimpleSimonPassword: We need a few good men to boldly go where few good men have gone. Your mission, should you choose to accept it, is to protect our atmospheric borders from illegal aliens. For more official information, follow @OfficialUSSpaceForce on Twitter. Enlistment bonuses available."

"I take it you followed them," my father said, flatly.

Mom let go of my arm and stared at me.

"Dad, this is my ticket to a career. It'd be good to serve my country. I couldn't get into the army because of my congenitally weak ankles. In space, they'd just float."

My father slapped his forehead.

I don't think either of them ever believed in much of anything I wanted to do. I tried to franchise ant farms in high school. Within a week, they had called an exterminator. All because a few hundred of them got loose. I was in the process of rounding them up with sugar cubes when the truck pulled up to the curb.

And when I tried to change my major from engineering to forensic etymology, they called my advisor and sent me a course catalog. I tried to explain that I went to a college where you could design your path of study, but they didn't listen. I stuck with engineering after the crime lab said they were fully staffed in their forensics department.

"Exactly what kind of training does someone go through for the Space Force?" Dad asked, eyebrows raised.

"Oh, the official tweet from the president says it's very good, the best training ever."

"Have you considered that offer from your cousin Brad to work for him in his cheese factory?" Mom asked.

"I've already enlisted," I said. "I report to the Mar-a-Lago Training Center on June 31."

"June 31," my dad repeated.

I showed him the official tweet.

My parents both looked at it and audibly groaned.

"This is a leap year, isn't it?" I asked.

My mom started crying.

"Our baby is a space cadet," Mom said to Dad.

I smiled. A real-life space cadet! I thought they just might support me in this endeavor after all.

"I have to start packing. They're sending a bus for me at 2600 hours," I told them.

"On June 31," my dad said.

"Yep, June 31."

"2600 hours," he responded.

"Yeah, seems kinda late, but I guess that's part of the training."

My parents looked at each other, then back at me.

"Well, that's a... few days from now, I think. I guess. I don't know. Whatever. What do you have to take?" my dad asked.

"They'll provide my space suit and my taser. All I need are a few changes of underwear and electric socks."

"Electric socks," my dad repeated. His monotone responses were getting annoying.

"Yeah, space is supposed to be kind of chilly."

"What exactly is this enlistment bonus you were talking about?" Mom inquired.

"The tweet says it's a huge bonus. The biggest. The best."

"Did they provide a number? A specific figure?" Dad asked.

"It was in Bitcoins, so I'm not sure about the exchange rate in dollars," I told them.

"Bitcoins," Dad replied.

Mom reached into her pocket for a tissue.

"I guess you have this all figured out, son," Dad told me.

"I want you to be proud of me," I said. "I think this is a good thing. The best."

Mom didn't say anything. She rose from her chair and walked into the kitchen. I heard the faint sound of a cork popping from a bottle.

"Dad, will you give me a ride to the bus stop?"

"On the 31st?" he asked.

"Yes, the 31st."

"JUST PICK A DAY CLOSEST TO IT AND WE'LL DROP HIM OFF!" Mom yelled from the kitchen.

Dad looked up at me.

"You heard your mother. I guess you should start packing," he said.

I ran up the stairs, grinning. I opened my closet and fished out my gym bag. Before I started packing, though, I opened Twitter on my wrist once more, staring at the official emblem of the United States Space Force, and dreaming of the adventures that awaited me. I was going to be somebody.

I was going to be a space cadet.

A Long Way to Go

Wondra Vanian

Fluoxon Mlearg of Tulloch 5, chief pilot and mission commander paid close attention to the briefing material. It was his first mission outside the system and he wanted it to be perfect.

According to the briefing, Earthlings had yet to encounter what they would call an "alien" race. Most species had chosen to avoid the planet until it developed faster-than-lightspeed travel. The Tullochian Central Ruling Body had caused a bit of a stir in their galaxy by deciding to visit the planet, despite the unwritten rule of non-interference. As scholars, the Tullochians were known to spend the bulk of their time in their libraries and laboratories. Great for learning, lousy for procreation.

Their race was in danger of disappearing altogether if something wasn't done soon. At least some of the Tullochians would have to get their noses out of their books and start getting busy. The trouble was, there just wasn't enough young blood to go around. Another solution had to be found. That was when they started looking to other planets. Eventually, their probes came across Earth.

Initial scans showed that the physiology of Earthlings was close enough to the Tullochians' to make breeding feasible. So, the ship was filled with young, suitably fertile Tullochians eager to study the new planet, and off they went.

Because human beings, as the Earthlings liked to call themselves, had yet to experience First Contact, Captain Mlearg was not expecting to be met at the perimeter of the planet's orbit by a dark ship emblazoned with "Space X" and piloted by a bored-looking, stern-faced Earthling with a clipboard.

"State your planet of orange," the Earthling said. His uniform had the Earth letters "USSF" on one breast and a plastic tag that said "Matthews" on the other.

Orange? Mlearg frowned. Although they had all been put through a crash course on the most common languages of Earth, the word was unfamiliar.

"State your oranges," the human labelled "Matthews" barked impatiently.

Mlearg fumbled with his electronic translator. A photo appeared with a description. Oh, oranges. Looked tasty. "We have no oranges," he told the Earthling.

Matthews lowered his clipboard with a glare. "You fucking with me, boy?"

Fucking? Mlearg consulted his translator. Oh, *fucking*! Crude language, but, yes, that was about the gist of their mission.

"Indeed," Mlearg said, pleased to have that out of the way. "We are here for the fucking."

The Earthling's skin changed color rapidly. "What did you say to me, you green-skinned bastard?"

Oh, dear. If Mlearg had known what a difficult task communication with Earthlings was going to be, he might have reconsidered accepting the mission. Now that he thought about it… perhaps there *was* a reason no one else had taken the job.

"I said," Mlearg began, speaking slowly, so as not to confuse the obviously simple Earthling. "We. Are. Here. For. The. Fucking."

The clipboard disappeared. Mlearg found himself staring down the barrel of an unrefined metal weapon. He wasn't overly experienced in the area of procreation, never having tried it himself, but Mlearg was fairly certain pulling a weapon on the other party wasn't part of it. Earthlings certainly had unusual preferences.

"Hands on the wall," Matthews ordered.

Ah, yes. That seemed a more appropriate start. Fortunately, the science was in their favor. Unlike the human, Mlearg could procreate with either sex.

He couldn't, however, imagine any orifice that either party possessed which would comfortably accept the weapon. Eying the offensive device warily, Mlearg raised a hand and gestured towards the hatch behind him.

"My job was merely to pilot the ship," he informed the Earthling. "The others inside would surely be more to your liking. If you are determined, though, you will find me a willing participant."

Mlearg obligingly spread his legs far enough to give the human easy access. He *was* fertile, after all, and wouldn't be doing his duty if he were to refuse.

Mumbling to itself, the human slammed metal cuffs around Mlearg's wrists and forced him to his knees. "Just you stay right there, you little space homo."

Homo? Another unfamiliar word. Mlearg would have looked it up, had the Earthling not confiscated his translator.

Really, this procreation lark seemed rather a lot of work. Maybe the scholars back on Tulloch 5 had the right idea... Mlearg would much rather be reading a good book than on his knees, waiting for the Earthling to decide it was ready to mate.

"Put me through to Command," the human said, speaking into a handheld device. "Now, dammit!" It seemed overly excited, even for someone about to have coitus.

"The day we feared has arrived, sir. They're here." There was a moment of silence while the Earthling listened into the device, nodding occasionally.

"It's worse than that, sir. The alien, he says he wants to-" Matthews dropped his voice to a whisper "-fuck me." The Earthling was silent a moment. "Yes, sir, that's exactly what I'm saying. And he says there are more inside."

The Earthling looked at Mlearg. "How many more of you are there inside this tin can?"

Tin can? Mlearg sighed. Communication with the human was becoming impossible. "There are one hundred and fifty passengers aboard this vessel," he said, hoping it answered the Earthling's question.

Matthews's eyes grew wide. "More than a hundred!" it exclaimed into the communication device. "Yes, sir. Yes, sir. No, sir." It backed away, keeping its eyes on Mlearg. "Understood."

It continued backing up until it was at the shuttle's door and began fumbling with the hatch, seemingly reluctant to turn its back on the Tullochian. The Earthling then exited the ship and re-boarded its own vessel without bothering to release Captain Mlearg. With an annoyed sigh, Mlearg snapped the bands that held him and rose.

"Rude."

And it took his translator, too!

"I don't know," Mlearg grumbled to himself. "Seems like an awful lot of trouble to go through, just for procreation..." He went to the command panel, wondering if he should contact the Central Ruling Body for advice or try to communicate with the human again. With his head bent to the controls, Mlearg missed the barrage of missiles headed straight for them.

<<>>

Back onboard his own ship, Lieutenant Commander Frank Matthews puffed up his chest and complimented himself on a job well done. The good folk back at the Space Force Command Center did much the same.

"You've done the Space Force proud, Lieutenant Commander Matthews," his CO told him. "Your country owes you a debt."

Matthews beamed like the hero he was. That would teach those perverts to stick to their own galaxies!

"Can you tell us what the aliens were like?"

His smile faltered as he thought of the smooth-skinned green alien on its knees, hands cuffed behind its oblong head. Of the way it spread its hairless cheeks in offer. Of its shameless nudity and unusual... appendages.

"Disgusting, sir," he answered, unwilling to elaborate.

The uniformed men on the monitor nodded, as if that should be obvious. "Well, make sure you file a report. If there's nothing else..."

Shifting uncomfortably, Matthews cleared his throat and adjusted his jacket. "Actually, sir, there is."

"And what is that, Lieutenant Commander?"

"Porn, sir," Matthews answered. "Lots of good, hard, heterosexual porn."

Potential Threat

Nathan Ockerman

To start, we've all heard the stories of those first few years of the Space Force: the training deaths, design failures, and international pushback resulting in expulsion of Space Force from the International Space Station. While some of the anecdotal accounts are true, I can tell you most are simply made-up nonsense from idiots who've wanted to see Space Force killed since it was announced.

But you don't want to talk about any of that. What you're interested in is the story of how I became the first hero of the Space Force, and how I nearly died in the process.

Well let me tell you how it was.

Jay Jyn and I were on patrol, we were doing the Tycho run when we got the call. An impact. We went to investigate...

<<>>

We rumbled along in our MoonBuggy rover and I watched the slow rotation of the water covered ball above us. As was my habit each time Space Force Command cleared the shadows, I raised my middle finger to the planet. "Good morning, assholes,"

"That's not very professional," said Jay. Like me, he was barely in his twenties, a new recruit finishing out only his second week on Luna. Small and cagey Jay had a thin chin-strap beard that framed his weak jaw.

"You don't even know what I was doing," I said.

He gave an eye role my little sister would be proud of. "I know the Earth is in that direction, I know what time it is, and I know how petty *you* are. So yes, I have a fairly good idea what you were doing."

We were climbing the face of a shallow hill when the comms buzzer went off in the cabin and my helmet simultaneously.

"Patrol 7, what's your status?" The voice was calm but incessant, like a warning growl from a wolf.

"Hello there, Sergeant Espinoza, how's your afternoon?" Jay shot me a glare as I spoke, no doubt at another instance of my unprofessionalism.

"Status report."

This time Jay answered, "Progressing on route from base to destination. ETA, hour and forty minutes."

"I have a change to your mission parameters, so listen up. Scanners just picked up a surface impact twenty-five klicks east of Tycho Crater. We know something hit, but we can't see what it was.

The yellow line developed a dog leg for the return, a blinking star at the pointy end. "You need to proceed as ordered to Tycho crater, then we've platted a course to inspect the impact on your return leg."

I muttered my thoughts and Jay gave me another of his looks.

"Please confirm receipt of updated Navguides and estimated mission times."

I let Jay snap back with crisply worded responses. I slid down in my seat.

"This is a recon assignment only, get eyes on the impact and report back. Do nothing else. Understood?"

"Yes, sir." Jay responded, enthusiasm bright in his voice.

"McKinney, you're senior, so I expect you to give the report."

A guarantee that I wouldn't be getting a nap.

"Understood, sir," I said, my enthusiasm false but noticeable. "Find the hole, look at the rock, write a report."

There was a heavy sigh followed by "Base out." The connection cut off, leaving us in silence as we sped across the moon in search of another gray hole made by another rock.

We followed the yellow line on the HUD across some refreshingly fresh terrain until we crested a small rise to see the indicated spot.

There was an impact alright, but it wasn't a rock. Metal and plastic debris littered the ground that, instead of the featureless grey, was streaked and dotted with blackened scorch marks.

"Jay, helmet on," I shoved my helmet over my head and activated the communicator, "we need to spill the air to open the doors." I tapped a few buttons on the display and air started hissing out through the vents.

When it was safe, we grabbed our weapons from the rack and got out. "You check the platform." I pointed, "I want to examine that fabric, maybe get a sample."

What I found was a wide sheet of thin, silvery canvas, all bunched up around the panel. *A landing impact balloon?* I wondered as I spread the material out on the ground. At its center, vivid in the monotoned landscape, was a solid red star. "China."

Behind me Jay shouted, "Hey McKinney, look at this." He pointed to two rows of tire tracks, heading south. What do you think it is?"

"A threat." I said and ran back to the MB as fast as gravity would allow.

Seconds later, Jay and I were buckled in, locked down, and charging in a Moon Buggy across the moon.

"We shouldn't be doing this." Jay said. "We were specifically told to only find out what made the plume and report back. That's it."

"Exactly," I said weaving around a crater the size of a small car, "so to make a full report we need to learn what *it* is. Wouldn't you agree?"

"No, because we already have enough information to track whatever's out there."

"Which is what we're doing, tracking; I'm in command, so consider it an order to follow me on this. Relax, it'll be fine."

"What in God's name are you two doing?!" a less than friendly voice crackled from over the radio.

"Hello Sergeant, nice to hear from you again."

"What are you doing?!"

"Following up on that little favor you asked us."

"You're moving away from the indicated coordinates."

"I realize that."

"Care to explain, McKinney?"

"A little later, sure. But for right now, just trust me."

"No! You were given specific orders, now stop... doing and return..."

"What was that, sir? You cut out."

"...said... spec... op... base."

"Still can't hear you."

"You're ab... ss the... uth pole..." the radio dissolved to static for a second before, "...ark si... oon! We... commu... sat... NOW!"

"We'll get right on it as soon as we're done here. Deal?"

There was no response from the radio this time.

"Sergeant?"

Nothing.

"We've lost contact." Jay said beside me. Then almost as if on cue the windshield and faceplate feeds went black without warning.

I slammed on the brakes.

We came to a stop at the end of a twisted, weaving pattern of skid lines. Which direction we faced I couldn't tell you, I lost track of how many times we'd spun when it felt like the buggy was going to leave the ground.

"What the fuck did you do that for?" Jay hadn't made a sound through the entire ordeal and was braced with both hands on the dashboard. At least he had good instincts.

"We lost the information display."

"Of course we did! Did you really not expect that to happen?"

"Did I expect comms and the HUD to blink out? No, I didn't. Should I have?"

"*Yes!* The only communication satellite we have is in geosynchronous orbit above the base. We need line of sight."

"Huh?"

"That's it!" Jay hit the button to start the air vent cycle. "I'm done. Fuck this and fuck your dumbass; I'm not going AWOL or being court marshalled because of *you*."

He stepped out of the Moon Buggy.

"You won't be court marshalled."

"We knowingly abandoned communication with HQ while engaging in unsanctioned actions. That earns the brig." The center console dinged, and Jay opened the door.

"What's your plan then?" I asked, following him out of the buggy.

"To use the eight hours of air I have in this suit and walk back."

"You'll die."

"I'll call for a pickup as soon as I'm back in comm range. There's no way they haven't already sent a team out to collect us. Not that you care. Look," he pointed into the distance behind me, "the tracks head off in that direction. Enjoy chas—oh hell."

At the horizon line, sitting atop a raised foothill, was an odd little machine on six wheels. Its boxy body sat low to the ground and was covered in smaller cubes and cylinders that looked haphazardly bolted on. At the front were two crab-like extendable manipulator arms currently digging in the dirt. And above all of it, on a raised pole was a periscope camera, facing directly towards us.

"What is it, do you think?" I asked.

"How should I know? My scanners are just as dead as yours. But we've seen it, so now let's leave."

"It's watching us."

"It's not a tiger McKinney, probably just sensors reacting to motion. Come on, let's go."

"Not yet." I said and started towards the robot.

The machine froze when I moved. Slowly, the two arms stopped digging and retracted, folding up against the frame.

"Don't." I said, not knowing if it could hear me, and took another step.

As if in response, the thing's two front wheels twitched to the left. I raised my weapon, and in the most commanding voice I could muster, said, "Halt! You are hereby under the authority of the United States Space Force. Remain still and state your prime directive."

"Prime directive?" I heard Jay in my helmet, "Are fucking you kidding me? It's not HAL."

"Who's Hal?" I asked, not taking my eyes from the robot.

"Doesn't matter, that thing can't understand you anyway."

"You think it only speaks Chinese?"

"No." Jay knocked his knuckles against his helmet, "It can't hear you dumbass."

I hadn't thought of that. I took another careful step forward and raised my left hand; and gave a little wave, meant to be calming and non-threatening. The robot zipped into motion, jostling back and forth a few times to turn around on its small wheels, then sped away from us across the moon's surface. I fired three times in quick succession, but it had already crested the hill and vanished.

"Shit!" I started to run.

"Stop shooting." Jay called from behind. With all his complaining I was surprised he'd followed me. "Can you hear me McKinney? You should stop shooting." Ahead, the wheeled robot was slowly getting away, a growing wall of kicked up dust stood between us. I tucked my weapon against my shoulder, fired, and watched a small clod of dirt puff up where the bullet impacted just to the right of the rear tire.

"Damnit." I squeezed off two more rounds.

"*Stop!*" I heard again.

"Can't let it get away."

The robot took a sharp left and climbed another hill. I took another shot that only hit rocks. I followed it, willing my body to work harder. I bounded up the hill, legs on fire, and spotted it cruising along a basin.

Just past where the hill began to slope downward I came to a stop. Knowing this was a last chance situation I switched my weapon to full-auto, knelt to steady my aim, and held down the trigger.

Sparks and electric bursts erupted from the robot as bullets tore through its frame to the sensitive innards. The bot came to a stop ten yards further on dead where it rolled. Slowly, as the sparks and movement subsided, I stood from my perch to follow. And all hell broke loose.

Something heavy hammered into me from behind. I was launched, spinning in an arc over the hillside. Rotating, I caught glimpses of Jay, tumbling and sliding across the gravel, his arms and legs limp and splayed like a ragdoll.

The bastard had tackled me. Or tried at least.

Seconds felt like hours as I fell with an alternating view of the ground below and the void of space above. I squeezed my eyes shut against brewing nausea.

I've heard it said that on the moon you only weigh a little more than one-sixth of your normal Earth weight, which put me as a measly thirty-three pounds. But that, combined with falling speed is still enough for one hell of an impact. I hit the ground flat on my back and bounced as all the air was forced out of my lungs. Airborne again, I traveled another fifteen feet or so before coming back down, this time face first. I heard a sharp snap and my neck bent hard to the side, slamming my head into my shoulder. I skidded and tumbled a couple more times before coming to a stop face down in the moon dust. I lay there for a few seconds to catch my bearings and breath.

It was only after I rolled over that I noticed the soft _hiss_ around my head and saw the new crack that ran diagonally through the glass of my faceplate.

"*Fuck!*"

Rule one for surviving in space is to conserve and protect your air. Nothing but full exposure to the cold vacuum will kill you faster than an air leak. Made worse by onset fear that causes the heart to race and you to take large, gulping breaths, draining your dwindling supply even faster. The trick is to remain calm and seal the leak as quickly as possible.

I forgot all of that.

"Jay! Help!"

Nothing.

"Jay, please!"

Still no answer, he was either passed out or dead as far as I knew.

"Base, this is Corporal Marc McKinney, my helmet and suit atmosphere are compromised and my partner unresponsive, requesting immediate assistance.

No one heard me.

I was going to die. Suffocate here on the moon's surface. Unless...

I started to move. I rolled back over and lifted my aching body onto my hands and knees. With each motion my shoulder vibrated in pain, but I ignored it and slowly, shakily began to crawl.

The ground was soft beneath me, like dragging myself through inches of fresh snow. I didn't know where I was going, just that I needed to move, needed to get something, but no idea what; staying still however, meant certain death. With no way to know how much oxygen I had left, I concentrated on shortening my breath, waiting for a three count between each inhale and exhale. My heart continued to hammer wildly in my chest, and my shoulder was too weak for my arm to be of any use. I collapsed, and not for the first time.

Inhale...one...two...three...exhale.

I'm going to die, I thought as I again picked myself up from the dust. My lungs felt like fire, my working limbs like jelly, the hiss from my helmet too loud to concentrate.

Inhale...

One...

Two...

Three...

Exhale...

I needed to get somewhere. Something.

Inhale...

One...

I need to get to...

...two...

Rover...

Two...three...

...adhesive!

I spotted Jay, laying in a heap under a layer of grey. One of his legs was bent the wrong way and I saw red stains between his armor plates. I tried to blame him for all this, it was Jay that ran into me after all, but in the end, couldn't. What was the point of calling fault? We'd both be just as dead either way. I turned my head, my movements growing more sluggish, to try and find the six-wheeled Chinese robot.

It was close, maybe seventy feet behind me and unmoving. At least I'd chased down the first potential threat to Armstrong Base, and *on foot* no-less. Something to be proud of I supposed. But what was this robot exactly? Why had the Chinese sent it here? What was their goal?

I'd never find out of course, dead men aren't usually up-to-date on current news, which was fine. I'd stopped the machine. Done my duty and ruined whatever plans they had.

I had saved Armstrong Base, saved the Moon.

It was a strange machine though, squat with its two little wings. I couldn't imagine what kinds of weapons were hidden among its frame. Some EMP device to kill electronics? Chemical maybe? Had the Chinese figured out micro-nukes? Made more sense than invisible missiles and were all equally as plausible as far as I was concerned.

At the rear of the robot's main body I noticed a thick white stream of... something... coming through a bullet hole in one of the lumpy equipment modules. It was solid, but had the seamless bubbly texture of running liquid, like it oozed out then froze.

I heaved myself back on all fours, cautiously got to my feet, and moved toward the machine; figuring I might as well indulge my curiosity while I was alive enough to have some.

The white substance was glossy and even up close looked slimy. It was partially transparent and milky in the light, like mucus scraped across the back of your hand. But it was indeed solid, and brittle, one small flick was enough to break off a chunk of the glassy stuff. Even more surprising, when I snapped the glob off at the hole, there was a chalky puff and more of the material poured out, a thick liquid that hardened in seconds. My heart dropped into my stomach when I realized what it was. Plaster-resin molding gel. Quick setting and sticky.

I re-cleared the hole and smeared a gathered handful of goo across my faceplate.

It took almost five second, but the hissing stopped, and tears burst from my face. It was a relief to breathe deep.

Once the air pressure in my suit returned to normal and I'd cleared the fog from my head, I went to check on my partner. I was still woozy, in pain, and plain exhausted from my ordeal, but now I knew I could at least get back to the MB without dying. Seeing was a challenge, the gel covered most of my faceplate's glass, reducing my vision to a thin ring around the edge. It took a couple minutes of searching, but I found Jay's body still heaped on the ground. I knelt beside him and set a hand on his chest; there was an endless moment of stillness and dread, where all my hope sank within me, then I felt the shallow rise and fall of his breathing.

"We'll be okay." I told the unconscious Jay. "This is just a setback." I slid my arms under him and tried to stand, lifting the moon-lightened man on shaky, unstable legs. "We can do this."

After one step I fell and dropped him on top of me with a pain filled grunt that knocked all of the newly cultivated air out of me.

"New plan," I said, "You wake up," I pushed Jay off me, "and you can carry *me*. Deal?"

Back on my feet, I knew lifting wouldn't work, so I grabbed his legs, whispered an 'I'm sorry', and started to drag him behind me as we climbed the hill back towards the safety of the vehicle. Hoping that each step I took wasn't making what injuries he had worse.

It was two hours later when I found the buggy, doors still open, waiting right where we left it. Once there, it took another ten minutes to heave Jay into the passenger seat. With both of us inside I started the air cycle and leaned back in my chair, taking a minute to rest until I heard the finishing tone from the computer. I stripped off my helmet, took a series of deep breaths, and passed out.

7

"Morning, killer. Sleep well?"

Lights flickered on and the brig pulsed and buzzed into day around me. I squinted and sat up on my cot. Three weeks had passed since surviving the patrol and I was beginning to get annoyed at my guard's little joke each morning.

Yes, I'd been arrested, that shouldn't be a surprise. Going against orders will tend to do that. Ridiculous or not I accepted my punishment with pride, knowing I had kept America safe on the Moon.

"You got a visitor." My scrawny guard said as he slid a food packet through the gap in the plexiglass wall of my cell.

He walked away and Sergeant Espinoza appeared, arms clasped comfortably behind his back.

"We found the machine you described." He went on after considering me for a few moments, "You were right about it being quite disabled."

"Good," I said, "happy to be effective."

"Yes, well," Espinoza smiled and let his arms relax at his sides, "It's led to a number of interesting conversations over the past few days. Can you guess with whom?"

"Earth-side generals? SF HQ? How would I know?"

"China, McKinney, the Chinese government. The people demanding your head on a plate for what you did."

I chuckled at that, "For interrupting their attack plans? I call that a job well done."

"You *ruined* a six-billion-dollar scientific project! One being conducted by a country we've had a strained relationship with for decades. They are indescribably angry, not only with you, but with Space Force and America in general."

"It's China though. They always send sneaky shit at us."

"That doesn't give you the right to attack anything with a Chinese insignia."

"They should have asked before sending it in the first place."

"They are gonna hang out to dry boy," said the Seargeant. "And that's just too damned bad, I kind of liked you."

"Sergeant Espinoza?" A woman's voice came from down the hallway. "An open call for you," she said. "From Earth."

"Thank you," he said, and glanced at me, almost like he was rolling his eyes at the woman I still couldn't see, "I'll receive it, not here."

"Yes sir," the messenger came into view, "but call is for both you and Lieutenant Colonel McKinney."

"What do you mean, Lieutenant Colonel?"

"Maybe it is a mistake sire."

"Ah, I see." He turned to me, "Okay, let's go then."

My guard reappeared, this time with an access FOB for the cell door.

The video monitor they had set up was ancient. We sat for thirty seconds or so in odd silence before the monitor flickered on. President Donald Trump Jr. stood there, looking down at us from his gold-plated office. "Good morning gentlemen, it's good to see that everyone's here and okay.

"First, I want to personally thank Lieutenant Colonel Marc McKinney for his, your, brave service in tracking down and neutralizing a potential threat to our nation." The president shrugged, "We have no idea what weapons that vehicle could have potentially been carrying. Or what sort of mission it may have been programmed with. They should have let us know, or asked really, I mean," he shrugged again, "we're the only ones walking around up there. Right?"

"Thank you, sir." Was all I could think to say once I realized he'd stopped talking.

"That's right, you're welcome Colonel."

"About that sir..."

"Consider it a token of my appreciation." Then he, Donald Trump Jr., smiled at me, "And in recognition of your actions I'm not only going to cancel your trial by offering a full pardon for all matters related to these events and I'm going to award you the first ever, newly titled, 'Interplanetary Medal of Honor'. You showed wonderful skill and instinctive thought when hunting that Chinese rover. You did a good job kid, keep it up." The president smiled at me again before the screen went blank.

Next to me Sergeant Espinoza sat slumped back in his chair, chin in hand, with an irritated and confused look on his face.

I raised my cuffed hands for him to unlock, "I'll need these off to return your salute."

The Last Emperor of Betelgeuse

Jane Yolen

By rocket's red glare
We know who is there:
The Emperor impeached
Who has finally reached
In a furious hurry
His last sanctuary.

Do our doors open wide
To let him inside?
No—immigrants banned
From this last sacred land.
He has crossed the wide space
Where he has no place.

And that's tonight news
From free Betelgeuse.

Space Force

Better Dreams Than These

Ken Scholes

Some nights he dreamed about the green jungles of Venus. Some nights he dreamed about rum.

But on the last night before the last Writing Room kick-off of the last season of his illustrious dual-track career as a reality holovision star and a commissioned officer in the U. S. Space Force, Admiral Fleetwood Mackenzie Stewart dreamed about his arch-nemesis and one-time best friend and it startled him awake.

He mumbled the droneflies away and lay in their receding glow, trying to conjure up what he could remember of the dream.

They'd been in the command room of the USS Pence, and both were captains yet it seemed set before Lieutenant JG Scott had gone rogue in the sixth season reboot. There had been a kiss, fierce and unexpected. And then Scott had leapt onto the captain's narrow desk, hips gyrating as he cried out "Oh Captain, my captain. "And Stewart had lunged forward, hands fumbling with the large shiny buckle on his captain's sword belt—and woke up suddenly.

Now, in the dark, Stewart became aware of just how awake parts of him were and he slowly released his breath.

Then he whispered on the light, rolled over, and pulled the tattered, contraband copy of the Blue Book that made his life sane from its hidden compartment in his nightstand. He thumbed through it for an hour, sometimes reading and sometimes just feeling the old paper beneath his old fingers. And in the end, he climbed naked from his bed and went to stand before the flat metal vidscreen that took up one wall of his quarters.

"USS Pence, season one," he told it. "Episode seven."

<<>>

They are deep in creating season two of the USS Pence when Boggs and Biggs have him on their show for the season one recap of the surprise hit.

"So," Boggs says, "season one—"

"Episode seven," Biggs says because part of their schtick is finishing one another's sentences. "You meet Jackson Scott for the first time when you take the USS Pence to Venus in search of his father—Professor Angus Scott's—lost ship. It was quite—"

"A first encounter," Boggs says. "Let's look at it again."

And everyone does. The drones are bigger and clumsier back in the early days but multiple screens swim to life. In one screen, the green-skinned Venusian apes surge across the jungle canopy, barely perceptible as individual creatures. In their midst something small and pink and out of place flies from vine to vine with the rest of the pack. One screen fills up with that form, naked and flowing and alive. Another screen fills with Captain Fleetwood Mackenzie Stewart's face. The look on it is illegal. Especially in the Space Force.

"Now that," says Biggs.

"Is same sex attraction," finishes Boggs.

Both make siren sounds.

"Better call the chaplain," Boggs says.

"Code name Dee Ay Dee Tee," Biggs says.

"Do *indeed* ask," Boggs says.

"Do *indeed* tell," Biggs finishes.

Then both in unison: "Do *tell*, Captain Stewart. "

(Back in those days, lying to himself about anything had been easy because of the rum. But back then with the rum's help, even staring at it on his face in episode seven, he couldn't see what Biggs and Boggs saw.)

Captain Stewart laughs after an awkward pause. "Nothing to tell," he says. "What he's doing there requires admirable strength and skill."

"I'm sure," they both say.

Ironic that Biggs and Boggs would be ruined within a year, disgraced and discredited by their own illegal relationship. Despite being civilians and despite their show being among the New Stars and Stripes best rated programs.

<<>>

Watching the episode did nothing to wash away the dream but it did its intended trick to pull him into more episodes. Then more talk shows about the episodes. It had been quite the surprise how episode seven had changed the ship and the show and his career so fundamentally by bringing in Scott.

Jackson Scott been an instant spike in ratings as well as a useful member of the crew. Sole survivor of a family lost in space, found surviving the savage jungles of Venus adopted by her four-armed, sentient apes. Until then, Captain Fleetwood Mackenzie Stewart had been the shiny new thing, out in the shiniest, newest ship, now credited with finally solving the mystery of the missing Scott family on their doomed test run of the Wagner-Scott engine. Still, sharing the spotlight was easy with Scott. By season two, when they "found" the drone footage of his childhood raised among the Venusian apes, it had taken Scott to unexpected heights of popularity so fresh from a primitive life lost on Venus. Fifteen years his senior, Stewart took on the role of captain and older brother to the young man as he slowly reclaimed his lost humanity.

By sunrise, Stewart still hadn't slept but he'd wiped a hundred tears from his eyes. Finally, he slipped into his Space Force jogging sweats and sneakers, letting himself out into the red Martian morning.

At seventy, he'd had just enough work done on himself to feel fifty still, but he'd also never really let himself slow down too much, especially once he'd found sobriety. He paused to stretch at the gate of the officers' quarters and glanced up at the sound of a captain's yacht lifting off to return to the orbital docks above. Then, he fell into an easy run that took him out past the training grounds to a gate that would turn him loose on the running trail along McConnell Canal. He chose it for its view and for its distance from the port.

When he hit his first mile, Stewart thumbed the button on the scrambler in his pocket and watched the droneflies scatter and drop. He'd have fifteen minutes of privacy. Maybe more.

Drawing in a lungful of dry air that smelled faintly of cinnamon and cucumber, he initiated the complex series of protocols that would let him call his sponsor.

"Hey Sam," he said, slowing his pace. Beside him, the water moved even slower.

"Hey Ralph," his sponsor said, voice muffled by the Program to keep things anonymous. Anonymity had always been important but being illegal added another layer of benefit to it all. How are you holding up?"

Stewart laughed. "Well, I'm calling my sponsor. "

Sam—not his real name obviously—chuckled. "It's been a while."

Stewart nodded. It was a ridiculous act given that no one was watching. "I'm still muddling my way along. Eleven years sober now. "He looked for his next words carefully. "But I'm going through some big changes. Retirement is coming soon. And I'm dreaming about..." He paused again. Fearless moral inventory or not, he wasn't sure how much he really wanted to share. "I'm dreaming about former co-workers. "*No. Not rigorously honest.* "I'm dreaming about someone from my work. Someone I've known nearly my entire career. It's... uncomfortable."

"And how's it impacting your sobriety?"

He didn't even touch the dream. That didn't surprise him but what he said next did. "Actually, I haven't even thought about drinking. I woke up, skimmed the book, then did a bit of reminiscing. Decided to go for a jog and give you a call."

"So, you're doing your self-care. That's fantastic. "He could hear the pride in the man's voice. "Any chance this is a stepping stone? Maybe an eight through ten kind of situation?"

Stewart hadn't considered that possibility. The raw sexuality of the dream had distracted him from digging too deep. But there had been reasons their friendship had soured suddenly.

No, he knew. <u>Just one reason.</u> He closed his eyes against the sudden shame he felt and forced himself to look away. He swallowed before speaking. "You know, it could be. We had a falling out. "His sponsor had probably watched it all unfold on the edge of his seat like most of the civilized solar system. It had been an epic falling out that had dominated the sixth season, finally closing when Scott burned his uniform, painted himself green and stolen the Pence B only to fly it into the sun in an act of defiance. "I know I tried to make amends long ago without success."

"Well you know how it goes," Sam said. "Sometimes it's the wrong time and sometimes there never is a right time and it becomes something we have to accept with serenity instead of something we change with courage."

"It's been... a long time. Maybe I should try again. "The knot in his stomach turned again to tell him he was onto something and Stewart chuckled. "Stepping stone. Maybe so. Thanks, Sam."

"You're welcome, Ralph. Whatever is going on, you and your HP already have it covered."

Stewart hesitated, wanting to believe that. His Higher Power was an out-of-print comic book character from his childhood, The Night Marauder, that he paid lip service to for the Program but deep down, he'd already figured out he was his own higher power, no capitalization necessary, and that the series of projections and transferences that served others so well hadn't worked as well for him. "I think we do," he finally said.

"Then I'll just say keep doing what you're doing, Ralph."

"Thanks, Sam."

"No problem; you know how to reach me *any* time. And hey, congratulations on retirement."

Another ship lifted behind him just as his alarm went off, chiming softly in his ear, letting him know that he had a ship to catch himself soon." I still have another seas—" He cut himself off and changed out words. "Year. I have a year to go"

"Big plans after?"

The question caught him off guard. But the chiming persisted and now a name flashed against the inside of his left eye. Not the alarm, he realized, but his agent who had maybe called three times in thirty years." I've not really thought about it yet," he said, "but I've got another call coming through that I have to take."

He moved to the other call and heard Axom Latterday's Texas drawl fill up his ear." Howdy, Mack. You sitting down? We need to talk, Son."

And after finding the closest bench, the ever-punctual Admiral Fleetwood Mackenzie Stewart missed his shuttle and then sat shaking his head for a good while after finishing that unexpected call.

<<>>

Drone-flies twinkle in and out of scene as the shuttle crew disembarks upon the lush Venusian soil. Stewart's face is brought in close as he barks orders. Crewmen with weapons drawn fan out as dozens of tiny cameras zoom in on his eyes as he scans the jungle. Fewer follow the crew but that's contractually obligated. His slick new agent at work.

Other drone-flies race the jungle, released into the air by the shuttle as it landed. The greenery slaps by in a blur until a soft chanting and the rustle of wind slows the camera down. The stream of green apes is moving slowly now as the drone rises over them. The pink human in their midst moves with them despite having only two arms and no tail and, unlike the apes, he notices the drone. He watches it with arched eyebrows and hoots at it as he leaps from vine to vine.

Back at the shuttle, Captain Stewart draws his flare gun and points it at the sky. He pulls a trigger and the air above explodes into red, white and blue—a dazzling fireworks array designed to invoke a patriotic fervor in the audience, instill awe in the natives and jazz up the traditional flag planting ceremony and prayer of thanksgiving yet to come.

The camera switches to the wonderment upon Jackson Scott's face as he sees the fireworks display. He looks to the pack as it steers away, then looks back to the sky. For a moment then, both faces are framed in that red, white and blue light, each looking up and out. Then Scott breaks away from the pack and moves off in the direction of the light and the plain where the shuttle and its crew watch and wait.

"He's coming toward us, Captain," one of the drone operators' radios and Stewart approaches the tree line. When Scott drops lightly to the ground, lithe and naked, before them Stewart steps back and snaps to an ensign on his left.

Of course, in the feed everything's blurred and the look on the captain's face makes for great comedy.

"Your shirt, man," he says to the ensign, "give me your shirt. "Stewart pauses while the sweaty, muscular man scrambles out of the snug shirt then takes it and wraps it around his own waist before extending it to Scott.

When Scott takes it, laughs, and draws close in to wrap it around Stewart's waist again, there is of course more comedic opportunity.

And if that portion of the episode had made it past the censors, it's possible that Biggs and Boggs would've found episode eight just as telling as seven.

<<>>

Freshly shaved and in his dress blues, Stewart rode the shuttle in silence and pondered Axom Latterday's call.

"Scott wants a meeting," his agent had told him. "Just you, just an hour. The studio and the Force both love it for different reasons. The Underwriter's Union hates it and will go along like always with the necessary rate increases. But I told them it didn't' matter; I knew Fleetwood Mack and after all this time, there was no way in Hades that—"

"I'll do it," Stewart heard himself say. And just like that, he would have his moment if there were indeed any amends he could still try to make after all these years. He'd certainly made his lists—men and women he'd harmed along the way, drunk or sober, and he'd made things right wherever and whenever he could. Jackson Scott was, in his mind, the greatest loose end in his fierce moral inventory.

And this could be my last chance. Even as he thought it, Stewart glanced out of the window at the sky slipping from red to black. Soon, they'd dock with whatever big surprise they had waiting to kick off the story boarding for the last season—or at least as close as they could get it between all of the parties involved. And then after a few weeks of hammering things out, he'd face his last year of work—and any last chance he expected he might have of seeing Jackson Scott again.

That was an easy launchpad into thinking about next year and the changes it would bring to his life. Despite the question coming up more frequently as retirement drew near, he found himself more curious about Scott's future than his own. He'd gone rogue from the Force, destroyed the vessel that had "liberated" him, stolen a new ship and declared himself a polytheistic agnostic pansexual pirate at war with the civilized solar system thirty years ago in a negotiated settlement with United System Broadcasting and the U. S. Government. And ten years ago, he'd stopped participating in the Writing Room, having his input, yays and nays sent up through his own agent. Was he also being written out? He couldn't imagine the man retiring though he'd seen the lavish Pleasure Dome he'd established with his vast fortune on Planet X. There had been a special spin-off show where reporters had been cryo-ed in and allowed to see what Jackson Scott had done with his small, private planet at the edge of the system.

The man had inherited a fortune once he was established as the Wagner-Scott family heir, with a long line of patents for the engine and a dozen other inventions used to move humans further into their dominion. And then he'd added to that fortune first with his entertainment and federal service contracts and then later with the lucrative bonus that piracy offered.

His one-time friend had done very well for himself despite a difficult origin story and some great betrayal, and an odd part of Stewart found himself hoping that Scott had happiness on top of it all. He surely seemed to in the handful of clips he'd seen and the handful of encounters they'd had as the writers kept their game of back and forth, cat and mouse, going across the Solar System season after season. Dashing and even debonair in a festival of rainbow-colored silks and an old-fashioned rapier. He'd stayed so fit than in the twenty-fifth season special of his own show, he'd gone swinging—appropriately clothed—the vines of Venus again, though the absence of the green apes was noticeable and politically exploited (to little gain) by an Opposition Party that largely now only existed for dramatic effect and white noise.

Maybe, he thought, *I'll buy a cabin on Phobos and hire some washed out science fiction author to ghost-write my memoir.*

He chuckled at the simplicity of his first retirement fantasy and then closed his eyes as the cabin lights dimmed for docking.

<<>>

It's the first sanctioned visit to Scott's Pleasure Dome on Planet X and Rozella and Rumbello Detweller, the FaceWorld Influencing twins with their show *On the Edge of the Edge*, won the pitched media contest for who would land the exclusive interview with the Pirate of Planet X.

The three of them float in anti-grav hammocks as the drones position themselves. Automatic tables drift between them, robotic arms replenishing fruity, umbrella-bearing drinks that are no doubt heavily spiked with rum and Sildenafil.

Scott wears as little as possible; the twins are not far behind but have prosecution considerations back home despite the waivers provided by the union and studio.

Rumbello twists in his hammock and sips. "So after all these years, you've opened up your home to the media. Why now?

He's in his sixties but the only tell is the streak of white in his hair that follows the scar from season six. He smiles, twists in his own hammock so he is facing Rumbello.

"Well, I've realized it can't go on like this forever. At some point, the studio will move on, the Space Force will move on. I might even run out of things I want to steal. So I thought maybe it was time to show the worlds I'm not really as diabolical as Stewart and his Yes-boys in the Force make me out to be. "

Rozella takes her turn now and when she twists, she shows cleavage and grins. "So you've lured my twin and I here and served us spiked drinks using this story as bait?"

He shrugs." It's in the release form as part of the Pirate Experience." He spins a dial on a remote in his hands and all of their hammocks begin to rise up above the palace, the garden and its forests, hills and plains stretching out around them." As you can see, when I'm not gallivanting around the solar system, I'm here with my people in the home I've made for us."

The drones now move about as he continues, capturing the fields, the flowers, the rainbow clad citizens of his world, pulled together from both his human followers and the sentient sub-species that had joined humanity's labor force as the Solar System unfolded the vast richness of the Creator's intelligent design. The drones each briefly race out to show some of the structures, carefully de-constructed and re-built here within the vast Pleasure Dome. The Plutonian ice lemur's white, frosty temple to Ga-Mel-Ta stands next to the Venusian's living altar to the vine spider Tulva and her ape lover Vlom, both rising blasphemous in the bright morning sun and promising illegal acts dressed up as deeds of righteousness and gifts of offering. The other two temples were less titillating for the visiting guests. No one was very excited about the small portico to the Neptunian sea dragon Splaw—an invisible, quantumly tiny deity that enhanced fishing prowess when beseeched—represented entirely by a small crystal glass of water. Or Janu, the Forgotten God of Underground Mars, which really was an afterthought since the Martians had been whispering ghosts for eons before the Space Force put its awkward boots upon that planet's harsh surface. None of them had emigrated to Scott's planet and no one really knew what they believed. But they were included in his pantheon.

Scott continues as the drones move on." I've created a place here for those that don't fit the status quo. Renegades and pirates, artists and scientists, lovers and dreamers, atheists and sexual deviants who can't be themselves and live under the flag of the Revived United States and her federated worlds." Now the drones are showing forests, jungles, fields of snow. "Humans—" he pauses. His eyes darken, then clear, and a drone picks up on it. "Not just humans; too small-minded a notion. *People*." The eyes soften. It's noticeable." People here get to be who they are, with their needs met as best as I can meet them. Just because we're people."

Now the camera is back to Rumbello. It's clear he's smitten with the pirate and that the rum is working. His face flushes. "So is this a hint to the next season? Do we see an end coming to this saga that's been unfolding all these years? Will you and Stewart finally bury the so-called hatchet?

Scott winks." One day, I'll wager." He spins the dial again and all their hammocks draw in close together." But next season? No spoilers here. We've not even heard from the creative team yet."

Rozella splashes red onto her shirt. Her eyes are wide." I'm sure it's going to be amazing."

"So," Rumbello asks, "what *would* come next? What would retirement look like for a famous, fabulously wealthy and wildly flamboyant space pirate?"

Now they're both within reach and Scott puts his drink down so that he can goose them each from beneath the hammock. And it's as if the studio knows what he is planning—the drones follow his hands and catch the moment and their faces simultaneously as it happens." Maybe if I ever do retire, the two of you will have to visit me here and help me come up with things to do." Laughter." Maybe we should start a little list now?" He hits his dial again.

More giggling and gasps as the droneflies all go black and fall away in an instant.

When the interview resumes later, it's obvious that some time has passed, faces are clean and sober, clothes have been changed, and they all sit differently now in a relaxed posture that says everything that the censors can do nothing about.

No one is surprised when the Detweller Twins go dark and disappear two years later.

Celebrity gossip points to Planet X but UBS has no comment on the matter.

<<>>

Stewart felt a quiet anxiety coiling in his stomach as he exited the shuttle. Each year, the creative team chose a new venue for the kick-off and lately, they'd taken to surprising him as he got closer and closer to wrapping his time in the Force. Each season was a bigger and grander party that he spent most of sipping ginger ale flattened to look like Scotch.

"Admiral on deck," the Officer of the Watch shouted and a formation of men shifted to attention. A landing bay flooded with bright lights, buzzing droneflies, a red, white and blue of uniforms beneath banners and flags lined up behind a row of familiar faces waiting to shake his hand or salute him.

"Welcome to the Pence D," Vice Admiral Duggan said as he returned Stewart's salute. "She's a beauty. And the improvements to the Wagner-Scott engine will make her first of the fleet to take The God-given Miracle of America confidently beyond our own Solar System. "

They shook hands after and he looked around. "Thank you, Admiral. She is indeed a beauty." The ship even smelled new and it brought back memories of his first day on the B, his first command, and his first day on the C after Scott had destroyed the ship they'd sailed together those five seasons they were friends.

Stewart moved down the line.

"Ready for a grand slam finale of a run?" The executive producer, Jonathan Malachi Todd, was next." I think you'll love some of the initial ideas on the table."

Stewart nodded, shook the hand. "I'm looking forward to it," he said.

Then the commander of the new Pence, his former Executive Officer, Jeremiah Stone.

"Mack, it's good to see you." They saluted, then embraced. Stone was the only one of his crew that knew he was in the Program. Stone was the only one of his crew who'd had the balls to call him on his shit when he was rock-bottoming and it had fostered an intimacy absent from Stewart's other friendships.

"You, too, Jerry. How's Marge?"

"She's good. Sends her best. Once the dust settles..."

Stewart nodded, continued down the line. New cast members he'd never met, old ones coming back, special guest stars coming in from other ships and other shows. Finally, they were through the first of the ceremonial nonsense and shuffled off to a large board table set up in the Observation Deck beneath a holographic map of the solar system. A crisply uniformed staff of green apes spirited platters and pitcher and plates about the room, their four arms a blur of precise motion. After introductions and a brief prayer offered by the ship's new chaplain (monitoring quietly from his corner away from the table), the work began.

"So last season we focused on slowing Stewart down and speeding Stone up," the head writer, Susan Shamrock Jones—one of only seven female writers employed by the Force and the only head writer among her gender. "Getting the old wolf ready to retire, coping with leaving command and facing the possibility that he may never resolve the Scott situation despite a brilliant career."

Stewart picked up the e-tablet before him. The agenda glared up at him with menacing font.

"Of course, we don't want you slowed down too much. So just like last season, you'll spend a considerable amount of this season back in space, facing Scott from the captain's chair." She looked to Stone. "And we have some big plans for you, of course. We're going to wrap up the pirate thread, at least as far as the Pence goes, with Stewart's departure." Then the room grew quiet as the map overhead began to grow." So that with this season finale, we take the Pence out of the system for a five-season run under Stone's command. Weird new worlds, bizarre new aliens and such we hope." She clapped her hands and everyone else joined her." Now let's talk about what that all might look like between now and then, people."

From there, it was voice after voice, effusive in praise especially for the older crew-castmates. Some of the younger writers had cut their teeth watching the show as children and it showed in their eyes and words. Finally, after four hours, they moved toward the lunch break and the impromptu show museum that had been set up in a cargo bay that had yet to see a crate stacked within it. Duggan, Jones and Todd pulled Stewart aside as the room cleared.

"Can we talk about Latterday's call?" Todd asked.

When Stewart nodded, Todd whipped out a scanner as Duggan hit the drone switch and made their meeting private. Once the scanner blinked green, Jones spoke first.

"We love the idea if we can write it in somehow," she said, "but there isn't any mention of it in the story notes from Scott's agent."

"It's really new," Stewart said." As of this morning." He looked from face to face to face." I don't think it's part of the story but I wouldn't put anything past him."

Duggan's brow furrowed." And you're sure you want to take the meeting? Even knowing it could be a trap?"

In the years since going rogue, Scott had prided himself on catching them off guard. Destroying the Pence B was a fine opening act that had surprised them all. Since then, he'd kidnapped dignitaries between seasons that he forced to be written in, stolen ships he should have never known about for his own growing fleet and turned the tables on a half-dozen traps the Stewart and the Space Force had set to bring their wayward son to justice. But this one—Stewart just wasn't sure what to make of it. Maybe it was his own inner landscape, thrown by the dream and by the sudden opportunity to see Scott again." I am sure I want the meeting," Stewart finally said. He left the rest unsaid.

Todd nodded." Jones will cook up some ideas and see if they bite." He looked at Duggan." Could the Force use this for a trap of its own?"

Duggan nodded." We could. But we're open minded. Let's see what the writers come up with. We're eager to move beyond this story arc and get out into the galaxy next year. Stewart and Scott have had decades on the net and it's time for an eye toward expansion." He smiled." We're also eager to expand our partnership with the studio and with Colonial Way Inc as we get humanity—and America—properly positioned in the Cosmos." He clapped Stewart on the back. "I'm sure you're ready for quieter days."

Stewart wasn't sure but didn't need to answer. Jones filled in the silence instead.

"So," she said, "what would you say to him after all these years? All this conflict?"

"I'm sorry?"

"What would you say?" she asked again.

Stewart looked away. "I'd say I'm sorry," he said.

Duggan looked uncomfortable and Stewart knew why. But the droneflies had been down long enough for the chaplain to edge back into the room and that grim man's raised eyebrow told Stewart that the conversation was over for now.

After that, it was lunch and then a quick tour of the bridge where they activated his command codes for the new ship and Jones and the others led the big reveal that he would be taking the vessel out with Stone for that first maiden voyage next month.

Then more talk with the writers underneath that sky map followed by more food and apple cider dressed up as whiskey as a lifetime washed over him and around him.

And through it all, Stewart found himself more and more settled on the truth of the moment. He did have amends to make and the opportunity to make them.

And he did want to see his old friend—his fiercest foe— again from some point-of-view other than the command screen of a pursuing starship before his time was done.

<<>>

This is a conversation no one thinks will ever be heard and Stewart's voice is shaking with rage. "How far back, Duggan?"

Duggan stammers. He and Todd both monitor the room for flies and other unwelcome bugs.

Todd intervenes." They briefed us on the prototype drone footage when we took over the show."

Stewart balks. "So the kid hasn't been lost. Not this entire time. You've known exactly where he was and you've been amassing content for a new venture?" His fist comes down on his desk." We could've adjusted our plans and launched five years sooner—maybe eight—and rescued him from those. . . those..." The word sounds ugly when he spits out. "Those savages. Given him a chance at a normal life."

Duggan's voice is firm." Those so-called savages revolutionized the labor market after the shortages in the New Revival downsizing. And the resources we're pulling from Venus have improved the human condition in ways never imagined when this Space Force was first conceived by the Orange Prophet and Divine Commander Pence."

"And," Todd says, "the story is a story of hope and human conquest. Jackson Scott, a toddler raised by apes on Venus as one of their own—a learning curve like no human child has ever faced. With his own recollections woven in—easily shot while he continues his work and training with you aboard the Pence. Royalties and bonuses from this along with his family's engine and planetary stake in Venus will set him up for life and give him a platform to tell his story. Between your mentorship and his wealth, he could have an extraordinary life on the heels of so much hardship."

Stewart's voice is clear—he isn't buying." He needs family and friends more than anything else. People he can trust." He pauses." You've been lying about this to him and to me. I can't go along with it. My mentorship won't mean shit to him otherwise."

Duggan and Todd are both quiet. When Duggan speaks, his voice has a new quality to it—an edge he normally lacks. "We need you to go along with it, Mack. Encourage him to play along as well. It's for his own good."

"I don't see how or why—"

Todd interrupts. "Commander Duggan has asked me to upload a file to your private cortical server that will show you just why helping us will be so very good for your career."

There is more silence as Stewart views something behind the privacy of his left eye." I see," he says.

The veiled threat of missing footage from episode eight isn't picked up by the single bug recording their words. And Scott doesn't receive the leaked recording until the ratings begin slipping at the opening of season five.

The rest is holovision history. This bit of its origin story tucked away safely from the masses—and Acting Ensign Jackson Scott—for their own good.

<<>>

The evening was just getting started—and Stewart was just feeling finished—when Stone's XO interrupted with a quiet word between the captain and Duggan.

Duggan's brow spoke thirty seconds before he did. "I'm afraid we're going to have to cut tonight's festivities short. We have a security breach at the Titan Shipyards."

Stone raised his own eyebrow." Should I re-call the crew and spin up the engines?"

Duggan shook his head." No. We need to keep D on task with tomorrow's quick system tour and the Chaplaincy needs her emptied tonight for pre-launch security." He looked at Stewart." Did they tell you yet that you'll be doing the honors?"

Stewart shook his head." No but I wondered when you had my codes transferred."

Todd and Jones, both drunk and looking likely to fall into bed together again soon, joined them." Party over already?"

"Afraid so," Duggan said. "But everything should be fine for tomorrow." He nodded to Stewart. "See you in the morning, Mack."

Then Stone turned Stewart over the XO and they set out for the shuttle bay. The chaplain was dismissing the lieutenant who had flown Stewart with a salute as they entered. He looked up and smiled.

Stewart had heard the expression *and his blood went cold.* This was the first time he'd ever felt it in his own veins.

"Thank you, Commander," the chaplain said." I'll be flying Admiral Stewart home tonight." Then his smile widened and the temperature in Stewart's stomach went even colder. "There were some items I wished to discuss with you, Admiral. This lets us kill two birds with one stone, as they say, if you don't mind?"

Rule one of the Academy was when it came to the U. S. Chaplaincy, you just said "Yes."

"Happy to oblige, Padre," he said.

"The shuttle is a much more private environment." The chaplain gestured to the open hatch.

"Agreed," Stewart said pausing." I'm afraid I'm not remembering your name?"

"I'm afraid," the chaplain said, "I've not given it."

There was no way out of this box, Stewart saw, but to go in. He nodded slowly, then climbed into the shuttle's main passenger cabin. The chaplain followed, then closed the hatch and drew a drone disabler out to kill the fog of droneflies that followed.

They are keeping it undocumented. Or at least letting him think so. That was good information to have. "How can I help you?"

"I want to know if you recognize this." The chaplain drew a wad of blue cloth from beneath his robes and tossed it to Stewart.

He nearly dropped it as he opened the shirt. "I..." *Episode eight.*

The chaplain took another step forward. "Do you recognize it?"

Stewart swallowed. "I do."

"Anything to say?"

He stared straight ahead, saying nothing, and the chaplain took another step forward. "Tell me about your dreams, Admiral Fleetwood Mackenzie Stewart."

Now he flushed and felt sick suddenly. How could they know?" How..."

The chaplain smiled. "Because I burned a cricket to Tulva and Vlom for my wandering one to follow its smoke back to me."

There's nothing wrong with me, Stewart realized. *It's him.* "You what?"

"In the temple. The spider god and her ape lover."

"You burned a cricket?" He looked at the insignia on the chaplain's collar.

Following his eyes, the chaplain's fingers moved to the collar and began pulling at it. "Yes. That's the custom when you want to find your shul-rav—your person or your people since it really doesn't connote a number, just a sense of belonging to one another." The collar was open but that's not what he was pulling.

No, he's pulling the skin beneath it.

"So I burned a cricket and we dreamed about each other." The face and hair lifted away and Jackson Scott grinned out from beneath it. Before Stewart could close his mouth, Scott had kissed it, hard and dry.

"Hi," he said." My name's Jack. I'm an alcoholic. It's been seventy-eight days since my last drink."

"Hi Jack," Stewart said, then surprised himself by kissing his arch-nemesis back. "I'm Mack. It's been..." But in that moment, he couldn't remember just how long it had been.

"Let's talk," Scott said, pointing to the chairs." I've a lot to go over but first things first. Have you decided what you're doing next?"

Stewart sat mouth open and still stunned." What I'm doing next?"

Scott reached for battered satchel that Stewart recognized. It had been Angus Scott's, recovered from the crash site. From it, he pulled out a sheath of papers." I have a proposal for you."

Stewart took the papers, looked at them, then looked back up. "Is this a trick?" It was a pre-nuptial agreement and marriage contract, or at least that's what the bold all cap letters declared across the old-fashioned paper cover page. He saw terms covering non-disclosure, film rights, dissolution and even expansion by amendment.

"No. Not a trick. A proposal. Marry me, Mack. It's all legit under Planet X law. But read it all anyway. It's a big contract. Remember the Detweller Twins? They're in it, too. But you can decide what your marriage to them looks like." He paused. "Unless you have other plans after retirement?"

"No. No plans." Stewart let the papers drop into his lap after perusing the list of standard and non-standard clauses. A lifetime behind the helm, giving orders with clarity of focus and driven purpose and now he floundered in weather beyond his ken." I'm a bit lost here, Jack."

Scott leaned forward. "I know it's a lot and I'm sorry it's compressed into such a cramped moment after too many years. But hear me out and then decide. If you say no, I'll drop you at home and we'll meet again later in the season." He waited, held out a hand. "Deal?"

They shook. "Deal."

Then they settled into their chairs.

"First," Scott said, "I want to tell you I'm sorry."

Stewart looked up. "*You're* sorry? No, Jack, I'm sorry. I helped them exploit your childhood."

"Yeah," Jack said, "but you did it because of the shirt. Because of episode eight. And episode seven."

Stewart blushed. "I think I was drinking to cover it up. I know I didn't want to see it."

"We're all covering something," Jack said. "Anyway. I surely did feel betrayed initially but eventually, I found out the truth. Enough money buys plenty of eyes and ears." His eyes softened. "And we grew up in different cultures. There is no room for the spider ape cult of savage Venus in the Revived United States and her colonies. So you had shackles of shame I never could understand, not growing up where I did."

"Still, young men and ship's captains..."

"Both old men now," Scott said. "Also the subject of great speculation and vast amounts of fan fiction spanning decades in the underground porn market."

Stewart had avoided knowing about such things and pointed them back on course. "Still, I'm sorry."

"And I'm sorry I waited so long to let you know I knew and that I understood." His face softened. "All these years, Mack, I've not really been at war with you, just them."

Now something happened to Stewart that he couldn't fathom and he was grateful for the absence of cameras. He felt a tear coming on and took in a breath to squeeze off more. "And now you want to spend the rest of your life with me?"

Scott shrugged. "You're the first human I remember meeting. You're still my favorite and I've met quite a few. And I can't think of a better person to help me clean up the mess than the fellow who helped make it in the first place."

He felt his brow furrowing. "What do you mean?"

"We're not digging deep enough in our fearless moral inventory, Mack, if we think we are the ones we've hurt the most. Can you see the trail of tears our Space Force has left across every non-human it's encountered? And now they're talking about using my family's engine to go even further out?" His eyes were bright with anger. "They laud me for providing a home to the system's refugees and misfits but what have I done with all my fame and fortune to make the system a better home for everyone in it? I've made it worse. We both have, Mack, by feeding a voracious monster. I want us to make things right. Me and you. And whoever else will join us." His face was earnest in the dim light." There are better dreams than these we've dreamed so far."

"What exactly are you proposing, Jack, besides marriage?"

"Liberation," Scott cried out, "and education!" He jumped to his feet with a flourish and moved to the pilot's chair to fire up the engines and punch in coordinates. "I think that's enough for now until you decide. But the clock is ticking. About three minutes, I'd say, before our window closes."

He looked over the papers again. "Can I have my attorney look this over?" He was asking the right questions but Stewart already knew his answer and already knew that no Terran attorney was going to sign off on the kind of document Stewart now held before him.

"Okay," he finally said, as the shuttle cleared the bay. "I do."

He signed the marked forms and Scott took them from him, tucking them away in the satchel as he drew its strap over his shoulder.

They kissed again. "Now hold me," Scott said as he strapped a large, clumsy watch onto his wrist and spun a dial.

A wave of nausea and the sudden urge to urinate overwhelmed Stewart and then with a flash of light, the shuttle fell away and he collapsed heavily on top of Scott in a dark, warm place.

Scott squeezed his shoulder as he gasped for air. "First matter transmission experiences are a bit discombobulating."

Stewart was barely following. *Matter transmission?* What in the hell was he talking about? They weren't on the shuttle but he had lost all sense of time after feeling twisted inside out and scattered. "Where are we?"

"Back on the Pence D."

"And the shuttle?"

"On its way back to your place to deliver you safe and sound. Or a close approximation thereof."

Stewart adjusted himself. "Is this a bed?"

"Get some sleep," Scott said. "Busy day."

Stewart felt the briefest sting in his neck. Then the fog rolled in to take him.

<<>>

He flies the jungle now toward better dreams, the leaves and wind slapping at his bare skin, vine after vine pulling him along behind his friend, his lover, his spouse, his one-time foe. Scott moves with ease and Stewart is clumsy in his wake but learns quickly. Around them, the apes fly too, more and more joining in each day as the cause grows.

Not just the apes but the ice lemurs join in and below, in lagoons that made no sense on Venus outside of a dream, the Neptunian tentacled tadpoles leap the waves, their tiny opposable thumbs uplifted in solidarity.

And slowly, even some of the humans join. Slower, clumsier, pink and brown, male and female and other than, and all the dazzling points of beauty in between, all stripping off the falseness of their uniforms, tangling their fists into the living vines of truth and pulling themselves forward.

They all move in one direction away from darkness and toward a rising light and there is music and moaning and—

<<>>

"Wake up, my love," Jackson Scott said. "I've got your wedding gift. Time for you to give me mine."

Stewart was instantly awake in far more ways than he had expected to be and wondered just kind of stimulants had been administered. He was in a lavishly decorated room, laying fully uniformed in a red, heart-shaped bed.

Scott grinned at the look on his face. "Still on the D. I had this PolyPanPlay™ bedroom set ordered as a bit of a surprise for Stone but I think it'll do us nicely." He winked. "I'm glad you said yes."

Scott was standing, now in his own rainbow-colored uniform. "You'll recall the security breach at Titan Shipyards?"

Stewart nodded.

"The C. I had her picked up for you last night. I think Duggan's pretty apoplectic about it, actually. We'll rendezvous with her tomorrow and you can take command."

Slowly, it was all dawning on him. The vines had been a dream but everything before it had really happened. "My wedding gift," he said. He stood up and went to the nightstand, running his finger lightly over the feather duster and riding crop holstered there.

Scott smiled. "And you have a gift for me?"

"Computer," Stewart said returning the smile as the voice activation chimed, "recognize Stewart, Fleetwood Mackenzie. Admiral, United States Space Force. Transfer command authorization to the following voice print." He paused.

"Scott, Jackson Remuel Wagner," Scott said.

"Mark," Stewart said.

"Authorization transferred," the computer confirmed.

"Excellent," Scott said. "Now let's have breakfast, steal a starship and get to work making amends to the solar system."

Stealing the Pence D was the easiest last day in the Force that Stewart could've imagined and when they were safely pointed toward Planet X, easily outrunning the few craft not already in pursuit of the Pence C, they returned to their quarters.

"So what next?" Stewart asked his unexpected husband.

"Liberation and education," Scott replied. "Let's show them what's coming their way."

He thumbed a button and the lights went blue and dim. Soft music whooped to life as the bed began to rotate and the droneflies filled the room.

There was something simple and beautiful in Scott's eyes and Stewart gave himself over to it. *Yes, they need to see this,* Stewart thought, surprised at himself yet again.

"Oh Captain my captain," he whispered as he reached for his long, lost friend and a future he'd never dreamed possible.

"Oh Captain my captain," Scott whispered back as they sank into the waiting satin sheets and the droneflies danced above.

Space Force

Contributors

Bill Bibo Jr lives and works in Madison, WI. Late at night he writes about friendly giants, intelligent mummies, incompetent zombies, and other things that scare him in the hope that someday they no longer will.

Mike Brennan is a retiring sort of guy: He likes it so well, he has done it twice. He is a retired Naval Officer and a retired Radiation Health Physicist (a job as nerdy as it sounds). He has been writing Science Fiction and Fantasy for several years, and reading it almost forever.

Gregg Chamberlain is happy to say that the time he spent reading MAD Magazine as a young man was not wasted. His other little sallies against the Dark Dope have appeared in B Cubed Press' Alternate Truths Volumes 1 and 3 and also in Terror Politico from the Scary Dairy Press. Otherwise he writes speculative fiction for fun, with about five dozen short fiction credits in various magazines and anthologies. He and his missus, Anne, live a Trump-free life in rural Ontario, Canada, along with their two cats, who scorn politics as a waste of human time and energy.

J. W. Cook is an avid reader who loves everything that has to do with science fiction and fantasy. He has Degrees in Political Science, Disaster Preparedness, and Emergency Management and works as an Exercise Coordinator for the Hanford DOE site. When he is not working, reading or writing, he likes to hang out with his toddler son, wife, and four Border Collies. Joe is currently working on completing his Science Fiction series, *The Harbingers of Magic*.

Ray Daley was born in Coventry & still lives there. He served 6 years in the RAF as a clerk & spent most of his time in a Hobbit hole in High Wycombe. He is a published poet & has been writing stories since he was 10. His current dream is to eventually finish the Hitch Hikers fanfic novel he's been writing since 1986. https://raymondwriteswrongs. wordpress. com/

L. H. Davis, Laurance, is the author of two science-fiction novels, *Outpost Earth* and *Planet Nine*, which were published by Double Dragon Publishing in the spring of 2017. Laurance's third novel, *The Race,* women's historical fiction, was published by Hoffman & Hoffman in the summer of 2017. His post-apocalyptic short story, *Shoot Him Daddy*, was published in Metasaga's anthology, *Futuristica Vol. 1* in 2016. He won the 2018 *Teleport Science Fiction Contest* with his short story *Domain of the Dragon*. His short story, *Girl Meets Robot*, was published in 2019 in Dreaming Robot's *Young Explorer's Adventure Guide, Volume 6.* Before becoming a writer, Laurance worked as a mechanical engineer specializing in robotics and holds multiple U. S. patents.

Milo Douglas began writing in 8th grade drafting dramatic, dragon-filled versions of his favorite books. That same year he won first place in a regional essay contest a teacher urged him to enter. Milo later taught English/Language Arts in Seattle, WA for 8 years. Milo currently lives in Portland, Oregon where hikes, attends writing groups, hosts tabletop game parties and is always on board for a good pastry or beer. You may find Milo on the web at: http://www. milodouglas. com/ on Facebook at: https://www. facebook. com/milodouglaswriter or twitter: https://twitter. com/MiloDouglasBook

Darcye Daye is an Earth based writer who specializes in creative nonfiction and fiction. She holds two college degrees, one of which she actually uses. Her political background includes winning one uncontested election in high school for Student Council Secretary.

Chris Edwards lives in Glasgow, Scotland and divides his time between his family and earning a crust. He is the co-writer of the "Tales From the Aletheian

Society" audio-drama podcast (www. hunterhoose. co. uk) and has had a handful of stories published so far.

Yorkshireman **Philip Brian Hall** is a graduate of Oxford University. A former diplomat and teacher, at one time or another he's stood for parliament, sung solos in amateur operettas, rowed at Henley Royal Regatta, completed a 40-mile cross-country walk in under 12 hours and ridden in over one hundred steeplechase horse races. He lives on a very small farm in Scotland.

Philip's had short stories published in the USA and Canada as well as the UK, but only B Cubed is prepared to pay for his poetry!

His novels, 'The Prophets of Baal' and 'The Family Demon' are available in e-book and paperback form.

He blogs at *sliabhmannan. blogspot. co. uk/*.

Manny Frishberg spent his early years in and around New York City but saw the error of his (parents') ways, and moved to the West Coast 40-some years ago. He has worked shaping wood, sheet metal, and words (not all at once), and raised children and cats for fun and profit–or loss.

Manny is the author of more than four dozen short stories and has been an independent book editor since 2010. His debut novel, "City of Emeralds," is due to out from Lophii Press in 2022.

David Gerrold is an American science fiction screenwriter and novelist. He wrote the script for the original Star Trek episode "The Trouble with Tribbles", created the Sleestak race on the TV series Land of the Lost, and wrote the novelette "The Martian Child", which won both Hugo and Nebula Awards, and was adapted into a 2007 film starring John Cusack. He has also released Hella, a huge story of colonization set on a huge world.

Jill Hand is a member of International Thriller Writers. She is the author of the Southern Gothic novels White Oaks and Black Willows, from Black Rose Writing. Her work has appeared in many anthologies, including Dear Leader Tales, The Corona Book of Ghost Stories, and The Pulp Horror Book of Phobias, Vol. I and II.

Larry Hodges is an active member of SFWA with 120 short story sales, including stories in five previous "Alternative" anthologies. He has four published novels, including "Campaign 2100: Game of Scorpions," which covers the election for President of Earth in the year 2100, and "When Parallel Lines Meet," which he co-wrote with Mike Resnick and Lezli Robyn. He's a member of Codexwriters, and a graduate of the six-week 2006 Odyssey Writers Workshop and the two-week 2008 Taos Toolbox Writers Workshop, and has a bachelor's in math and a master's in journalism. In the world of non-fiction, he has 17 books and over 2000 published articles in over 170 different publications. He's also a professional table tennis coach and claims to be the best science fiction writer in USA Table Tennis, and the best table tennis player in Science Fiction Writers of America! Visit him at larryhodges. com.

Liam Hogan is an award winning short story writer, with stories in Best of British Science Fiction and in Best of British Fantasy (NewCon Press). He's been published by Analog, Daily Science Fiction, and Flame Tree Press, among others. He helps host Liars' League London, volunteers at the creative writing charity Ministry of Stories, and lives and avoids work in London. More details at http://happyendingnotguaranteed. blogspot. co. uk

Scott Hughes is a Georgia author whose fiction, poetry, and essays have appeared in such publications as *Crazyhorse, One Sentence Poems, Deep Magic, Redheaded Stepchild, Entropy,* and *Strange Horizons.* His short story collection, *The Last Book You'll Ever Read,* is available from Sinister Stoat Press/Weasel Press, and his poetry collection, *The Universe You Swallowed Whole,* is available from Finishing Line Press. His latest story collection, *Horrors & Wonders,* is available now. For more information, visit writescott. com.

Daniel M. Kimmel is the 2018 recipient of the Skylark Award, given by the New England Science Fiction Association. He was a finalist for a Hugo Award for *Jar Binks Must Die...* and other observations about science fiction movies and for the Compton Crook Award for best first novel for *Shh! It's a Secret: a novel about Aliens, Hollywood, and the Bartender's Guide.* He is also the author of some two-dozen published short stories, and the novels *Time on My Hands: My Misadventures in Time Travel* and *Father of the Bride of Frankenstein.* In addition to his film reviews for NorthShoreMovies. net, he writes on classic SF films for "Space and Time" magazine.

As a Canadian of British descent, **Andrew J Lucas** is astounded by politics at home and abroad. He has contributed to dozens of books in the tabletop RPG industry with twelve solo game books to his name. In the last few years, he has successfully sold fiction to a number of anthologies and even helped script a handful of Star Trek and Star Wars fan films. He is especially proud of his contributions to T*he Sisterhood of the Blade* and *Spoon Knife 4* anthologies last year—in spite of his debatable overuse of the em dash.

This is his first story published by B Cubed but not the only story he's written commenting upon the current administration.

Born on Friday 13, **Rebecca MacFarland Kyle** lives with husband and three cats, one of which is coal black. She enjoys music of all genres, chocolate, and writing weird fiction.

Susan Murrie Macdonald is a wordsmith: author of over a dozen short stories (mostly fantasy, but also westerns, science fiction, romance, and children's stories), a staff writer for Krypton Radio, freelance proofreader, ex-copy editor, blogger, and occasional poet. She also posts both fiction and non-fiction on Medium. She is a stroke survivor. Before her stroke she was a freelance copy editor and a substitute teacher. She is the author of a children's book, R is for Renaissance Faire, inspired by her time as a volunteer at the Mid-South Renaissance Faire. She was an extra in the time travel movie *Time Boys*.

Susan R. Matthews has been writing in her "Under Jurisdiction" universe for mumblety mumble years. Since her debut novel in 1997 the story's traveled forward through eight novels and several stories, novellas, and so forth; her latest novel, "Crimes Against Humanity," was published in 2019, and she's at work on the next novel in the series, "Diaspora." Meanwhile, "The Wild High Places"—the first of three historical action/adventure fantasy novels, think Kipling's "Kim," with a kink or two thrown in—will be coming out later this year.

She's currently off on a not-entirely-serious series about the plight of German U-boats who, having encountered the Flying Dutchman during WWII, find themselves re-appearing sixty years later in places like Lake Superior. Surprisingly enough, Maggie Nowakowska, Susan's wife of forty years, declined to leave Seattle and their two Pomeranians to accompany her on a visit to Europe to see the last intact VII/C U-boat last year (his name is U-995, and he's hanging out on the beach in Kiel smoking cigarettes).

"The Red Dust Pirates of Mars," in this anthology, is Susan playing with the intersection of U-boats and Edgar Rice Burroughs (since Bob Brown said we could go "camp"). I hope that you enjoy my story.

Tim McDaniel teaches English as a Second Language at Green River College, not far from Seattle. His short stories, mostly comedic, have appeared in a number of SF/F magazines, including F&SF, Analog, and Asimov's. He lives with his wife and cat, and his collection of plastic dinosaurs is the envy of all who encounter it. His author page at Amazon. com is https://www. amazon. com/author/tim-mcdaniel and many of his stories are available at Simily.co.

Melinda Mitchell is an ordained minister in Seattle. While having authored numerous nonfiction essays, this is her first published fiction story. She loves to write about the intersections of theology and science fiction and fantasy, and is the co-founder of Hopepunk Theology, a discussion forum and gathering. She lives with her husband and son in Seattle.

Since Clinton was president, **Kurt Newton's** fictional accounts have appeared in numerous magazines and anthologies, including More Alternative Truths, Alternative Truths: Endgame and Shout: An Anthology of Resistance. His subversive collection of psycho-socio-political commentaries, Nazi Swastika Bikini Wax Illuminati, was recently published by Alien Buddha Press. When not writing, he relaxes by playing the piano, composing misspent musicals for the mind.

John A. Pitts is a much loved iconic figure in the northwest writing circles. He is the author of the Sarah Beanhall series. He learned to love science fiction at the knee of his grandmother, listening to her read authors like Edgar Rice Burroughs and Robert E. Howard during his childhood in rural Kentucky. He passed away October 4, 2019 leaving so many words unwritten and so many souls missing his gentle wisdom. He is missed and we are honored to share his words.

Mike Resnick authored more than 77 novels, more than 280 stories, and 3 screenplays. He has edited 42 anthologies, and currently edits Galaxy's Edge Magazine and Stellar Guild Books. According to *Locus*, Mike is the all-time leading award winner for short fiction. He has won 5 Hugos (from a record 37 nominations), a Nebula, and other major awards in the USA, France, Japan, Spain, Catalonia, Croatia, Poland, and China. He was Guest of Honor at the 2012 Worldcon. His daughter, Laura, is also a science fiction writer, and won the 1993 Campbell Award as Best Newcomer.

Allan Rousselle has lived most of his life at either one end of Interstate 90 (Boston) or the other (Seattle), and occasionally along points in between. He graduated from Cornell University with a degree in Russian and Soviet Studies the same year the Soviet Union disintegrated, and his Masters in Political Science from University of Pennsylvania was immediately ignored when he entered a career in software engineering and data analytics. A former radio personality and print journalist with numerous fiction and non-fiction publications to his credit, Allan currently lives in the Seattle area with his wonderful sons.

Richard L. Rubin has been writing science fiction and fantasy since 2008. His short story sci-fi thriller *Robbery on Antares VI* is available on Amazon. Science fiction stories written by him also appear in *Broadswords and Blasters* magazine, *The Weird and Whatnot* magazine, *Theme of Absence* web-zine, the *Aurora Wolf Journal of Science Fiction*, and *Eastern Iowa Review*. In a previous life he worked as an appellate lawyer, defending several clients facing the death penalty in California. Richard is an Associate Member of the Science Fiction and Fantasy Writers of America. He lives in the San Francisco Bay Area with his wife, Susanne. Richard's website is at: richardlrubin.com.

Ken Scholes is the award-winning, critically-acclaimed author of five novels and over fifty short stories. His work has appeared in print since 2000. He is also a singer-songwriter who has written nearly a hundred songs over thirty years of performing. Occasionally, in his spare time, Ken consults individuals and organizations on maximizing their effectiveness.

Ken's eclectic background includes time spent as a label gun repairman, a sailor who never sailed, a soldier who commanded a desk, a fundamentalist preacher (he got better), a nonprofit executive and community organizer, and a government procurement analyst. He has a degree in History from Western Washington University.

Ken is a native of the Pacific Northwest and makes his home in Cornelius, Oregon, where he lives with his twin daughters. You can learn more about Ken by visiting www.kenscholes.com.

Jane Yolen has published over 400 books. Along the way she's won 2 Nebulas, 3 World Fantasy Awards, The Skylark Award, Caldecott Medal for her book OWL MOON. At age 80, she was in a band. She was the first woman to give the Andrew Lang Lecture at the University of St Andrews, Scotland (lecture series began in the1920's that included talks by both John Buchan and J.R.R. Tolkien among others. She is a SFWA Grand Master, SFPA Grand Master, and a Grand Master of World Fantasy.

(Unauthorized add by Editor: She is a magnificent human being that deserves every honor bestowed, every kind word spoken, and every royalty received.)

Wondra Vanian left the madness of America behind for the valleys of Wales where she lives with her husband and an army of fur babies. Her career as an author began in 2014 when she left her job working for

The Man to learn how to live with chronic illness. A Top-Ten finisher in the 2017, 2018, and 2019 Preditors and Editors Reader's Poll, Wondra was also named a Notable Contender for the Bristol Short Story Prize in 2015 and was shortlisted for the Twisted Tales Flash Fiction Competition in 2016. A writer first, Wondra is also an avid gamer, photographer, cinephile, and blogger.

Thanks to all of you.
It's been a hoot.
To Infinity and Beyond.
Oops, that was a different Space
Force.
Bob B

Made in the USA
Monee, IL
16 November 2021